MURDER MILE

Tony Black is an award-winning journalist who has written for most of the national newspapers. He is the author of *Paying for It, Gutted, Loss, Long Time Dead* and *Truth Lies Bleeding*. For more information visit www.tonyblack.net.

'Tony Black's Edinburgh makes Ian Rankin's version seem sedate, polite and carefree ... DI Rob Brennan, in his second outing, makes a strong case to assume the mantle of Edinburgh's leading fictional detective, vacant since the retirement of Rebus ... he's immensely well drawn, and Black's dialogue and atmosphere crackle with authenticity.' Marcel Berlins, *The Times*

'An authentic yet unique voice, Tony Black shows why he is leading the pack in British crime fiction today. His deeply disturbing previous books have been labelled tartan noir, but *Murder Mile* is in a class of its own, from gripping beginning to shocking end. Atmospherically driven, the taut and sparse prose is as near to the bone you are ever likely to encounter in crime noir. Powerful.' *New York Journal of Books*

'Comparisons with Rebus will be obvious. But that would be too easy ... Black has put his defiant, kick-ass stamp on his leading man, creating a character that deftly carries the story through every razor-sharp twist and harrowing turn. DI Rob Brennan is my new star on the capital's murder mile. And you can't help but think Rebus would approve.' *Daily Record*

'Black renders his nicotine-stained domain in a hardboiled slang that fizzles with vicious verisimilitude.' *Guardian*

'This up-and-coming crime writer isn't portraying the Edinburgh in the Visit Scotland tourism ads . . . a convincing portrayal of Edinburgh low-life and police rivalries.' *Sun*

'Black has already delivered four fine novels to establish himself at the front of the Tartan Noir pack and this fifth sees him pushing the police procedural as far as it will go . . . a superior offering in an already crowded Scottish crime market.' *Big Issue*

Also by Tony Black

Paying for It
Gutted
Loss
Long Time Dead
Truth Lies Bleeding

MURDER MILE

TONY BLACK

arrow books

This paperback edition published by Arrow Books 2012

10 9 8 7 6 5 4 3

First published in Great Britain in 2012 by Preface Publishing

20 Vauxhall Bridge Road
London SW1V 2SA

An imprint of The Random House Group Limited

www.randomhouse.co.uk

Addresses for companies within The Random House Group Limited
can be found at www.randomhouse.co.uk

The Random House Group Limited Reg. No. 954009
A CIP catalogue record for this book is available from the British Library

ISBN 978 0 09956 883 4

The Random House Group Limited supports The Forest Stewardship
Council® (FSC®), the leading international forest-certification organisation.
Our books carrying the FSC label are printed on FSC®-certified paper.
FSC is the only forest-certification scheme supported by the leading
environmental organisations, including Greenpeace. Our
paper procurement policy can be found at
www.randomhouse.co.uk/environment

Typeset in Times by Palimpsest Book Production Limited,
Falkirk, Stirlingshire

Printed in Great Britain by Clays Ltd, St Ives plc

For Cheryl
(Now I know what all the fuss is about)

Prologue

THE CAR ROUNDED THE BEND a little too fast and the tyres aquaplaned on the wet road; it was enough to send the girls on the back seat from giggles to screams. They were not real screams, more for show, silliness. They were the type of screams that presented themselves after a night of hilarity and heavy drinking. The aim was to keep the boys focused; focused on them. It had the desired effect.

'That's my hearing gone,' said Ben.

The girls giggled again, started to scream again.

'I'm not kidding, that's me fully deaf now!'

The driver lowered the revs, dropped speed. The night was wet, the rain had stopped but there was a lot of water sitting in potholes and puddles by the side of the road that splashed up every time the tyres made contact.

'You pulling over?' said Ben.

'Eh?'

'You're slowing down . . .' He had to raise his voice, the girls had started to sing on the back seat now. 'I'm only saying, if you're stopping . . .'

'I'm not stopping . . . I want to get home.' Garry nodded to the pair behind them, singing, and now attempting to dance in the confined space.

Ben turned to face the driver, bunched his brows. 'Go on, mate, just pull over for a minute or that . . . I need a slash.'

Garry frowned, 'Oh, for fuck's sake, Ben. Can you not wait?'

Headshakes. 'Want me to pish in your glove box?'

Ben started to fiddle with the handle beneath the dash-board, opened the glove box. 'Maybe there's an empty bottle in here; mind you, I was never a very good aim . . . especially after a few pints.'

Garry snapped, 'Right. OK.' He flicked on the indicators, applied the brake. The girls were jolted forward, giggled again as their stretched arms reached out to balance them.

'Whoa . . . what's up?'

'We stopping?'

The car pulled off the road, into a lay-by. It was a deserted stretch, not another car had been seen for miles on this road. There were no houses, not a barn or any other kind of farm building within sight. They were in the wilds, a deserted place, hidden beneath an inky darkness.

Ben opened his door, 'Call of nature, ladies.'

More giggles.

As he got out of the car Ben put his foot into a deep declivity in the tarred road. His shoe got wet, he shook it, cursed. 'Bloody hell.'

'Hurry up, eh!' yelled Garry.

'Give me a minute, I just got out.' As he went, he looked around. It was cold, much colder than he had imagined it would be. It was darker too, there were no street lamps on

2

the country road. He tensed for a moment, then raked fingers through his hair.

Behind him the girls called for the stereo to be turned up, started singing along to a Rihanna song. They were getting out of the car, beginning to dance as Ben headed to the lay-by's bourne. When he got to the fence he could make out the girls in the lights of the car; he didn't want them to see him taking a piss and climbed over the fence. There was a beaten path through the high grass, he followed it.

The grass was wet, soaking. Ben's trousers started to dampen, then he felt moisture seeping through to his shins but he walked on; he could still hear the music from the car, the girls singing along. The night air was cold on his face, each breath he took seemed to chill his lungs. He started to rub at his arms as he walked.

The illuminated hands of Ben's watch caught the glare of the moon; it wasn't quite a full moon, but near enough. He could see the outline of the city of Edinburgh – further down the bypass – and the orange fizz of the street lights glowing and flickering like the place was on fire. It was a strange sight; he thought he had seen the city from just about every angle, in every guise, but this was a new one. Ben felt unnerved, uncomfortable in this territory.

The path petered out and he was suddenly walking in heavy, waist-high grass, then he found the incline of the ground subsiding, his shoes slipping. He looked back, he couldn't see the car any more – it was above his line of vision. The wind raised his hair as he walked. For a moment he wanted to bolt back to the others; he couldn't explain the feeling – it was like an unconscious fear of the dark. Like when he was a child and he didn't want the light to be turned out at bedtime. He wondered what was out there, in the blackness.

He shook it off and said, 'Get a grip, Ben.'

He started to undo the buttons of his fly; the relief was instant.

'Ah, bliss . . .'

There was enough light from the reflective mirror of the moon for Ben to see the steam rising from the ground as he emptied his bladder. His arms – bare in only short shirt-sleeves – started to feel colder as he stood still. He heard the wind emit a low whistle, then the rustling of branches. He looked around. Where was he? Middle of nowhere. He checked himself, it was a field, some farmer's pride and joy off a B-road. He didn't care, though, he just wanted away. He felt spooked there, freaked out. It was too quiet now. Where were the others?

'Guys?' he called to them.

Silence.

He stood still for a minute, then quickly gave himself a shake and started to button up.

It was too quiet, they wouldn't have left without him, would they?

'*Guys?*'

There was no answer. Thoughts swirled in his mind.

They were taking the piss, they'd have driven off – it would have been Garry's idea, to put the shits up him – what a laugh, eh.

Ben began to jog towards the path; the place looked different facing the other way. His head spun too. He could feel the effects of alcohol rising in him as he jogged. His stomach cramped, his vision blurred. He upped his pace, but soon realised there was no path now. He knew there

4

had been a path, but he couldn't find it. It was too dark to see, the moon slinking behind amethyst clouds.

He stumbled.

'Fucking hell.'

Ben expected to have seen the lights of the car by now, heard the stereo and the girls giggling and dancing, singing along. But he heard nothing.

What was going on? he thought.

'Where the hell am I?'

He called out again, 'Garry . . . Steph . . .'

Nothing.

He felt his foot sink into another deep hole. 'Shit!'

There was a loud squelch as Ben removed his foot from the soggy ground. He tried to shake off the water, the mud, and then he tried to wipe it on the long grass. As he dragged his foot, he looked about; it was pitch dark. The path he had followed was nowhere to be seen, hidden in the blackness. He knew the others were playing games with him; if they hadn't driven off, then they were sitting with the lights out and trying hard not to giggle.

'Put the lights on, eh . . . I'm lost here!'

There was no reply. His breathing ramped.

'Fuckers.' As he started off again he continued to curse his friends. The ground was wet and treacherous; he wondered if he would be better staying still but immediately brushed the thought aside in favour of keeping moving. He had managed only another few yards when the cloud covering receded and the moonlight came out again. As he looked ahead to the newly lit field, he stopped still. He felt as if he'd been struck in the chest.

'What is that?'

There was a pale, white object sticking out of the ground.

5

It looked familiar to him, but in such an unfamiliar setting he couldn't be sure.

Ben slit his eyes, tried to get a better view. The object remained elusive. He edged a step or two closer, tilted his head towards the light but he still couldn't see it clearly enough. As he took further paces, another cloud passed over the moon and the light weakened once again. His vision diminished and he was suddenly aware of a heady scent. The smell caught in the back of his nostrils and throat, it was like something from the science labs at school, he thought.

His hand shot up to his mouth, it was an involuntary action. Was he going to gag? His stomach grew heavy, he sensed the bile rising. Then the light returned and he was facing two bright yellow eyes.

Ben's heart stilled.

He screamed out.

The sky brightened some more and the fox he had been staring at took off for the long grass. When he regained his composure he realised the pale, white object he had seen was indeed familiar: it was a woman's leg.

'Ben, you all right?' It was Garry.

'Ben . . . *Ben* . . .' And the girls.

The car headlights were shone into the field. Ben took another look at the pale, white leg. It was attached to a pale, white body.

He looked away quickly.

Ben's shoulders tensed, his throat constricted.

As his stomach heaved, he bent over and vomited on the ground.

Ben was still retching when the girls appeared, running towards him through the lit-up grass.

'Ben . . . what is it?'

6

He tried to straighten himself in time, to stop them from seeing what was there but he was too late.

The girls' loud, frightened screams were for real this time.

Chapter 1

THE FLUORESCENT GREEN OF THE alarm clock stung DI Rob Brennan's eyes as he awoke, but it was the ringing phone by the bedside that did the real damage. He reached out, knocked it off its cradle and heard it clatter to the ground. His next instinct was to turn round and see if his wife was still asleep beside him, but she wasn't there; he remembered now.

Brennan eased himself upright, leaned over the edge of the bed and retrieved the receiver; his voice rasped as he spoke, 'Yes, Brennan.'

'Hello, sorry to wake you . . .' It was DS Stevie McGuire – the lad still hadn't learned how to handle him, thought Brennan. He didn't like people who opened conversations with the word 'sorry'.

'What is it?'

The line crackled a little. There was a pause, Stevie preparing his words carefully – he knew that much then. 'Boss, there's been a call . . .'

'There better have been more than a bloody call if you're getting me out of my kip at this hour, Stevie.'

The DS coughed gently, was he thinking of another apology? 'Yes, well . . . There was a call and we had uniform check it out. By all accounts it's not pretty.'

Brennan's interest was aroused. He massaged the back of his neck with his hand and then he rose from the bed, walked towards the window and stuck his fingers in the blinds. It was still dark out. 'Go on.'

'The early reports are a female, sexually motivated.'

'Have you been to the scene?' Brennan knew he hadn't; if he had he wouldn't be relaying the uniforms' report. He was reaching, making assumptions.

'No.' Stevie sounded defensive now. 'The victim's half naked, bound and tied.'

'So it *looks* sexually motivated, Stevie.' He let the implication hang.

'Yes, sir.'

Brennan removed his fingers from the blinds, turned towards the bed. The wind outside worried the window latch. 'Where is she?'

'Just off the bypass . . . Straiton will be about the nearest if you're mapping it.'

'She's in the wilds?'

McGuire's tone softened, he seemed to be relaxing again. 'A field . . . The boffins are setting up, or on their way there now.'

Brennan gouged a knuckle into his eye, rubbed. He was awake now, but not fully functioning. It was cold in the room, it would be colder outside; the chill air should wake him, he thought, if the job didn't get there first. 'OK, Stevie, pick me up in fifteen.'

'Yes, sir.'

He hung up.

10

Brennan returned the phone to its cradle and looked at the pillow lying beside his; it didn't look slept on. His thoughts zigzagged for a moment. He turned away, flicked the light switch on, immediately his eyes creased in a defensive move as the shadeless bulb burned. He let his vision adjust for a moment or two and then he headed towards the wardrobe. He stood firm footed as he tried to grasp what his next move should be. He grabbed the first shirt he came to – pale blue, button-down collar – and matched it with the first pair of trousers he found – grey, chino-style – they had been put away with the belt still in the loops and were saggy kneed; he dressed quickly.

In the bathroom the strip light was even brighter. Brennan ran a cold palm down his chin but knew a shave, even a quick run over with the electric razor, was out of the question. He looked at his stubble, it had started to lighten, there were white spikes poking through; he wondered why the greying hadn't reached the hair on his head yet. In a moment the passing thought was expunged from his mind; he had more serious matters to consider now. The demands of the job always came first and he felt vaguely guilty to have let himself forget that, even for a second. There was a woman lying dead in a field – that was his focus now.

Outside the bathroom, Brennan stood in the top landing staring at his daughter's bedroom door. A light flickered on the inch or so of exposed jamb – she had fallen asleep with the television on again. He'd told her about that a dozen times but had always been ignored. He sighed; there was another talk he needed to have with Sophie – one he didn't want to have – and he wondered how she would react.

Brennan grabbed his jacket and overcoat from the banister, headed downstairs. He looked at his watch as he

11

went, it read 3:42. McGuire would be arriving in under five minutes. In the hallway outside the kitchen door Brennan put on his jacket, fastened the buttons, then fitted himself into his overcoat. He felt bulky as he thrashed about looking for his cigarettes. He tried all his pockets but they weren't there.

'Fucking hell,' he mumbled.

Brennan turned the handle on the kitchen door, walked in. He saw his wife straight away; she was sitting with her face towards the wall, smoking one of his cigarettes. He looked at her for a moment, tried to discern some kind of meaning from the tableau but could find none.

'Joyce . . .'

She had heard him come in, couldn't have failed to, but she refused to acknowledge him. He stared on, she was still for a moment longer and then she brought the filter tip of the cigarette up to her lips and inhaled deeply. Brennan continued watching her for a few seconds longer and then retreated through the door, closing it gently.

In the hallway, he shook his head and made for the front door. He opened up and stepped outside. At the end of the driveway Brennan felt his mind jam with incoming thoughts, none of them aligned with what he knew he should be occupying himself with. Was this the way it was going to be now? Day after day fading into one another, into insignificance. Did nothing matter any more? Certainly nothing he did made a difference. Every emotion he felt was pastiche – a throwback to childhood or adolescence when feelings meant something, indicated a mood shift or a new sensation. There were no new sensations in adult-hood. Nothing was new. All that was left was the husk of experience. Life was drudge. Endless routine. It took something painful – the shock of hurt, tears – to bring back the unsettling realisation that you could still feel.

Brennan wondered if this was why he stayed in the job. It certainly wasn't the rewards. There was no satisfaction – even capturing a killer and seeing justice served came after the event, after the killing. He could never do anything about that. His job was making sense of the mess, sweeping up after it; but never halting anything. He saved no one. If he knew this, understood this, then what did that make him: a ghoul? Did he simply get off on witnessing other people's hurt? Did it make him feel more alive – just alive, in any way – to be so close to death and to people's encounters with death?

Brennan stamped his feet, tried to knock out the cold. He felt his lungs itch for tobacco. When he got like this, a cigarette always helped. He didn't know why; all he knew was the simple act of lighting up took him out of himself. He put his thoughts into the cigarette, then watched them burn up. Wullie had always said, 'Never trust your mind, Rob . . . It's a tool, a bloody good tool, but don't let it rule you.' You had to listen to your gut too, and if there was a choice between gut and head, the gut was always right.

As the VW Passat rolled into view, McGuire raised a hand above the wheel and signalled to Brennan. The car stopped next to the kerb, dislodging some rainwater from the gutter. McGuire had the passenger's window down, was leaning over, 'Think we're going to have our work cut out with this one, sir.'

Brennan grabbed the door handle, stepped in. 'Is that what you think?'

McGuire turned, his face indicated angst, his eyebrows

rose in an apse. 'Revise what I said about *looks* sexually motivated, sir . . . We've got genital mutilation and some seriously sadistic carving. And that's just the tip of the iceberg.'

Chapter 2

'WHO HAVE YOU BEEN SPEAKING to?' said Brennan as he got inside the car and slammed the door.

'The doc . . .'

Brennan fished in the glove box for cigarettes, there were none. He eased himself further back in the seat, roved the street with his eyes. 'Is he on the scene now?'

'Well he was five minutes ago . . . I just called him.'

'I hope you told him to hang around, I don't want him fucking off to his pit for a few hours' shut-eye before private practice kicks off.'

McGuire's stare lingered on the DI for a little longer than looked healthy, he seemed to be sucking in his lips. 'Would you like me to call him again, tell him to hang on?'

Brennan returned the look, it was the one that said, *I shouldn't have to tell you, Stevie.* He slammed the glove box shut. 'Don't suppose there's any fags in this motor?'

'Sorry, sir.'

'Don't be . . . you're far too free with your apologies, laddie.'

Brennan couldn't remember when he had started calling people laddie. He certainly hadn't done it before he was forty; it would have seemed too unnatural. He wondered if it happened right around the time when people had stopped calling him son. He remembered Wullie calling him laddie when he started in the job; he didn't mind it from him. There were others who had made intimidation of junior officers into an art form though; they made you feel like you should think yourself lucky to be part of their club. Brennan had laughed them up; he was part of no club.

'So do I have to wring it out of you?' said Brennan.

McGuire turned, they were leaving Corstorphine now. 'Well, it's only been fifteen minutes since we last spoke but the SOCOs are on site and just about set up . . .'

'Spare me the details, Stevie . . . stick to the stuff it might be useful for me to know before we arrive, eh.' Brennan felt himself frowning, he was giving the DS a hard time and he knew it, but this was a murder investigation. He could let up when they had the killer in custody.

'It's a young girl, in her teens.'

'White?'

'As a ghost, by all accounts.'

'ID?'

'No ID, sir. It's dark out there, they're off the road, we might turn something up when the day breaks.'

Brennan shook his head, there should have been flood-lights up there already. Every minute was precious at this point in an investigation – without a lead in the first forty-eight hours it halved your chances of an arrest. McGuire was still talking, the DI held up a hand, 'Hang on, Stevie, who's out there for us now, Lou?'

'It's Collins, he was on call.'

'Fucking Collins . . .' Brennan picked up his mobile, dialled the DS.

Ringing.

He answered quickly, 'Collins.'

'It's Rob.'

He yawned into the phone. 'Hello, sir.'

Brennan raised his voice a notch, dropped some steel in his tone. 'How many uniform have you got out there?'

'Jesus, I haven't counted . . . half a dozen maybe.'

'Double it, and get the klieg lights out. I want the surrounds searched, and by that I mean thoroughly. If there's a fucking field mouse taking a dump on our scene I want it photographed and catalogued, got it?'

'Boss, you did read the Chief Super's memo about the OT, didn't you?'

'Listen, leave Benny to me . . . get the search done.'

He hung up.

DS Stevie McGuire was shaking his head, he looked solemn, as if he might begin to chant. 'Playing with fire aren't you?'

'This is my investigation and I won't be running every move I make past the bean counters.'

'Your call, sir.'

Brennan looked out the window; they had reached Liberton already, 'Bloody right it is.' He kept staring out into the empty city, it was bathed in a surreal glow from the street lamps. Brennan liked this hour, it reminded him of the early morning fishing trips he'd taken with his brother Andy, when they were boys; he was thinking about those times more and more now. He was thinking about too much now, he knew he needed to regain focus, keep his life outside the job.

By the sounds of it, he was dealing with a deranged killer. Murder was never pleasant, but mutilating a young girl and leaving her in a field required a warped mind. If he was to capture this killer, Brennan knew he would have to train himself to think like him. He had done this before, put himself in the mind of a maniac, tried to figure out what drove him, but he had always withdrawn quickly. It was no place to dwell for too long, but it was a fact that you could only make so much progress with generalities – you needed to get personal, understand the criminal – only then could you hope to know them, and through knowing, capture. Brennan had to be the killer – become him in mind – to feel his emotions, his thought patterns. But never to become like him. The task was to take what you could from the insanity and level it against your own mentality. It was never easy, never enjoyable.

McGuire negotiated the Straiton roundabout, said, 'It's not far up here by all accounts.'

Brennan had already spotted the police crew up ahead, pointed, 'There.'

'Oh, yeah. I see them.' McGuire put on the blinkers, started to drop down through the gears and pull off the road. As they entered the lay-by Collins spotted them and raised an arm, flagged them into the side. He approached the driver's door first.

'Morning, Stevie . . . Sir.'

The pair nodded, McGuire spoke, 'Is the doc still about?'

'Aye, Pettigrew, miserable bastard's been bending my ear for the last half hour.'

'What's his problem?' said Brennan.

Collins made a fist, shook it up and down, 'The guy's a wanker . . . that's his problem.'

Brennan didn't acknowledge the remark, exited the car. A chill blast caught him as he stood in the road. He fastened his top two buttons, turned up his collar and called out to Collins; the DS moved round to the other side of the car.

'Boss?'

'Got any smokes?'

He looked relieved, 'Aye, sure.'

Brennan removed an Embassy Regal, cupped his hand around the tip as Collins lit him up. He took two swift pelts on the cigarette then looked around the scene. It was miles from anywhere, and yet still close enough to the sprawl of the city. In an hour or two the bypass would be clogged with commuter traffic.

At the front of the lay-by an old Ford Escort was parked. There had been a car just like it at one of the first crime scenes that Brennan attended as a junior officer. It was a lock-up in Fountainbridge: the engine was running behind the door when he arrived. The door wasn't locked, but something had been stuck in the hasp on the other side. He battered the door with his shoulder to get in, then saw the man in the front seat. He'd blocked up the top of his window, around the hosepipe leading from the exhaust, with a damp towel. Brennan saw the man's face again, his skin pale, his eyes rolled up inside his head. He remembered the taste of the fumes, how they burned his lungs as he grabbed the door, lunged in, and dragged the man out. It was pointless, though; he fell limp and lifeless on the concrete floor of the lock-up. Escorts had always seemed like bad luck since then, thought Brennan.

'Whose car's that?'

'The Escort . . . that's the bloke that found it.' He looked

19

in his notebook, 'No, sorry, his mate was driving . . . Garry Johnston, that's who the car's registered to.'

Brennan flagged him down. 'Where are they now?'

'At the station, giving statements. There were two girls with them, they were a bit hysterical, thought they'd be better on a cup of tea.' He made a motion simulating the act of cup to mouth, 'Think there might have been a jug or two taken as well, if you know what I mean.'

Brennan inhaled deep on the cigarette, took another couple of quick drags and handed it back to Collins. 'Stub that in the ashtray, eh.' He nodded to the Passat.

'Sure, boss.'

DS Stevie McGuire was getting out the driver's door, zipping up a windcheater. He followed Brennan as he took off for the SOCOs' white tent.

'Didn't take them long,' said McGuire.

'Never does, like the boy fucking scouts that lot.'

At the edge of the lay-by, all the way to the gap in the verge, blue and white crime-scene tape had been put up. A uniform was still unravelling a roll of it as Brennan and McGuire ducked underneath and made their way to the SOCOs. Brennan felt the wind lash at him, there was a spit of rain in the air now – he hoped it wouldn't get any heavier, he didn't want important pieces of information to be washed away.

At the tent opening McGuire lifted the flap, motioned Brennan to go ahead first. 'After you, sir.'

He didn't think it was something to thank the junior officer for.

Chapter 3

BRENNAN KNEW BEING HUMAN WAS hard, tough. We were animals, but we were no longer allowed to be. We had come down from the trees and learned to walk upright – but, given the right circumstances, how many of us would revert to the primordial swamp? He knew it was in him, the atavistic tripwire had been crossed before: he'd struck people; thrashed some. None that hadn't deserved it, but how far had he been from the ultimate conclusion of violence? Some way, he thought, some way indeed – but he wasn't exactly sure how far.

Brennan remembered an old TV interview with the late John Lennon: he'd been asked about a line in a song of his about war and destruction; he'd said count me out, but then added count me *in*. The songwriter concluded he had to add the line because he knew he was all too human. That was the problem thought Brennan, what was *in* us was there, whether we denied it or not. He knew you only needed to turn on the news any night of the week to see evidence of the fact that, no matter how much we liked to pretend otherwise, we were animals.

If you removed the authority figures, the men in uniform, the boundaries of acceptable behaviour and consequences, then lawlessness was never far away. Desperation played a part too, like a magnifying glass on tinder, but the definition of desperation was open to interpretation. A hungry dog will fight and kill another dog for a scrap of food; human appetites were more complex, but they could trigger the same bestial reaction. None of us was immune to acting on our instincts, we could no easier be separated from them than the salt from the sea; it was our nature. We constructed an artificial image of ourselves, allowed a social duplicity to emerge when we believed in an evil strain in the blood – but, did we all have dark hearts?

We had domesticated ourselves – like we had domesticated the wolf – but the savagery we were capable of made the DI uneasy in his own skin. As he looked into the tent the SOCOs had erected he did not want to be a part, however insignificant, of the human race. It reviled him – the fact that he could draw this conclusion, intellectualise it, was no consolation. Thought and action, it seemed, bore little relation to each other. There was a wider, more sweeping force at play and none of us – man nor beast – was beyond its reach.

Brennan and McGuire were halted inside the white tent by a SOCO; he was fully suited in white overalls and held out two small boxes to the DI and the DS. Brennan removed a pair of blue covers for his shoes; when he had them in place he dipped into the other box and removed some lightweight rubber gloves. McGuire followed him. They both declined an offer of facemasks.

In the far corner of the tent, two men in white overalls stood chatting to Dr Pettigrew; he was a broad man with a small head and a short neck that looked like they'd been pressed into the bulk of his body. The doctor indicated to the ground with a yellow pencil for a moment or two and then returned to writing in a blue folder. He seemed calmer than usual, certainly for the time of day. Brennan nodded to McGuire, the pair approached the doctor.

'Good morning,' said Brennan.

'I wouldn't go that far,' said Dr Pettigrew.

Brennan declined a rejoinder. As he spoke to the doctor he became vaguely aware of the slight bundle at his feet; it was a corpse but seemed far too insignificant to have been a vessel for life. Brennan stepped away from the doctor, rounded the body and kneeled down beside it. He sensed DS McGuire behind him, he seemed eager to keep his distance.

'All right, Stevie?'

A nod, shake of the head.

Brennan turned back to the victim; a thin, pale-green plastic covering had been placed over the body, it fluttered every few seconds in the breeze that got under the tent flaps and exposed white, glass-smooth skin.

'I hope you haven't had your breakfast,' said Dr Pettigrew. When Brennan looked up, the doctor was smiling – a row of yellowed teeth on display.

This time Brennan bit, 'Don't worry, I won't splash your brogues.'

As he removed the covering, in one swift sweep, Brennan was shocked by the whiteness of the victim's body. The only relief from the harsh pallor was occasional patches of pale-blue and black skin. The girl, a young girl, lay contorted to one side. Her legs were splashed with blood and mud and her dress had been pulled up, over her head. Her stomach was exposed, but where the pale skin showed it was in sparse patches as dark blood had dried over the main share of the surface. Deep welts marked where a thick blade had struck her stomach and the tops of her thighs. Her genitals had been crudely hacked out.

Brennan turned back to McGuire; the DS looked drawn as he raised a hand to his cheek; his mouth sat slantwise and uncertain in his face. 'Stevie, go and keep an eye on Collins, eh.'

He nodded. Retreated at a jog to the tent opening.

Dr Pettigrew watched the DS go, eyes flitting about, eager for information. 'The skin colour is due to . . .'

Brennan interrupted, 'Loss of blood, yes, I know.'

'Then I don't know why the hell you need me here. It's not like I couldn't do with the extra time in bed.'

Brennan rose, he felt a flash of heat in his chest, for some reason he hoped the victim hadn't heard him and then he remembered she was dead. He fronted the doctor. 'You're here for the same reason I am – a young girl has been murdered.'

'Yes, I-I'm aware of that.' All the power had been sapped from his voice but the sound of it seemed to rally him. He pointed to the corpse, 'I didn't need to go to medical school to tell you that!'

Brennan felt the heat in his chest rise to his head, he gripped his jaw tight. The muscles in his neck firmed. Was he the only one left on the squad who cared about these people? 'Then perhaps you can put some of that medical training to good use and give me a time of death.'

The doctor eased himself back on his heels, scratched under his chin, 'Well, rigor mortis has set in . . . clearly. I'd say it's starting to subside now . . .' He hoisted up his belt as he continued, 'I'd say she's been dead a good sixteen hours anyway.'

Brennan stored the timing away, he was searching for a particle of optimism, but found none. He returned to the corpse, pointed to the doctor. 'Give me that.'

Dr Pettigrew removed a pencil from his top pocket and handed it to Brennan. He leaned forward and slipped the tip of the pencil under the hem of the girl's dress that was covering her face. The doctor was watching him as he withdrew the dress; it was stiff with dried blood.

'Jesus,' said Brennan.

'Quite a sight, isn't it.'

The DI scanned what was left of the victim's features. Her face was no more than a mass of black ruptures and contusions. She had been beaten soundly, pummelled. The girl lay at an unnatural angle, ligatures at her neck seemed to have turned it too far from her shoulders. Her mouth, parallel to the ground, was slightly open – a clump of what looked like red cloth was stuck between her teeth. At first Brennan thought the skin of her face had been flayed, there was so much blood, but then he became aware of why: her eyes had been gouged out. The swelling had hidden the sockets, but he was sure the eyeballs had been removed.

'Her eyes . . . are they?' he said.

'Removed,' said Dr Pettigrew, 'plucked out.'

Brennan shook his head, he didn't want to stare at what was left of the girl's face any longer. He returned the covering and stood up.

'Can you hazard a cause of death?'

'Take your pick, the broken neck or the abdominal punctures.'

Brennan returned to stare at the victim, her thin white arm protruded, seemed to reflect too much light. Only a few hours ago the girl was somewhere else, living her life. What had happened? How did a young girl, a teenager, turn up brutally murdered, hacked to death, in a field on the outskirts of Edinburgh? No matter how many times he had to encounter the bestial side of life and death, Brennan remained confused by it all. Each death, each life cut short, snuffed out, was another scar on his soul.

He turned back to Dr Pettigrew, pointed a finger. 'I want that girl thoroughly looked at. What is that in her mouth?'

The doctor leaned back, crossed his arms over his chest and creased his narrow forehead as he bawled out. 'We can't get the red cloth, her jaw's clamped on it. But, I'll tell you this for nothing, Inspector . . . you have a seriously deranged psychopath on the loose.'

Outside the tent Brennan removed his blue shoe coverings and handed them to a passing uniform, stomped towards McGuire. The DS was leaning on the bonnet of the Passat, staring into the night sky. The wind caught Brennan's coat as he pulled the rubber gloves from his hands, secreted them in his pocket. He stopped still for a moment, felt his shoulders tightening inexplicably, then he shook himself, buttoned his coat and approached McGuire.

'What do you think?' he said.

McGuire steadied himself on the bonnet of the car. 'I've never seen anything like it.' He fastened his eyes tight, thin radial lines appeared at their edges. 'It's just deranged . . . utterly callous.'

Brennan moved round beside him, hitched his thigh on the edge of the car's wing. 'It looks . . . *practised*.'

'What do you mean, sir?'

'The ligatures, the hacked genitals and the eyes . . . it's all specific.'

McGuire turned to face him, 'You think this is pathological, like some kind of ritual?'

Brennan looked out to the field, there were more SOCOs arriving, directing photographers. 'No, not ritual, more like a release. What I'm saying is, it's systematic – and controlled – our killer knew what he wanted out of this.'

'I hate to admit it, sir, but Pettigrew's right then – we've got a psycho on the loose.'

Brennan eased himself off the bonnet of the car, the springs wheezed beneath him. 'It's more than that, Stevie, we've got a psycho who's acted on his urges.' He crossed the ground towards the car's door. 'And it's down to us to stop him acting on them again.'

Chapter 4

NEIL HENDERSON WATCHED THE PRISON officer
pack up his belongings, tipping the little plastic containers
into the brown paper bag. He was sneering, the bastard was
sneering at him, he thought.

'Got something to say to me, pal?' said Henderson.

The officer shook his head, dropped his chin onto his
chest and jangled some coins into the bag. He looked to
be enjoying himself too much, continued to sneer.

A spasm twitched on Henderson's lip as he spoke, 'No,
come on, out with it.'

The officer closed a drawer, turned a key in the lock
and then returned to Henderson's possessions. The bag
was full now, he rolled over the top, made it into a neat
bundle then passed it through the chute. He was still
sneering as he made a little wave through the glass. 'See
you soon, sunshine!'

Henderson double blinked. The muscles in his neck tightened, became firm rods. He wanted to punch the window,
smack the screw bastard. They were all the same, screws

and filth; just out to rumble you, give you a hard time. They got off on it. He spat out, 'You'll be fucking lucky!'

A laugh now, he was laughing at him. His Adam's apple rose and fell as he spoke through the laughter, 'Want to take a wee bet?'

Another screw came into the picture, a fat bastard with pools of sweat under his armpits, they were both laughing in sync. The one who called him sunshine rubbed his hands together, then pointed at his palm. 'Could make a few quid at this, Drew.'

'Yeah, yeah . . . Only this prick hasn't got a penny. What's he gonna bet with?'

The prison officer tugged at his earlobe, tilted his head and pretended to look thoughtful. 'Have to go out and rob someone . . . Now there's an idea, Hendy!'

Henderson inflated his chest and yelled, 'Fuck off.'

'That's what you do, isn't it?'

'I said, fuck off.'

The other screw joined in, he leaned over the counter and widened his eyes, raised his voice. 'Robbing and beating the shite out of innocent old punters. You followed him home from the bookies, didn't you. Wonder if that old boy's family will be waiting for you out there?'

The other one jumped in, 'His son's a rugby player, I heard.'

They were winding him up, just sticking the needle in. Henderson grabbed his belongings from the chute; the bag was bulky and the brown paper wrapping rustled loudly as he tugged it free. When he had the package under his arm he raised a single digit on his right hand and said, 'Get fucked.'

The tone suddenly changed, the screws weren't having

29

a laugh any more. The big one pointed at him through the glass. 'I hope you do, mate. I hope you get well and truly fucked, because you know what, you deserve it. You're an animal.'

'You don't know what you're talking about. You know fuck all about me.'

The screw nodded, his meaty neck quivered under his chin. 'I know your type. And I know a leopard doesn't change its spots.' He leaned closer, got right up against the glass, 'You'll be back in here in under a month. How do I know that? Because you're all the same. You're scum, Henderson. Just trash.'

Henderson's pulse raced, he dived for the screen, got close enough to face the screw but was yanked back by his shoulder, another prison officer turned him away. 'Move it!'

The pair beyond the glass were still staring. What had started out as a bit of innocent patter had turned ugly. It always turned out like that, thought Henderson. 'Get fucked the pair of you!' he yelled.

'I said move it!' The screw poked him in the back.

Henderson thundered along the corridor, his heart was still beating hard. He wanted to attack the screws; he wanted to show them who he was, that he didn't take that kind of shit from anyone. Least of all a couple of lard-arsed screws. He was Hendy the Leith boy; he was known. Folk knew that name, knew who he was. He wasn't to be messed with.

As he walked his rushing blood calmed, seemed to settle. When he got like that, he couldn't control it. He just wanted to lash out. He couldn't change that, it was who he was. He put his energy into his stride, but the prison followed him. The prison smell haunted him. He would never forget that smell; on his first night he'd asked an old giffer what the smell was. 'The stench of a thousand reeking bastards,' he'd told him, 'their farts and shits, their BO and their utter fucking despair!'

There was no escape from it, the prison got under your skin. It polluted you. If it wasn't some radge talking about who he'd offed on the outside it was some nut-job looking to make a name for himself by offing someone on the inside. You had to be on your toes, every minute of the day. There was no way of avoiding it; if you didn't play the game then they thought there was something wrong with you. That's how rumours started. He remembered the bloke who'd got moved from Kilmarnock, he never fitted in, never made the effort and then folk started to say he was a nonce. A beast. He was battered into a coma.

That's what prison had taught Neil Henderson, to be tough; to get the first punch in. No one was looking out for you in the pound. You were on your own. And if you let your guard down for a second it could be fatal. Life was like that, too. That's what they all said. 'Get your retaliation in first!' That's what he'd been told, and that's what he believed.

'You got someone coming for you, Hendy?' said the screw.

'I don't know, not a fucking mind reader am I.'

The screw shook his head. 'Have you no family?'

Henderson shrugged.

The screw rattled some keys. 'What about a girl?'

'What the fuck's it got to do with you?'

The conversation came to an abrupt halt as the prison officer opened the first door into an enclosed area that had been partitioned off. He pointed to a sheet of paper on a clipboard, said, 'Sign.'

'What's this?'

'For your possessions.'

Henderson grabbed the brown paper bag tighter. 'You better not have nicked anything . . . I know what I came in here with, got it all up here,' he tapped his head.

'You saw it counted out, now sign it or you'll be in another night. That what you want?'

Henderson grabbed the pen, signed. When he was finished he let the biro fall, it swung on its chain, rattled off the wall. The screw picked it up and placed it on the counter. 'Always the arsehole, right to the end, eh. You learnt nothing in here?'

'Oh, I learnt plenty, mate . . . fucking plenty.'

The screw turned down the corners of his mouth, he seemed to have something else to say but kept it to himself. It was a look that Henderson had seen many times before, it had started at home, when he had a home, then it was school, the workplace, the street, pubs. Everywhere. Someone always seemed to be ready to tell Neil Henderson how to lead his life, where he was going wrong.

A key turned in a large lock, then another. A bolt slid across the door and then light and a cool breeze flooded in. Henderson tipped back his head to inhale the luxury of clean air.

'Don't get too used to it out there, sure we'll be seeing you again soon.'

Henderson smiled. He was too pleased to see the outside world to manage a riposte. As he stepped over the prison threshold he felt a weakness in his knees. He was out. He was back in the real world. For a second he felt exhilarated and then he felt a tightening in his gut. Something twisted there, like a rag being wrung out. He wondered what it

32

was. Fear? Panic? It was nothing, surely. Just the shock of being out, of getting away from that shit-hole. There would be no more, he was out.

'You fucking beauty!'

He looked up Gorgie Road, he could go anywhere, do anything. He sniffed the air like a dog that had been kept in for too long. Beer, he wanted a bevy. He could grab a pint and then, at the weekend, he could see Hearts. The glorious Jam Tarts.

Henderson was free, he felt it like a rush. He raised his bag and ran towards the bus stop.

Chapter 5

ANGELA MICKLE HAD WOKEN WITH a humming in her head, she didn't quite know if it was the humming that came from a hangover or the humming that precipitated her withdrawal from heroin. She'd shot up but knew the slim takings she'd managed out on the Links the night before weren't going to be enough to score again soon; and she would need to score again soon.

Her arms itched, her throat was dry and the humming in her head made her feel woozy. There were bruises too, finger marks on her arms; her last punter had been too rough, but he'd paid extra for that. She touched her lip, it had been split, she remembered the knuckle cracking off her teeth. She'd told him, bawled him out, but he said he was taking what he'd paid for and that was that. 'Scream all you want you dirty whore, who's going to hear you out here?'

That's what he'd said.

He'd driven her to an old factory site in East Lothian, miles from anywhere and threatened to leave her there if she didn't play along. As Angela gripped herself, felt her bruised ribs, it didn't seem like such a good idea now. Even for the extra twenty pounds.

She looked at herself in the mirror that sat on the floor beside the mattress where she lay. Her dirty blonde hair needed washed, there was blood smeared in it. Her lips were cracked and scabbed, she couldn't go out looking like this. But she needed to go out, to score. It was a Friday, punters were always looking to score at the end of the week, they were flush with wages. That's what Hendy had told her; he had looked after her.

Angela knew she couldn't go out in the daylight, there was too much aggro now from residents on the Links. Nosey bastards; Edinburgh was full of them. It was a town full of square pegs. It wasn't her town any more, it didn't feel like the place she'd grown up in, but she couldn't see herself going anywhere else now; not any time soon anyway.

Angela raised herself from the mattress; she felt a little sick rising in her stomach, it reached her throat and she threw up on the floor. Some milky-white vomit splashed on the mattress and her foot. She leaned over and felt the knots in her stomach again.

'Got to fucking score,' she said.

As she edged over to the wall, tried to steady herself, she became vaguely aware of noise from beyond the front door of her flat. It jarred with the humming in her head, made her feel worse. But it was Leith, there was always noise in Leith stairwells. This was something different, however; it sounded like a celebration.

'What the fuck's going on?'

Angela pushed out her thin legs, they were bruised and scraped. At one stage her punter had kicked her out of his car, she'd landed in an overgrown bramble bush; she remembered now. So much of what she did seemed a haze at the time, but it always came back to her the next day. That's when she wanted another hit, to block it all out. Angela Mickle didn't want any reminders of what her life had become.

There was a knock at the door; heavy thuds.

She felt her heart kick. Little needles tingled at the back of her eyes. It didn't feel like fear, but it was confusion. She tried to push herself forward. Her hands steadied herself on the wall as she placed one foot in front of the other, slowly at first, but then she found something close to a rhythm.

The knock came again. Louder this time.

'Angela, open up, eh?'

It was a man, who?

She wasn't expecting anyone, the rent was paid – it had been short but she wangled her usual five-finger discount from the landlord. He was starting to get greedy, had asked her to see to his friend as well.

'Angela, fuck's sake . . .'

She got close to the door, cupping her stomach in her hand like she was holding in the contents. The voice sounded familiar now; as she reached the spy-hole she peered out. Her vision was too blurred to make out any more than the shape of a man's frame. She paused for a moment, remembered her beating the night before. She felt scared, but she also wanted to block everything out and there was only one way to do that; only one way to get the money to do that. She slid the chain, turned the key in the lock and opened up the door.

'Hello, Ange.'

It was Henderson.

'*You*?'

He stood there, smiling. He had a television under his arm, one of those thin flat-screen ones. 'Look, I brought you a pressie.'

'But, when . . . I thought you weren't due out for another six months.'

Henderson put a foot in the door, 'Aye well, they let me out a wee bit early.'

Angela stepped back, let him in. 'But how . . . why?'

'I dunno do I . . . something about overcrowding or that, needed the cells.'

As Henderson walked through the hallway, Angela closed the door behind him. He shook his head at the state of the place, he seemed to have something stuck to his shoe – a used condom. 'Fucking hell, Ange . . . This place is a rat-hole.'

She stood in the doorway, shivering. 'Well . . .'

'*Well*, do something about it . . .' Henderson shook the condom from his shoe. 'Have you been turning tricks in here?'

Angela shrugged. 'Maybe.'

'No fucking maybe about it.' He moved towards the window, opened up. 'This place fucking stinks. Bad.'

Angela took a step forward, 'Where did you get the telly?'

'What kind of a question's that?' Henderson turned round, looked at her. He stood facing her for a moment, showed her an open palm. 'A man in a pub, of course.' He turned away from her, leaned towards the shelving unit by the window and swept the contents off with the back of his hand. Angela shrieked as a cup smashed on the floor.

'This place is a tip . . .' said Henderson, he pointed at

the cup. 'I'd get that cleaned up . . . you going about in your bare feet and all that, you'll get cut.'

Angela moved over to the shelves, started to gather up the shards of pottery as Henderson plugged in the television. 'Good job I brought the cord as well . . . Bloodywell knew you'd have no cord for the aerial!'

The picture on the television came clear and sharp, Henderson stepped back, looked pleased with himself.

'Not fucking bad, eh.'

Angela nodded as she emptied the broken cup shards into an open drawer. She moved to stand beside Henderson. He put an arm out, 'Don't crowd me out, come on.'

She put a hand into his jacket, 'Hendy, I'll look after you.'

He faced her for a moment, removed her hand from him. 'I don't need any looking after, Ange.'

'But, I will . . . y'know, if you look after me.'

Henderson grinned, tipped back his head. 'I'm not holding, if that's what you were thinking.'

'I need a shot, Hendy. I need it bad, I had a rough time last night.'

He flicked the television channels, found the lunchtime news slot. 'That's the nature of the business you're in love, I'd say it's you that needs me.'

She nodded, 'I do. I need you, Hendy.'

'Aye well. Maybe we'll see about that.' He pointed the remote control at the screen, shushed Angela as he increased the volume. 'Check this out, that's Edinburgh.'

The newscaster started to relay the details of a murder scene.

'*Police are remaining tight-lipped about the discovery of a body on the outskirts of the city. No identification has been*

38

released for what is believed to be the body of a teenage girl found in a field near to the town of Straiton . . .'

The camera zoomed in. Police officers stood outside a white tent as men in full-body overalls came and went.

'Oh, my God!' said Angela. She stared at the screen, raised a hand to her mouth and began to tremble.

'Funny seeing your own town on the telly isn't it,' said Henderson. 'Look there's some filth daftie looking stupid!'

Angela raised both her hands to her mouth, then quickly put them to her ears, turned away from the screen. 'Off. Off. Off.'

Henderson scoffed, 'What?'

'Turn it off.' Angela moved towards the mattress on the floor, threw herself down and began to sob. 'Turn it off. I don't want to see it. I don't want to see that place.'

'What is it?' Henderson walked round to her side, pointed the remote control at the television, 'Right there you go, it's off. What the fuck's up with you?'

She sat up, screamed at him. 'Why did you have to come back? . . . Why? . . . Why did you have to bring that in here?'

'It's just a telly!'

She rose on her knees and started to lash out with her fists, 'You brought that here . . . That place.'

She was still lashing out, screaming hysterically as Henderson brought an open palm across her face. She fell sideways onto the mattress and was quiet.

Chapter 6

DI ROB BRENNAN WALKED INTO the café on Shandwick Place, nodded to the woman behind the counter and produced a low-voltage smile. She already had the dazed, tired look of someone who was ill-at-ease with their lot; it was barely lunchtime. In Edinburgh, Brennan expected no less; working at a till could hardly afford you enough to cover the bus fares.

'Coffee please, black,' he said.

She nodded, retreated to the machine on the counter behind her and started to batter ten bells out of it. Brennan eased himself to the side of the queue of people; the place was filling up.

He had been home, caught a few hours' sleep, but his mind never really relaxed. He could still see the image of the bloodless girl, dead in a field on the outskirts of the city. He knew it would never leave him. There were cases that he had worked when he was still in uniform, still buddied to a proper officer, that haunted him to this day. Death was always with him.

Brennan looked around the café; most people were dead anyway, he thought. Couples of varying ages stared out into the bright, over-lit, open-plan area. Few of the assembled made eye contact. Or even attempted conversation. Their mouths opened and closed like fish as they gnawed on shortbread biscuits and supped beverages that they didn't really want anyway.

They were dead. If any were alive once, they didn't know it, or, had forgotten it. What did life mean to a fool? What did it mean to him? Brennan's days had been full of death; brutal, sometimes barbaric death – as he looked around this slim section of the public, he questioned the worth of his occupation. Would any of these drones miss what they had if it was suddenly wrung out of them? If their precious life was snuffed out – what difference would it make to the world to lose one more of these lifeless cabbages?

Brennan shook himself. It was a pathetic indulgence that he had allowed himself: weighing the value of a life. Who was he, God? He knew it meant nothing – no more than the flip remark that death comes to us all. It was a stupid thing to do and he understood that, regretted it at once.

The victim was only one half of the equation – the perpetrator was the other. Any notion that the victim had to be of an exalted value to the human race missed the point. It was the act, not the consequence Brennan knew he had to concern himself with now. It was the cold cruelty. The malevolence. The evil. That's what fired him. No matter how indifferent he was to the mass of men and their lives of quiet desperation, he could not conceive of killing anyone himself; it took another type of man to do that – the type he had sworn to protect all others from.

'Black coffee,' the woman on the counter shouted out.

'Yeah, mine. Thanks.'

Brennan took it, held it steady as he returned to the car. He opened the door, stepped in behind the wheel. A little coffee escaped from the brim of the Styrofoam cup, slid down the side and scalded his fingers.

'Shit.'

He quickly swapped the cup into his other hand, pulled out the holder on the dash and slotted the coffee cup in it. The DI exhaled deeply, gathered himself for a moment, then tugged over his seatbelt and drove off.

At the edge of Princes Street, the tram works – that eternal gutting of the city – had diverted traffic up Lothian Road in a snaking one-way system. There were new temporary traffic lights in operation. He couldn't keep up with the changes in the city's road layouts. There was a burning, sneaking assumption lurking in him that said the council was orchestrating this as a revenge for the public's rejection of its congestion charge.

Brennan banged on the rim of the wheel, said, 'Come on for fuck's sake.'

The traffic was stationary. He had a full view of a tram – immobile – that had been installed at the foot of the Castle, on the main shopping thoroughfare. The idea was to give the city a taste of things to come; Brennan knew there would be snowballs in hell before a single tram got rolling. He readied himself to curse again as the light changed; he engaged the clutch and geared the car forward.

'About bloody time.'

On Queensferry Street, Brennan removed a cigarette from his packet of Embassy Regal; he had reached the point where he didn't care about giving up now. He had once tried to cut back, tried smoking milder brands, but now he was so entrenched in his own form of personal nihilism that he had abandoned the idea. He pressed the lighter in the dash and waited for the ping.

By Fettes, Brennan had smoked three-quarters of the cigarette and his coffee was now cool enough to drink. He stubbed the dowp on the tarmac and walked with his coffee cup held out in front of him. The door was opened by a waiting uniform. He nodded a thank you.

Inside, the desk sergeant greeted him. 'Morning, Rob.'

More nods, the standard greeting. 'Doesn't feel like morning.'

'You were on the early start out at Straiton . . . Saw it on the lunchtime news.'

'Aye, so did I.'

'You don't sound chuffed.'

'Would you be, Charlie.' It wasn't a question. More of a statement to confirm his position.

The older man leaned forward; the bright lights above the desk caught on his pate and momentarily blinded Brennan. 'The Chief Super's been running around like he's got a bee in his bonnet.'

'Really?'

A look to the left, a tweak of the nose. 'I keep expecting the wee baldy fella to show up and Benny to start slapping his head!'

Brennan permitted himself a laugh. Chief Superintendent Bernard Hill had only been in the station a few months and had already earned himself the moniker *Benny*.

'I better get up there . . . Though I suspect it'll be no joke.'

Charlie pinched his lips like he was about to whistle, rested his chin on his knuckles. 'Aye, well . . . He's already pulled the station roster, counting the overtime up, that'll be down to you, no doubt.'

Brennan dipped his head. He felt the blood stiffen in his veins. He had a murderer to catch, he didn't need to have his every move costed and budgeted. He turned for the stairs. On the way up he passed a young WPC, she was carrying a blue folder and tried not to catch the officer's attention; he remembered what it was like to be her age, at her stage on the career path, and afraid of senior officers. At that stage, Brennan had wanted to ascend the ranks, purely so he could be the one giving the orders. Was it just ego? he thought. Had his ego pushed him to this point?

At the top of the stairs Brennan took a sip from his coffee cup. He glanced down the corridor towards the Chief Super's office; he was in, his secretary was sitting by the door typing up some no doubt important piece of documentation, like an RSVP to the Provost's latest black-tie event. Brennan stared for a moment longer, he thought about the short distance that the Chief Super's office was from his own and whether it was a distance he wanted to, or indeed ever would, cover. He had once spoken to Wullie about why he had never progressed beyond DI and the old boy understood intuitively where he was coming from. 'You're too smart to go chasing rank, Rob . . . You know already that, up or down, the ladder's shaky, son,' he had said. Brennan had a smile to himself as he thought of Wullie, he missed him around the place. There were far too many careerists and glory hunters on the scene now.

As he turned to face Incident Room One, Brennan heard his name called from the other end of the corridor. He glanced over his shoulder but already he knew the voice belonged to Benny.

'A minute, please, Rob.' The Chief Super stood in his doorway, buttoned up, spick and span as ever.

Brennan stared at him for a second or two, took in his worth. Hill was about the same age as he was, but he was shorter. The Chief Super had a weaker frame and he wore glasses; he didn't look the type to go far in frontline policing. He leaned over his secretary's desk, removed his glasses for a moment, then ushered Brennan like a toreador, 'Well, come along.'

'Coming.' The DI nodded, started a slow trail towards his superior's outer-office door. Once inside he closed the door gently, nodded and smiled towards Dee the secretary, and proceeded to the door marked Bernard Hill, Chief Superintendent.

'Take a seat, Rob.'

'Is it going to take that long? . . . I have a murder investigation on the go.'

The Chief Super returned his glasses to his nose, it was a delicate bulb nose and looked to be rimmed in red, like he had been battling a cold for too long. He indicated the seat with the flat of his hand. 'Please.'

Brennan obliged him, pulled out the chair and lowered himself onto it.

'I wanted to grab you before you went through . . . There's been some developments.'

'Oh, yes.' Brennan felt himself shift his weight in the chair. 'What would they be?'

'We have ID'd the victim.'

Brennan tensed up, 'What? . . . When did this come in?'

'Look, calm down . . . It's just in this minute, I'm literally just off the phone to the lab, I was on my way to call you.'

Brennan's stock of anger subsided a little, 'Well . . . Are you going to fill me in? I *am* the investigating officer.'

The Chief Super peered over his glasses at Brennan, his eyes were damp and red-webbed but the look was a definite warning. 'Well, we cross-matched the victim's dental records from those on the missing persons list, locally that is, there weren't so many – we got a lucky break . . .'

Brennan felt himself gripping the arm of the chair tightly. 'Really, lucky for who, sir?'

'Well, not the young girl. Or her family . . . Which reminds me, would you, eh . . .'

Brennan nodded. 'Consider it done.'

'Good. Good. Her name is Lindsey Sloan, like I say, a local girl . . . There's a file obviously.' The Chief Super removed a blue folder from the top of a pile on his desk and handed it to Brennan. It seemed a slim volume to contain the details of a life that had ended; it would be added to now though, in minute detail. It struck him that most victims attracted more attention in death than they ever did in life; the thought gored him.

'I'll alert the parents.'

Brennan rose.

'Oh, if you don't mind . . .' The Chief Super indicated the chair again. 'I'm not finished.'

'No?'

'No, I'm not. I wanted to ask if you'd seen this?'

He passed a sheet of paper over the desk towards Brennan, who turned it around, scanned the rubric. It was the memorandum about the complete ban on overtime. Brennan took a deep breath and stared out of the window; he caught sight of a road sweeper leaning on his broom.

'Well, you did see this?'

'Yes.'

'And?'

'And, what, sir?'

The Chief Super looked perplexed, he removed his glasses again, started to fumble for words. He tapped a pile of papers on the other side of the desk. 'This is the duty roster, it's what we are budgeted for this month.' He picked up another pile of papers, 'And this is what has been added to it from your little escapade last night . . . Where am I supposed to find the savings?'

Brennan rolled his eyes towards his feet. 'I think that's an administrative issue, sir . . . As I said, I'm running a murder investigation.'

The Chief Super gasped, his neck seemed to shorten as he threw himself back in his chair. 'I don't believe I'm hearing this. Do you read the papers?'

'Yes, full of crime, sir.'

'I was referring to the recession . . . The country is in dire straits in case you haven't noticed, and we are public servants, we have to do our bit. Do we understand each other?'

When he was younger, Brennan knew, he would have flared up after a remark like that. But not now. For some time he had come to the conclusion that life was an endless succession of such blows. Wullie had called it 'eating crow'. Brennan knew the bird was a staple of every man's diet, and it was a measure of the man how much he could consume without reacting.

He answered, 'I think we understand each other, sir.' His heart beat faster now, he felt it pounding beneath his shirt front, but his chest cavity felt strangely empty. He was trapped, but he knew it was futile to struggle in the trap.

It only made things worse, made the job more difficult for you.

The Chief Super painted a thin smirk on his face, 'Good, I'm glad we understand each other. Because any further misunderstandings will have very serious consequences, Inspector.'

Chapter 7

BRENNAN KNEW THAT LIFE WAS never going to be easy for him. For some it was. For the brutes whose only aim was to get snout to trough, life was simple, a joy even. For the thinking, the intelligent, it was a complex affair. He recalled an interrogation of a repeat offender – a gangly youth he'd watched grow into a stocky recidivist – who said he'd been in trouble his whole life because he 'just had one of those faces'. Brennan knew he had one of those faces too; but there was more. There was something inside him – an energy he was dimly aware of. He would often feel it rise in him, force him to rebel, and even when he held it in check – ignored it, sublimated it – it was still there. It shone out of him, it showed in his face, and the brutes scented it like pack dogs detecting adrenaline before an attack.

Brennan had tried to deny his self, who he was inside – to have an easy life – but it didn't work. It merely weakened him, his energy attenuated. Denial of his true self only brought in doubts, and ultimately lowered the innate respect

49

he had for himself. By the age he was now, Brennan knew he should have accepted his lot. Both physically and spiritually – he was what he was. There was no point fighting it, denying himself. But he sometimes longed for an easier path from birth to death – how could he not when the ignorant brutes had it so good?

He felt controlled like a marionette on strings. Life was all about control – who had it, who controlled whom – it dictated the level of your contentment and happiness. If you were a controller, the world felt like it was yours, even a small world. But if you were controlled, even a little, you were nothing but someone's plaything. Brennan had sometimes wondered about leaving the force, the city, hauling up somewhere alien to him. Somewhere where no one knew him, where he could be free, untrammelled. But it was only a dream. There was no escape from his lot and he knew it. The inner scream could rage, roar louder, but it had to be suppressed. Exhibiting doubts was a weakness, and if they saw weakness on the force, it made their control of you even stronger.

The door's hinges wheezed as Brennan entered Incident Room One. At once heads turned in his direction: he managed to ignore them for his first few steps but when Lou and Brian turned round to greet him in unison, the DI halted. He saw McGuire down the other end of the room at the whiteboard with Elaine Docherty, one of the WPCs; they seemed to be very close but separated instantly as they caught sight of Brennan; he tipped back his head to beckon McGuire over.

'Right, listen up.'

The room stilled. A few rose from chairs, others eased themselves onto the corners of desks. Files and coffee cups were put down.

'There have been some developments in the last few minutes . . .' The silence was interrupted by a cackle of low voices. Brennan raised his own voice, 'We have a name for our victim. She is a local girl and was on the missing persons' list so we tied the dental together pretty quickly.'

'What's her name, boss?'

Brennan turned over the blue folder in his hand, opened up. He was surprised to see a colour photograph of a smiling young girl; she looked nothing like the bloodless corpse he'd seen a few hours ago. 'Her name is Lindsey Sloan, I'll be giving the details over to Stevie and he can fill you in . . .' Brennan leaned forward, passed the folder to the DS.

'Have the parents been notified?' said McGuire.

Brennan shook his head, 'That's a job for you and me this afternoon, Stevie.'

'I can hardly wait.'

The DI continued his impromptu briefing. 'Now, I don't need to tell you that the scene of the crime was particularly gruesome. Let there be no doubt in anyone's mind that we are dealing with a deranged killer . . .' Brennan spotted the far entrance door to the room open, DI Jim Gallagher sauntered in and pulled out a chair; as he sat he swept a hand over his thick-set jowls. He was not part of the squad; Brennan eyed him down the length of the room, 'Something for us, Jim?'

Headshakes, a smoker's cough into a fist. 'No, just passing through. Carry on . . .'

Brennan ignored the interruption, 'Right, what's everyone got for me?'

Lou was first to speak, 'Well, everything's up in the air now that we have an ID, surely.'

'Nothing come out the field?'

'Cow shit, sir,' said Collins.

'That it?'

'Not a mark; there's some footprints but they're looking like the kid's . . .' He turned over a page in his notebook, 'Er, Ben Russell.'

'What's he had to say for himself?' said Brennan.

Collins deferred to McGuire.

A shrug, 'Not much, they were out clubbing, he stopped for a pish, found the victim. He's a student, the whole lot from the car were, I don't think they've got a parking ticket between them.'

Brennan swayed on the balls of his feet, pinched the tip of his nose with thumb and forefinger. 'They never saw anything on the road . . . car, punter, fucking milk-float?'

'Not a thing, boss.'

'Right, Brian . . . you're up,' said Brennan, he pointed to the DS, clapped hands together. 'Come on, chop-chop, eh.'

Brian rose, 'I just checked with Dr Pettigrew about an hour ago, the postmortem's not been done yet.'

'What?'

Brian shrugged, 'He's due in later on . . . I tried to tell him you wouldn't be pleased.'

'Fucking right I'm not . . . So, is that it?'

Brennan watched Jim Gallagher get up and walk back to the door, he was putting a cigarette in his mouth as he went, mouthed a silent 'Catch you later' to the DI. Brennan scanned the rest of the room, looking for a grain of information.

'Unbelievable. Right, who's doing the door-to-door?'

McGuire looked in his file, 'Smeeton's heading it up. He's out now. Still early days yet, boss.'

Brennan frowned, 'Try telling that to the press office when the hacks start on us . . . Call Smeeton, tell him to update us on the hour, sooner if he turns anything up. And that goes for the rest of you as well, anything comes in I do not want to hear about it second hand. Got it?'

Together, 'Yes, sir.'

'Good. Right, that's it. Off you trot.'

Brennan walked towards the whiteboard at the other end of the room. Some pictures the SOCOs had taken had been stuck up there; he removed the photograph of Lindsey Sloan from the file McGuire held and stuck it beside the others. He was writing her name beside the picture when McGuire spoke.

'Pretty girl?'

Brennan nodded, placed the cap back on the pen. 'What was Jim Gallagher after?'

McGuire shrugged. 'Search me.'

'Let me know if he starts sniffing about, I don't want him big-footing us.'

McGuire ran a thumb over his chin, 'Is that likely?'

'He's a glory hunter isn't he. Find out what he's working on and let me know, eh.'

McGuire nodded. 'Aye, sure.'

'And whilst you're at it I want you to get hold of a profiler.'

'OK, we're owed a favour by Northern, I'll get them to send down McClymont.'

Brennan shook his head, 'No I want Joe Lorrimer.'

'Who?'

'He's Strathclyde. They might not owe us any favours, though.'

McGuire creased back the corners of his mouth. 'Benny won't like it coming out our budget.'

'Fuck Benny,' said Brennan. 'I'll deal with him in my own way.'

Chapter 8

DI ROB BRENNAN KNEW PEOPLE didn't like you when you were police. When they found out, they were over cautious around you. They'd hold back, make jokes about watching what they said; but they weren't joking. The job followed you everywhere, and when someone knew what and who you were their attitude changed. It was always perceptible – pointed, blatant. There were some officers in the ranks who became different people out of uniform, off duty. They changed their personalities and became like class clowns, over eager to please, joking and affecting a false bonhomie. It never helped, thought Brennan, it worsened the situation. People were instinctively wary and raised their guards higher, they thought you were trying to inveigle some useful information out of them or, worse, catch them out.

This was something they never told you about at the training academy; they told you how to think, feel and react on the job, to get the end product they wanted, but the toll the job took on the individual didn't concern them. Training was pointless, there were some aspects of the job you just couldn't be taught. Brennan remembered a spell on traffic as a young uniform, he was with another new recruit, a young woman from Stirling called Elsie. They were supposed to be no more than a speeding deterrent, it was a confidence builder for the pair of them – out on their own without a senior officer, free of the buddy system for the first time.

An old Cortina had come haring over the brow of a hill.

'Jesus, look at the speed of him,' said Elsie.

Brennan had run to the side of the road instinctively, 'He's going to hit that truck if he doesn't straighten up.'

There was a stationary row of traffic on the other side of the hill and the Cortina veered from side to side when the brakes were applied.

Elsie raised her voice, 'Rob, he's going to hit it!'

Brennan felt helpless, what could he do? Suddenly there was a loud thud, a dull noise, a dunt. Not what he had expected. The Cortina connected with the rear of the dump-truck which shuddered slightly but remained largely unmoved.

'Oh, my God,' said Elsie, her voice was a shrill wail.

The pair of them jogged to the site of the collision; the driver of the truck was getting out of his cab as Brennan arrived first.

'Stay inside, sir.'

Brennan saw the two front wheels of the Cortina raised off the ground, the front end of the vehicle was wrapped round the axle of the dump-truck like tinfoil. About a quarter of the bonnet had survived, the windscreen had been destroyed; at least that's what Brennan's first thought was.

As he got closer to the car, he saw the driver was still

in the front seat, but he could see now that the windscreen had not shattered, it had popped out and severed the driver's head clear from his shoulders. The torso, though intact, was showered in bright blood. On the back seat the head had come to rest in a pool of crimson.

'No. No.' Elsie appeared behind him, became hysterical.

'It's OK.' Brennan didn't know what to say. She was in shock. He turned her away from the car. 'Don't look, don't look.'

But she had looked, she had seen a severed head, doused in a profusion of blood, the arteries of the neck still pumping it out. Brennan remembered Elsie now, she was barely twenty at the time. She left the force soon after. As he recalled the accident he knew there were some things no one should have to see, and knew he had seen more than his fair share of them.

'This is the worst part of the job,' said McGuire.

Brennan turned in his seat; they were coming into Pilrig. 'I can think of worse.'

McGuire flitted eyes towards the DI, seemed to be assessing him. He quickly returned his gaze to the road, negotiated a speed bump. 'Well, what I mean is . . .'

Brennan cut in, 'I know, Stevie, it's not a favourite task of mine.'

'There just never seem to be the right words.'

'To tell a parent their child is dead . . . no, there never are the right words.'

It was one of those unseen aspects of the job, the kind of thing that Brennan had done a thousand times without blinking. There was no way of knowing how to conduct yourself in such situations, he had seen parents fold, crumple, dissolve before his eyes and he had seen others

57

react with utter disbelief. Some had even laughed, thought it was a joke. No two were the same. They all required a different approach, it was about looking into their eyes and delivering the worst piece of news they had ever encountered and understanding that any reaction – even violence – was justified. There was no training manual that could teach you how to do it.

Brennan knew his world – life on the force – was tough, aggressive. It was the pressure of policing, it caused those on the job to change whatever they were before they joined up and become like the rest. It was the culture, but it was a self-defence mechanism too. You smoked, drank, cursed and talked crudely, acted aggressively because that's how the people that inhabited this world acted. The stress levels rose, the tension rose, and you had to find a way of releasing the valve that held them inside.

What continued to surprise Brennan, the longer he was on the force, was the sympathy, the heartfelt sorrow that officers showed those in grief; it affected those on the force every bit as much as the family. Even old hands, those who had learned to compartmentalise the job, showed their hurt, their disgust, from time to time. Grief could seep out over a pint or after revealing the death to the victim's family, but the abreact came and, when it did, it drew a squad closer together. The family's pain touched you, became your pain.

Brennan knew that another family's hurt was about to become his own. It was a perverse form of vicarious sadism, to know that he was about to share the burden of strangers' misery, worse was to know he had done it before and continued to do it. How could he remain human, how could he continue to function? At times like this, the job was a test of sanity. He could halt his reaction, lock it away and forget about it. But he knew he was kidding himself, it would still be there, and would surface at some moment when he was unawares. It didn't matter how it was triggered, over a crossword puzzle, a familiar patch of carpet that reminded him of the victim's home, it didn't matter, it would be waiting, and that was that.

'Over here,' Brennan pointed to a small end-terrace house on the road McGuire had just turned into. The garden was neatly tended and the property looked to have been well cared for, one of the few in the street. 'One with the silver Corolla outside.'

'I see it,' said McGuire. He pulled up behind the car.

Brennan nodded, released his seatbelt. 'Well, we can be glad the press haven't got here before us.'

McGuire tutted, 'We're ahead of the posse for now you mean.'

In the street two teenage boys kicked an empty can of Cally Special between themselves, they laughed loudly as they went; the noise from the can and their laughter rattled up and down the street. Brennan looked at them in their skinny jeans, arse cheeks on show beneath exposed underwear and then he looked at the Sloans' house. He approached the pair, adopted a gruff tone, said, 'Pack that clatter in.'

The boys stopped still, turned to each other and passed a long stare between them; one of them kicked the can again. Brennan produced his warrant card, closed in on the teenager. 'Pull your head in, son, or I might be tempted to run you in.'

The boy flicked his long fringe, sparked up, 'What for?'

Brennan jutted his head forward, 'Insulting a police officer, jay-walking, having ginger hair or cheek and bloody impudence . . . the choices are endless. Tempt me.'

The boy swept back his fringe, pushed his friend roughly to the side; they stropped off towards the other end of the street. Brennan watched them go – waited for the inevitable single-digit salute – then walked towards the house. McGuire was already at the gate, holding it open with an outstretched arm. He tipped his head towards the DI, said, 'Ready for this, sir?'

'As I'll ever be.'

The doorbell chimed, a dog barked behind the frosted glass. It was a small dog, the white blur of its outline was seen at their feet as the door was opened by a man in his fifties. His hair was grey and wiry, sitting flat on his crown but sticking out from behind his ears. His skin looked mottled, he seemed tired, like he hadn't slept for days.

He coughed, then, 'Yes.'

Brennan showed his card again, 'I'm Detective Inspector Brennan and this is my colleague, DS McGuire . . . may we come in and talk to you?'

At once the man shrunk before them, his knees seemed to have buckled. 'Oh, Jesus. God, no.'

Brennan reached out, steadied him with a hand on his elbow. 'It would be best if we came inside.'

The man turned slowly, there was a call from further in the house, a woman's voice. 'Davie, who is it?'

He didn't answer, merely led the officers through the narrow corridor to the living room. Brennan took in the surrounds, it was a small house, nothing flash, but had been well taken care of. The carpets were new and the furnishings didn't look to be that old; in some of these council properties the décor was like stepping back in time. It said a lot about the family, he thought. They cared about

60

appearances, and those that cared how they looked often cared what was said about them in such neighbourhoods; of course it could just be that they thought they were a cut above the rest. One wage, never mind two, was a rarity in these homes.

'What's this?' A woman was standing in the middle of the floor, she drew her cardigan tight. On the couch behind her sat a man in a tracksuit and trainers. The man who had answered the door went to her side, placed an arm around her.

'It's the police, love.'

She shook her head, said, 'No. It's not my Lindsey . . . Have you found her?'

'It would be better if you sat down, Mrs Sloan,' said Brennan.

The man in the tracksuit stood up. He was a thin, angular man with outsized hands that sliced the air like rotor blades as he showed he was holding some papers, said, 'I should probably be on my way now, Mrs Sloan.' He fumbled with the papers, looked unsure of what to do with them, then bunched them together and placed them on the couch behind him. He seemed at a loss now his large hands were empty, stood rubbing them together in front of Brennan and McGuire.

Mr Sloan spoke, 'That's fine, Mr Crawley.' He turned to the officers standing in his living room. 'This is, I'm sorry I don't know your first name . . .'

'Colin . . .'

Mr Sloan took his lead, 'Colin is from Lindsey's old school . . . The kids were putting out posters, with her picture and, well . . .' He lost all enthusiasm for his explanation, exhaled slowly, turned to his wife. Mrs Sloan's lower lip trembled, her husband guided her to a chair, eased her into it. He watched her for a moment, ran a palm over her back and then went to the window ledge and removed a packet of cigarettes. 'Do you mind if I smoke?'

Brennan shook his head.

'It's a terrible business,' said Mr Crawley. He continued rubbing his hands, seemed suddenly conscious of the action, then stopped abruptly and placed them in the pockets of his tracksuit. 'She was never one of my pupils but the school is a small community and when we heard, well, the kids wanted to do something.' He turned to the couch, leaned over and picked up one of the small posters the pupils had been sticking up in the neighbourhood. 'They designed them themselves.' He held it out.

Brennan looked at the man for a moment then reached out a hand to take the poster. He was from Edinburgh High; Brennan knew the school well – his daughter went there – the thought brought the Sloans' grief even closer to home. 'Thank you.'

Mr Crawley smiled and nodded, made his way to the door, said, 'I'll see myself out, Mrs Sloan. God bless.'

Brennan watched him leave the room, thought about questioning him but knew this wasn't the time or place; he waited for the sound of the front door closing, the room seemed to bristle with energy. The Sloans focused on the DI as he spoke, 'I'm afraid I have some very distressing news for you.'

Mrs Sloan cried out, 'Oh, no.'

Mr Sloan watched her lower her head into her hands and sob. 'Is it . . . Lindsey?'

Brennan nodded, 'We found the body of a young woman that we believe to be your daughter this morning.'

62

Mrs Sloan started to rock gently on her chair, her husband approached her, placed a hand on her head. She buried her face in his side and gripped him round the waist. He continued to pat the back of her head. 'What happened?'

Brennan caught McGuire's gaze shifting to meet his, he turned back to Mr Sloan. 'We're still trying to ascertain that; there will be a postmortem later today, or tomorrow.'

The word seemed to pass a bolt through Mrs Sloan, she sobbed uncontrollably.

Mr Sloan raised his cigarette to his lips, his face was firm, stoic. 'I don't understand. Why?' He shook his head, 'I mean, who would want to . . .' He looked down towards his sobbing wife, started to rub her back again. His eyes grew red and moist.

Brennan knew they needed time to take in the information. 'Is there anything we can do . . . Someone we can call maybe?'

'No. We're all that's left.'

Brennan rose, 'When you feel ready, I'd appreciate it if you'd get in touch,' he removed a card from his pocket, passed it to the man, 'there are one or two formalities.'

He took the card, stared at it. 'I just don't understand.'

Brennan stepped back, 'When you're ready, just give me a call. I can have you collected.' He motioned McGuire to the door. 'Please, we'll see ourselves out.' He stalled for a moment as McGuire passed through the door; the man was still holding out his card, staring at him. 'I'm just so very sorry for your loss, Mr Sloan.'

Outside Brennan removed a packet of Embassy Regal, lit up. He walked to the end of the garden path, closed the gate delicately behind him and peered back into the Sloans' little home. He knew their lives would never be the same, he felt a hollowness open up inside him as though he'd been presented with all his sins. As he walked back to the car he began to feel queasy, the whole situation weighed on his heart.

'Everything OK, boss?' said McGuire.

Brennan closed the car door, inhaled deep on his cigarette. 'I want everything there is to know about Lindsey Sloan.'

Chapter 9

DI ROB BRENNAN CHOSE TO remain silent on the drive back to Fettes Police Station. He had allowed himself a rare moment of introspection after revealing to the Sloans that their daughter was dead. He felt their grief, but didn't want to lug it around with him. There was sympathy and there was empathy; the latter meant taking on too much of the grief and he needed to keep a clear head if he was to catch their daughter's killer. Though he knew it wasn't healthy, he locked away the meeting with the Sloans; he would address his true feelings about what had happened at a later date. Of that he had no doubt.

When they reached the station Brennan realised he was holding the stub of a cigarette he had forgotten to smoke; it had burnt down to the filter tip and there was a dusting of ash on his trouser leg. He quickly brushed it off, placed the dowp in the ashtray as McGuire parked up.

'What now?' said the DS once he'd stopped the car, removed the key from the ignition.

Brennan felt his brain itch, 'Did you get hold of Lorrimer?'

McGuire raised an eyebrow, looked ready to say '*Who*?' then, 'Oh, profiler, Strathclyde . . . aye, he's coming through.'

'When?'

The DS turned away, exhaled. 'Well, he said soon as . . . I'm hoping tonight or tomorrow.'

'Call him, get a definite time. And don't tell Benny, we'll wait until Lorrimer's on the job before we do that.'

'Yes, boss . . . anything else?'

Brennan released his seatbelt, 'I'm sure there will be, just let me get a look at the files before we plan the next move.'

The pair left the car, headed for the front door. Charlie was manning the desk again, nodded to them from behind the pages of the *News*. He seemed unchallenged, content. Brennan didn't know whether to envy him or feel sorry for him. He had his foot on the first step as his mobile started to ring. He looked at the caller ID, it was Joyce.

'I'll catch you up there, Stevie.'

Ringing.

'Hello.'

'I want you out tonight,' she sounded nervy, distraught.

'Joyce, what are you on about?' Brennan turned around, passed Charlie and headed out to the car park.

'I want you out of our house and our lives.'

A vision of Sophie flashed before Brennan's eyes, 'Well, that's never going to happen and you know it.'

'We'll see about that . . . How well do you think your affair will go down with the divorce courts?'

'Joyce . . .' His affair was almost a year ago, he hadn't seen Lorraine in that time and he had no intention of changing that. 'Why are you bringing that up now?'

There was a gap on the line, some shuffling. He heard her inhale a cigarette. 'I've changed the locks.'

'*What*?'

'You heard . . . And I've packed up your things. There's two suitcases sitting in the garage, you can come and collect them when you like, but don't try coming to the house.'

'I want to see Sophie.'

Joyce tutted, 'Since when? You don't normally have any time for her.'

Brennan felt confused, his thoughts spiralled. Of course he had time for her, it was the job alone that kept him from seeing her. 'You've no right to do this . . . You've just no . . .'

'I've every fucking right. Every right after what you did to us!'

'Joyce, get a hold of yourself.'

'I'm perfectly fucking together,' she was roaring now, roaring into the phone.

'Can we talk about this at least? I mean, where am I supposed to go?'

'Why don't you go to your slut, Rob? . . . Huh? Why don't you go there?'

She hung up.

Brennan stared at the phone for a moment, then quickly turned towards the station. He hoped no one had seen him engaged in the call; his home life was something to keep separate, the two worlds could never mix. He pocketed the mobile and started to walk back towards the building. His thoughts filled with Sophie. How would she feel? How would she react? He tried to press delete on those thoughts but their impressions remained. He felt hollowed out like

67

the hull of a shipwreck. He halted in mid-stride for a moment and tried to gather himself; a blackbird swooped on the car park, raised its yellow beak and set off again. Brennan watched the bird, wings spread, as it crossed the cloud-covered sky and felt he was watching a part of himself being carried away.

The DI steadied himself some more; this wasn't the time or place for ratiocination, for dissecting the failure of his marriage. The job always had to come first, always. He returned to the station, his gait slow, but sure.

Upstairs, in Incident Room One, there was some activity but Brennan's gaze alighted on McGuire and WPC Elaine Docherty smiling at each other like there was no one else in the room; he approached the whiteboard, turned to DS Collins, 'This all we have on the Sloan girl?'

Collins leaned back in his seat, 'Sally, anything to stick up?'

'No, not yet. Once they've done the postmortem there will be.'

Collins returned to the DI, 'That's it for now, sir.'

'What about Smeeton's door-to-door?'

A shrug of shoulders, 'There weren't any doors really, nearest house was a couple of miles away . . . and it was a pitch-black night, remember.'

Brennan shook his head, returned to the board. The background details were sketchy, they had an address and a place of work but there were no friends, boyfriend listed. 'Collins, what's happening with all this fucking white space?'

The DS rose, approached the board. 'Well, Lou is down at the travel agent where she worked, talking to her colleagues, and he's going to follow up any names that come from there. And Bri is going through her history, school and previous jobs . . . There's nothing standing out, though. She seemed very ordinary.'

'Check out everybody she's had contact with in recent years – youth club, local pub . . . if she knew a bus driver with a fucking speeding ticket I want him brought in. Got me?'

'Sir.'

'And Collins . . .'

'Yes, sir?'

'Interview her classmates from school . . . She's not long out the place, she's likely kept in contact . . . Facebook generation and all that. Anything, no matter how insignificant, fire it up to me.'

Collins nodded, he looked as if he was about to say something, raised a finger towards the board, but Brennan cut him off. He spoke in hushed tones, 'What the bloody hell is going on here?'

Collins turned round, Brennan watched over the DS's shoulder as the Chief Super and DI Jim Gallagher walked down through the incident room.

Gallagher nodded, 'Rob, how's it going?'

'Fine, Jim . . . is this a social call?'

The Chief Super hitched his glasses higher on the bridge of his nose as he looked at the board. 'Everything ticking along all right, Rob?'

Brennan nodded, 'Yes. Just fine.' He watched the Chief Super peer over the details that had been written up in marker pen then quickly remove his gaze as he caught sight of the bloody photographs.

'Right, well, got a moment, Rob? Something Jim and I would like to talk to you about?'

Brennan felt his spirit shrivel inside him; he looked over at Gallagher, he was smiling. Not a real smile, a false, painted-on one. They were up to something and Brennan knew it. He pointed towards his glassed-off section at the other end of the room.

'This way, then,' he said.

The Chief Super headed for the office, Gallagher laid up behind Brennan and let him go first, motioning him to go ahead with the palm of his hand. Brennan paced out, but he didn't like the thought of Gallagher descending into obvious politesse – it made him feel wary.

The Chief Super took Brennan's chair, sat. The two DIs stood there like schoolboys before the headmaster.

'Is somebody going to tell me what this is about?' said Brennan.

Gallagher laid a blue folder down on the desk, 'You better take a look at this.'

Brennan reached forward, picked it up; it contained details of an unsolved murder case. There were pictures of the victim, bound and tied, her name was Fiona Gow. As Brennan scanned the files he immediately saw the similarities to the murder of Lindsey Sloan.

He said, 'These deaths are five years apart . . . you think they're connected?'

Gallagher readied himself to reply; the Chief Super stepped over him. 'We don't know, Rob.'

Brennan bristled, 'Then why are you showing them to me?'

'We believe,' said Gallagher, 'there may be a connection.' He leaned forward, plucked a photograph from the file. 'Look at the ligatures, the genital mutilation . . . and the eyes.'

'It's almost identical,' said the Chief Super.

Brennan had to agree, but he kept his thoughts to himself. He could see where this was going; he now knew why Gallagher had been snooping around in his earlier briefing. 'I'll need this confirmed by the lab.'

'Of course. But I can tell you now, this was my case, Rob, and the killings are identical,' said Gallagher.

The Chief Super edged an opinion in, 'I would have thought you'd welcome Jim's input in this situation, Rob.'

Brennan leaned forward, closed the file. He was staring at Gallagher, but talking to the Chief Super when he replied, 'You never solved this case, did you, Jim?'

Gallagher faltered, his mouth opened but no words came out. He seemed to recover quickly though. 'We came close.'

'Not close enough, Jim. If you had we might not have Lindsey Sloan's name chalked up out there.'

Gallagher's face flushed, he seemed to inflate. The Chief Super rose, stepped between the two men. 'Right, well, I was going to suggest some co-operation on this case between you both, given the undeniable similarities . . .'

'That's not what we discussed . . .' burst Gallagher.

The Chief Super flagged him down, 'Rob, I'd like you to take Jim onto your team, he'll report to you . . .' He looked at Gallagher, 'For the time being.'

Brennan's head buzzed, he felt like an angry wasp had got in there. He looked at Gallagher and then back to the Chief Super. He didn't know which one to despise the most. He knew Gallagher had cooked this up, it was trophy hunting, he was after the case because it was the biggest one going. Benny, though, he was just playing the only game he knew: divide and rule.

Brennan held himself in check, kept his tone low and flat. 'And if I object, sir?'

'Object all you like, Rob,' said the Chief Super as he reached for the door handle, 'it won't make a blind bit of difference.'

Chapter 10

NEIL HENDERSON AWOKE WITH A blowtorch burning behind his eyes. His head throbbed, soundly and persistently. His mouth felt like there was something in there, something alien, a sponge perhaps or blotting paper -- something that absorbed all the moisture. He had forgotten how hard it was to return to old habits. Even alcohol; your resistance was never the same after a short spell away. It took time and repeated bouts of abuse to build up tolerance; he wondered how long it would take him.

Henderson rose on the mattress, Ange was still sleeping at his side; she had passed out long before him. He remembered her hysterics, the fit of near panic, and the terror on her face as she shrieked out. What the hell was wrong with her? He had seen all kinds of bad trips, he'd seen withdrawals where punters thought their demons had taken them over -- it was all inside their heads. Henderson knew Ange was losing it; Christ, she had just about lost it before he went away, so where did that put her now? He turned, eyed her bare back where she lay on the mattress, her shoulders shivering.

'You've got some problems girl.'

He lifted the covers, exposed her naked frame. 'Still got a fine arse on you, though.'

Of course she had, he thought, the girl was only twenty. It would take a fair few years yet – even at her rate of intake – to totally wreck herself. He ran his hand over her backside, down the edge of her thigh. 'Few bawbees to be made off that yet!'

Henderson pulled back the cover, started to shake Angela by the shoulder. She turned over and fumbled her way to his side of the bed; as she grabbed his groin, lowered her head, the move seemed altogether mechanical, too practised.

'Hey, hey . . . What the fuck you up to?' said Henderson.

Angela carried on, seemed barely aware of his presence.

'I'm talking to you.' Henderson grabbed her hair, twisted a handful of it; it took some tightening of the knot to alert Angela, wake her from her daze.

'Ahh . . .'

'Sort yourself out, eh,' said Henderson. 'Sit up, I want to talk to you.'

Angela reached hands to her head, her eyes widened. Immediately she seemed to have wakened, fell into a coughing fit.

Henderson flared his nostrils. 'Look at the fucking kip of you, who's going to pay for a skank, eh?'

Angela rubbed her head, 'What was that for?'

'To wake you up . . . Seen the time?'

Angela looked towards the window; it was dark outside. Time she should be out on the Links, scoring punters. Henderson tweaked the tip of her nose, 'You hearing me?'

74

'Aye, I hear you.' She pushed his hand away, withdrew to the far side of the mattress. 'You got any fags?'

'Fags is it?' Henderson put one foot out of the bed, tried to hook a toe under his jeans then dragged them over. He took a packet of Club Kingsize out of his pocket, sparked up, then chucked the packet at Angela. 'This better not be the start of you scrounging off me, you know I can't be doing with that kind of patter . . . There's no free rides in this world, Ange.'

She took out a cigarette, put it between her lips and lit it. 'I'll get out there in a minute, Hendy . . . Just have a quick fag, eh.'

Henderson got off the mattress, pulled his jeans on; the belt buckle rattled as he fastened the buttons. When he was fully dressed he went round to Angela's side of the room and crouched down.

'See that way you went off there, when I put the telly on . . .' he watched her press the cigarette into her mouth and inhale deep. 'What was that all about?'

She shrugged. 'I dunno.'

Henderson grabbed her face in his hand, 'I'm not playing fucking games with you, Ange . . . I want to know.' She yanked her face away. He saw the imprints of his fingers in the white flesh of her jaw line. He wagged a fist at her. 'I mean it, if I'm going to be looking out for you, I need to know that you're fit for it and not going to be getting fucking locked up . . . Not worth my time, is it?'

Angela looked away, pinched her lips. Her eyes flickered as she raised them towards the ceiling. Her reply came hard and flat, 'I'm fine.'

Henderson knew she was keeping something from him; experience had taught him that when whores had secrets there was a good reason for it. Someone else was stamping their mark on them; they had a few quid stashed away; or a secret punter that was paying big. He didn't know what it was that Angela had to keep quiet about but he knew he needed to find out. He grabbed her by the throat, pinned her to the wall.

'Now you better fucking loosen that gob of yours, or I might be forced to close it once and for all . . . You get me?'

Angela whimpered, her eyes reddened – intricate little red lines like fine cracks in pottery appeared over the whites. 'It's nothing . . . nothing.'

Henderson gripped her throat tighter, forced his thumb deep into the crevice of her neck; Angela started to splutter, gasp for breath. Her face darkened as he brought the cigarette up to her eye.

'How many fucking punters do you think you'd score out on the Links with one eye, eh?' He moved the glowing amber tip of the cigarette to within an inch of Angela's eye, pointed it like a dart. 'I'll fucking do it . . . I will.'

'OK. OK. Let me go.'

'And you'll tell me?'

'Yes. I will. I promise.'

Henderson released his grip on her neck; Angela fell forward and landed face down on the mattress. She shot hands up to her throat as she coughed and gasped for breath. She was still spluttering as Henderson loomed over her and inhaled deeply on the cigarette he had threatened to blind her with.

'I'm waiting,' he said.

She coughed again, some long trails of spit escaped her mouth.

'I've not got all night!'

Angela forced herself up onto her knees, her thin fingers traced the line of her throat as she tried to massage some of the pain away. She looked ready to fold again, pass out. Henderson reached over and yanked her to her feet; he was surprised by how light she was.

Angela shrieked again, as she stood, shivering and naked before him.

'Right, talk . . .' he said.

She wiped a tear from her cheek, 'I-I can't . . .'

Henderson lit up, he drew back a fist.

'OK. OK,' yelled Angela.

'I'm losing the fucking rag with you, girl . . .'

She gripped her waist in her arms, spoke softly. 'Can I show you something?'

Henderson's face shrivelled into confusion. 'Show me what?'

'It's just, I've never told anyone before.'

'Told anyone what?'

Rain started to patter on the window; Angela looked away, slowly got down from the mattress and walked towards the other side of the room. By the doorway sat a small coffee table with a drawer in the top; she opened up and removed a *Yellow Pages*. Underneath the directory sat a little mauve-coloured diary. 'I wrote it in here.'

'Wrote what?' said Henderson.

She held up the diary, she seemed to have trouble even looking at it. Some more tears rolled over her cheekbones. 'What happened . . . out there.'

Henderson stubbed his cigarette in the smoked-glass ashtray by the mattress and walked towards Angela. He snatched the diary out of her hand. 'This is like a notebook.'

Angela watched him turning over the pages. 'It's a journal . . . I used to keep it, before I met you.'

Henderson held it up, 'Well, what the fuck's in it?'

Angela looked towards the window, it was dark out and the rain was getting heavier. 'I need to go. We've no money.'

'What about this?'

'You asked what it was about . . . It's in there.'

'So I have to fucking read this?'

Angela nodded, moved away. She pulled on her black mini-dress and stuck her bare feet into her heels. As she put on her coat she saw Henderson flicking through the diary.

'You won't tell anyone, will you?'

'Tell anyone what?'

'What's in there.'

He looked at her, smiled. 'I haven't read it yet . . . so I guess that all depends, doesn't it?'

Chapter 11

NEIL HENDERSON WATCHED ANGELA TEETER towards the front door of the cold-water flat in Leith. He didn't know what to make of her. The tart had gone downhill, rapidly, since he went inside. They were all the same, none of them knew how to look after themselves. She hadn't even put on a bit of lipstick: what kind of punter was she going to score without even a bit of lipstick? Some of them, he thought, just weren't worth the bother.

The door slammed as Angela left; he heard her heels clacking as she descended the steps.

Henderson drummed fingers on the little mauve-coloured diary she had given him. The girl was next to worthless; how was a man supposed to earn a crust off a wreck like that? He knew she was going to be more trouble. All that time and effort he'd put in on her had been wasted.

When he had met Angela she was in a bad enough way; crying her eyes out in the street after being stiffed out of her last tenner by some bitch off the Links. They were like

79

a pack of animals those girls; any new meat on display and they fired into it, ripped it to shreds.

Henderson grimaced, 'Fucking pack of slags.'

He'd shown them though; there had been three of them, old boots who should have known better. A few smacks in the face, some bust noses and black eyes were enough to teach them. A couple of nights in dock till the bruises subsided and a few quid out their takings and they didn't think about messing with Angela again.

'Easy money,' said Henderson. He grinned to himself.

There had been times when it really was easy money, he'd had three of them on the go, all bringing in a pretty penny. Then one of them shot herself an overdose and that was her. The other got stiffed by a guy who worked at the bookies – a week of hand jobs went unpaid until Henderson made a visit, followed him home and leathered him in the street. How was he to know there was filth living in the same row? She'd been a good earner though, Casy, until she fucked off when he went inside.

'Never had a fucking day's luck,' said Henderson. 'Not a fucking day of it.'

He was turning the diary over in his hand when he decided to take a look inside, see what all the fuss was about.

'Stupid bloody bitch,' he said as he opened the slim volume.

On page one was written: Angela Mickle, Porty Acad.

'Jesus, she was still a schoolie.'

He read on. There was a lot of puerile nonsense about boys in her class, pressure from her parents to study for exams and falling out with friends.

'Bloody daft lassie,' said Henderson as he skimmed the first few entries.

He skipped back and forwards, looking for the part that Angela had made such a fuss about but couldn't find anything. It was all about school and stealing money out her dad's jacket to buy cigarettes. It was inane. Nothing to cause the reaction of the night before.

Henderson was beginning to think he'd been had. It seemed the diary covered a period of about six months. After a month or so, she'd joined the gymnastics team, had a new coach who had said she had promise. There were a lot of entries about the gymnastics classes, the training and the after-school club. It bored Henderson.

He got up and took a cigarette from his packet of Club, sparked up.

What was she going on about with this diary?

Was she taking the piss?

He thought Angela had pulled a fast one; that she had used the diary to shut him up, to get away from him. She was probably at the bus station now.

'The fucking bitch!'

He returned to the small book, scanned it faster, looking, searching for whatever it was that might have happened to her. His attention was roused now, because if there wasn't something there – something worth his while wading through all this schoolie nonsense – then he'd been had.

Near the end of the diary Henderson noticed the hand-writing had changed. It stopped being florid, it lost the big looping curls and smiley-faces above the 'i's. It became a scratch, sloped hard to the left and failed to keep a straight line, even though the diary had lined pages.

The entries changed too.

He read:

It was gymnastics class again today. I don't know how

much longer I can keep this up, the Creep has started to act very strange since the night he tried to kiss me. I told him I didn't want to do it, but he's said that if I don't then I won't be on the team any more and he'll tell everyone that I am a slut.

Henderson's eyes roved over the page, tried to find another mention of the Creep.

He told me that I was the best gymnast he had ever coached and it would be a shame to throw it all away just because I was being immature. I'm not immature, I just don't want to let him touch me. He said I wouldn't know what I was missing and that all the other girls in the squad would think they were lucky to be in my shoes.

Henderson found himself tensing up as he read the diary entries. He crossed his legs, watched his ankle sit at a jagged angle to the rest of his body.

'The dirty old fucker,' he said.

Who was this Creep? he wondered. He'd heard about pervs, they called them beasts inside. They were scum, the lowest of the low. Beneath contempt. Hated. This guy was a teacher as well, a square peg . . . the thought mangled Henderson's mind.

He raised the book higher, swapped hands and massaged his left wrist for a little while. He couldn't quite take in what he was reading, but he was sure it was a juicy story. He wanted to see if she did do the dirty old bastard.

The handwriting started to deteriorate even further now.

I told him no and I told him to stop but he didn't listen. He forced my top over my head and started to bite at me. I was crying and pushing him away. I remember trying to scream but I couldn't seem to get enough air into my lungs and then he was on top of me and breathing hard. His breath smelled, I wanted away. I dug my nails into his face and I saw the blood run down his cheek, it made him jerk backwards and he touched his face. He said something to me, called me something but I couldn't hear what because I was running . . .

Henderson was startled by a knock at the door; he put down the diary.

It was getting dark in the flat and he put on the main light as he edged past the mattress and crossed the narrow corridor to the door.

'Who is it?' he yelled.

There was no reply. He bent down, flicked open the letter box. He could see two legs in blue denims. As he scanned up he saw they were attached to a young man.

'What do you want?' said Henderson.

'Er, I was looking for the lassie, y'know, Angela . . .'

Henderson straightened himself, he saw the youth was no threat; he opened the door. 'Oh, aye.'

The young man stepped back, clearly not confrontational. Henderson looked him up and down, he was about to speak and then he suddenly felt a blinding pain strike in the side of his head; he fell to the floor.

'How's it going, Hendy?' A large amorphous black mass loomed over him. 'Forget about our wee arrangement, eh?'

Henderson started to regain his focus, realised he was bleeding from the mouth. The youth was walking away from him, counting cash as he slowly moved towards the stairwell. Henderson felt his collar grabbed, he was jerked to his feet.

'Money y'cunt, I want it.' A finger was pressed in his chest, it was attached to a bulky arm that led to a shaven head with a face like a pug; he recognised it belonged to one of Boaby Stevens's boys.

Henderson nodded, rapid. 'You'll get it, tell Shaky it's coming, eh.'

The finger moved from his chest to the flesh beneath his chin, pressed so hard it threatened to appear in his mouth. 'I've no fucking doubt about it, Hendy. What you holding?'

Henderson emptied his pockets. His words were strangled as they came, 'Just this.'

The man in the black leather jacket stepped back, roared, 'That's fuck all . . . It's two-grand you're in for, not fucking . . .' he counted, 'Fifty-five sovs, that's not paying a day's interest is it?'

Henderson edged towards the flat, spoke, 'Look it's coming, I've got a decent payoff on the way. Just give me a few days, eh, pal.'

The pug leaned forward, 'I'm not your fucking pal.' He drew a fist, planted it in Henderson's stomach. He fell to the ground, coughed once and then vomited hard.

'I'll be back, and you better have the fucking money.'

Henderson's vision blurred as he watched the man stride down the hall, he was so broad he almost filled the corridor. At the start of the stairs, he turned, pointed to Henderson and said, 'Don't forget now . . . your fucking life depends on it!'

Chapter 12

DI ROB BRENNAN KNEW THERE was a dark shadow which followed him around; it was the ever-present fog of his failure. It clung to him like the grim scent of death that pervaded the morgue, seeped into your clothes, your hair and had colleagues remarking, 'Have you been to the dead place?'

Brennan knew he should have gone further, he knew he deserved it. He deserved better than having to answer to the likes of Benny, but then, he knew it was never about what you deserved in the ranks, in life. With each year that passed he felt the shackles of his station tighten. He would never rise above DI, he knew it; and he knew why. It was because he was real – a real person. He knew himself and he knew he wasn't prepared to compromise on who he was for anyone – even if it kept him down.

Brennan saw the types that rose – Wullie had called them floaters, 'Shit doesn't sink, son,' he had said. Floaters were the careerists and corporate gimps, the glory hunters, the desk jockeys, the bull-shitters and whorers, the Napoleon complexes and the, sometimes barely, socialised psychopaths. None cared about the job; none knew how Brennan felt.

Once, he had read about a native American Indian chief who had been confused by the way white men looked. He couldn't understand why their brows were so furrowed, their eyes stared so intently, showing their need, their intense craving for something more than they already had. He thought they looked insane. The comment had struck a chord with Brennan, not because he was overawed by the chief's insight, but because he had given voice, put into words, what Brennan felt inside himself: everyone around him was insane. The game of life was hardly worth the candle. It wasn't that he rated himself a higher being, or felt embayed with some inveterate wisdom of his own, not at all – Brennan knew he was every bit as likely to be pulled into the maelstrom. A loss of focus, a weakness, giving in . . . any one of a thousand daily challenges not met and he would be in there, in the drink with all the floaters, swimming for his life.

Brennan sat outside his home for the best part of an hour, staring at Sophie's window and waiting for the light to go out. When it did, the flickering of the television screen continued and Brennan smiled to himself.

'Don't leave it on all night, love.'

He took another draw on his Embassy Regal and flicked the ash into the tray on the dashboard. He looked at the keys for his home in his left hand. Joyce had changed the locks, but she didn't need to. He would have gone quietly. On the same keyring were the little keys he carried for his handcuffs; he lifted the metal ring and slid them off. For a moment he stared at them; he remembered the first time he'd put cuffs on someone, it was a drunk after Glasgow Rangers had played Hibs and he had chased the lad up Easter Road before pinning his arms behind his back. It had been a disaster; after getting one of the cuffs on he had failed to get the second one tightened in time and the drunk had lunged at him, swinging the open cuff and taking a lump of flesh out of his eyebrow.

Brennan grimaced with the memory, he leaned forward, checked in the rear-view mirror to see if he still had the scar. It was there; they were all there. He wondered how many scars he couldn't see. It was the invisible ones that worried him the most. He knew he was thinking too much about the past, and that was never a good sign.

Brennan stubbed his cigarette in the ashtray, opened the door and stepped out. He held his keys in his hand and wondered about mailing them through the letter box; he thought better of the idea, he didn't want to alert anyone to the fact that he was there, least of all Sophie. It would be too painful to have to explain why he was collecting suitcases of his clothes from the garage, why her mother – his wife – couldn't even look at him, never mind speak to him. He bunched the keys in his fist and proceeded down the driveway.

It was his property, his home and yet he felt like an intruder there now. He paused in the driveway; the building sat grey and weary against the night sky. He didn't feel welcome there; he knew he had crossed a chalk line with Joyce and there was nothing else to do now but leave. He paced towards the garage door and opened up; at once he saw his two dark cases sitting in the middle of the floor. The sight of them caused his heart to sicken, he raised a hand towards his face and brushed the edges of his mouth as he slowly exhaled. A sharp, dramatic gasp followed, and then he placed the bunch of keys on the workbench and lifted the cases.

On the way down Corstorphine Road Brennan's thoughts felt like splinters in his mind. He knew his marriage was over, he had no desire left to fight for it; it somehow felt like the end of yet another long journey; one that had promised a great deal and yet failed to deliver on almost every front. A lot of his life had been lived in expectation, and so much of it had been met with disappointment that he almost felt like laughing at the naivety of his youthful dreams and hopes.

'Get a fucking grip, Rob,' he said.

Princes Street had been opened again. He followed the thoroughfare to the end and snaked down Leith Street towards the Walk. He had secured a studio flat in Montgomery Street, it was a temporary measure he told himself.

'The most burgled street in Edinburgh,' had been his reply when he was informed of all that was on offer.

The agent hadn't argued, 'It's all we've got.'

'Take it or leave it, then?'

A shrug.

He took it.

As Brennan parked up he looked down the street towards the Walk; he knew Wullie was down there, not far away. For some reason the thought gored him. He didn't know why that should be at first and then he remembered a visit to Wullie soon after his retirement; he recalled how shocked he had been at the state of the place, and the state of him.

Brennan smirked, 'Partners in crime again, eh, Wullie.'

He took a recent purchase, a bottle of Macallan, from the passenger seat and placed it in the pocket of his overcoat, then got out of the car. At his new front door Brennan lowered his cases, ferreted for the keys the agent had given him earlier.

The Yale fitted in the lock and turned easily. He went inside.

The flat had been mis-sold; it was a bedsit.

There was only one room, about three-quarters the size of the living room he had in Corstorphine. In one corner was a sink unit with a small white boiler above it. A grey plastic draining board leaned against the wall next to the stainless-steel sink. Beside that was a heavily-bracketed shelf with a Baby Belling cooker. Brennan walked over, opened the door, it came away in his hand.

'Well you've seen better days,' he said. He put the door back, 'Mind you, haven't we all.'

He turned, scanned his new surrounds. There was a large window, covered with a set of psychedelic seventies swirl-print curtains. Brennan shook his head; he could see a street light burning through the thin fabric. In one corner was a bed, without bedding, and in the other an old couch that looked like it had been emancipated from a skip. He went over and patted the cushion; a cloud of dust rose into the room – little particles of effluvia were illuminated in the orange glow of the street lamp.

'Bloody hell.' He put his hands on his hips, stood firmly on the flats of his feet. 'What a kip house.'

Is this what he had come to? Is this what his forty-one years of life had amounted to?

Brennan didn't know where to look next; even as temporary accommodation, it couldn't have been any worse.

He spied a foldaway table and two chairs, walked over and opened out the table-top. He removed his overcoat, then his jacket and loosened his tie. As he sat down he reached for the bottle of Macallan and a cup from the drainer. Just about everything in the room was within grasping distance.

He poured out a good measure of the whisky and started to roll up his sleeves; after the first sip he grimaced, then smiled.

'Well, at least the company's good.'

He delved into his briefcase and removed the blue folder with Fiona Gow's name on the front and opened up.

On top were photographs of the victim. Fiona Gow had been a pretty girl; she had short, straight blonde hair, she had been described as 'leggy' by the press.

'Poor lassie,' he said.

He leafed through a few of the pictures, until the scenes of crime shots appeared and then bunched them together, removed them from the file, and placed the lot face down at the corner of the table.

The girl had been a hairdressing apprentice, had a day-release class once a fortnight and was said to be 'popular' in the case notes. She was also described as a bit ditsy, and no one could remember her ever having had a bad word to say about anyone. She seemed the epitome of the girl next door. The murder seemed utterly pointless, unless she had been targeted at random.

Brennan scanned more of the notes, there were further details on her schooling – Portobello Academy – her social status, she went clubbing on the weekends. A forensic serology report identified the presence of blood on her body that wasn't hers; it was a rare group: B.

DI Jim Gallagher seemed to have talked to just about everyone who had ever known the girl, but had turned up very little that was going to be useful to Brennan.

'Where's the pull, Jim?'

Nothing in the notes indicated a cohesive investigation, it was all perfunctory. A couple of local sex offenders had been called in, interviewed, but neither had the blood group B and both had supplied alibis for the time of the murder. They were released and that was as close as the squad had got. As far as suspects went, that seemed to be it.

Brennan leaned over on the table, took another sip of whisky. He felt his brows start to ache, he rubbed at his forehead. Something bothered him; he reached back to his jacket, removed his mobile phone and called Gallagher.

Ringing.

'Hello, DI Gallagher.'

'It's Rob.'

There was a stalled breath's silence on the other end of the line, 'Hello, Rob.'

Brennan toyed with the idea of demanding a *sir*, but let it pass. 'I'm going over your file on Fiona Gow here . . .'

Gallagher cut in, 'Oh aye, definite links I'd say.'

'You would, if you were angling to take the case off me, Jim.' Brennan let his remark sting. 'And you are, aren't you?'

Gallagher wheezed, 'Look, it's nothing personal, Rob . . .'

'*Sir*.'

'What?'

'I'll have the proper honorific, since *I* am leading this investigation.'

'Yes, sir . . .'

Brennan knew he'd made it clear that he had Gallagher's number and felt content to change direction. 'Anyway, this file . . . a bit light isn't it?'

'Well, the lab reports are with the Chief Super . . . And

there's a profiler's report on my desk but, truth is, we never really dug up that much.'

'You're not kidding, Jim.'

The line fizzed, then, 'Well there would be a reason for that, which I think you know.'

'Enlighten me.'

'I think we have a serial killer on our hands, and they don't get that tag because they're easy to find, sir . . .'

A car revved on the street outside, Brennan put the phone to his other ear, 'Nothing in this life comes easy, Jim. We'd have a damn sight more serial killers if it wasn't for the likes of us. But let's not get carried away with the terminology – Pettigrew's meeting us at the morgue tomorrow at 7 a.m.; get yourself down there and let's see what he turns up.'

Chapter 13

DI ROB BRENNAN HAD REACHED the stage where it no longer mattered what life threw at him. It couldn't affect who he was any more. There was a time, he still remembered it, when life's defeats and disappointments – the hurts and the devastations – felled him. It all seemed strange now – why? He was still here, after all the slings and arrows of outrageous fortune. None of his woes had killed him; killed a part of him, yes. He had lost the ability to feel wounded, hurt; they seemed like futile emotions to him now – like something children went through, not grown men. Not, for certain, police officers; men like him.

So what did that make Rob Brennan – insensitive? He didn't think so, that part of him hadn't changed. He still loved his daughter, nurtured fond memories of the brother he had lost. It was another part of him that had changed – the part that he showed to the outside world. His carapace had hardened. He knew this made him look insensitive, loutish to some, but there was nothing he could do about it. The act, the process itself, was instinctual. When he thought about it, he wondered if there was any real point to it. He could no longer feel, he could no longer be hurt, so why put up the shell? He surmised, after careful thought, and having assessed the trait in others, that it wasn't for his benefit; it was for the rest of the world. Brennan's outward subfusc was a warning flag, a marker for those who thought to seek the sympathies of a fellow traveller on life's road: not here, it yelled. Move away, try someone else. If that was the case, so be it, he thought; we all wore masks anyway, at least his honestly reflected reality, as he saw it.

Brennan lay in the sagging bed, staring at the nicotine-stained ceiling of his bedsit. It was a high ceiling, hinted at an opulent past life before subdivision and the looting of architraves and ornate, wrought-iron fireplaces. He pitched himself on his elbow, glanced towards the billowing curtains, blowing in what appeared to be a breeze but could only be a draught because he hadn't opened the window. He stared at the waves and folds in the fabric for a moment, surmised a fierce wind blowing across Leith Walk was to blame.

He sighed, a long deep sigh that seemed to come from the core of him; it caught him unawares. Was he so surprised to be here? There had been many times when he had thought of leaving Joyce, if he was honest with himself he had only stayed because of Sophie. Their lives had become separated – as much as any two lives could be whilst living under the same roof. It didn't faze him to say goodbye to all of that. The house, the car, the family holidays; they all meant nothing to him. He didn't need anything. Even as he looked around the dingy bedsit he could only regale himself with the complete lack of comfort. Why did he need any of it?

Brennan felt like he had jumped from a slowly-moving train and he was now lying at the side of the tracks watching the carriages snake past. He recognised all the carriages, they were the accoutrements of success and fulfilment and yet, to him, they were all empty. He was happy to watch them fade into the distance, pass over the horizon towards a destination he would never reach. He wondered why he had ever chosen to get on the train at all, but he dismissed the thought at once. He wasn't the man who had made those decisions; when he looked back at the Rob Brennan of the past, he hardly recognised him. Who was he? Really? Who was this man who had joined the police force? Because he had decided the fate of both of them – the young and the old Rob Brennan – and now one questioned the other's motives.

Brennan rose quickly, ran water in the tiny stainless-steel sink and splashed it on his face. He straightened himself, ran the splayed fingers of his hands through his hair. For a moment he stood in front of the tiny cracked mirror and stared at himself.

'Thinking like that, now that would never do, Rob . . .'

He was being dragged down by his own thoughts. He knew the mind loved to show you your flaws, to take you back to past mistakes and flash snapshots of more to come in future. It had to be halted, distracted.

Brennan pulled his trousers from the arm of the chair and fitted himself into them. The suitcases were still closed, he reached for the nearest one and raised it onto the table, opened up. Inside the clothes sat in a jumble.

'Bloody hell . . .'

He shook his head. As he rummaged for a shirt he realised how ridiculous he had been. What did he expect? Joyce to have freshly laundered, neatly ironed and folded his clothes? It was laughable. He had been thrown out by his wife and the sooner he came to that realisation, and what it meant, the better. There was no point going over it, trying to locate the triggers. They were unhappy. He had strayed and she had found out. That was it. Delving any further into the matter was a worthless exercise. He had to move on.

Brennan was smacked awake by the brewery fumes on Montgomery Street as he left the stairwell. He had heard there was only one brewery left in Edinburgh and longed for it to go the way of the others. When he was a child, his brother had hated trips to Edinburgh because of the brewery stench. The smell always made Brennan think of the past, of Andy, and he resented the incursion bitterly.

The car started first time and Brennan engaged the clutch, pulled out. The streets were surprisingly empty; he was not used to getting anywhere in the city easily, least of all by car. At the end of Montgomery Street he turned onto the Walk and was in second gear by the roundabout; there was no need to stop and he progressed past the John Lewis store, checking out a billboard for a new movie as he went.

The morgue was located in the Old Town, the hotchpotch of pends and wynds that huddled around the foot of the castle. Brennan felt out of place in this part of town, it felt too touristy, too synthetic. It was where out-of-towners came to sample whisky and take photographs of themselves in See-You-Jimmy wigs. He didn't think anybody lived there, there were flats and there were new apartments, but they were rentals surely. There was certainly no local pub, no community spirit. It was an empty, vapid place; the perfect location for the morgue.

Brennan rounded the High Street, swung into the chicane

that sat between the Parliament and the palace of Holyrood; on the next bend he spotted the granite massif of Arthur's Seat, swathed in a morning mist.

DS Stevie McGuire was already sitting out front when Brennan pulled over. He rolled up his window and got out of the car when he saw the DI.

'Morning, sir.'

Brennan nodded, 'Stevie.'

'No signs of life, I'm afraid.'

Brennan frowned, looked him over.

Realisation dawned, 'Sorry. You know what I mean.'

'Pettigrew has confirmed a 7 a.m. start, aye?'

'Sure has . . .'

As they chatted, a green Vectra pulled up and DI Jim Gallagher raised a salute. He was smoking a cigarette and some ash fell as he lifted his hand from the wheel. As he left the car he removed a necktie from his jacket pocket and started to thread it through his collar.

'Rob, Stevie.'

The pair nodded in reply.

'Quite an early start, isn't it?'

Brennan watched Gallagher struggle with his tie, 'Obviously a bit of a challenge for you, Jim.'

The DI seemed to infer something from Brennan's tone, he curled his eyebrow down as he dispensed with the necktie. 'Look, Rob, do you think we could have a chat . . .' He looked at McGuire, 'No offence, Stevie, I just want a private word with the boss.'

McGuire looked at Brennan, appeared to detect no opposition and raised his open palms in the DI's direction. 'Be my guest.'

Gallagher touched Rob's elbow, nodded to the end of the

street. Brennan watched another car pulling up, it was Pettigrew's Mercedes. 'Look, whatever you have to say, Jim, make it quick, eh . . .'

'Aye, sure, sure . . .' He removed a packet of Lambert & Butler, offered one to Brennan.

'No thanks.'

'Sure.' Gallagher seemed nervous, anxious to get his words out but desperate to make a proper build-up that would confer their true import. 'I just wanted to say, Rob, that I don't want to get off on the wrong foot with you.'

'Bit late for that isn't it?'

Gallagher bit the tip of his cigarette, produced a Zippo lighter; the smell of petrol came sharp in the morning air. 'Look, I'm not here to step on anyone's toes, Rob.'

Brennan removed a hand from his jacket, hushed Gallagher quiet. 'You're not big enough to step on my toes, Jim.'

The DI pocketed his lighter, his face firmed. The open, expressionless façade seemed to slip, gave way to a harsh-eyed stare. 'You've no right to play the Big I Am with me, Rob.'

Brennan smirked, leaned over Gallagher, he was the taller of the two men by some way. 'Jim, lad, let me tell you something, if I catch a poacher on my land he can think himself lucky if he gets away with an arse-full of lead.'

'You're all wrong, Rob . . .' Gallagher inhaled a deep drag on his cigarette, 'I'm all about the team, me.'

'Your team only has one player.'

'Oh, come on . . . We've a lunatic to catch!' He stepped to the side, waved to Pettigrew as he opened up. 'Rob, you've no rank on me, and you're not the most popular DI in the force either. I wouldn't go throwing up a genuine offer of friendship.'

A smile spread on Brennan's face, 'Why not?'

'Let's just say it could backfire.'

'If you've got a threat to put on me, Jim . . . Let's have it.'

Gallagher dropped his cigarette, pressed it into the ground with the sole of his shoe. He was staring down as he spoke, 'I don't make threats, Rob.' He edged towards the morgue. '. . . I don't need to.'

Chapter 14

BRENNAN WATCHED DI JIM GALLAGHER approach the morgue, make his way up the steps. He waited for a moment, took a breath of air and started the slow trail behind him. DS Stevie McGuire was waiting for him, said, 'What was that all about?'

Brennan held back for a moment, watched Gallagher enter the front door and strike up a conversation with Dr Pettigrew, then, 'Just Jim being Jim . . . Look, did you check him out like I asked you the other day?'

'His caseload, aye, aye . . .'

'Well?'

'Nothing spectacular, he seems to be flitting over to Glasgow quite a bit, helping out CID there with some tit-for-tat gang stabbings. But mainly he's looking at the cold cases like our Fiona Gow.'

'That it?'

McGuire scratched at his ear, 'He's counting his days, can't be far off the pension now.' He dropped his hand, 'Is there something I should know about, boss?'

Brennan reached over, touched McGuire's shoulder. 'No. Not at all. I'm just a bit wary of him.'

'In what way?'

'He's an old hand, you don't get to his age in this racket without knowing where a few bodies are buried.'

McGuire's eyes sunk in his head, his voice trailed off in a dull monotone. 'Sounds tenuous?'

'I just don't trust him . . . Why is he taking such an interest in our case when he seems to be able to pick and choose the cases he works these days?'

A bin lorry started to roll down the street, the noise threatened to drown them out; McGuire pointed to the morgue, raised his voice, 'Look, we should go in.'

'Yeah, I know . . . Just keep an eye on Jim, let me know if he pulls any fast ones.'

Inside the building Brennan removed his overcoat and jacket, folded them over the crook of his arm, then walked the few paces to the cloakroom and hung them up. Gallagher and Pettigrew were already in there.

'Morning, Rob.'

Brennan nodded to the doctor. He was tempted to have a dig about taking his time to get round to this postmortem but figured there would only be a grating reply about having to do private-practice work to pay for the Mercedes. He stilled his nerve and watched as Pettigrew bunched his brows on the way out the door. Gallagher stood square-footed in the middle of the room for a moment longer, a thin-eyed stare on Brennan, and then jerked his head to the side and followed the doctor out.

'Ready to roll?' said McGuire as he hung up his coat.

'Let's go.'

The steps down to the morgue were hard granite, the

officers' heels clacked on every one like hammer blows. No one spoke, the only sound came from the doctor as he lunged through the swing doors and made his way to scrub up.

Brennan and the other officers fitted themselves into green gowns and waited for the doctor by the edge of the room. The smell of the place was already settling in Brennan's nostrils; he knew it would be on his clothes and skin for the rest of the day. His colleagues would notice and question him on it. After a visit to the morgue Brennan always felt like taking a shower, a long burning-hot shower, and smothering himself in a lather. The place had come to signify not only death but stagnation to him; when he went there he felt like it inculcated something that was alien to life itself, that seeped into him, right down to his bones.

'Right,' said Pettigrew, 'get going shall we?' He snapped his rubber gloves into place and opened the door to the refrigerated section; the corpse of Lindsey Sloan was lying there. Brennan looked at the trolley; it had the same kind of wheels as a supermarket one, a little larger perhaps, but the similarity always struck him. Since first making this observation he had always chosen a basket in Sainsbury's.

Pettigrew asked McGuire to grab one end of the trolley and the pair removed the stretcher with the corpse on it towards the mortuary slab. The slab was grey as concrete and when the covering was removed Brennan noticed how similar the victim's flesh was in tone.

There was a different, more pungent odour now. It pervaded the large room and Brennan watched as McGuire raised his hand towards his mouth and tweaked the tip of his nose a few times.

Pettigrew looked at the clock on the wall as a young man

walked through the door and muttered apologetically, 'The buses were late.'

'Get scrubbed up, and be quick about it.'

The pathologist's assistant threw himself into a gown and started to scrub up. He seemed jolly as he joined the others. 'Morning folks, how goes it today?'

Nods. A chorus of 'Good morning.'

'Right,' said Pettigrew.

His first scalpel cut pierced the sternum and exposed a layer of yellow subcutaneous fat. The tissue was attached to the flesh and always struck Brennan as being far too bright, much brighter than any butcher's meat. He watched as the pathologist removed the dead girl's organs, weighed them, and replaced them in the body cavity. All the while his attendant washed away what blood there was with a hand-held hose; the blood ran down the slab and through a hole onto the cement floor where it met a drain and was carried away.

No one spoke for a while as the procedure was carried out. Brennan was the first to break the silence, 'What about that, when are you going to look at that?'

He was staring at the victim's head.

'I have a procedure,' said Pettigrew.

Brennan lowered his voice, it seemed too loud for the room. 'Just the mouth, please. The cloth.'

The pathologist walked from the middle of the slab to the top. He creased up his eyes as he bent over, poked a finger into the girl's mouth. 'Yes, there's something in there.'

'What is it?' said Brennan.

'I can't really see . . .' He moved away, withdrew a slender grapple-hook, like a dentist's instrument from his top pocket. 'It's soaked with blood of course . . .'

'Can you remove it?'

As Pettigrew eased the item from the girl's mouth it looked like a tight red ball, a crumpled-up piece of cotton. He laid it down on the table to the side of the slab and started to ease it open with his fingers and the chromium instrument.

'Yes, looks like undergarments,' he said.

The others watched as he unravelled cotton panties.

'He's gagged her with them . . .' said Gallagher.

'Suffocated her, you mean,' said Brennan.

Pettigrew continued to poke at the blood-caked panties. 'Hang on a minute . . .' There was something wrapped up inside.

'What is it?' said Brennan.

The pathologist hovered over the small bundle. 'There's more here . . .' he pointed with his gloved finger. 'Look, it's flesh, brittle flesh . . . Hang on.' He took a long-nosed pair of scissors, eased them under the dark, pulpy tissue. The material was brittle, hard. As he snipped through, dark patches of blood crumbled and fell onto the table. Pettigrew leaned in again, picked up the thin, tight strips of flesh. 'Oh, my God . . .'

'What is it?' said Brennan yet again.

'I think I've found the genitalia.'

Gallagher spoke, 'There's no doubt this is a sexual predator now.'

Brennan looked to Pettigrew; he was laying aside the scissors.

'Well, it's hard to tell . . . but . . .'

Brennan prompted, 'But what?'

Pettigrew raised his hands, waved one over the victim's head. 'Well, there is the eyes . . . they're not there. They've been appropriated.'

Gallagher tapped on the slab with his forefinger. 'I told you! It's a trophy take. We had this on the Fiona Gow case too.' He turned to Brennan. 'We're after the same guy . . . Tell me you doubt it now.'

Chapter 15

DI ROB BRENNAN STEADIED HIMSELF before the whiteboard in Incident Room One, knew he was staring into an abyss. He tapped two fingertips on his cheekbone, removed his hand, buried it in his trouser pocket, and nervously started to thumb the wedding ring he was unsure he should still be wearing. His mind was pervaded with confusion. The body of a young woman had been found, mutilated in the most grotesque fashion. As he looked at the photographs of Lindsey Sloan's ivory-white corpse he wondered what it was that he was missing. The answer, he told himself, was a clear line of enquiry to follow. Nothing had presented itself. The team had been door-to-door, checked the victim's background and spoken to her known associates. The girl had no obvious enemies, lived a quiet life. She was not a typical murder victim. It was as if she had been plucked from the street and singled out for her brutal death in some sick lottery. The more he played with the events of her death, the more it baffled him.

Lindsey Sloan had a life, a family; she was someone's

daughter. Thoughts of his own daughter now emerged; he knew he had to call Sophie soon. He would have to explain why her stable family unit had been blown asunder. Why her father was no longer going to be a part of her daily life. The thought stabbed at him. Brennan couldn't bear inflicting any kind of pain on her; he could not comprehend the true hurt the Sloans now faced. He wondered if he would be strong enough to take such a blow.

'Christ, Rob,' he whispered.

He was losing focus; was it because he had none? The case had him mystified. He knew there were always pieces of the puzzle that remained elusive, in every case, but this case seemed to be unlike anything he had ever known. How did a young girl end up in a field, strangled, with a broken neck and multiple wounds? What had she done? Who had she encountered that was capable of such evil? There had to be something he'd missed; there had to be somewhere to begin the search. The clues were out there, they always were – he knew this. He also knew Lindsey Sloan's murder was not a one-off; this killer had struck before, Jim Gallagher had all but proven this. And all the received wisdom indicated this kind of killer would strike again; unless he was stopped.

DS Stevie McGuire appeared at Brennan's side; he had closed a hand around a blue file, folded it beneath his arm. 'That was Joe Lorrimer on the phone,' he said.

The sound of the DS's voice broke Brennan's concentration, brought him back to reality. 'Oh, aye.'

'He'll be with us later today.'

'Good.' Brennan was not in the mood for conversation; he returned his gaze to the whiteboard, brought his hands together and worked them like he was lathering soap.

'There's not much to go on, is there?' said McGuire. He seemed insistent on pulling the DI into a discourse.

'Not much at all.'

McGuire raised the blue file in his hand, 'I've been through the Fiona Gow file . . . no answers there either.'

Brennan turned, frowned. 'Where is Jim?'

'He's gone for a bite. I asked him for the profiler's report on Fiona Gow, but I can't see what it's going to add.'

Brennan turned round to face the DS, eased himself onto the edge of the table next to the photocopier; he was resigned to debate the case's slow progress. The tabletop creaked as he settled himself, folded arms. 'It'll add fuck all, even if it ties in with Lorrimer's judgements, without a break.'

McGuire nodded, tapped the blue file off his thigh. 'Jim seemed happy enough to have the two cases linked up.'

'He would, wouldn't he . . . Jim's after this case, wants to take over.'

McGuire brought a hand up to his face, rubbed. His skin sat in folds below his eyes. He looked tired, strained. 'Why though? Surely he's past all that at his stage.'

'You think? Never heard of going out in a blaze of glory? . . . Look, I don't trust Jim's motives, there's something not right about his interest in this case so just keep a bloody close eye on him, Stevie.'

McGuire looked unconvinced, agitated. 'I don't know, sir, are you sure you're not just, well I don't know, being defensive?'

Brennan felt the implication dent his armour, he didn't want to admit McGuire might be right, he didn't like Gallagher imposing himself on his territory. But he didn't want to deny his gut either. 'I guess we'll see.' He rose, straightened himself, leaned back as he attempted to loosen the anxiety in his neck. He returned to the whiteboard, tapped at the picture of Lindsey Sloan.

McGuire had the Fiona Gow file open now, started to stick up her pictures. 'They're remarkably similar in terms of . . .'

Brennan cut it, 'You mean they're nothing like your typical murder victims? They never led chaotic lives, they were stable. They didn't come from poverty, they were workers. They weren't promiscuous . . . So where do we start?'

McGuire lit up. 'If you proceeded on the assumption that most victims know their attackers, then we're looking at a very bland bunch of possibilities.'

'Or we're not looking in the right place at all.'

McGuire closed the file again, turned towards Brennan. 'Perhaps she did know her killer, only he fits quite plainly into wider society.'

Brennan looked over McGuire's shoulder, towards the window – a white cloud sat like a smear against the grey sky. He understood perfectly what the DS was saying, he understood that the facts pointed to him being right too, but something stopped him buying into the assumption. 'You could be right, Stevie . . . or totally wrong.'

'What do you mean?'

'What if it's random? What if our killer selected these girls on the basis of some random criteria that could mean any number of girls out there might be plucked off the street.' He raised a finger, pointed out the window. 'I mean, who's to say he didn't select them because they were about the same height and weight . . . used the same bus stop . . . smoked the same brand of ciggies . . .'

'That's nuts.'

'Exactly!'

McGuire looked confused, his eyebrows lowered, stretched his brow. 'I don't get you.'

'What I'm saying is, Stevie, that's how we need to think to catch this guy. He is fucking nuts. His thought processes aren't the same as yours or mine. If we're going to catch him we're going to have to stop thinking like this is a normal murder investigation, because it clearly isn't.'

McGuire pinched his cheeks, exhaled a heavy breath. 'We need Joe Lorrimer in here as soon as.'

Brennan nodded, widened his eyes. His thoughts had already shifted. 'I need to make a phone call.' He walked towards his glassed-off office at the other end of the room; as he went inside he closed the door and drew down the blinds. It wasn't exactly privacy but it was as close as he was going to get. The call he had to make was gnawing at him; he knew it wouldn't be well received but there was no way of avoiding it. After all, he was still a father.

Ringing.

'Hello.'

'Joyce, it's Rob.' There was silence on the other end of the line. He let the fact that he was calling register, settle in his wife's mind for a moment, but she didn't bite. 'We need to talk.'

A tut. 'I don't think so.'

Brennan felt himself gasp for air, he was full of mixed emotions. He didn't want to go through this rigmarole with Joyce, their marriage had ended long ago and they both knew it. They had been inhabiting their house in Corstorphine like ghosts, barely encountering each other, rarely sharing words beyond the bare minimum to make their coexistence tolerable. He simply wanted out now, but that didn't mean he wanted to face the recriminations, have his affair cast up, or say goodbye to his daughter.

'There are certain formalities, Joyce.'

She was lighting a cigarette now, he could hear the lighter clicking. 'I have a lawyer for that.'

Brennan didn't rise to her gambit. 'Good. That will make things easier.'

'All you have to do is stay away.'

He couldn't let that go. 'If by that you mean not see my daughter, you're mistaken.'

'Do you think she wants to see you?'

Brennan's gaze veered out of focus, but found nothing to alight upon in the middle distance. He felt slightly sick, what had Joyce said to her? Had she told her about the affair? The mounting tension constricted his vocal cords as he tried to speak again. 'I swear Joyce if you've polluted her mind . . .'

'What? Fucking what, Rob?'

'I'll fight any order . . .'

Her tone and pitch increased. There was no escaping the anger she directed at Brennan. 'You destroyed this family . . . You're no longer a part of it. You cannot do us any more harm.'

A number of replies queued on his lips, but he never got a chance to give voice to them; the line died. She'd hung up. Brennan put down the phone. The realisation of what had just happened seemed to make him numb; his impressions sank into his mind but none of them came close to anything so coherent as thought. The predominant truth he faced was that he had hurt Joyce; more than he thought possible. He knew it wasn't hurt at the thought of losing him – he believed she no longer cared about him, or their marriage – it was the hurt of a wounded ego. Her husband had rejected her, in favour of another woman. She abhorred him for it and feared the ignominy. She felt too old now to start again, to find a new life partner and the thought infuriated her. Brennan knew he was the focus for the full brunt of her ire. In the days and weeks to come she would burn him in effigy; bottles of wine would be consumed with friends, or alone, and she would give vent to her spleen. He had ruined her life; Joyce's outward misery now had an inward direction: she could dump the whole lot on him. And he knew she would.

Brennan rose, he tapped his shirt pocket, removed an Embassy Regal and his lighter. As he walked out of his office, McGuire was sitting at his desk; he stood above him, said, 'I'll be at the front door, shout me if anything happens.'

'Unlikely, but OK.'

Brennan started out for the exit, got as far as the coffee machine, turned and pointed to McGuire's shirt front, 'Fix your tie, eh. We can at least look like we give a shit.'

He stomped towards the stairs; as he went, an angry energy seemed to seep from the tensed stock of his body. Things were not going well, and when that happened, he knew he became difficult to live with. He knew this, not just because other people had told him, but because he found it difficult to live with himself.

The soles of Brennan's shoes slapped noisily on the stairs as he descended. By the window on the first landing he caught a chink of sunlight breaking through the clouds – it painted an irregular ribbon on the wall. For a moment he was gripped by its form and then the sound of familiar voices droned up from the lower staircases.

'Leave him to me, there's more than one way to skin a

112

cat, Jim.' It was the Chief Super. 'There's plenty to call into question from his file if needs be.'

Gallagher replied, 'Well, I just want you to know I'm doing my best.'

'That's all we can ask.'

'But, it might not be good enough if he decides to . . .' The DI abruptly curtailed his conversation as Brennan stepped in front of him.

'Ah, Rob, just the man.' The Chief Super held out a blue folder, handed it to Brennan. 'This is the profiler's report on Fiona Gow . . . Jim and I have just been going over it.'

Brennan knew it was bluster, the pair of them had been caught red handed, they were discussing him. His facial muscles conspired against him and released a thin smile. 'Have you really . . . nice lunch was it, Jim?'

Gallagher nodded, the sunlight slanted across his face. 'Yes, thanks.'

'Always nice to have a bite with friends, I say.'

The Chief Super pushed up his glasses. 'We were discussing the case, Rob,' he said. 'And we have come to the conclusion, partly based on this morning's revelation, that we need to call in a profiler.'

Brennan widened his grin. 'I already have one.'

'You do? Who?'

'Lorrimer.'

The Chief Super stepped forward, the sun's glare bounced off his brow and his glasses. Brennan couldn't see his eyes behind their lenses as he spoke, 'Joe Lorrimer's Strathclyde . . .'

Brennan at once knew he had walked into an ambush he'd created for himself. His thoughts played tag as he searched for a way out. 'He's the best there is.'

'And what about the cost implication?'

'Like I said, I think Lorrimer is the best man for the job and . . .'

The Chief Super cut him off, 'You really didn't listen to a word I said earlier did you?' A disbelieving frown crossed his face as he lowered his chin towards his chest and eyed Brennan from above his glasses. 'We'll have a talk about this in my office, I think . . .'

The Chief Super turned for the stairs. Brennan caught sight of Gallagher grinning, he had the pleased look of a sheepdog that had just jumped through a hoop. 'This way, Rob,' said the Chief Super.

Brennan managed two steps before he was called from below.

'Rob?' It was Charlie from the front desk. 'Some people here to see you.'

'He's busy,' said the Chief Super.

'Oh, I think he'll want to see them, sir . . . It's the Sloan girl's parents.'

Chapter 16

NEIL HENDERSON SAT IN A dingy old drinker at the edge of the Grassmarket. It was as far from his usual stomping ground as he could get, but he needed a break, an escape. He had thought he would be delighted to get out of prison, back to the real world where there was no night-time lockdown, no sly groping in the showers or food that wasn't fit for swine. He didn't miss the danger, the cons with sharpened spoons or the screws who were looking for any excuse to batter their black batons off your head. He didn't miss the lack of privacy or the boredom, the endless days stretching on and on, each one as miserable as the next. And for sure, it was a blessing to be able to score without having to put your snout in hock for weeks on end, or trade chocolate bars for a one-skin spliff that had precious little puff in it. He could score and shoot up, get fired into a bag of Moroccan rock if he wanted; but somehow, it wasn't stacking up like he had hoped it would. It hadn't taken Boaby Stevens long to find him and now he had to get his money in a hurry. If he didn't he knew they'd be scraping him off the ground beneath a flyover.

Henderson had had plans in the past, dreams. None of them had ever materialised. He wondered if he was jinxed; if he was one of those people who was going to go through life with nothing. When he was nine or ten he'd been told by his mother's then boyfriend, a thug called Dinger, something that had stuck in his mind like a jagged shard of glass since. 'See you, laddie, you're going nowhere but the jail.'

'Why's that?' he'd asked.

Dinger sneered at him, 'Cause that's the only place your type ever go.'

He had been angered, wanted to hit him. That's how Henderson solved everything then, and now, he thought. Nobody got lippy if they knew there was the chance of a split nose in the offing. He'd fronted up, even though he was only a boy. 'And what's my type?'

These days, thought Henderson, that kind of thing was meat and drink to adults; they didn't bother with a bit of cheek, but back then it was enough to get you leathered. Back then, when Henderson was a lad, he remembered it was enough to get you more than leathered.

Dinger and Henderson were alone, the man grabbed him by the ear, threw him down then lifted him by the neck and marched him upstairs. His knees dragged on every step as he screamed out – he knew something was wrong – then a hard slap dazed him into quiet.

In his bedroom he was still a little woozy, but from where he lay on the edge of the bed he saw Dinger's neck, pink and fat above his collar. He had red hair, it was cut short and tight to the nape with little spikes sticking up. 'Shut your fucking hole, laddie.'

He remembered every word he had said, right up until the moment he'd tried to forget, he couldn't remember anything after that. He'd blocked it out.

'What are you doing?' He watched Dinger fiddling with his belt buckle. 'Tell me, I want to know.'

There was no reply. Henderson, the nine- or ten-year-old, was tense as a rod when Dinger turned around. There was a strange smell in the air – Dinger's face had turned red, as he started to open his shirt buttons.

'What's going to happen?'

No answer.

'Why are you looking at me?'

Still, no answer.

The boy felt his stomach start to tremble and there was a whooshing feeling in his chest that he couldn't explain. He looked up at the man, he was opening the rest of his shirt buttons. His chest was freckled and red. He looked at the boy with a twisted grin on his face, said, 'Get your trousers off.'

Henderson didn't move. He was cold, frozen. Even as the heat rose in his head he felt chilled to his insides. He couldn't speak.

The man slapped him across the face.

He felt a flash of pain, tasted blood in his mouth as he fell from the bed, and then his trousers were pulled down.

'There is a special treatment for boys like you, do you know that?'

He still couldn't speak. His cheek brushed the carpet, the fibres scratched at the corners of his mouth as he called out in agony. He couldn't believe the pain he felt. As he now remembered, his face contorted into a grimace.

Henderson stared across the Grassmarket bar, raised his

pint to his mouth. His hand was shaking a little but steadied as the golden liquid in the glass touched his throat. He looked about, wondered if there was anyone there who had caught him in deep thought; they would have been able to see what he was thinking of. It was his greatest shame.

For a long time, Neil Henderson had thought he was the only person in the world to have undergone such treatment. His mother's boyfriend had told him he deserved it and Henderson had believed him. He had felt like a truly degenerate little boy, one who required a special punishment. For some time he was a different child, he remembered how everyone had said so. He was quiet, withdrawn. There was no more trouble, for a while. He never told anyone about the trip upstairs but felt somehow, even now, that everyone should have known. It was such an awful occurrence that he felt that all grown-ups should have seen the signs, spotted them in him, and known what had happened. He simply couldn't believe that it had happened and that no one, not a soul, had any idea of it except him.

It was Henderson's secret, he kept it to himself. Even now.

There had been times when he had wondered about the man. He had fantasised about finding him, taking him on a little trip of his own to somewhere desolate. He had devised numerous tortures he would inflict upon him. He would tie him up, nail-gun his knees so he couldn't move, then he would slowly remove strips of flesh from his freckled chest with a Stanley knife. He'd bludgeon his face with a claw hammer and blowtorch his testicles, before finally castrating the bastard with a cold blade. He would take his time, make sure it hurt. Make sure there was as much agony inflicted as was humanly possible by one man on another. He wouldn't hold back.

Henderson raised his glass again, drained the last mouthful and called over the barman. 'Hey, mate, another pint in here.'

The barman nodded, moved down to Henderson's end of the bar and took up the glass. He returned with it fully topped up.

'There you go. Might want to go a wee bit slower with that one,' said the barman, leaning over to face him.

'What you on about *slower*?' Henderson snapped.

'I mean, that's your last in here . . . You've had a bucket already.'

Henderson looked up at the barman, he was older than him, quite a few years older than him but obviously fancied his chances. He knew he could take him, even after a fair drink, but he was still basking in his post-prison glow. His mouth shut fast; the barman retreated.

Henderson took his pint to the corner of the bar, selected a secluded table and sat down. He took a couple of small sips, it made him want a cigarette. He hadn't yet adapted to the smoking ban, and didn't like going outdoors for a drag. He massaged the brow of his head with his fingertips and let out a sigh.

His mind had wandered earlier; he knew why.

He didn't like to think about the incident he had tried to lock away for so long but he had been forced to stare into the black heart of himself because of Angela. Reading her journal had raised the dead in him; but the bastard Dinger *was* dead, there could be no revenge now. Henderson understood why Angela had been so hysterical when she saw that item on the news the other night, the item with the body that turned up in a field off the A720. It had been a rekindling of old memories for her; but she *could* take revenge.

'What was it with her?' he mumbled; immediately checking himself. No one in the bar had heard him. He looked back to his pint glass, raised it to his mouth and swallowed another mouthful.

He had started reading her journal thinking it was going to be the spicy confessions of a teenage schoolgirl, but as he read on it turned his stomach. He felt surprised by his reaction; surely it would be natural to feel sympathy for her. After all, she had gone through the same kind of indignity that he had: an adult they should have respected had taken advantage of them. But he didn't – he felt nothing for her except contempt. For years he had stored up his anger; a social worker had once described him as 'self-loathing' and the description had struck him because he knew he did loathe himself. Now he loathed Angela too, because she was no better than him. They were both worthless, but she could do something about it and he couldn't.

Henderson took out the little mauve-coloured diary and placed it on the table in front of him. It had already started to open at the page he had creased with rereading so many times. He stared at it for a moment longer, took another sip of his lager, and then he raised the diary and read once more.

The next I remembered was waking up in the field . . .

There was a field on the news – it had set her off, he saw that now.

He thought back to the story from the television report. There had been a murder in a field outside Edinburgh, off the A720. He knew it was a young girl, they had said that

120

on the television. There was no name, at least the filth hadn't released one. He tried to remember what else had been said but all he could see in his mind's eye was the footage from the field, the reporter all suited up and freezing by the side of the road. He cursed himself for not paying more attention. Then he cursed Angela for distracting him, arking up and having a carry on. It was her screaming and messing about that distracted him.

He picked up the diary again. None of it seemed real to him. This was a story about a teacher, some gymnastics coach, who had tried it on with Angela and ended up taking her out to a field. And now there had been a story on the news about a girl who had been murdered in the same field.

Henderson tried to concentrate, to think. It was as if the same group of disparate thoughts came back to irritate his mind like mosquito bites.

He returned to the entry.

. . . I could hardly move my hands because they were tied, but I pulled and pulled to get free. I felt this fear, it was like terror in me. I tried to blot it all out – like this was all happening to someone else, in a film maybe. It was cold and I had to wee. I remember when I did wee, I felt it run all down my bum and I knew I had no knickers on. I wasn't able to see very well at first, but I think it was just my eyes getting used to the dark like when you play hide and seek as a kid. I saw the moon first and then I saw him, I recognised the Creep straight away, he had the scratch marks on his face where I went for him. I don't know what he was doing, just standing there and then he leant over and picked something up, it was my tights from my gym bag, he was rolling them on his hands and then he tried to tie them round my neck. I wanted to say, 'No, go away' but

I couldn't speak. When he leant right over I knew I had to do something or he was going to kill me. I don't know how my hand came free, he couldn't have tied me properly, but my hand was on a stone, a big rock and I grabbed it up and hit him on the side of the head. He fell onto me, I thought I was going to be crushed, but I wriggled out from under him. I thought I'd killed him but I just kept running and running.

Henderson turned the last page, there were no more entries. He closed the little mauve-coloured diary and placed it in his inside pocket as he stood up and headed for the door.

Chapter 17

THE DOOR'S HINGES SANG OUT as Neil Henderson returned to the flat he shared in Leith with Angela Mickle. He hung his jacket on the hook and staggered through to the front room, belching loudly as he went. He found Angela splayed out on their filthy mattress, her works sitting on the floor beside her. He angled himself above her, swayed a little as he looked down. There was a white line of dried spittle around her mouth and her skin looked pale as whey.

'Ange,' he said.

There was no answer.

He leaned a hand on the wall to steady himself, tried again, 'Ange, doll . . . you awake?'

He could tell she was out of it, she had shot up, but he wanted to be sure she wasn't unconscious. He slid his hand off the wall, kneeled down beside the mattress. As he did so he realised he had put his knee in a pile of sick. 'For fuck's sake.'

He pitched himself on his toes, leaned over to pat Angela on the back. 'Ange, you all right there?'

Her back felt warm, wet with sweat. He rested his hand there for a moment longer; he could feel her lungs expanding as she took breath.

'Fucking out for the count you are.'

He raised himself, went over to the window and stared out. It wasn't dark yet but it would be in a couple of hours or so. He took a packet of Kensitas Club up from the window ledge; there was a blue plastic lighter inside next to the cigarettes. He sparked up, blew smoke into the room.

As he looked around, Henderson shook his head. 'This what I came out for?' He felt a desire to spit, 'Not much better than the fucking pound this place.'

He closed his eyes tight as he remembered his latest stint in prison. It took him a great effort to knock the thoughts of the place out, but when he did he reopened his eyes and brought the cigarette up to his mouth, inhaled.

Henderson sat down in the wicker chair by the window; the chair had split and as he lowered himself down a stray wicker prong poked into his leg. 'Jesus fuck!' He snatched at the spike, snapped it in his hand. He was ready to kick out but held back; his head was spinning a little now with all the alcohol and he wanted to gather his thoughts for when Angela came around.

He knew what he wanted to say to her, he had it all planned out. At least, after catching the number 26 bus from Princes Street it had all seemed clear. When he missed his stop, after dozing off, and had to walk half the way down London Road and onto Easter Road his plan had faded a bit.

'Could do with a fucking can.'

Henderson looked over the grimy flat, the paper peeling from the walls, the plaster blotched and stained, the curtains ripped and worn. He had been in worse, but not much worse. And anyway, that wasn't the point. There was money to be made out there. People were always making money in Edinburgh, the town was awash with it. Flash bastards in big Range Rovers, the ones with the tinted windows that came down the Links. He had made good money off the Links, off his girls. But all he had now was Angela, and a two-grand debt to Boaby Stevens.

'Fat fucking lot of use you're going to be to me.'

There was a groan from the mattress.

Henderson raised his voice a notch, 'I said fat fucking use you are!'

Angela's head moved a little, the dirty blonde hair on the pillow was stretched out as she looked up. Henderson saw she was still spaced, had no clue what day of the week it was never mind anything else. How could he put her out to work in a couple of hours like that. Who'd pay for it?

He rose from the wicker chair; it seemed to stick to him as he got up and he turned on his heels and kicked out, the chair went flying across the room. 'Right, come on, get yourself up,' he yelled.

'What?'

'You fucking heard, you're not lying in that pit any longer, get your fucking self up or *I'll* get you up.'

Angela's head dropped to the pillow. It was like incitement to Henderson. He reached over her and grabbed a handful of her dirty blonde hair. She screamed out as he yanked her to her knees in one firm jerk.

'You not fucking hear me, or what?'

'Hendy . . . Stop.'

'Are you ignoring me, eh? That it?'

She raised her hands to his, screamed out again. 'Stop it, that hurts!'

Henderson bunched a fist, 'I'll give you fucking hurts in a minute, if you're not on those feet and walking the fucking Links.'

Angela dragged herself up; Henderson released his grip. For a moment she stood, naked, in front of him and then she crossed her hands over her breasts.

'Oh come on for fuck's sake, I've seen it before, along with half of fucking Leith.'

Angela looked away, turned for the door. She was unsteady on her feet, balancing herself on the walls with the palms of her hands as she went.

'Where are you off to?'

'I need the toilet.'

'You better not have any gear in there . . . I want you out on the streets tonight.'

She slammed the bathroom door behind her and Henderson slumped on the mattress. As he landed he felt something pressing in his back pocket; he clasped his cigarette in his mouth and reached round to remove the little mauve-coloured diary. He was still reading it as Angela returned. She had put on a short black dress; she didn't speak when she saw him reading.

'I understand, you know,' said Henderson.

'What?'

He kept turning the pages as he spoke, 'About what happened with this teacher guy.'

Angela looked out the window. 'I don't want to talk about that.'

'Oh, but we have to.' He removed the cigarette, pointed the tip of it at Angela, 'We very definitely have to talk about him, Ange.'

Her shoulders rose and fell, then she looked at the nails on her hands for a moment before bunching fists. 'I can't . . . that's why I gave you the diary. I just can't talk about it.'

Henderson pitched himself on one elbow; he knew he was going to have to draw what he needed out of her. He had to be cautious; if he scared her, she might bolt and she had something that was valuable to him now. 'I never told anybody this before, Ange . . .' he paused, looked at the tip of his cigarette.

'Told anybody what?'

He looked up, met her eyes. He knew his voice had started to quiver. 'What you got me to read here . . . It happened to me too.'

She shook her head, 'It couldn't have.'

'I mean, not the way you describe it, but . . .' Henderson got off his elbow, sat upright on the mattress, leaned his back on the wall. He started to tell her about his own experience, the one he had locked away. When he had finished, Angela was staring at him with doleful eyes.

'What happened to him?' she said.

Henderson got up, went to the other side of the room and took out another cigarette from the packet of Club; he offered one to Angela. 'He died.' The words came out flat, cold.

'How?'

Henderson shrugged, 'Does it matter? He's dead. And my mam's dead as well so who's left to fucking tell.'

Angela lit her cigarette. She inhaled the smoke deep into her lungs and then released it quickly. 'I'm sorry about that, but what's it got to do with me?'

Henderson moved in front of her, placed a hand on her shoulder. 'I never got the chance to pay the bastard back . . . But yours, you can.'

'How?'

He pointed to his chest, 'With me . . . I can sort the fucker out.'

Angela turned her gaze to the floor, 'I don't want to have anything to do with him. He's as good as dead to me too . . .'

A huff, loud tut.

'Ange, it's not about you . . . Or me even. Remember what we saw on the telly the other night, this bastard could still be at it. You want that on your conscience, eh?'

She got up, walked over to the window and started to press the cigarette to her lips. He could see he hadn't got through to her, she wasn't interested. Henderson felt the desperation of his situation attach to him like a stranglehold.

'Ange . . .'

'*What*?' she snapped.

'You hearing me?'

'Aye . . .'

'Well, what do you say?'

She turned to face him. 'What the fuck do you want me to say, Hendy?'

He crossed the floor, placed a hand on her shoulder. There was only one thing she had to say; if she didn't he'd have to rethink his plans. 'Just tell me where to get hold of the bastard. That's all. I'll take care of the rest.'

Chapter 18

DI ROB BRENNAN KNEW HIS problem: he wouldn't play the game. He would never be one of those who faded into the background, became part of the office furniture. It was easy for them – the type that had no conscience or guilt attached to playing the game. Kissing the boss's arse or denying their true thoughts and emotions were their primary responses. To Brennan, each time he succumbed was like a death in him. A part of what made him, gave him strength, simply collapsed; imploded with the defeat. He knew he had always fought back, but he wondered: with enough attacks on him – in quick succession – could he be felled? Just fold; never come back. Life was all about the blows, about the myriad knocks and how you took them. He knew it would be easier to be a wimp – a drone – but it wasn't in him. Brennan couldn't deny who he was and so the fear, the worry of the time-bomb going off inside him, remained. He carried it everywhere and lived in the constant presence of its slow tick, tick, tick.

Gallagher wasn't the first to try and put one over on him;

Brennan had been on the force long enough to have outmanoeuvred more than one like him. They didn't know what they were taking on – it was no game to him. When the job is burned so deeply into a soul, it becomes more than the sum of its parts. It was more than an occupation, a vocation even, to Brennan. It was his life. He had sacrificed so much to the job that he no longer knew where the job began or ended. It was all the job. The job was everything.

He tried to put himself in Gallagher's mindset, imagine what being on this murder squad meant to the DI. He hadn't once heard him voice a sympathetic word for the victim, her family. Brennan knew that didn't necessarily mean anything – there were others on the force, younger than Gallagher, who had learned to bury their emotions deep. But somehow, he had never found himself questioning anyone else's compassion; it was assumed. With Gallagher there was a lack, a want. It wasn't a clinical disengagement either, like he had seen the morgue workers adopt; it was as if the emotion was absent. The thought sat like a marker in Brennan's mind; to him the job was inseparable from his emotions, instincts, feelings – he relied on them to make his way through every case. People were fickle, could spark up or alight on a completely new course at any moment – there was no predicting where they would lead you in an investigation and Brennan relied on his wits. It challenged his logic to watch Gallagher.

The DI had manoeuvred himself into the Chief Super's ambit; that wasn't such a big deal, thought Brennan. Benny was a typical careerist, he watched out for himself. He nurtured lackeys and brown-nosers, but only so long as they were not a threat. If they evinced any attempts to climb the greasy pole to his level, he quickly quashed such incursions. Gallagher was no such threat – he was nearing the end of his days in the job, he was in handover mode. So what was in it for Benny? It wasn't the clean up, because Gallagher had little or no chance of attaining that on his own, his previous failings on the Fiona Gow case had proven that. And Benny was too proud, too pompous to be swayed by any old-school experience that Gallagher might pass on in an avuncular, back-slapping manner; Benny was an egotist, he'd be far more likely to see himself as teaching the old dog new tricks. There was only one possibility that Brennan could countenance: the Chief Super saw Gallagher as a way of keeping one errant DI in check. Benny was using Gallagher to teach Brennan a lesson. And the lesson was, Benny was the boss.

Brennan knew his next meeting with the Chief Super was likely to be an uncomfortable one. There would be some wrist slapping, dressed up as a retreat from the proper arse-caning that he should have delivered; then there would be a detailed account of what was expected of DIs on Benny's watch; finally, there would be the 'I've no choice in the circumstances' speech that ended with the repositioning of Gallagher at the front of the murder squad. It was a subtle mix of management psychology and testosterone that Brennan had encountered more than once before. Wullie had said, 'They're all out to hack the billiards off you, Rob . . . It's a miracle if you get out the force with a full set.'

Brennan had no intention of putting his knackers in a poke for Benny or Gallagher; he liked them where they were. There was only one way to avert that outcome, however, and that was wrapping up the murder of Lindsey Sloan sooner rather than later. He wondered if he'd get the chance.

At the foot of the stairs the desk sergeant stood with an arm resting on the banister; he eyed Brennan and ran a dry tongue over his lower lip as he indicated upwards with a nod. 'He gone?'

'Benny? . . . Aye, thanks for the bail out, mate.'

'What's got his goat?'

Brennan felt his chest expand as he took breath. 'Does he need an excuse?'

Charlie lowered his arm from the banister, stepped closer. 'Watch that bastard Gallagher, he's sleekit.'

Brennan was glad that somebody shared his opinion, but Charlie was too much of a fount of gossip to confide in, much as he liked the man. He played possum, 'Come on, Jim Gallagher . . . He's old school.'

Charlie huffed. 'Who told you that?'

'You telling me different?'

'The pair of us joined up around the same time; now, I'm not saying you can read too much into this but do you think he got to be a DI by being a better cop?'

Brennan lowered a consoling hand onto Charlie's shoulder, joked, 'Maybe he just had the marbles, mate.'

Charlie bit back. 'If it was about marbles, *mate*, I'd be sitting in Benny's chair now.' He turned for the front desk, reeled. 'Ask Wullie Stuart what he thinks of Gallagher, he's not a fucking fan either.'

Brennan felt a smirk pass up the side of his face; he was glad to have Charlie confirm his suspicions, but people like Charlie were rare on the force, and getting rarer. It would take an army of supporters like him to ward off the Chief Super and Gallagher, and Brennan knew, in reality, he was on his own.

He set out for the interview room, trying to refocus his

thoughts onto the more pressing matter of what he was going to say to the Sloans about the brutal murder of their daughter. Brennan felt a band begin to tighten around his chest as he walked; he knew it was stress – the job got you like that, took a grip of you when you least expected it and tried to warn you that something wasn't right. Brennan didn't need any reminders.

A few moments ago, he had been staring at the pictures of the Sloans' daughter – pale-white against the dark of a field in night-time. They were pictures no one should have to look at; when he thought of the girl's fate the trivia of his own life seemed to disperse, evaporate.

Brennan reached the door of the interview room and stalled, he felt his jaw clench and he forced himself to release it. He wanted to greet the couple with an open expression. As he walked in Mr Sloan was sitting tense with the heel of his shoe tapping on the chair leg; the man was lost in thought, staring out the window at the empty, sun-crossed street.

'Hello again, thank you for coming in,' said Brennan.

Mr Sloan stood up, his wiry grey hair sat flat on his head as he spoke. 'Hello, Inspector, hello . . .' He sat quickly, returned to a cigarette he had burning in the ashtray.

'Can I get you something to drink, a coffee or a tea perhaps?'

Mr Sloan shook his head. 'I think we'd sooner just get this over with as quickly as possible, if that's all OK with you, Inspector.'

'Of course.' Brennan turned his gaze to Mrs Sloan. She was a slight, bunched-up woman with timid movements; her eyelids were dipped towards the tabletop. 'You've been to see the pathologist, I believe.'

Mrs Sloan shut her eyes.

'Yes, we have,' said Mr Sloan.

'Can I just say again, how very sorry I am.'

'We know, thank you.' He raised the cigarette to his lips, inhaled deeply.

Brennan sat down, hooked his feet beneath his chair as he leaned forward with his hands flat on the table. 'I know it's all happened so quickly for you both, and you probably haven't had a chance to take any of this in, but I want you to know we're doing all we can. There isn't a soul on the force who isn't determined to catch . . .' He realised he'd blocked himself in with his choice of words, 'What I'm saying is, we're working as hard as we can.'

Mr Sloan nodded. 'I know . . .' He turned to his wife, 'We both know that, don't we, love?'

Mrs Sloan sat impassive.

'Can I ask, are you ready to answer some questions about Lindsey?' said Brennan.

'I think so, yes.'

Brennan tapped delicately on the table surface, he felt his shoulders tighten at the prospect of addressing the victim's demise. 'Can you tell me a little about Lindsey . . . What kind of a girl was she?'

Mrs Sloan answered, her reedy voice came as a shock the first time Brennan heard it. 'She was our daughter . . .' she raised her eyes, 'what do you want us to say? Everybody loves their daughter, adores her. Do you have a daughter, Inspector?'

Brennan nodded, 'Yes. I do.'

Mr Sloan grabbed his wife's hand, 'Lindsey was just a lassie, she was working away and doing her thing . . . She would never have harmed a soul.'

134

'Did she have a wide circle of friends?'

'She was a popular girl at the school, but she'd been working and seeing a few boys lately; she never had that much time for her old friends I don't think, except for maybe one or two she went out clubbing with.'

Brennan locked his feet under the front legs of the chair, sat back. 'Any regular boyfriend?'

Mr Sloan rolled his eyes towards the ceiling, 'There was a boy, think he was a trainee mechanic . . . He was a nice boy, we had him to the house, y'know, but that was months ago. No, I don't think she had a steady boyfriend, Inspector.'

Mrs Sloan lowered her head, there were tears rolling down her cheeks; her husband turned towards her, started to rub at her hand.

'Are you OK to continue, Mrs Sloan?' said Brennan.

Mr Sloan answered, 'We'd sooner get this by with.'

Brennan laced his fingers, he knew the questions he wanted to ask, he knew the information he wanted to draw from them, but he could see they were deep in their grief and it wasn't the time to pry much further. He kept the tone of his voice low and flat, 'You said Lindsey had some friends she went clubbing with . . . Where was that?'

'Just the clubs, you know, up the town . . . I don't know their names.'

'Have you any idea what part of the city they went to?'

'Aye, it was George Street and all that New Town bit.' He looked to his wife, smiled. 'She liked the trendy bars, our Lindsey.'

The DI made a mental note, asked if it would be all right to speak to some of her friends and then he changed subject. The picture he was getting of Lindsey Sloan was

135

remarkably similar to that of Fiona Gow, but he had found nothing to link the pair, no commonality.

'Can I ask, Mr Sloan, did Lindsey ever change schools?'

'No, no. Always the one school . . . Edinburgh High.'

Brennan flinched, his mind reeled for a moment, then steadied itself as he recalled the case notes had said Fiona Gow had gone to Portobello Academy. 'What about clubs, or games at school?'

'No, I don't think so. She wasn't into that sort of thing.'

'Gymnastics,' Mrs Sloan's voice had firmed. 'She liked her gymnastics for a wee while there at the school but she gave it up.'

Brennan leaned in, 'She gave it up?'

'Said it wasn't her thing. She took her notions, Lindsey, one minute it was all this, the next she wasn't interested . . . A typical teenager,' said Mrs Sloan, 'How old is your daughter, Inspector?'

Brennan took a sharp intake of breath as the question came his way, 'She's sixteen . . . Sophie's sixteen.'

'What a lovely name.'

'Thank you.'

'You should cherish her, Inspector.' Mrs Sloan looked out to the street, she had no more tears, but her hurt was so palpable it could almost be touched.

'I think, Inspector, we should call it a day, for now,' said Mr Sloan.

Brennan rose, his chair scraped noisily along the floor and he winced, but Mrs Sloan didn't falter. 'Thank you, you've been very helpful,' he said.

The man put his arm around his wife and eased her from her chair, led her to the door. The pair looked frail, older than their years, as they shuffled slowly out of sight.

As Brennan watched them go he felt a pinch in his throat; he had seen too many good people destroyed by the evil that was out there. He wanted to help them, wanted to right their wrongs, but he wondered what use he could possibly be to them now. Their daughter had been taken, there was nothing he could do to alter that; he couldn't bring Lindsey back. The thought hacked into him, tugged out his pity and replaced it with a febrile anger.

Chapter 19

AS DI ROB BRENNAN WALKED into Incident Room One his attention was drawn towards WPC Elaine Docherty. She was standing next to the coffee machine, throwing back her blonde hair and laughing loudly. It was a scene that looked out of place in the sombre setting. Beside her, DS Stevie McGuire placed a hand on her arm – they seemed to be sharing a joke, the moment looked intimate – but the vision shattered before Brennan's eyes as McGuire spotted him coming and made a quick retreat. Brennan let his stare linger on the pair for a moment longer, he watched the WPC pick up a blue folder and press it to her white shirt front; she quickly exited the room, averting her eyes as she passed him. McGuire closed his mouth like a zipper and manoeuvred himself clumsily behind his desk.

Brennan approached. 'Stevie,' he said.

'Yes, sir.'

The room fell into hushed silence; Brennan looked around him, heads that had sprung up dropped suddenly as his gaze roved around the room. He saw at once this wasn't the kind of conversation they should have in the open. 'Never mind, I'll see you later,' he said.

'Sir.'

As Brennan strolled through the room he felt as though he had brought in an air of anxiety; either that, or the team was unsettled. He knew they needed a break. They had been working hard, had done everything the DI had asked of them, but nothing had turned up. They needed some encouragement, a reminder that their roles were worthwhile. They were a murder squad and if that wasn't something to be valued, Brennan didn't know what was. He had his own troubles and wondered if he'd been neglecting the team. Was it his fault that there hadn't been a break? Had he missed something? He checked himself; knew that wasn't the case. Brennan had watched doubts creep in before, they didn't carry any weight, they didn't mean anything. They were merely reminders, prompts that kept you on track. Without the doubts, his actions – the team's actions – went unchecked and that was something he would never allow to happen. The process was continual, non-stop. If doubts crept in, they kept them on their toes, and that was something to be welcomed.

Brennan halted himself in the middle of the room, looked around. The place was busy enough, but there was none of the adrenaline high that came of getting close to solving a case. He needed to prod them, cajole.

'Right, listen up everyone,' he said. 'I know we've not had a break on this case yet, but we're still in the early days.'

A chorus, 'Sir.'

Brennan took in the team's gaze; he had their attention, it was important to hold it. 'You're doing fine, no one has put a foot wrong and as long as we keep at it, keep doing what we're doing, then we'll get that break. That's all it takes, I've seen it a million times before: a case can rest on a single scrap of information that turns everything on its head. Keep looking. Keep turning over the stones, because that's how we'll get this bastard.'

The team stood around, some shuffled; they were waiting for more. Brennan didn't want to overdo it, but conceded to the call. 'I've just spoken to the Sloans, they're good people.' He paused, drank in the team's interest; he knew that they understood him. 'That family deserves our best, so let's bear that in mind.'

Heads dipped, some looked at each other, exchanged mournful expressions. Everyone in the room absorbed the import of Brennan's words; he saw that they knew what he meant: he was proud of them. There were times on the force when he wanted to throw things, turn over filing cabinets, clear his desk; but not now. He looked at his team with such affection that the thought touched his mind like a kindness.

Immediately Brennan withdrew into himself; it wasn't right to show his sentiments. 'Right, that's all. Back to work.'

The DI strode towards the whiteboard, eyed the photographs that had been stuck up of Fiona Gow and Lindsey Sloan. He stood with one hand in his trouser pocket and with the other he removed the black marker pen from the thin shelf and started to fiddle with the cap between thumb and forefinger. His mind was flitting to and fro, between the meeting with the Sloans and what he knew about the case as it stood. The Sloans had not given him much to go on, but what could he expect? They had just lost a daughter,

140

he had felt their anguish every second he had been with them. It was painful to watch. The woman was ruined; she would never be the same again. How could she? How could anyone recover from that? What they were going through was not something you could adequately comprehend; his mind darted towards Sophie once again. She would be getting out of school soon, there would be no one to collect her from the gates because she was too old for that now. But was she? The girls on the whiteboard weren't much older than Sophie. Brennan felt an urge to pick up his daughter, hold her in his arms and keep her safe. The urge had presented itself before; at first he had thought it was a side-effect of the job, but now he knew it was nothing to do with it. It was about being a parent, about wanting to hold on to your child for ever. He had seen that in Mrs Sloan and he knew her devastation was drawn from the realisation that she could never keep her daughter close to her, and now she would never see her again.

Brennan removed the cap from the marker as in his peripheral vision he spotted DS Stevie McGuire and DI Jim Gallagher approaching. McGuire seemed to be striding ahead of the older DI; he looked back towards him as if he wondered why he was being followed or just what Gallagher was going to ask the boss. His eyes told a story all of their own: he clearly had Gallagher down as a challenge to his position as head boy. He reached Brennan first, said, 'Well, how did it go?'

The DI turned from the whiteboard, put a stare on Gallagher then moved his gaze towards Stevie. 'Not well.'

'Did you get anything?' said Gallagher, his voice rising with an unnatural inflection.

Brennan stood before them for a minute, let them digest

his manner and then turned to the board. He wrote the word 'nightclubs' and suffixed it with a large question mark. 'She did the George Street scene,' he said, his voice was matter of fact, blunt.

'Pricey on a travel agent's wage,' said McGuire; he said it to the DI but was looking at Gallagher as he spoke.

'Trainee travel agent,' said Brennan 'but we don't know how much of a regular she was. Maybe she was drinking lemonade, maybe someone was buying her drinks for her . . .'

'I'll check it out,' said Gallagher. He sounded over-eager, his vowels clipped and prim as a schoolmaster. He turned from the board, brushed past McGuire and had the receiver of a telephone raised to his ear when Brennan stopped him.

'No, I want Stevie on that. I've something else for you, Jim.'

Brennan faced the board, raised the marker and drew a sharp line from the picture of Lindsey Sloan, topped it with an arrowhead and wrote the word 'gymnastics'.

He turned to face the others.

'What's that all about?' said Gallagher.

'Just about the only thing her parents could remember her taking an interest in at school . . . There might have been some kind of club, some kind of social scene. I don't know . . . But that's the whole point. I want to know.'

'She's a wee while out the school, sir.'

'I know that,' Brennan's voice rose, 'I also know we've got nothing out of the group of friends she's been associating with so far, or the old school pals we contacted. Her Facebook buddies and so on. This might be a stretch, Jim, but it's a new line of enquiry and I'm not going to ignore it . . . Get on it right away and report back to me.'

'Sir.' Gallagher stepped aside, he sucked in his broad

stomach as he eased himself round the desk and moved off to the other side of the room. He was still looking at Brennan as he sat down behind his desk, but quickly busied himself with the telephone when the DI kept a long stare on him.

McGuire had been watching the exchange of looks. He closed in on Brennan, tapped his chin with the knuckles of his right hand as he spoke, 'I heard there was some kind of kerfuffle earlier.'

'What?'

'On the stairs.'

Brennan sniffed. 'Bloody Charlie . . .'

'Come again?'

'That who you heard it from?'

McGuire made a half smile. Said nothing.

'Oh, I get it. Look, it's nothing for you to worry about . . . You've got more important matters to concern yourself with, laddie.'

The sergeant's eyebrows shot up together. 'Like what?'

'Like what's going on with you and Elaine Docherty?'

McGuire's smile disappeared completely, his chin dimpled like the skin of a lemon as he replied, 'I don't know what you mean.'

Brennan let his mind skim the possibilities, could he have picked it up wrong? He was sure he hadn't, but decided to give McGuire a break. Chances were a subtle word would be enough for them to get the message, and after all, he was hardly one to be preaching about office romance when his own affair with the force psychiatrist had cost him his marriage. 'All right. Maybe I've got the wrong end of the stick, Stevie.'

'I think you must have, sir.'

Brennan let the remark slide, but tagged a warning notice

143

to it; he didn't like his DS lying to him. 'But I suppose we'll see, in time.' He dipped his chin to his chest, smirked. 'Right, about this Sloan girl . . .'

'Yes, sir.'

'I want you to go back to her friends, get the details of all the clubs and pubs they visited when they were out on the town.'

McGuire butted in, he had a biro in his hand, raised it. 'The night she disappeared, you mean . . .'

'No, Lou and Brian have covered that. We know her movements on the night she disappeared pretty thoroughly and . . .' he trailed off, his eyes glazed over as he chased a line of thought.

'What is it?'

Brennan leaned his back on the wall, tapped the marker. 'You can cross-reference all of this with the Fiona Gow case file.'

McGuire turned, pointed with his pen up the room. 'Right, Collins has it just now . . . But what am I checking in there?'

Brennan's voice was flat, unemotional. He was working his thoughts out on the hoof. 'She was a hairdresser, wasn't she . . . They all like a good night out. Check if she was part of the same scene too.'

'Pubs and clubs, then?'

Brennan shook his head, 'Pubs, clubs, names, faces . . . If they bought a pair of fucking dancing shoes from the same shop I want to know.'

McGuire was biting the tip of his pen now. 'Boss, they were five years apart.'

'I know that, Stevie, and I know the club scene changes fast but there might be something in it.'

McGuire nodded. 'Well, we won't know until we try.'

'Exactly.' Brennan eased himself off the wall, leaned past McGuire and looked down the room. 'Who checked the last club the Sloan girl visited?'

'Er, Collins . . .'

Brennan called out, 'Collins . . . Come here a minute.'

Collins rose slowly, strolled down the middle of the room, eying everyone's desktop as he went. He was chewing gum and had a cigarette behind his ear, but when he reached the whiteboard he looked attentive. He thinned eyes, took in the new additions. 'Yes, sir.'

'The last club the Sloan girl visited . . .'

'Called The Rondo, boss.'

'Aye, get anything on the CCTV?'

'Not a morsel . . . All cheesy quavers and glow sticks.'

Brennan pounced. 'Right, get yourself hooked up with one of the WPCs and get down there tonight. And tomorrow night. Ask about, casual like, not heavy handed.'

'Oh, nice one. Paid to go on the piss.' He grinned at McGuire, but as he checked Brennan's expression, Collins backtracked, 'I mean, not actually on the piss, but . . .'

'Just remember what we're doing here, eh?' He paused, stared at McGuire again, but addressed Collins. 'Why don't you take Elaine Docherty with you?'

'Yes, sir.'

McGuire looked away, Brennan saw him struggle to maintain his earlier indifference to the WPC; he knew for sure he'd been lied to now.

Brennan turned back to Collins, said, 'And go over that footage again, anything that sticks out, check it!'

Collins's answer came quickly. 'Nothing stuck out, sir, she was with friends, dancing and that. We ID'd them all.'

'Check again; if anyone's looking at her funny – hoick them in.'

'Clutching at straws isn't it?'

Brennan fired up, waved the marker pen to emphasise his point. 'Fucking right we're clutching at straws. And we'll keep clutching till we get a result.'

Chapter 20

DI ROB BRENNAN TURNED THE key in the ignition of the VW Passat and pulled out of Fettes Police Station. He had a cigarette burning in his left hand as he negotiated the gears. The sun had started to shine through the clouds, but there was little warmth in it. In puddles by the sides of the road, little iridescent patches of light played like lantern-glow. Brennan looked out to the sky, large cumulus sat like a bulwark against the blue of the expanding horizon. He knew by the time he reached Craigleith Road the weather could have changed, but he wound down his window a few inches and swapped his cigarette to his right hand in a move of defiant optimism.

In Ayr, where Brennan had grown up, he remembered nothing but sunny days. Bright, warm afternoons with long walks along the beach and games of football, with Andy playing in goal. They had enjoyed a happy, stable child-hood. Was it only nostalgia, he wondered, that made him look back so fondly? Perhaps. He knew he missed his brother, but you couldn't bring back the dead. Brennan had often thought about an afterlife, about heaven and hell and all the variations in between, but dismissed it entirely. He had seen enough of this life to believe that nothing could be worse in hell. He found his mind returning to the SOCOs' photographs of Fiona Gow and Lindsey Sloan. How could hell not be on Earth?

Brennan dredged up some lines by the Ayrshire poet Robert Burns that he'd learned in boyhood. Burns had created a vision of depravity that still loomed large in Brennan's mind, it was where 'sat Auld Nick in shape o'beast'.

As he drove Brennan recited from Burns: 'Coffins stood round, like open presses . . . That shaw'd the dead in their last dresses.'

The poet was supposed to be a great humanitarian, and yet he had created such an inhumane vision.

'A murderer's banes in gibbet airns; Twa span-lang, wee, unchristaned bairns; A thief, new-cutted frae a rape.'

Brennan thought it was as if the whole country had always been rotten, and here in Edinburgh was the mouldering core. As he drove, he eyed the crowd: how many knew there was a brutal murderer among them? None, except him. It was a burden he always carried, knowing that there was more to the city than people ever imagined. It was not the place of sweeping spires and cobbled streets, of mawkish sentimental Scottishness; it was a hard place. And no one knew it better than him.

With each day that passed Brennan now felt himself drawing further away from Edinburgh in spirit. The city dragged people in, the tourists flocked at Festival time and Hogmanay; the disenfranchised Little Englanders decamped there when the equity was high enough on their commuter-belt maisonettes. But the place had no root, no heart. Its historic residents had long ago got the message that if you were poor you were not welcome. They'd been pushed to the outskirts of the city, to massive dumping grounds where they were left to fester, helped along by criminality, drug abuse and state-sponsored indolence. The game was up in the capital, thought Brennan, the place was choking on its own filth and he despised his role in the mess.

As the car drew closer to Edinburgh High the DI found himself trapped by a wave of guilt; how could he let Sophie grow up in a place like this? Lindsey Sloan had attended the same school as his daughter only a few years ago and she had ended up mutilated, murdered. What had happened to the place? A year earlier he had visited the murder scene of another young girl, she had been hacked to death, dismembered, and dumped in the lee of a high-rise. He had thought of Sophie then too, worried about where she was for an instant, but dismissed the notion that any harm could come to her because she wasn't at all like the victim, wasn't in her demographic. He knew now that he had been wrong to think like that; Sophie was every bit as likely to be a victim now. The battle lines were growing every day and it worried him. How could he keep his daughter safe?

As he got closer to the school Brennan saw the gates were fringed with parked cars; worried parents picking teenagers up from school. He knew Sophie wouldn't thank him for turning up like this but he needed to see her, needed to talk to her without Joyce around. He took the car into the staff car park, pulled into an empty space by the front of the building. He had a good view of the door he expected to see his daughter walking through at any moment.

As Brennan stilled the car's engine he watched a group of teenage boys jogging from the football field, banging their boots off the wall to shake away clumps of mud and grass. It was still warm and he decided to step out of the car, remove his jacket. As he did so, a thin, angular man in a tracksuit emerged from the playing fields and raised an oversized hand. For a moment Brennan searched his memory for the man's identity but his name remained elusive.

'Hello again, Inspector,' said the man. He could clearly tell Brennan wasn't sure who he was. 'Colin . . . Colin Crawley, we met at the Sloans'.'

'Oh yes, of course . . . Hello.'

The man was sweating, his face flushed red. He wiped the back of his sleeve over his brow, said, 'Been taking advantage of the good weather, bit of five aside with year six.'

Brennan nodded. 'Good idea.'

As the man stood before the DI he swayed a little, his hair was stuck to his brow. 'I heard about the dreadful business with . . .' he leaned forward, lowered his voice, 'Lindsey.'

The DI became aware of a slow trail of students leaving the building; his attention diverted to the front door as he scanned the blur of blazers and schoolbags for his daughter.

'But of course, you'll be here for Sophie.'

Brennan turned to face the man, he hadn't mentioned his daughter went to the school. He felt his brows tighten as he stared at Crawley.

'Mrs Sloan mentioned you have a daughter here . . .' he looked away, brushed at a grass stain on his elbow, 'Just a dreadful business for them . . . we had a memorial service, for the school. Seemed the least we could do.' He broke away, took a step to the front. 'Oh, here she is . . .'

150

It was Sophie. As she came through the door with two other girls, she halted in her tracks to stare at her father. She put a hand in the pocket of her blazer and turned down her head as she walked towards the car and got in without speaking.

'You'll have to excuse me,' said Brennan.

Crawley raised a supplicating hand towards the car, 'Of course.' He stood waving them off as Brennan reversed out of the parking space.

Sophie spoke, 'What were you doing with Creepy Crawley?'

Brennan smirked, the nickname seemed to fit. 'Just passing the time of day, love.'

A tut, frown. 'And could you have parked any closer? . . . All my friends saw you.'

'Is that a problem?'

'I don't need a lift, I have a bus pass.' She started to roll down her window, 'And this car stinks of fags.'

Brennan gave a wave out the window to Crawley; he was going inside now. 'Well, we won't be in it for long, I thought I'd just take you for a milkshake or something.'

'Christ, Dad . . . I'm sixteen.'

She said it like she was twenty-six, or forty-six, thought Brennan. He turned to her, 'And?'

'I don't drink bloody milkshakes!'

The DI turned on the blinkers, pulled out. 'OK, Starbucks then. I'll buy you a coffee. Does that suit you?'

She slumped in the seat, tucked her schoolbag on the ground beside her feet but didn't answer.

The traffic was slow-moving, cars full of teenagers pulling out every few yards. 'This is a nightmare,' said Brennan.

'I never asked you to come and collect me . . . It's so embarrassing.'

'Maybe I should put the sirens on, eh?'

Sophie sprang to life, 'Don't you dare.'

Brennan laughed as he caught her eyes burying into him, raised his hands from the wheel in mock surrender. 'I was kidding. Kidding.'

At the Starbucks on Palmerston Place, Brennan ordered himself a black coffee and a latte for Sophie. They took the last two remaining seats in the café and sat; Sophie disconsolately resting her head on her hands in front of him.

'Mum said you've moved out.'

The words came as a shock to Brennan, 'Just like that?'

'Pretty much.'

He eased a spoon into his coffee cup, stirred. 'It's not as simple as you make it sound you realise . . . I mean.'

'Oh, please. Don't go dumping all your guilt on me.'

'Sorry?'

'I know all about this kind of thing, Wendy Cuthbertson's mum and dad split up in, like, third year . . . And Claire's split up last year. I was beginning to wonder what was taking you so long.'

Brennan removed his spoon from the cup, looked for a saucer to place it in but found he didn't have one. 'I don't know why, but I expected you to be a bit more . . .'

'Broken up? . . . . No.' She spooned a layer of foam from the top of her latte and smiled, 'It's no biggie.'

Brennan constantly found himself blindsided by his daughter; Wullie had once remarked that he thought each generation he'd seen had got softer; as Brennan listened to his daughter's assessment of his marriage break-up he wondered if the opposite wasn't true. She seemed unmoved by the event.

'I'm not sure that's how your mum and I feel . . .'

Sophie rolled eyes, 'Mum's neurotic at the best of times.'

Brennan made sure to keep his expression clear, he was not getting into an exchange of insults with his daughter behind his wife's back, even if she was right. Joyce did indeed live on her nerves.

'But anyway, when I saw you at the school, do you know what I thought?'

Brennan shook his head, 'No, what?'

'I thought you were here about that girl that got murdered.'

'Lindsey Sloan.'

'Yes, that's her . . . Everyone's talking about it at school.'

The DI felt himself shift uncomfortably on his chair, he was uneasy about discussing the case with his daughter; it didn't seem right. He did, however, feel a pull towards the possibility that there might be something to be gained from her. All information, even gossip, had to be weighed up on a murder investigation. 'And what are they saying?'

Sophie rolled her eyes again, she had her mother's eyes, large and round. 'Oh, just stuff . . . I don't think anybody knew her, except the teachers, she was years older.'

The DI felt some relief that Sophie was distanced from the case, 'I see.'

'Yeah, but, everybody's getting lifts to school and picked up . . . They'll think that's why you were there.'

Brennan knew the facts of the case and knew that parents, and the public in general, were liable to become irrational when a crime touched their lives. None of them seemed to comprehend that it is out there all the time – every single minute of every single day. 'I think that's a bit of an over-reaction, she wasn't killed at school.'

Sophie had exhausted her attention span. 'I've finished my coffee.'

'Well, would you like another?'

She looked across to the counter, 'No, I don't think so.'

Brennan put his hands around his cup, swirled the remains of his coffee. 'Look, Sophie, the reason I came here was to tell you that everything's going to be OK.' She looked nonplussed. 'What I mean is, just because your mum and I are splitting, doesn't mean we won't both be around for you.'

Her eyes darted from counter to window, then back to her cup. She lifted it, started to pour out the last dregs of liquid onto a paper napkin.

'Sophie, do you understand?'

'Yes.'

'Good. It's important to me . . . And your mum.'

'Can I go home now?'

Brennan put down his cup, waved to the door. 'After you.'

Chapter 21

AS DI ROB BRENNAN PULLED into the Corstorphine street he once shared with his family he felt his emotions eddying inside him. At his side, his daughter stared wearily out the car window, barely covering her desire to be free of him and return to the lone sanctuary of her bedroom. She went there to block out reality, drowned out the world with music. He knew Joyce would be waiting for her to return, they hadn't been long – just one quick coffee – but it would be enough to set her off. His wife had made her position clear, the trench had been dug at their daughter and Brennan had encroached on her territory. He watched as Sophie gnawed on her scalloped nails, she was oblivious to the coming changes in her life; perhaps it was for the best. Brennan envied her insouciance.

The DI brought the car to a halt, said, 'Right, you're home.'

Sophie smiled, 'So we are.' She leant forward to retrieve her bag from the floor. 'Bye then.'

'Look, love, if you need anything, even just to talk, then give me a call.'

She nodded, gripped her bag. 'Mum's waiting.'

Joyce stood at the doorway with arms akimbo; Brennan knew it was a stance reserved for him. He made to wave, got as far as raising his hand from the steering wheel as his wife turned away, moved inside the house.

'Remember, call anytime. OK?'

'Bye, Dad.'

He engaged the clutch, found first gear and pulled out. At Shandwick Place the city streets filled with a slow, somnambulant trail of office drones. They slopped down the pavement in silent procession towards home and freedom from the workaday world. Brennan knew life was toil – endless hours given over to mundanity and minutiae. He knew his life was; the job wasn't all high-speed car chases and adrenaline rushes like Hollywood portrayed.

From an early age the importance of work – the concept, the philosophy – and the consequences of going without work had been drilled into Brennan like a Calvinist dirge. His father had known no better – he had lived all his days to slave away, save the pennies and stay in work. There was no greater achievement on Earth to him. He had longed for Brennan to go into the family firm, but his eldest son had resisted, left that honour to his brother. Andy had resented him for it and he wondered if he had made another choice how different things would have been between them.

As he thought of his father, he knew he was lost now in retirement. Leisure time was wasted on him; the subtle joys of art, music, literature, of a film or even sport didn't interest him. Work, toil had been his all and any suggestion of an alternative to that assumption was treated with scorn, contempt. Brennan knew there was more to life. There was a whole other world out there that had been denied to him and that he wanted to explore. He had adopted his father's values at an early stage and – despite his antipathy to them – made them his values. He'd simply assumed so many of those formative influences that it was only now with age and experience that he could see where he went wrong.

Brennan now wondered if he really wanted to continue in life as a policeman. Had it only been a subconscious act of rebellion? A move to disturb his father, and yet at once conform to his code of ethics? It was his age, and awareness, that made him think these thoughts. He knew at its root was his unhappiness: he was seeking an explanation for it. Was there one? Were there many? Brennan knew the cards were stacked against him – there was no alternative really. Had he rejected his father's doctrine and taken another path, surely he would have arrived at the same point. For people like him, life was thrown at you in clumps; it was about taking the small knocks in the hope of avoiding the bigger ones. Lassitude and draining of the soul as though it were a weeping sore were the trade off his father taught him you paid against penury and ignominy. You took the repetition day after day, faced it like a man, because it's what you are conditioned to do. When your senses, your intellect rebelled, you quashed them with alcohol, drugs, sugary foods or created distractions with football, boxing or car-crash television. In time, it became a routine, a coping mechanism. He knew the urges and wants remained, but the fight for them was lost so long ago that they were conceded without struggle.

Brennan knew he wasn't alone in feeling this way. It was the human condition – a malady specific to this point in the evolution of the race. We were nothing more than a brooding, amorphous mass of discontent. The streets ran to overflowing with evidence of it and that was why Brennan knew he had no alternative but to carry on, day in and day out. Much as he despised his station, it had grown to define him; perhaps there was nothing else to him now.

The DI had toyed with the idea of dropping into the office to check on the progress of the squad but dismissed the notion outright; if there had been any developments they would have called. He knew he headed back to a grim and empty bedsit but it suited him; he was in no mood for company. A loud siren wailed, cutting through the hum of traffic and clatter of pedestrians as Brennan pulled into Leith Walk. He dropped gears, took the central reservation and snaked back towards Montgomery Street. A lone drunk was yawing from side to side in the road with a red and white striped carrier in his hand; Brennan recognised the bag as coming from the off-licence. As he parked up he kept an eye on the man as he ranted and roared his way down the street. The chip shop was open and Brennan bought a haggis supper to avoid a trip to the supermarket, then headed for home.

Black bin bags were stacked on the street outside his front door, a dark lacustral ooze seeped from them towards the gutter; he stepped over and put his key in the lock. Inside the stairwell smelled damp, a gritty silt crunched under his shoes as he climbed the stairs. Once inside his flat, Brennan found the place in semi-darkness; the day was limping wearily into night. He placed his dinner on the table, removed his coat, and poured himself a large Macallan. As he begun to pick at the chips in their greasy wrapper, his phone began to ring, he wiped his fingers on the paper tray and reached for his mobile.

'Brennan.'

It was DS Stevie McGuire. 'Hello, sir . . . Was wondering if you were coming back in today?'

Brennan blurted a blunt reply. 'Not without a bloody good reason.'

'Right, it's just there was something I wanted to set the record straight about.'

The DI felt a gravid pause settle between them on the line. He knew at once what McGuire was referring to but decided it was for him to open the bidding; he pushed away his haggis supper, said, 'Now what would that be, Stevie?'

'You were right about . . . Elaine.'

'WPC Docherty . . . I see.' Brennan was torn between blasting McGuire for his stupidity, or blasting him for lying to him. In the end he decided to do neither.

McGuire spoke, 'I shouldn't have deceived you. That was wrong, you played me straight and I ballsed up.'

He sounded sorry, but Brennan was unsure if he had fully learned his lesson. 'Stevie, don't you ever fucking lie to me again, even a pissy wee white lie, do you get me?'

'Yes, sir.' His voice had lowered to a whisper. 'Where will this . . . go?'

Brennan knew what he was asking, and it wasn't the same as what he wanted to know. The DI would be within his rights to drop McGuire from the murder squad; at the very least he had been tested on his loyalty, and found wanting. It was not conducive to a solid working relationship. He edged forward on his chair, the floorboards creaked beneath him. 'How would you like me to answer that question, Stevie?'

A pause.

'Sir?'

'What I mean is, should I laugh it off . . . play it like we're all boys together?'

159

'Well, I don't want to . . .'

'Or should I change the habits of a lifetime and play it by the book; now what would that entail I wonder? To be honest with you Stevie, I don't fucking know what to do. Because after an initially shaky start it has to be said, until today I thought I had your undivided loyalty.'

The DS's voice rose now. 'Rob, I mean *sir*, you do. You know you have my loyalty. I made a mistake, I've apologised.'

Brennan let a gap of static extend on the line, said, 'How serious is it, with you and WPC Docherty?'

Another pause, a huff. 'I'd be compounding the error if I said it wasn't serious, boss.'

Brennan ran his fingers through his hair, he was grateful for McGuire's honesty but the reality of his statement hit like a hammer blow. He had put WPC Docherty on undercover with Collins and he didn't want to lose McGuire either, especially with Jim Gallagher unsettling the squad. 'Jesus Christ, Stevie couldn't you keep it in your pants?' his voice rose like a howitzer. 'This is all we fucking need.'

'Sir, I'll stand down if . . .'

'Shut it, Stevie. Leave the thinking to me, eh . . . Be in early tomorrow morning, we have things to discuss.'

He hung up.

Chapter 22

NEIL HENDERSON STARED ACROSS THE bare boards of the grimy Leith flat he shared with Angela Mickle towards the front door and drummed fingers on the tabletop. He had spent the last day and night dreading a knock. He knew he had just about run out of time to repay Boaby Stevens and one of his boys would be around again soon. The next visit would mean a serious beating, breaking bones, something visible so others got the message that you didn't miss payments to Shaky. Henderson felt tense, nervy. As a key turned in the lock he sat bolt upright; it was Angela. She staggered through the front door after her night on the Links. He watched as she leaned herself against the wall, slipped off her heels and removed her jacket. She looked exhausted, but at the same time, she looked too wrecked to even know it. She was out of it, as usual.

Angela had collected a dark bruise on her neckline; Henderson thought to ask her about it but then realised he didn't care enough to bother. He watched as she limped a few steps to the stain-patched grey mattress and threw herself down, he saw the soles of her feet were dirty and he wondered when she had last washed. The thought jarred in his mind; her shelf-life on the Links was just about up. No one was going to pay for a filthy junky, he thought. It was time for him to start looking for a new source of income.

Henderson strolled over to where Angela had flung herself and now lay semi-comatose on her stomach. He kicked at her foot, 'Hey, how much did you make?'

She waved a vague hand towards her jacket that lay rumpled on the floor beside her shoes. Henderson followed her actions, then walked towards the bundle and picked it up, rifled the pockets. 'This it?' He removed two handfuls of tens and fives, threw down the jacket; some coins and condoms spilled on the floorboards. He took the money with him to the other side of the room; by the window he sat down on the broken wicker chair and started to count out the cash. It was less than ninety pounds.

Henderson shook his head, he felt a burning sensation behind his eyes, not quite a pain, more of a hot flash. 'Jesus fucking Christ, girl . . . Not even a ton? What the fuck have you been doing all night?'

She flapped a hand over her head, she was out of it. Gone. He knew it would be a few hours before he got any sense out of her. She had been out on the Links, got just enough money to shoot up and then grabbed a couple of quick punters to have a few quid to hand over, make it look like she'd been busy. She was suiting herself, not him. Her priority was the smack and he wasn't even in her sights after that had been fired up. Henderson felt the hot flash behind his eye burn deeper into his head, his jaw gripped tightly. He was going to get something out of her though, something that he wanted, even if it meant beating it out

162

of her. He rose again, hitched up his trousers and removed his belt. He held the buckle in his hand and began to wrap the strap around his fingers, once, twice, until it was good and tight. He looked at the belt; it was thick leather; he smiled to himself then raised it high above his head: as he brought it down heavily upon the table the loud whack of its contact made Angela sit up.

'What you doing, Hendy?'

He walked over to her, stood with the belt in his hand, tapped it off his leg. His heart pounded beneath his T-shirt.

'Hendy? . . . What are you doing with that?' Her voice trembled, her eyes darted between the flapping belt and the fist that held it tightly.

Henderson smiled, a weak smile at first, then it grew up the side of his face like a smirk. He felt Angela's fear, her terror growing with each second, and he drank it in.

'What did I say to you?' he said. He could feel the blood surging in his veins, his arms tensed.

Angela put her hands out behind her, started to edge backwards on the mattress, towards the wall. Her feet pushed her back in a slow, cautious movement. Henderson watched her feet, saw they weren't just dirty on the soles, they were caked in filth that rested in her high arches and sat between her toes. He raised the belt, his chest expanded briefly as his shoulder swung, and then he brought the leather down upon her legs with a loud smack.

Angela curled over and screamed, she brought her hands towards her legs. Henderson lunged forward and grabbed her by the hair, 'What did I say to you?'

She was crying now, tears streaming down her red cheeks. 'I don't know. I don't know.'

Henderson raged, 'Too fucking right you don't. I've lost

163

count of the times I've told you . . . I've fucking lost count.' He brought the belt up to her face, paraded it in front of her eyes. 'I'll take the fucking skin off you . . . Every fucking inch of it. I mean it. Do you fucking doubt me?'

Angela raised her hands from her legs, tried to grab at Henderson's arms as he struggled with her. He knocked her arms down, forced the fist with the leather strap into her mouth and she fell heavily to the exposed floorboards. For a moment she was lifeless, lying like a doll on the floor and then she started to shift her head from side to side, moaning all the while. Henderson stood over her, dangled the leather on her face; as he did so he saw her open her mouth; her teeth were bloodied.

Henderson knelt down, draped the belt over Angela's neck and positioned his hands either side of it. As he pressed down he watched her struggle, her legs thrashed, her nails dug into the belt as she tried to free herself. Her face tightened and grew dark, her eyes started to bulge. When he was sure she was about to pass out he released the belt but kept his knee in her chest.

'Now, I want that teacher's name, Ange . . . and I fucking-well want it now.'

Angela coughed, spluttered. She pushed at the knee on her chest and Henderson lowered it into her windpipe. 'I'm telling you, if you think he was a bastard, you want to see me when I get going . . . Now give me the fucker's name or it's the end of the road for you, Ange.'

She continued to struggle, her eyes tightening then bulging out once more. She smacked at the knee in her windpipe and tried to speak but no words came. She looked like a trapped animal, thought Henderson; he enjoyed the power he had over her.

'Now if I let you up you better tell me what I want to know . . . I mean it,' he slapped the belt off the floorboards beside Angela's head. 'I'll fucking take the skin off you if you mess me about, Ange.'

Henderson withdrew the belt, stood up slowly, cautiously. He watched Angela's every move as he rose. She shot hands to her throat, then started to cough. She lay on the ground spluttering for a few moments and then the colour started to return to her face. Henderson continued to watch her, feeling nothing but contempt. He would gladly end her days, he thought. She was nothing. Worse than nothing. She'd been on the streets since she was seventeen, and by her twenties she was worn out, worthless. Nobody was going to be paying for her skanky arse in the years to come, she was finished. He watched her pitch herself up on her elbow, lean over and start to gag; she was always puking up. Fucking puking up or shooting up, he couldn't face looking at her. He gripped the belt tighter in his hand, felt an urge to bring it across her face, but resisted; she could do one thing, just one thing that would pay her way.

Angela coughed, fitted. Her eyes were veined in a red spider's web as she slowly began to speak, 'Crawley . . .'

'What did you say?'

She hesitated, tried to gather her breath. 'The teacher, he's called Crawley.'

Henderson felt himself draw a wide smile. He watched as Angela toppled over once again, started to gag on her own vomit. He let her be sick, then pushed her onto the mattress with the heel of his shoe. As she curled into a foetal position he started to thread the leather belt back through the loops of his jeans. He laughed out, said, 'Aye, well, you came good in the end, Ange . . . Told you it wasn't going to be hard, didn't I?'

Angela brought her arms around her, started to shiver. Her eyes were closed tight; it was as if she was reliving a memory she didn't want to see again. She looked like a small child in the grip of a nightmare. 'You won't find him,' she said.

Henderson halted, dropped the buckle in his hands, it dangled over the front of his jeans. 'What did you say?'

She was trembling harder now, brought her hands up to her head and gripped at her dirty blonde hair. 'He left the school,' the words looked like a struggle for her. 'Not long after what happened, he moved to another school.'

Henderson raised his hands, clenched fists, then dropped them at his sides. He put a heavy foot on the mattress and stepped forward, his eyes darted. 'What do you fucking mean moved schools?'

Angela's words were shrill and sharp. 'He moved. That's all I know. I don't know where he went. I don't fucking care.'

Henderson got down from the mattress, walked towards the window. He stood there fastening his belt buckle, hoisting up his jeans again and tucking in his T-shirt. A dog barked outside the window as he looked into the city streets. It was early morning and suited-up businessmen were lined seriatim at the bus stop. A woman on a bicycle passed them by. Henderson watched the day unfolding before him from his first-floor vantage point and then he stroked the stubble on his chin.

'He's not fucking far away though,' he said.

He heard Angela stirring behind him as he reached forward and removed a Kensitas Club from the packet on

166

the window ledge; there was only one cigarette left. He lit up, inhaled.

'*What*?'

Henderson continued to stare out into the city streets. A homeless man swooped the gutters for dowps, he gave up and started to beg at the bus queue. Henderson shook his head; a woman with a dog was crossing the road now.

'I said, he's not far away . . . Crawley.' He savoured the word, his new knowledge was power to him.

Angela pushed herself up on the mattress, brought her knees under her chin. 'I don't know that.'

Henderson turned from the window, pointed his cigarette at her. 'Aye, well I do. And it's best you leave the thinking to me.'

She rubbed at her shins, said, 'How, though? How do you know?'

Henderson had turned away from her again, he leaned forward, his nose pressing hard to the window. As he spoke, his breath frosted the glass. 'Because if he's up to his old tricks, like they said on the news the other night, then he must be in Edinburgh.'

167

Chapter 23

HENDERSON'S PLAN WAS A SIMPLE one, but it involved one more piece of help from Angela. After waking from a doze and watching her fitful dreams for a few minutes he realised he wasn't able to sit in the flat with her; he decided to let her sleep off her fix for a few hours. The place stank anyway, it was utterly rank. Worse than prison. There were pools of vomit on the floor; used works scattered everywhere; used condoms. How could he live like this? He didn't want to be there any more, but he had nowhere else to go, no money. Certainly not the type of money he needed to repay his debts to Boaby Stevens. The thought raced in him, haunted his every thought like an incubus.

Henderson took the money Angela had earned on the Links and went to the nearest pub, ordered up a pint of lager. The bar was quiet, only dole moles and an old jakey with a blue nose who was likely to be turfed out at any minute for singing 'Danny Boy'. Henderson retreated to the corner, selected a bentwood chair, glabrous with age, and positioned it against the wall. As he supped his pint he felt himself watching the window, the door; he didn't want to be caught in there – on the piss – when he had a debt to pay to Shaky. That would be like incitement; suicidal. He found himself anxious to leave, and, after only a few sips, started to gulp the lager.

Outside on the street again he felt even more self-conscious, found himself hugging the shop fronts as he headed back to the flat; he was desperate not to be seen. Once inside the main door he lunged up the stairs, holding the door key out in front of him. As quickly as he had opened up he closed the door again, pressed his back to it. He felt his heart beating fast beneath his denim jacket as he rested there. He was sweating, hard. He removed a hand from the door, ran the back of it across his brow, trailed wearily towards the front room.

Angela was still lying face down on the stained mattress. Her hair was spread either side of her head like she had brushed it out that way. Henderson put his key in his trouser pocket, started to undo the buttons on his jacket. He stood over her for a moment, scratched at his elbow then spoke, 'Ange . . . Time to make a move.'

She remained still.

'Ange, come on . . . Get yourself out that pit.' He reached down, pulled a clump of her hair.

She raised a hand, yelped. 'What is it?'

'Come on, get yourself out that fucking bed . . .'

'Why?'

'Cause I fucking said so.' He dug a shoe in her ribs, not hard, but enough to make her sit up.

Angela's eyes drooped as she tried to take in Henderson, standing above her with a mobile phone in his hand. She lifted her arm, ran fingers topped with chipped red nails through her long hair. 'What time is it?'

'Never mind that . . . Here take this phone.'

Angela reached out, took it. 'What's this for?'

Henderson had started to pace the room, his shoes thumping on the dusty boards. 'I want you to phone that school of yours.'

'What?'

'You heard . . . Call them up and ask where this Crawley prick went to.'

Angela stared at him; he had his hands on his hips, then quickly removed one to brush at the stubble on his chin. He moved forward, sat on his haunches as he spoke to her, 'Look, all you need to say is that he used to be your teacher and that you're having some kind of a reunion and wanted to ask him along.'

Angela looked weary now, she slumped on the mattress. Henderson leaned forward, pitched himself on his knees as he pointed at the mobile phone. 'Look, I've even put the number in there for you . . . See, scroll down, Porty Academy . . . Easy.'

Angela looked at the small screen on the phone, then back to Henderson. His mouth was twitching, there was sweat on his brows. 'What if they say no?'

He shot up from the mattress, 'They won't say no . . . if they say no it's because you've fucked it up, because you've put the shits up them.' He walked to the doorway, pointed at her. 'Get on that fucking phone now, call them and find out where this Crawley is because if you don't your life's not going to be worth two shits, Ange. I mean it.' He left the room and headed into the bathroom.

As she sat on the mattress Angela's breathing ramped

up, she stared at the little screen on the mobile and then she pressed the button Henderson had shown her.

In the bathroom he heard Angela's voice in the other room. She was doing what he had asked her. He didn't want to consider the junky whore messing it up; that didn't bear thinking about. He didn't want to picture some snooty school secretary refusing to answer a simple question either. He remembered what they were like when he was at school; they were all old boots. All middle-class square pegs that looked down their noses at you. Why would they do you a favour? Why would they help you out of a hole? They had never done anything for him before, that lot; or anyone like them. But Henderson knew that if he didn't find Crawley soon, he might as well hand himself over to Boaby Stevens right away.

He ran the taps in the bathroom and put his hands under the water, splashed his face. He rubbed the water on the back of his neck and then he ran more through his hair. It felt cold, relieving some of his tensions. It was short-lived though. As Henderson dried himself off with the towel, he realised that Angela had stopped talking in the other room.

She knocked on the bathroom door.

Henderson turned, opened up. 'Well?'

She stood there with her dishevelled hair flopping in her eyes and the black eyeliner she wore from the night before streaking her face. 'He's at Edinburgh High.'

Chapter 24

DI ROB BRENNAN AWOKE EARLY, found his eyes fix on the orange swirl of curtain that lapped into the room. The street lamp still burned outside, a blustery wind soughed against the windowpane which rattled in its frame. He slumped, rested his head on the pillow for a moment, then reached for his cigarettes. The first breath of nicotine tasted good to him, stilled the thoughts that were stirring in his head. Through the wall he could hear a games machine playing; already? he thought. He looked at his watch, it had barely gone seven. He was surrounded by wasters: students and the work-shy. How had he arrived at this point? he wondered. He knew the answer instantly, but didn't want to face it. He raised himself on the edge of the bed, took another long drag on his cigarette and brushed a weary hand through his unkempt hair.

Brennan looked at his feet, wriggled his toes into socks and rose. His trousers hung over the back of a chair, the belt still threaded through the loops. He reached for them, stepped in. His shirt and tie had been beneath them. The tie was in a Windsor knot, slackened, but held in the same place it was the day before by the button-down collar. He looped the crinkled garment over his head and tucked the shirt tails into his trousers. His shoes were on the other side of the room and the floor felt cold beneath his feet as he crossed the boards.

Dressed, Brennan surveyed the room. On the table sat the remains of his visit to the chip shop the night before. He looked at the stale crust of the deep-fried haggis, the scatter of greying chips, and grimaced. He wanted coffee, but knew that was a long way off.

'What a way to live, Rob.'

He collected his jacket, a pile of blue folders and his mobile phone, headed for the door. It was dark on the stairwell, a lone lamp burned two floors up but Brennan guided himself down the steps with a hand on the banister. The gritty dusting of silt and refuse crunched beneath the soles of his shoes as usual.

Outside the rubbish bags sat ripped and torn, a large seagull stood propietorially over the spillage of potato peelings and empty microwaveable meal boxes. Brennan looked down the street, then raised his eyes: the sky was a milky albumen that threatened a day of rain. He crossed the road and opened the driver's door of the Passat. As he slotted the key in the ignition, a blast of chart music disrupted the morning's calm; he reached for the dial and switched it off.

On the road to Fettes Police Station he thought about the day to come, he knew he faced a grilling from the Chief Super about his appointment of the profiler from Strathclyde. Benny would – in all likelihood – use it as an excuse to install Gallagher at the front of the investigation. Brennan gripped the wheel, slapped a palm off the gear stick. That would suit the bastard nicely, wouldn't it? Gallagher might think he was working his way up the greasy pole, but Brennan had met his type before and still had a few moves of his own. He pulled out as a road-sweeping lorry edged into the middle lane, cursed: 'Fucking indicate, eh!'

He was still losing focus, and he knew it. He needed to batten down his thoughts, get back on the case. Two young girls had been killed, if he was to find their murderer then his focus had to be sharper. He was letting too many ancillary problems creep in and he had to halt that right away. There was a time when he had found no trouble separating the outside world from work, or even the machinations of co-workers from the task; but Brennan was questioning everything now. He was questioning his role in the world and it worried him, not because he wondered where it might lead, but because he knew the job deserved more. It demanded full attention and he was allowing too much that was irrelevant to seep in.

'Screw the nut, man,' he told himself as he pulled back into lane.

Ferry Road was already filling with commuter traffic and by the time he reached the Crew Toll roundabout the road to the city had become an immovable mass of cars, stuck bumper to bumper. Brennan watched the disconsolate faces of the drivers, yawning and frowning, as he slowed into the left lane and took the Crew Road exit to the station. At the car park he slotted the Passat in beside a blue Camry and stepped out. The wind was crisp around his ears as he headed for the front door. The place was still quiet at this time, how he liked it. It was one of Brennan's contradictions: much as he felt compelled to protect the public, felt the hurts of victims' families, he could only take so much company at one time. Small doses, that's how he handled people.

The DI made his way to the coffee machine, selected a large black and took his Styrofoam cup through to Incident Room One. His initial instinct was to check the whiteboard for new additions; it remained unchanged. He made his way through to his office, removed his jacket and tried his first sip of coffee. On his desk was a large envelope from the lab. It was marked for his attention and sealed. He pulled out his chair, sat. For a moment he tried to figure at the contents of the envelope but his mind remained blank – he opened it. On the first page was a yellow Post-it note from Bill Nailer in the serology lab; it stated: 'Interesting reading, I think you'll find, Rob.'

Brennan leafed through the report; it was short, only three pages. The first page was basic information, details from the victims. By the second page, the meat of the report was becoming evident. The test results were listed on the final page: the findings were conclusive.

'Interesting indeed, Bill,' said Rob. As he looked up, DS Stevie McGuire entered the office.

'What's that?'

'Serology report.'

McGuire loosened off his jacket, lowered himself onto the edge of the desk. 'Bill Nailer, yeah?'

'Aye.'

'Well, Bill knows his stuff.'

'You should have a read at it,' Brennan handed over the report.

'What's it say?'

'In a nutshell . . . They have blood samples that are not the victims'.'

'Gow or Sloan?'

Brennan leaned back, tucked his hands behind his head. 'Both. They found blood and skin under the nails of the Sloan girl and there was already a blood splatter from Fiona Gow on file. And, they match – it's a rare group . . . B.'

'Jesus, result indeed.'

McGuire eased himself off the desk, started to pore over the report. Brennan interrupted him, 'Leave that just now, Stevie . . . I want a word, before the others get in.'

McGuire closed the file, he removed his jacket, folded it over his arm. 'Look, boss . . .'

Brennan removed a hand from behind his head, 'No, Stevie . . . You listen, don't speak.'

The DS closed his mouth, turned down the corners. He placed his jacket over the back of the chair and was motioned to sit by Brennan.

'I'm not going to read you the riot act, so you can rest easy.'

'That's a relief . . .'

'But you can fucking rest assured I'm not best pleased with you, laddie.' Brennan was pointing his finger, he let it hang in the air for a moment then removed it.

'Sir.'

'When did this WPC Docherty business kick off?'

McGuire exhaled slowly, 'About a month ago, I suppose.'

Brennan shook his head, 'A month . . . For fuck's sake. And when were you going to tell me?'

McGuire raised his hands, showed palms.

'No, you were going to wait until you got us both nuts deep, eh . . .'

McGuire gnawed on his lower lip, 'I'm sorry . . . It's not something I planned.'

176

'No, you didn't think did you? Well, you better had now.' Brennan rose, walked over to the window. 'How do you suppose this looks, Stevie? . . . I mean, I've had Elaine on the squad from day one . . . She's out there in the field with Collins now, if I take her off it's going to show. Look bad. As for you, well, you were supposed to be my number two, my right hand man.'

McGuire turned in his seat, faced Brennan. 'I know. I know how it looks, and I've thought about it and I really am prepared to take the consequences.'

'Shut up, Stevie . . . You're in no position to judge. Fucking wee head is ruling the big head.'

McGuire dropped his eyes, turned from the DI.

Brennan put his hands in his pockets, jangled his keys as he stared out the window. He watched the clouds gathering over the rooftops and turned around. On his way back to his desk he raised his coffee cup and took a sip, then sat. McGuire was looking the DI over as he placed his hands either side of the desk blotter and spoke, 'Here's how it's going to play out, Stevie . . . I want you to call a halt to your relationship.'

McGuire leaned forward, interrupted, 'I don't think . . .'

Brennan slapped the desk. 'Shut up. I said you listen!'

'Yes, sir.'

'I want you both to call a halt to this relationship . . . For the time being. When we have concluded this case then – and only then – if you want to continue this relationship we will make sure WPC Docherty is removed to another work unit. Do you understand me, Stevie?'

McGuire looked up, 'Yes, sir.'

'I'm not fucking about, I am cutting you a break here.'

'I know that, sir.'

'If you throw it away, we're both screwed.'

'I understand.'

'Do you? . . . I mean do you really understand?'

McGuire placed his hands on the arms of the chair, raised himself. 'I understand, sir . . . This meeting never took place. You do not know anything about a relationship between myself and WPC Docherty and if you are asked to confirm at any point in the future that we have discussed such a thing, you would be entitled to deny it.'

Brennan grinned, 'I think you're learning, Stevie.'

Chapter 25

BRENNAN SCANNED THE BLUE FILES he had piled on his desk, tried to see if there was anything that he had missed. Nothing presented itself. He knew the information was coming in, but it was drip by drip when he needed a deluge. He had read about serial killer cases in the past, he knew that they followed a pattern. He was continually surprised by how similar their patterns were and by how closely they could be detailed after the event. The killers were slaves to routine, had habits and timetables that they followed. They were intricate planners, they had to be to avoid detection, evade the police. It was precisely because of this complexity that Brennan knew the cases could run on for months, years even. How long had the Yorkshire Ripper reigned? How many had he killed? Brennan knew the answers to those questions and they distilled fear in his heart. He had to stop this. But the longer the case went unsolved, the harder it would become to catch the killer.

Brennan sat at his desk in the glass-fronted office and

watched for the arrival of DS Collins. He was anxious to get feedback from the night before's visit to The Rondo in George Street. The chances of it turning up anything of use were slim, he knew that, but instinct and experience had taught him to keep trying, even when the odds were against you.

He caught sight of Collins, called him in. The DS was still carrying his coat and briefcase as he reached Brennan's office.

'So, how did it go last night?' he said.

Collins stood with his hands full, swayed on the balls of his feet as he exhaled a slow breath. He seemed to be searching for just the right words. 'Well, that depends what you were hoping to achieve, boss.'

Brennan bit, 'Meaning?'

Collins pointed to the chair sitting in front of the desk, 'Do you mind if I take the weight off? . . . Murder on the old plates those clubs, just standing around all night, y'know . . .'

Brennan nodded, 'Go on, then.'

'Well, if you wanted us to go out and try and fit in, we did that . . .' Collins ran a palm down his cheek, satisfied himself with the smoothness of his razor cut, said, 'But, if you were looking for more of a background report on the victims, I'm afraid I've nothing really to add to what I told you yesterday.'

Brennan got up from his desk, leaned a shoulder on the wall and folded his arms. He kept an eye on Collins, watched for any signs of optimism, but found none. 'OK, you and WPC Docherty slotted in, got to know the punters and staff, yeah?'

Collins rested his elbows on the chair's arms, tapped his

fingertips together. 'Yeah, we did. I have to say, boss, it's not a very teenage scene.'

'What do you mean?'

'Well, it's pretty well-heeled. Should have seen the motors outside on George Street, I lost count of the number of Porsches . . . Fucking fanny magnets they are.'

Brennan turned around, 'So an older crowd?'

'Yeah . . . Definitely.'

'An older crowd, sniffing around young lassies?'

Collins seemed to be weighing the possibilities in his mind. 'Well, not exclusively, but there was that element it has to be said. If I was going anywhere with this line of thought, sir, what I'd be saying is that Fiona Gow and Lindsey Sloan would have stuck out there, they would have been among the youngest.'

Brennan returned to his desk, removed his chair and sat down again. 'Makes you wonder if the door stewards knew them?'

'Checked their ID you mean?'

'It's more than possible . . . Likely even.'

Collins nodded, 'I don't know, these young lassies once they get a bit of makeup on and the high heels they look the part . . . I'd say they would have been more likely to have been known for being a couple of cracking looking girls.'

'Cracking looking underage girls.' Brennan leaned forward, tapped on the folders in front of him with his index finger. 'Keep at it, Collins. Talk to the stewards, softly, softly mind . . . These places heat up on the weekend so we'll give it a bit longer.'

Collins stood up, collected his coat and his bag. 'I'm happy to keep going out to the pub on the force's dime,

181

boss, but I just don't know what this is going to achieve . . . I mean, it's like looking for a needle in a haystack trying to find anything that might tie in.'

Brennan eased himself back in his chair, eyed Collins. 'Right now the fact that both those girls did the club scene is just about all we have.'

Collins returned his hand to his pocket, turned to face the door. 'There's the gymnastics stuff that Jim's following up?'

'That's an even longer shot I would have thought.'

'Well, how did he go?'

Brennan opened his office door, nodded to Collins. 'We'll ask him in the morning briefing . . . Meantime, keep on the pubs and clubs, let me know if anything stands out. If there's any talk, I don't know, a boyfriend we don't know about, a bouncer introducing them to their first joint . . . anything at all. If it stands out, if we don't know about it, I want it looked at. Someone knew those girls better than the friends we've spoken to, they could be the key that unlocks this whole case, they could know our killer and not know it themselves.'

'Yes, sir.'

Collins walked through the open door, returned to his desk. On the way he cast an eye in Jim Gallagher's direction, nodded, and stopped to engage him in chat. At the far end of Incident Room One, Brennan noticed a face he hadn't seen for some time step through the door. He looked disorientated, a little lost perhaps; Brennan walked towards the man, met him at the coat stand. 'Joe . . .' he extended a hand, 'Good to have you on board, mate.'

Joe Lorrimer turned around, locked eyes on Brennan and clasped his hand on his shoulder. 'Glad to be here.' He rested a briefcase at his feet as he removed his outdoor coat and hung it up. Brennan was waiting as Lorrimer reached down for his briefcase; he rose and the pair walked towards the DI's glassed-off office.

'So, have you had a chance to check out the file?' said Brennan.

'Aye, the trip was fine, Rob . . . Thanks for asking,' Lorrimer smiled as he looked at the DI.

Brennan returned the grin, 'Sorry, we're behind the eight ball here at the moment. You know how it gets on these cases . . .'

Lorrimer turned his head towards the carpet tiles, said, 'Well, I did wonder when you asked for me . . . I don't remember you being so keen to share the load with anyone in the past. But to answer your question, yes Rob, I have seen the files you sent over.'

Brennan was aware of the eyes in the office following them as he led the profiler through the room; he decided it might be best to keep their first meeting limited to invitations only. 'On you go inside, Joe.' He called out, 'Stevie, Jim . . .' he pointed to his room. 'Any sign of Brian?'

McGuire was leaning back in his chair, it creaked noisily as he sat forward, rose. 'He did a late one last night, sir.'

'OK, when you're ready, please, the rest of you in here.'

In Brennan's office Lorrimer took the chair in front of the desk, Gallagher took the only other spare; McGuire pitched himself on the window ledge.

'I'd like to introduce Joe Lorrimer,' said Brennan. 'Joe's going to be helping us build a profile for the case, but before we go any further . . . Stevie, maybe you could fill Joe and Jim in on the morning's latest developments.'

McGuire was slouching on the ledge, straightened

himself. 'Yes, of course . . . We had a serology report back from the lab, we have a positive rare blood group ID from both scenes.'

Gallagher slapped his thigh, 'Confirmation then, that's it!'

Brennan gauged his reply, thinned eyes. 'Certainly seems that way, Jim.'

'It's bloody cast-iron, you mean. What's the blood group?'

McGuire answered him: 'It's B.'

'Jesus, rare as hobby horse shite that is.'

'It's a rare group,' said Brennan. 'And it does tie the two cases together but let's not get carried away, it's not a perp' ID . . . we don't have a smoking gun quite yet.'

Gallagher seemed to take the statement as a slap down, he crossed his legs and ran a finger along the crease of his trousers. He remained quiet though looked to be desperate to speak up.

Brennan said, 'Right, Joe, sorry to throw you in at the deep end but do you have any initial findings you'd like to share with the group?'

Lorrimer picked up his briefcase, balanced it on his knees and opened up; he removed two blue folders. He placed the folders on the top of the briefcase as he closed it again and leafed through the files. 'Right.' He removed a pen from his shirt pocket and tapped at the page he had selected. 'If we're progressing on the assumption that this is the work of one killer, then that ties in with my initial recce of the files. The signatures – the ligatures, torture, taking souvenirs – all look to be identical to me.'

As Lorrimer paused, Gallagher spoke in a hushed voice. 'And can you say anything about the person we're looking for?'

Brennan turned to Gallagher, his words lit a fuse in him.

184

'This is no *person*, Jim . . . It's a fucking animal we're hunting.'

Lorrimer raised his eyes from the notes, seemed to sense the animosity between the pair. He halted mid-stride for a moment, then adopted the role of mediator. 'He's a bit of both, I'd say, Rob.' He patted the papers, 'Look, there can be no doubt this is an extremely disturbed mind we're dealing with here . . . The mutilation alone is worse than anything I've ever seen in my career, but the fact that it's been carried out in your own backyard and there is next to nothing known about his MO five years down the track shows the level of intelligence we're up against.'

Brennan squirmed in his seat, brushed beneath his chin with his forefingers, said, 'I wasn't a part of the Fiona Gow investigation.'

Gallagher's eyes widened, burned into him.

'Regardless,' said Lorrimer, 'what we have is a pattern killer who has evaded capture – twice. He's obviously intelligent and resourceful and he's going to be riding on a surge of confidence right now. That makes him more dangerous than ever.' Lorrimer closed his file, tucked away the page he was looking at and returned the biro to his shirt pocket. 'I don't think we'll have to wait another five years to see his next victim, Rob. We need to get this bastard . . . and soon.'

Chapter 26

DI ROB BRENNAN ROSE FROM his desk as his office emptied; he kept a close eye on Gallagher, followed him round the door, watched as his knees met on every step, his sloped shoulders rose and fell. At his desk he removed his chair, slid it silently on its runners over the carpet tiles and then lowered himself down with a sigh. He shuffled some papers, pulled a pen from his inside pocket and hunched himself over the middle portion of the broad desktop. Brennan had expected Gallagher to keep walking, head straight for the Chief Super's office but he surprised him. Gallagher continued to surprise him, he couldn't work the man out and that made him an unknown quantity. Brennan didn't like the unknown, it was a threat to him. He liked facts. He liked the world to make sense, and though he knew that was impossible he tried to make his small part in it as facile as he could. He felt his brows tighten, his neck stiffen; there was a deep itch working in the centre of his brain. He wanted to locate it, remove it, but the option wasn't there.

Brennan turned to face Joe Lorrimer who was standing, briefcase in hand, as the DI drew his gaze back towards the inside of the office. The room looked suddenly smaller than he remembered.

'So, where do you want me, Rob?' said Lorrimer.

Brennan waved a hand over his shoulder, in the direction of Incident Room One, 'Find yourself a spot; Stevie will sort you out with anything you need.'

The profiler nodded, stuck a finger in his collar and stretched his tie loose; he was looking out to the open-plan room when he spoke, 'I don't want to speak out of turn, mate . . . But do I sense some tensions on the team?'

A tut. Brennan pitched himself on his toes, he raised his hands on his hips and stretched out his back. As he walked towards the back window, the chimney stacks and rooftops made a jagged saw blade against the grey sky. 'Nothing I can't handle,' he said.

'It's not you I'm worried about, Rob.'

'Meaning?' The harshness of his voice surprised him, seemed to echo in his ears.

'An unhappy team doesn't get results,' said Lorrimer.

Brennan let his brain settle, absorb the words he was hearing and try to – if not process them – at least store them away for attention at a later date. There was nothing to be gained in the job from letting others know what was on his mind, even people he trusted. He took Lorrimer's concern as genuine, he had known him from his early days in CID and rated his abilities; he had hand-picked him for the role of profiler on his team and he understood his misgivings. The investigation was proving difficult enough without any added problems. Brennan turned away from the window, walked back towards the door to his office, pushed it closed, and turned to face Lorrimer. 'Can I get straight to the point?' he said.

'Of course. I wish you would,' Lorrimer grinned, scratched the side of his nose.

'I could do without the third wheel, to be honest.'

'Gallagher you mean?'

Brennan gnawed at his lip, 'Got it in one.' He rested himself on the edge of the desk, folded his arms.

'I take it you never asked for him on the team, then?'

'He clawed his way in, and I'm far from convinced we need him but he has the ear of Benny.'

Lorrimer tilted his head to the side, put out a palm, 'Benny?'

'Chief Superintendent Bernard Hill . . . He has it in his head, or should I say Gallagher put it in his head, that because he worked on the Fiona Gow case five years ago his experience is invaluable to us.'

'But you disagree?'

Brennan huffed, unfolded his arms and patted down his pockets. 'I can read case files, Joe. I don't need a . . .'

'. . . Third wheel. I heard you.'

The DI leaned back on his desk, retrieved a packet of Embassy Regal and a plastic lighter from beside his blotter. Pocketed them both. 'I don't like the way he operates, he's got his eye on taking the investigation off me and he's all over Benny like a hot fucking rash.'

Lorrimer lowered his brows, his tone seemed to drop in the same proportion. 'Are you sure this wouldn't be about something else, Rob?'

'What do you mean?' Brennan felt his stare cut into Lorrimer.

'I heard about you and Joyce . . .'

The mention of his wife's name stung, it was a shock to hear her brought into the conversation. He had been used to his personal life being put under the microscope at the station since his brother's death but the fact that it had happened in the past didn't lessen the impact on this occasion. Brennan looked up to the ceiling tiles, pinned back his smile. 'Bloody Charlie never misses a trick . . . Tell you on the way in did he?'

Lorrimer kept his gaze firmly fixed on the DI, shrugged his shoulders. 'I'm sorry, if it's any consolation.'

Brennan bit, '*I'm* not, if it's any consolation.' He turned round, the wooden desk creaked as he raised himself from its edge, faced the profiler. 'Look, Gallagher's stepping on my toes, that's all it is, Joe.'

Lorrimer didn't seem to buy it; he looked convinced that there was another explanation lurking beneath the surface of Brennan's bluster. 'You said yourself that he worked on the Fiona Gow case, Rob . . .'

'And?'

'I'm just saying, that must have been a hard case to work. He couldn't have been pleased to see the trail run cold . . .' Lorrimer massaged his wrist, ran a finger over the face of his watch. 'Maybe he's looking to make up for that lack of a result now, maybe he sees his chance and is a bit over anxious. Ever thought of that?'

Brennan removed his packet of cigarettes, drew one out and put it in his lips. 'Maybe.'

'You're not buying that though?'

Brennan made a half smile, tapped his stomach, 'I'm listening to this.'

Lorrimer took a step towards him, raised a finger, tapped on Brennan's head. 'Just don't let it interfere with that, eh.'

The DI smirked. 'Aye, sure . . .' he turned for the door, 'Going for a smoke now, Joe . . . But, there is one thing you can do for me.'

Lorrimer tipped back his head, 'What's that?'

He held the handle, rammed it down, but kept the door closed as he flicked his head towards the wider room, 'Gallagher's been doing a fair bit of time over in your neck of the woods, some gangland stabbings I believe, can you ask around?'

'Rob . . .' he tightened his features. 'I'm not conducting a witch hunt for you.'

'Who said anything about a witch hunt? . . . I'm just looking for a few folks' impressions of him.'

Lorrimer looked away, seemed unsure but obviously wanted to calm the waters between them. 'I'm promising nothing.'

Brennan opened the door, the hinges sang out. 'Time for that smoke, I think.'

In the corridor, Brennan glanced towards the Chief Super's office; the door sat open and his secretary was already battering away at a keyboard but there was no sign of Benny. The DI felt relieved; he could only evade him for so long though and he knew that when he did finally encounter the Chief Super he would have to explain why he had brought in Lorrimer when the force was owed the services of a profiler from Northern Constabulary. Brennan didn't want to be treated to another lecture on the perilous state of the nation's finances, he didn't want to be told about budgets and cost savings and economy drives. He had a murderer to catch and he would do that the best way he saw fit, without running to Benny every time he needed a petrol receipt stamped or a stationery requisition put through. He was a detective, not a micro-manager.

At the front desk Charlie sat hunched over a copy of the *News*, he had an involved look on his face, eyes slit behind his reading glasses, but when he spotted Brennan he rose from his seat and flattened his palms on the counter. 'I was just about to buzz you,' his voice pitched high like a child's.

'Oh, aye,' said Brennan. 'Sounds ominous.'

Charlie flashed the tip of his tongue through the tiny aperture of his pinched mouth as he turned over the newspaper. He folded the middle seam and pointed to an article that covered a whole page.

'Jesus Christ,' said Brennan; he felt the skin prickling on his face. There was a picture of the Sloans – they were holding a photograph of their daughter Lindsey.

Charlie leaned forward, rested on his elbows, said, 'And you've not even read it yet!'

Brennan picked up the article, his thoughts had started to play tag with the possibilities. He looked over the paper's edge, 'What does it say, Charlie?'

'Everything . . .' He cleared his throat, tapped on the page. 'Says they were told about the bastard's handiwork . . . the mutilation, the hacking, the strangulation . . . Leaves nothing out, pretty bloody gory read if you ask me.'

Brennan felt his hand rising to his mouth, he touched his face but everything had started to feel unreal to him now. All he could think of was the Sloans and how they must feel to have been given that knowledge, to understand that their daughter's last moments on the Earth had been spent being tortured. 'Where the hell have they got that?'

'Pathologist . . .'

'Pettigrew, that what it fucking says? . . . I'll hang him out to dry.'

Charlie pressed his weight to one side, the counter sighed beneath him, 'Might have been a flunkey, they've had some bother getting the right folk down there. Not a job I'd fancy myself it has to be said.'

Brennan started to switch off to Charlie, he was filtering the information he needed but there was very little of that. He had watched Charlie's enthusiasm to deliver a new turn of events, a fresh tale, and when he had removed all he could that was of worth to him he started to scan the article. The newspaper's layout highlighted the most salient comments.

'Lindsey was gagged and bound when they found her, when they examined her they discovered her private parts had been removed with a knife.'

The quote was attributed to Mr Sloan.

Brennan felt his pulse quicken, he knew none of this was going to help the family. Why had the paper done it? He knew none of this was going to help the case either, or him. He had managed to keep the investigation's details out of the press so far, he knew that any reporting would inflame the situation, create panic. The public could sometimes be a help in such instances – with sightings, backgrounds – but more often than not they were a hindrance. He didn't want to be weighed down with cranks or have women scared to walk the streets. He didn't want to read sensationalist head-lines from editors who wanted to sell newspapers based on gory updates and he didn't want to run a phalanx of hacks following his every move either. There was also the Chief Super to consider; he didn't want to give Benny any more reasons to question his handling of the investigation.

Brennan looked up from the *News* page, saw Charlie staring out to the car park. He started to fold up the paper, slapped it down on the desk. 'Has Benny seen this yet?'

Charlie slit his eyes slightly, dipped his chin. 'I haven't a clue. But you can ask him that yourself, Rob. Here he is parking up now.'

Chapter 27

DI ROB BRENNAN WATCHED THE back of the Chief Super's heels as he ascended the staircase with the copy of the *News* he had taken from Charlie. He didn't seem to be lifting his feet high enough, it looked like there was hardly the strength in his legs for the task as he kicked the rim of every other step and stumbled on. He made sighs and repeated outbursts of 'Jesus Christ Almighty' as he read the Sloans' interview; twice he halted in his stride and smacked the newspaper off his leg. At the top landing he turned to Brennan, thinned his eyes and forced the newspaper into his hands without a word. As he strode down the corridor towards his office he seemed to have discovered a new purpose in his steps – each foot thudding like heavy artillery fire on the carpet.

Brennan clasped the paper, folded it over and turned it under his arm. As he followed the Chief Super he tried to devise a stratagem to deal with the inevitable backlash that was coming his way, but his mind seemed strangely blank. On the one hand, Brennan sympathised with the Chief Super

– he didn't want to see this kind of thing in the press either. But on the other hand, he wasn't prepared to give Benny an excuse to attack his handling of the case. Brennan hadn't seen this coming; he hadn't warned the Sloans that talking to the media might hamper the investigation at this delicate juncture, but then they hadn't been very voluble when they appeared at the station. The idea that they would suddenly bare their souls to the press mystified the DI.

Brennan followed the Chief Super into his office, closed the door behind them. He watched as Benny removed his officer's cap and placed it on the desk, then slapped down a pair of black leather gloves. He leaned forward, put his hands on the desk and nodded Brennan to sit. As he manoeuvred himself into the chair Brennan felt his heart rate increase with the thought of the impending attack.

Benny sighed, shook his head. 'This really is the last straw, Rob.'

Brennan remained calm, there was nothing to be gained from sparking up or drawing down the defensive portcullis too soon. He had been in this situation before, with more brutal task masters than Benny, but he knew his position was precarious now. It had been precarious after the over-time breach, then worse after he had brought in Lorrimer, but the *News* revelation now made things perilous.

'It's as much a surprise to me as it is to you, sir,' said Brennan.

'Oh well that's all right then isn't it.' Sarcasm was a hard act to pull off thought Brennan – his wife was an expert at the dark art but Benny could do with taking a few lessons from her.

'When I spoke to the Sloans they were hardly loquacious . . . I didn't see this coming.'

The Chief Super paraded the length of his desk, turned briskly. 'And did you warn them not to speak to the press?' his tone was brusque.

Brennan played it straight, 'No.'

'*No*?' He made a show of almost choking on the word.

'I didn't think it was necessary.'

A loud tut. 'Well this article,' he pointed to the newspaper where Brennan had placed it on the edge of his desk, 'shows how wrong you were.'

Brennan watched as Benny's face flushed, his neck muscles looked tense above his collar. 'I would take the same decision again; as I said, the Sloans were deeply traumatised when I spoke to them, I never imagined for a second . . .'

Benny cut in, 'That they might unburden their grief on a sympathetic journalist!'

'Exactly. It seems out of character for them both.'

'But not out of character for you, Rob.'

Brennan felt a pressure forming behind his eyes. 'I'm not sure I follow your reasoning, sir.'

The Chief Super folded his hands behind his back, loomed over Brennan. 'I mean you have hardly been on top of this investigation from the start.'

Brennan felt the urge to leap from his seat, clamp a fist round Benny's pencil neck and squeeze till the lead popped out the roof of his head. He watched him, held his gaze firm, then released a slow trickle of words. 'Again, sir, I'm not sure I follow your reasoning . . . Perhaps it would be better to have this conversation a little later on, when you've calmed down.' He placed his hands on the arms of the chair, made to ease himself up.

'Sit down, Rob!' Benny's eyes glowed; Brennan could

see he'd pushed a button in him. When he spoke again, he was pointing at the DI with his outstretched index finger, 'Need I remind you of your little overtime stunt, which you undertook contrary to my expressed wishes . . . And then there's the matter of drawing a profiler from Strathclyde when you know full well the procedure we are operating in these straitened times is a quid pro quo with Northern . . . And now, *this* . . .' He reached out for the copy of the *News*, raised it in the air and then slapped it down on the desk, in front of Brennan.

The DI pushed himself further back in the chair; he crossed his fingers together but remained silent. He had overextended himself with his last remark and he regretted it now. The trouble was that he was irritated by Benny, he felt the man diminished the role of Chief Superintendent with his presence. Brennan had taken orders from people he didn't rate in the past, shiny arses, careerists, people who would have been better suited to the board of Markies, but he had never taken orders from anyone like Benny. The man was as prepossessing as a maiden aunt; he lacked the muscle for the job. When he thought of his situation, Brennan felt it was like being reprimanded by an effete children's entertainer, the type he had watched on television with his daughter years ago. Had it come to this? Is that really what was flying up the ranks these days? Brennan found himself staring out the window, switching off to the monotonous tirade that was being lavished on him.

'Are you listening to me, Rob?' said the Chief Super.

Brennan drew back his gaze, 'Yes, sir.'

'Then you will understand my predicament, will you not?'

'Predicament, sir?'

Benny exhaled a long breath, ran a thumb over the edge of the desk and removed himself to his seat. 'DI Brennan you are presiding over an investigation which is descending into farce.'

'I would dispute that entirely.'

'Would you now?'

'Certainly.'

Benny leaned back in his chair, he picked up a yellow pencil with a rubber on the end, twirled it between his thumb and forefinger. 'That's your opinion.'

Brennan smiled, a wide one. 'I'd be happy to have the case, and my management of it, looked at by an independent source if you are so dissatisfied.'

The Chief Super stopped moving the pencil, seemed to stare through Brennan. He knew that Benny had no real grounds to criticise, the investigation was going as well as could realistically be expected in the circumstances; his complaints were pettifogging and if he brought in the officers' rep he would be a laughing stock. Brennan knew also that the last thing anyone wanted in the force was to be looked at too closely; you never knew what they might turn up.

'Is that a veiled threat, Rob?'

Brennan slackened his grin, unhooked his fingers and splayed his palms forward. 'I don't know what you mean . . . sir.'

'I think you know exactly what I mean, but let me tell you this, Inspector . . . I will not be undermined in my authority, be it overtly or covertly, do I make myself clear?'

Brennan remained still.

Benny continued, 'I have now pointed out to you three matters of a disciplinary nature that have come to my

198

attention. You have a shaky record on this force and if there is a fourth incident you can be assured of some serious action.'

Brennan lowered his hands, placed them on his knees. 'Serious action . . . By that I presume you mean you would put Jim Gallagher in charge of the murder squad.'

Benny smiled now. He leaned back in his chair and patted the trim of the desk with his fingertips. 'I don't need any excuse to put Jim in charge immediately.'

'I don't understand. This is my investigation.'

The Chief Super folded his arms, pitched himself forward. 'No Rob, on my force, they are all *my* investigations.'

Brennan felt his temperature rise, the pressure behind his eyes became a slow, persistent thud that made him grip his back teeth in an effort to still the beat. 'What are you saying?'

'I think we need some new blood, Rob . . . And I think Jim could be just the man to inject that.'

Brennan felt himself drawing fists beneath the line of the desk; he stared at Benny, smirking before him, and felt an urge to rise from his chair and slap him about the head. He knew the game he was playing, his predecessor Chief Superintendent Aileen Galloway had played it too. If Benny thought he was going to get away with that though, he was mistaken; Rob had anticipated the move, and set up a road block of his own.

'I wouldn't advise that, sir.'

Benny laughed, 'Oh really, Rob.'

Brennan rose, started to button up his jacket. 'You see, I've called a press conference for tomorrow. I've got the Sloans appearing centre stage – alongside myself, as investigating officer – and we're going to make a televised plea.

Now, I'm no expert on the media, sir, but if you were to shuffle the deck right now I'd say there'd be a few hacks asking why it was Jim and not me fronting that up.'

The Chief Super's face stilled, for a moment his jowls hung grey and limp, and then he shook himself back to life. 'Why wasn't I informed of this?'

Brennan turned for the door, 'You just were, sir.'

Chapter 28

NEIL HENDERSON STOOD OUTSIDE THE gates of Edinburgh High and watched as the last of the school's pupils headed for home. He had watched the succession of family cars, saloons and 4x4s, coming to collect the pupils and felt something like envy creep into him. Everyone, it seemed, had a comfortable place in the world, except him. When he weighed his lot – thought of the grimy flat in Leith that he shared with Angela – he felt left out. The game of life had short-changed him.

How could it have been any different though? he wondered. As a boy, Henderson had followed his mother around the town like a beaten dog; she had no interest in him, he was merely an inconvenience – something that got in the way of drinking bouts and boyfriends. He didn't like to be reminded of those days, tried never to think of them, but the visit to the school grounds had brought them back. He was spending a lot of time looking into his past now and it did nothing but make his heart pound and head hum.

Henderson lit a cigarette, his first since arriving at the

school – the rain had prevented him from smoking for the best part of an hour. He was wet, his hair sitting in dark rat tails above his damp collar. He let his fingers linger over the lighter flame for a moment, then quickly buried it in his pocket. The tobacco tasted good, calmed him. The smoke seemed to swirl around his head, block out his thoughts. He took some more deep inhalations, filled his lungs on every gasp.

Henderson knew there was a risk attached to what he was about to do. He had just left prison; if the filth were to hear of his actions, he'd be looking at another stretch. Would that be so bad though? he wondered. His life hadn't exactly played out as he'd hoped since he got out. It was early days, of course it was, but his appraisal of the future didn't look any brighter. Angela was in no shape to be walking the Links, she was an overdose waiting to happen, couldn't be relied upon. And his debt to Boaby Stevens was being called in. The passing image of Shaky's pug-faced enforcer felt like a dig in the ribs. The next encounter would be worse, he knew it, and the picture it put in his head played as clearly as a movie now. Henderson felt a quake pass through his body, shook him to the bones. He brought the cigarette close again, snatched three quick draws and exhaled the white trail of smoke through his nostrils.

At the time the debt had seemed manageable to Henderson, and it was – with two girls on the Links every night. But not now, not with Ange in her advanced state of atrophy, with her mind and body shot. It was a miracle she was bringing any money in at all; he shook his head. 'I wouldn't fucking pay for that,' he muttered to himself.

Henderson knew he needed to find Shaky's money, fast. The film spooled in his mind again, showed him lying beaten and broken, bones poking through his skin. He'd had beatings before, for a time when he was a youngster they were a daily occurrence, but he'd moved on from them quickly. As a bullied young boy, Henderson had learned that if he couldn't beat the bullies, he could join them; and he dispensed a more brutal form of beating than he'd ever been exposed to himself. He smiled as he remembered the torture he'd doled out as a boy, and later, to the women on the Links.

'The fucking tarts.' He wasn't going to be brought down with Ange, or snuffed out by Shaky. 'No fucking danger.'

Henderson started pacing the gates; he was growing impatient, wanted to get it over with. He always felt this way before an act of violence, it was as if the impending thrill built up in him and then it could only be released by committing to the damage he had promised to deliver. He scented the blood, he was sure of it.

At the school the cleaning staff started to arrive, old women in tabards with water-bag legs pushing mops and buckets around the place. Henderson sneered at them, they were trash. His mother had cleaned offices in the city, she had worked her fingers to the bone for a pittance; he wasn't going to follow her. He'd had it good before and he would again; all he needed was a break.

He knew the minute he had started to read Angela's diary that there was a chance for him to make a few bob for himself. This was a teacher she was going on about, a square peg. Henderson remembered the teachers from his school days: they were all full of themselves, thought they were better than him, thought they were better than everyone. He still despised them. The same social worker that had described him as 'self-loathing' had also detailed his 'reluctance to accept authority' – he agreed with her. He didn't like being told what to do by stuck-up twats who looked down their noses at you. And here was one of them, trying it on with a schoolgirl. Even though it was only Angela, and in Henderson's eyes she was worthless, the teacher, Crawley, had no idea about that. As far as Henderson saw it this was a square peg acting out of turn and he was going to have to pay the price for it; his price.

Henderson watched as the teaching staff started to exit the school building. They were just as he remembered them, just as they always had looked. It was all jackets and ties, pinafores and packed-lunch boxes tucked under the arm with a copy of the *Guardian*. They all headed off to their Volvos and their Audi estates, some clutching armfuls of exercise books that they'd spend the night poring over with a red pen. He remembered the way they went on about that, the marking. How they'd spent their whole night on it and how disappointed they were with some of the work. They always meant him, thought Henderson. They always hated him. He smiled, it didn't seem to matter that much now. It might have then, years ago, but things were different. He knew what they were really like, he'd seen through them.

As he stood at the gates he felt a speck of rain fall on his face, he looked up to the sky. Dark clouds had gathered over the roof of the school and perched there like gargoyles; there was another downpour on the way. He put up the collar on his denim jacket, it felt cold and damp against the skin of his neck. He didn't want to get another soaking but Henderson knew he had to see this job through now. He couldn't wait any longer, he had waited long enough. There was the problem of people losing interest too; he hadn't seen or heard any more on the television or in the newspapers about the murder out at Straiton. People were funny these days, they had short attention spans. All it took was a new signing at Hibs, or someone to make an arse of themselves on *Britain's Got Talent*, and the news was full of nothing else. He shook his head at the idea of more middle-class men in suits from the press attempting to thwart his plans.

He leaned in closer to the wall, tried to shelter himself as the rain picked up its pace, fell harder. He had asked Angela for a detailed description of Crawley. She had been reluctant at first, even the thought of it seemed to rattle her out of her wits, but she conceded in the end, with some encouragement. He hadn't even needed to take his belt off again.

Angela said Crawley was a games teacher, always wore a tracksuit and was lanky. He had large hands that looked too big for his long arms and they flapped about when he spoke and when he walked. He sounded odd, like he would stick out.

Angela had said, 'He is – he looks like a rat – he's got a rat's face, pointy.'

Henderson replayed her description now, tried to make sure he had all the information in place. He couldn't afford to mistake him for someone else, or, worse, miss him entirely. There was too much at stake for that.

'He's got pale hair, it's thin and wispy, and sits low on his forehead. And he sweats a lot, like he's just been out for a run. His hair's always sticking flat to his forehead too, when he's sweating . . .' She trailed off then.

Henderson had watched her start bubbling with tears, and when he asked her for more of a description she folded over on the mattress and held her sides. He realised that was his lot. It would have to do.

The main door of the school building opened and a man carrying a gym bag appeared; he wasn't wearing a tracksuit but Henderson was sure of his identity at once. He dropped his cigarette on the ground, crushed it under his foot, and started to cross the car park in pursuit of the man. He put his hand in his pocket, gripped the Stanley knife's haft. He watched his subject pitch up on his toes to manoeuvre himself around the wing mirrors of two closely parked cars, then he placed his bag on the ground in front of the driver's door of a silver Corolla.

Henderson watched and followed in silence. He let Crawley open the door, shove his gym bag over to the back seat, and then get inside the car. He broke into a jog as he heard the ignition being turned. As he reached the side of the vehicle he grabbed the handle of the Corolla's passenger's door and stuck in his head.

'Mr Crawley?' he said.

A wide-eyed stare greeted him. 'Yes.'

Henderson had the Stanley blade out of his pocket as he jumped into the front seat. He took the blade, forced its edge into Crawley's line of vision – made sure he had a good look at it – then rested it on the pink flesh of his neck. 'We're going for a wee drive, Mr Crawley.'

The teacher's face lost all its colour, his thin lips began to tremble. Henderson noticed he did indeed sweat a lot, a line of perspiration rolled towards the Stanley blade.

'*W-what*?' he said.

'You fucking heard . . .' Henderson drew back his fist, put the butt of the knife into the cheekbone. Crawley yelped in pain and dropped his head towards the wheel. 'Now get

206

fucking moving before I take your throat out with this.'
Henderson shook the blade before the teacher's face.

Crawley settled his hands on the wheel and engaged the clutch.

Chapter 29

NEIL HENDERSON KEPT THE STANLEY knife tight in his hand as Crawley drove out of the school gates. His palm grew sticky around the warm piece of metal, he felt his fingers ache. There was a passing moment when he wondered if he had done the right thing, or if he had made a mistake that was going to deliver him straight back to the prison he had just left. The thoughts goaded him, raced around inside his head so fast that he started to feel a dull ache in the back of his skull. What choice did he have? he asked himself. He couldn't rely on Angela to come up with enough money to keep Boaby Stevens quiet, for even a little while, and he had no other prospects. Henderson felt forced into his actions, driven by circumstance: he had to free himself of Shaky; maybe after that he could think about what he was going to do with his life. Right now it wasn't an option – he almost laughed at the thought of backing out. Options like that were for other people, the square pegs; folk like teachers. Though not Crawley, he had no options left.

Henderson gripped the knife even tighter, but his whole hand stiffened; he shifted the blade into his other hand and stretched out his fingers on the stiff one. As they pulled into the traffic, he caught sight of Crawley moving his eyes towards him. He didn't like Crawley looking at him, he didn't like Crawley full stop; he had a face like a rat, pointy; just like Angela said. 'You just keep watching the fucking road,' he roared, smacking the Stanley blade off the dash; the noise made the teacher flinch.

'Y-You'll never get away with it.'

Had Crawley grown bolder? wondered Henderson. Had he started to puff himself up now that they had driven further from the school? He hadn't quite reached cockiness yet but Henderson wondered if he was already being too soft on him. Should he sound more threatening? Should he carve him a little? Maybe just a nick on his cheekbone to shut him up? The trouble was, he had never been in this situation before; it was new territory. Henderson knew exactly what to expect when it came to noising up scrotes on the inside, or tarts down the Links, but real people were a different matter. He didn't know how to handle them. He toyed again with the idea of marking him, raised the blade to his face a few times but withdrew it. That was going too far, at this stage. He wanted to mark him, wanted to do worse; he steadied himself, calmed it down. He told himself there was no need to be anxious; after all, this was not a real person – he just looked that way. Crawley was a beast, and everybody understood what that meant. Beasts got what they deserved in the end and he was the man that was making sure Crawley got his.

The Stanley blade was for the end of the line though, thought Henderson. If Crawley got carried away, if he got out of order, he would get the knife right away – no question. But Henderson knew he needed to wield the threat of it right now to keep him in his place. He said, 'Never get away with it . . . Should be me that's saying that to you.'

Crawley's arms looked locked, frozen to the wheel. His hands were tight clamps, his knuckles white. He stuttered, 'I-I don't understand . . . Look, why are you doing this? It's kidnapping, you know that.'

Henderson watched the teacher's nervous eyes dart towards him, he forced the butt of the blade into his face – pushed his gaze front. 'Keep watching the fucking road . . . I know where you live and if I see you taking me the wrong way I'll put this knife in you. Do you understand?'

There was a pause as Crawley gathered his breath, tried to adjust his tone. 'Y-yes. I understand.'

'Good, then do as you're fucking told.' Henderson lowered the Stanley knife, pressed it against Crawley's shoulder. He had him under control now, he could see that. He felt his pulse begin to calm, his own breathing seemed less strained. He spoke softly, stretching out the intonation of his words, allowing a maniacal cadence to seep in. 'What you don't understand though, is that I know all about you . . . Mr Crawley.'

The teacher's cheeks flushed, he was sweating, his thin hair sticking to his brow as Angela had described it. He looked as if words queued on his lips but he held his mouth closed, kept his thoughts to himself.

Henderson continued his baiting of him, 'Oh aye, I know all about you . . . And your type. See, there was plenty of your type in the jail; know what we called them?'

Crawley didn't answer, kept staring at the road ahead.

210

Two hollows appeared either side of his mouth as he frowned. His lips looked pale and thin as he ran a dry grey tongue over them.

'We called them beasts!' said Henderson. He let the sound of the word fill the car, it seemed to echo all around them. He liked the effect, so he said it again, 'Beasts! That's what they call guys like you, folk that go after wee lassies . . . You like the wee lassies, don't you, beast?'

Crawley's lower jaw started to jut, trembled momentarily. He blinked quickly as he tried to regain the power of speech. 'Y-you've made a mistake. You have me mixed up with someone else . . .' He turned to face Henderson, his eyes pleading. 'This is a mistaken identity.'

Henderson laughed; he dropped his head towards his chest and then, as his laughter increased in tone and pitch, he broke into a coughing fit. He lowered the blade for a second, casually shifted it back to his other hand and then coughed over his knuckles. 'That's a fucking good one . . . No, it is, a right good one.' The laughter halted, Henderson forced the Stanley knife's haft into Crawley's crotch. 'After what you've been up to I should just hack the balls off you . . . Maybe I will.'

Crawley's voice was a wail. 'I haven't done anything . . . I haven't . . . I . . .'

Henderson gripped the Stanley tighter, dug it deeper into Crawley's crotch. 'Do I look stupid to you? Do I? Do I look like a fucking halfwit, a mug? Someone who's likely to get something like this wrong? I checked my facts, pal . . . Well and truly. And I know who you are and what you've done. And you're going to pay for it. Fucking sure you are.'

Crawley raised a hand from the wheel, it trembled as he

211

wiped at his dry mouth. He replaced the hand quickly; his jaw drooped, made a sharp angle with his neck and chest. He looked uncomfortable, too hunched up to drive. His eyes narrowed, grew redder. The hollows in his cheeks deepened, became two dark declivities mimicking the outline of his eye sockets. He seemed to be disintegrating before Henderson.

He spoke, the words rasping in his throat. 'W-we're here . . . This is my home.'

It was a neat semi-detached property that looked to have been newly renovated. The front walls had been rendered and double-glazing had been added. The garden was small, a driveway sat to one side, skirted by a small white pebble-dashed wall. As Henderson looked at the house it reminded him of the homes he had seen on television, on sit-coms and soap operas. It was a home where everyday folk lived, normal people; not beasts.

'Pull into the drive,' he said.

Crawley worked down through the gears, pressed the brake pedal. When the car was stationary in the street he selected first gear and slowly rolled the vehicle towards the driveway, turning the steering wheel tightly. When the car came to rest he switched off the engine and sat staring ahead.

Henderson still had the Stanley dug into the teacher's crotch. He twisted it as he spoke, 'Now, here's what we're going to do . . . You're going to get out that door there and walk towards the house. You're going to open the door and we're going to walk inside. If you make any funny moves, if you make any fuss, if you even think about legging it, then it will be the worse for you.'

Crawley moved his head to face him, 'Why? What will you do?' he said.

212

Henderson released a wide smile; it stretched halfway up his face, tightening the lines around his eyes and creasing his forehead. 'Well, right now, I'll carve you a nice wee red necklace, you can rest assured of that. But I don't think that's your main worry.' He looked out the car's windscreen towards the house. 'No, I'd be concerned about keeping my place in Happy Valley if I was you . . . Not many around here, or at the school, would be chuffed to know you were a beast, would they, Crawley?'

The teacher slumped forward on the steering wheel, his head rested on the rim. A slow breath exited from his mouth and then he spoke, 'I keep telling you . . . You have the wrong man.'

Henderson removed the Stanley, slammed the butt hard into Crawley's thighbone. His tone rose higher, filled with aggression. 'Look, I've told you, I know who you are . . . You know how? Because I know someone you know.' He brought his face closer to Crawley's, pressed his jaw out. His speech came on a flight of spittle, 'Did you think your wee trip out to the countryside, out to the field by Straiton, went without notice . . .'

Crawley jerked his head from the wheel, turned to face Henderson. His mouth was wide, his reddened eyes struggling to find their focus. '*What*?'

Henderson bit, 'Oh that struck a chord, eh . . . Fucking bet it did.'

'I don't know what you're talking about.'

'Oh aye, did you just forget about . . . Angela Mickle?'

Silence.

The name sat between them in the confined space like a small explosion. Crawley's damp eyes widened and his teeth clattered as he drew his mouth closed. Henderson could tell he had him now, he could do what he wanted; it was like throttling someone and then withdrawing at the last moment. The moment before you choked the life out of them: at that point they were weak, almost too weak to carry on. The teacher sat limp in the driver's seat as Henderson reached across him, grabbed the handle, and forced open the door. 'Right, get out . . . You and me have got some stuff to talk about in the house.'

Chapter 30

NEIL HENDERSON KNEW EXACTLY WHAT he wanted
to do with Crawley – he wanted to kill him – but that wasn't
going to work to his advantage at this moment. As he looked
at Crawley, backing away, his hands groping behind him
as he bumped into the tile-topped coffee table in the centre
of the floor, he wondered how a man like him had ever
managed to instil fear in anyone. But he knew he had.
Henderson remembered the exact lines Angela had written
in her diary. He remembered how she had looked at the
merest mention of the teacher's name, the terror on her
face. And she had been panicked, thrown into shock by
the television news when the story about the girl they
found in the field near Straiton came on. Crawley had
done that – this weak, scared man who stood before him
with his hands shaking and his brow wet with sweat.

Henderson gripped the Stanley blade tighter in his hand
and walked towards Crawley. He had abducted him from
a school playground; he thought about that for a moment,
it seemed almost like fate. Like the tables being turned.

This is what Crawley had done to those girls; he had captured them, taken them prisoner. But he hadn't taken them home, or anywhere familiar. He had driven those girls into the countryside, into the dark of night. He had taken them to a place where no one would see them, where no one would hear their cries, their screams. Henderson felt moisture pooling in his hand; he shifted the blade. He remembered the time his mother's boyfriend had taken him somewhere out of sight, what he had done to him there. He remembered the pain, the agony of it. For a moment, Henderson wasn't there in the room with Crawley, he wasn't himself; he was the young boy who had been taken up those stairs, watched as the door closed behind him and then cried when the door opened again and he realised the shame he would have to carry around for the rest of his life.

'You fucking bastard,' said Henderson.

Crawley turned away, looked towards the back of the room. There was nothing there, only the window and the curtains, a standing lamp and a small bookcase. There was no one to save him, there was no weapon he could reach for, there was nowhere to hide or to run to. He turned back towards his captor, his face draining white for a moment. His eyes roved, left to right. He jerked, his arms flew up in a spasm towards the side of his head and then he gripped his limp hair in his hands.

'Thinking about bolting are you?' said Henderson; he edged forward again, closed down the space between them. 'Not much fucking chance of that, I'd have the throat out you before you got a yard.' He started to laugh, watched as Crawley closed his eyes tightly; he looked like a child pretending that nothing would happen if he couldn't see it.

'What do you want from me?' he wailed.

Henderson locked down his prisoner; he could almost smell the fear in the room. He sensed Crawley's energy attenuating, seeping out of him, as he reached forward and placed the haft of the blade on the sleeve of his jacket. The movement made him tense, his shoulders squared. 'Is that what they said to you . . . Those girls?'

Crawley raised a hand, wiped at his eyebrows with the tips of his long fingers; some drops of sweat glistened there. 'What girls? . . . I've no idea what you're talking about.'

Henderson sparked, 'Don't fuck me about, you know what I mean.' He reached out, grabbed Crawley by the collar. His hot neck brushed against Henderson's knuckles as he pulled him towards the blade, forced it to the edge of his jaw. 'The girls you took out to the field, the ones like . . . Angela.' He said the name slowly, savoured each syllable, made sure Crawley would have no doubt about the word he uttered.

'Who?' said Crawley.

Henderson raised the blade again, pressed it into the fleshy part of his jaw line; a thin trickle of blood smeared the tip of the blade and then ran down Crawley's neckline. 'Don't fucking mess me about, you know fine well who she is . . . You took her out to the field and tied her up but she got away.'

'No. No. No.'

'Yes! Fucking yes. And she's been walking the Links since she got away from you Crawley . . . She got away when she hit you with a fucking rock.' Henderson brought the Stanley down on Crawley's head; there was a dull thud and then the teacher called out in pain. His knees seemed to fold, one at a time and then he slumped to the floor in a slow, swooning fall. He writhed like a maggot in a bait-bucket, his arms flailing before him as he tried to renegotiate his place in this strange new world. His balance had deserted him, he patted at the carpet with his large ungainly hands and groaned audibly.

Henderson leaned over, grabbed Crawley's hair, dragged him towards the middle of the room. He was still dazed, still fumbling, as Henderson produced the nylon rope from the inside of his jacket and started to tie him, first round the ankles and then, after pushing the arms behind his back, the wrists. Blood smeared on the carpet from the nick on Crawley's jaw which had opened wider, and from the fresh wound on his head. His eyes rolled about and his limbs fell limp. He mumbled, tried to speak, but words wouldn't come. When he opened his mouth to grab mouthfuls of air, Henderson noticed the blood on his teeth.

'You know all about getting folk tied up, don't you . . .' said Henderson. He yanked on the rope, saw it burning into Crawley's skin; he tightened it even more and said, 'I say you know all about tying up folk, eh.'

Crawley groaned, a broad rivulet of blood traced the shape of his forehead from hairline to brow. His head lolled on his shoulders and his facial muscles sagged and drooped. He looked dazed, his eyes glassy and moist.

Henderson prodded him, 'Wee lassies, you know about tying them up, don't you.'

Crawley started to mumble again, his words came coated with spittle. Some blood escaped the corner of his mouth as he spoke, 'I don't know anything. I-I don't . . .'

'Just keep that up,' Henderson yelled. 'See where it fucking gets you, pal.' He stepped back, dropped the trailing rope at his feet and raised his hands. 'Are you fucking daft or what? . . . Can you not tell when you're digging a hole for yourself?' Henderson steadied himself before the teacher; he shook his head as he took in his gaze. He settled before him, let the mash of his thoughts subside and then he lowered his hand to the floor and pulled the rope tight. He tested the tension, looked at his work; he seemed content that the knots would hold and so he cut the excess rope at the teacher's wrists. As he rose, Henderson dug inside Crawley's jacket pocket and removed his wallet. There was a thin bundle of notes there; he seized the cash, then looked towards the bank cards.

Henderson held up the cards, waved them in Crawley's face. 'Right, what's the fucking numbers for these?'

Crawley folded over, moaned. He had started to hyperventilate, gasping for breath as he lolled to and fro on the carpet. 'I don't know anything.'

Henderson looked away, balanced his thoughts, then placed the cards in his pocket. He took a step back from the centre of the room then made a lunging kick into Crawley's lumber region – the teacher called out in agony, rolled to his side as Henderson stepped back. 'I'll ask once more, but only once more, and only because you seem to be a wee bit slow on the uptake, Mr Crawley. Now, if you tell me what I want to know . . . I'll fuck off and leave you in peace – so, the numbers on these cards . . .'

Crawley started a coughing fit, his face darkened as he tried to raise his head off the carpet, his thin hair fell over his watery eyes. He seemed to have registered the request, said, 'There's only one number . . . The cards all have the same number . . . It's two-two-four-three.'

Henderson had been tightening his fists, waiting to lunge

forward and connect them with the teacher's head. He nodded instead, smiled to himself. He said the numbers over, 'That's it? . . . No others?'

Crawley gasped, 'N-no. That's the number I always have.'

'OK. OK.' Henderson leaned over him, grabbed his mop of a fringe and twisted it. 'Now, I am going down the road there to clean out these accounts . . .'

Crawley's eyes lit. His head tilted, still drooping on his thin neck.

'Don't worry, don't worry . . . I won't get it all today; see they have limits on these bank machines. But . . .' he raised a finger in the air, his voice lilted, became a song, 'so as you won't be alone tonight, I'll come back here and I can get some more out tomorrow, how does that sound?'

Crawley rasped, 'You said you were leaving . . . If I told you the numbers, you said . . .'

Henderson placed the sole of his shoe on Crawley's shoulder, pushed him onto his back again and started to laugh. 'And you fucking believed me . . . You've still got a lot to learn, teacher, sure you have.'

Henderson straightened himself, stepped over the bound Crawley and headed for the hallway. He closed the living room door behind him, released the handle and pressed the flat of his back to the panels. He allowed a moment to compose himself, still his breathing. When he lifted his head he saw the car keys on the floor by the window; they sat beside a fallen lamp with a tassel shade. He walked over and picked up the keys, dropped them in his jacket pocket and headed through the front door, closing it behind him, checking the lock held.

Henderson's feet scrunched on the driveway scree as he

walked towards the car. A low hedge partly screened the house from the street and the road but the neighbouring properties were in full view. His heart still pounded beneath his jacket, but the cool breeze that touched his brow seemed to calm him. He opened the car door and found the engine started on the first turn of the ignition; he reversed out. On the main road Henderson wound down the window, let the air lick the edge of his face as he pushed the needle towards thirty miles-per-hour. In a few moments he felt his pulse subside; he had calmed completely. He slapped the dashboard, congratulated himself. 'Nice one, Hendy . . . Fucking nice one indeed.'

Henderson followed the roads into the centre of Edinburgh, heading for Newington on the south side. The traffic was heavy, commuters clogging up the city arteries, but once he passed the main shopping precinct the congestion eased. On North Bridge he stopped the car just shy of the High Street, beside a Bank of Scotland branch with a cash machine; a homeless man sat outside, wrapped in a blue blanket, begging for money; on his way out the car Henderson sneered at him. He knew he was on the verge of clearing a substantial chunk of his debt to Boaby Stevens and he already felt the surge in his confidence. He saw the faces on Shaky's lot when he handed it over; they'd know he was someone who settled his debts, not just another loser that they were going to pick away at for the rest of his days.

Henderson slotted in the first of the three cards he had taken from Crawley and withdrew the maximum limit, then repeated the action twice more. He felt a compulsion to kiss the cash as he slotted it into his inside pocket, but he resisted; he didn't want to draw attention to himself. As he headed back to the car he looked up to the darkening sky and shook his head. He'd had a result, all he had to do now was hold his nerve and make the payment on his debt.

Henderson knew Boaby Stevens holed up in a pub in Newington called the Wheatsheaf; he turned the engine over, released the clutch and started out along Nicolson Street. As he drove, he went over the words he would use as he strolled into the pub: 'Hello, Mr Stevens, I believe you sent a messenger out my way.' He smiled to himself, imagined the look on Shaky's face as he counted out the money. 'Well, I couldn't have you thinking Neil Henderson doesn't pay his debts . . . And so, here you are.' He laughed now; the springs in the driver's seat started to judder. He was going to show them – he wasn't paying the full amount but he'd get it. He'd have the debt cleared, and be back on his feet. It was all working out.

'Nice work, Hendy . . . Fucking nice work,' he mouthed to himself as he drove.

At the box junction, he flicked on the blinkers, turned left and then left again on his way to the Wheatsheaf. The sky had darkened more now; it looked like rain as he pulled up on the double yellows outside the pub and killed the engine. A white van passed by; its headlights washed a pale glow over the road surface as Henderson stepped onto the windy street and trailed the paving flags to the pub's entrance.

Chapter 31

DI ROB BRENNAN MADE HIS way down the corridor towards Incident Room One. He got as far as the coffee machine before his legs started to feel heavy, his feet dragging on the industrial carpet tiles, and then his knees locked. The DI stalled where he stood, drew a deep breath and checked his watch face. There was still time to call a press conference and get the Sloans on board, he hoped, but what were the chances the Sloans would be keen to front-up a plea on television for help to find their daughter's killer? It was one thing to talk to the press in your own front room, it was something altogether different to sit in a television studio under the spotlights and face a pack of hungry hacks. Brennan also knew from experience that very few relatives of victims were ever keen to repeat the experience once they'd spoken to the press. What had seemed like a good idea, like a closure, seemed only to open the wound wider once it was over.

The DI pinned back his shoulders, forced himself to take the first step towards the incident room. His feet still dragged, but his heart was by far the heaviest load he carried. Brennan knew he had taken an almighty chance on the Chief Super accepting his word and failing to check the veracity of his press conference claim. If he had, Brennan knew he could well be looking at another enforced leave. The thought spun around inside his mind as he walked, each dizzying revolution reminding him how much he had gambled. Is that what it had come to now, thought Brennan, gambling with his career? There had been a time when the job was all, everything; now it had been reduced to a spin of a roulette wheel. He didn't know quite when, or how, he had reached this new low but he didn't like it. He was changing inside, his every perception was being challenged. Everything he thought he had once held fast to – his job, his marriage, his sense of himself – was in flux. He wondered how long he could go on balancing so many misconceptions. He felt lost to himself, confused. The only constant he clung to was his sense of justice; Brennan needed to find justice for those girls that had been murdered. They were young girls, not even old enough to have reached their prime; they were barely more than children. And they had been slain, brutally; their corpses dropped in a field. Not even buried or hidden, just dumped. It was as if the killer was taunting the force; taunting him.

Inside Incident Room One, DS Stevie McGuire rose from his desk in the middle of the room, nodded to Brennan and moved out to meet him. As he edged aside, his foot caught the cable of a telephone on his desk, making it jump. McGuire stalled, turned and disentangled himself; he was free of the cable as Brennan drew beside him.

'Boss . . .' said McGuire.

'What is it, Stevie?'

The DS put his hands on his hips, made a poor attempt at a smile. 'I was just going to ask *you* that.'

'Later, Stevie.' Brennan took a step to the side, started to walk down the centre of the two rows of desks that divided the room. His stride was lengthened as he approached DI Jim Gallagher – he was hunched over a blue folder, making jottings in a notebook. 'Jim, where did you get with the gymnastics lead?' said Brennan.

The DI looked up, his eyebrows made a dart in the middle of his forehead. His hair had been scraped back tight on his head, accentuating his male pattern baldness. 'Lead? . . . I don't know if I'd be using so strong a term as that, sir.'

Brennan felt the blood surge in him, let rip. 'Don't fuck me about, Jim . . . I want to know how far you've got, not dance around the houses with you.'

Gallagher lowered his head, creased the rolls of flesh into his neck. He put down his pen, slowly locked his fingers together. His gaze seemed to intensify as he spoke, 'I've looked into it; there were four identifiable names that could have had contact with Lindsey Sloan . . . Three of them were already interviewed by Collins, and those all came up blank.'

'And the fourth?' Brennan snapped.

'On holiday . . . As of today, it's end of term.' Gallagher presented the fact like a justification.

Brennan turned his head, looked down the room; the place had fallen into silence. His face creased like he was staring at the sun as he called out, 'Seems to be a distinct lack of activity around here!'

A rustle of papers, bustle of bodies on the move. The photocopier started to noisily draw paper from the tray. A

225

filing cabinet drawer opened. Brennan turned back to Gallagher, 'What about cross-referencing with the Fiona Gow case?'

'They were different schools,' he said, looking down to his desk and turning a page inside the blue folder, 'the Sloan girl was . . . Edinburgh High and Fiona Gow was Portobello Academy.'

Brennan watched the DI's movements, let him settle again behind his desk and then he withdrew a hand from his pocket, held it out to Gallagher with a shrug of his shoulders, 'Your point being?'

Gallagher shifted in his seat, let the page he was holding fall back to the folder. His words came delicately balanced on the back of a sigh, 'I don't see the two schools coming into contact . . . Five years apart as well. It's not like the boys and their footy teams, it's gymnastics.'

'So there was no inter-school competition?' said Brennan, 'No regional or district contest?'

Gallagher wiped his mouth, 'I'd have to look into it, it's a lot to check though, sir . . . five years of it.'

'Check it. If those lassies shared a changing room, I want to know about it. If they had an away day to the Commie Pool, I want to know about it. If they had sprained ankles and wore the same make of fucking bandages, I want to know about it. Am I making myself clear enough, Jim? Am I setting it out for you in the right language or would you like me to relay it through a bullhorn or a fucking loud speaker for you?'

Brennan's voice had risen above the clatter of the office once again; he felt vaguely aware of eyes burning into the back of his head; DS Stevie McGuire drew up to his side. 'Sir, can I have a word?'

Gallagher sat impassively. A fresh line of sweat had formed above his top lip, his eyes still burned into Brennan.

'What is it, Stevie?' He could tell the DS was trying to distract him, calm him down and persuade him to leave off Gallagher. There was little chance of that; Brennan had decided DI Jim Gallagher was going to be made to regret disrupting his investigation. He had compounded the pressure on the team and Brennan was going to make sure he returned the compliment with redoubled force.

'It might be better if we . . .' McGuire pointed to the glassed-off area at the end of Incident Room One. He raised his eyebrows conspiratorially.

Brennan tutted, turned away from him and marched down the room towards his office. He wrenched the handle and pushed the door open; it swung back in a wide arc as McGuire followed in behind him; he side-stepped the door, grabbed the handle and then closed it gently.

'Make it snappy, Stevie,' said Brennan. 'I've got a stack of things we need to be getting on with and this case isn't going to solve itself.'

McGuire took two steps forward, hooked a thumb in his trouser pocket. His voice sounded flat, 'I just took a call there from a Martin Gow . . . Fiona Gow's father.'

Brennan felt a twitch kick in above his eyebrow. 'And?'

McGuire unhooked his thumb, ran the fingers of his hand through his hair. 'There's some article in the *News* and . . .'

Brennan cut in, 'I know, Stevie, I know all about the fucking *News* article.'

McGuire's tone pitched up a notch, he spoke faster. 'Well, you'll be aware then that it mentions certain aspects of the case that, generally speaking, we'd have liked to have kept quiet about.'

'No shit.' Brennan removed a packet of Embassy Regal from his jacket, withdrew a cigarette and placed it between his fingers. The movement comforted him, he felt his pulse decrease slightly as he touched the smooth surface. 'Look, what did Mr Gow say, Stevie?'

DS McGuire puffed his cheeks, squinted towards the window. 'He wanted to speak to the officer in charge, I came to look for you but you were in with Benny and ... Well, I headed him off at the pass.'

Brennan touched his forehead, the filter tip of the unlit cigarette pressed against his brows. 'Jesus fucking Christ, that's all we need.'

'But ...'

Brennan dropped his hand, looked at McGuire. 'There's a but?'

'I'm afraid so ... He wants to come and speak to you. As soon as possible.' The DS reached into his shirt pocket, removed a yellow Post-it note and handed it to Brennan, said, 'Here's his number, he's waiting for your call ... Says he's happy to come in to the station when you're free.'

'Right, thanks ...'

'I thought perhaps I should have handballed it to Jim.'

Brennan pocketed the number, 'No chance.' He pointed the cigarette like a blade at McGuire, 'Jim is on a strictly needs to know basis ... Needs to know fuck all, that is, unless I say otherwise.'

McGuire rolled his eyes towards the ceiling. 'Message received and understood, sir.'

Brennan tucked the cigarette behind his ear, 'Look, Stevie, you talk to Mr Gow, tell him we're exploring links to the Sloan killing ... But be careful, eh, and get him in for interviews with the squad.' The DI started to do up his tie.

His expression said he had moved on from the last topic of conversation. 'I need you to do something else for me.'

'What's that?'

'Get onto the press office and tell them to contact all media – especially the television studios – and tell them I'm fronting a press conference downstairs tomorrow morning . . . That should give them enough time to get us on the evening news slot.'

'We're going public already?' McGuire's voice dipped again.

'We've no choice, the *News* beat us to it.' Brennan brushed down the shoulders of his jacket, 'We can maybe turn this around, though, make it work for us.'

McGuire looked doubtful, thinning his eyes and pressing out his lower lip like a petulant child. 'We've never done well with the media before, boss.'

Brennan nodded, straightened his cuffs and headed for the door. 'You can say that again. Look, it's not the way I'd like to have played it, Stevie, but we've no choice. And it's not like we've got leads coming out of our ears.'

'Yes, sir.'

Brennan grabbed the door handle, held it steady as he spoke, 'But remember, keep this out of Benny's earshot . . .'

'He doesn't know? . . . You'll have to tell him.'

Brennan shook his head now, 'No, Stevie, he knows. He just thinks this was a *fait accompli* some time ago.'

'I don't follow you.'

'Good. It's probably best you don't. And, don't forget to let the press office know that I am fronting this up . . . I don't want fucking Gallagher anywhere near those cameras, don't even want him in the room with them.'

McGuire smiled, 'You media whore.'

'No, Stevie, I don't want him sticking his size tens in and tipping the press off to the links with the Fiona Gow case, that would be all we need – a serial killer frenzy on our hands and a baying mob of hacks following our every move.'

'Got you.' McGuire watched Brennan open the door, step through. 'Are you heading out, sir?'

'Well observed, Detective . . . I'm off to see the Sloans.'

230

Chapter 32

DI ROB BRENNAN THOUGHT THE world was cracked, fragmenting. He felt the age he lived in had grown confused and uncertain. The world no longer knew right from wrong. It confused profits with rewards and seemed unsure of the value of anything. As he drove towards the Sloans' home in Pilrig his mind thrashed between the case and more petty concerns. He thought about the way the Chief Super had cautioned him – not for his conduct on the case but for his financial mismanagement of the force's resources. It was insane: he knew you could not put a price on policing the streets. You could not put a price on finding the killer who had left the cold bodies of Fiona Gow and Lindsey Sloan in a Straiton field. He shook his head, wondered how far off a privatised police force was. They had put the prisons in the hands of big business – and the court transport – was a private force much closer now? Nothing was beyond the scope of the bean counters, he surmised.

Brennan tilted with the sweep of the car as he overtook a double-decker bus with an advertisement for a new reality

231

show on its side. He realised he no longer knew what a good television programme was. Or a good book. A movie or a piece of music. He couldn't remember the last time he'd engaged with mass culture. It was for other people, alien to him; it seemed to him like nobody got Rob Brennan any more. He didn't fit the unthinking mould: they were all waiting to be told their tastes, spoon fed.

He turned on the car radio, a saccharine pop song burst from the speakers and assaulted his eardrums; he turned it off, sneered into the windscreen.

'Fuck's sake.'

Where were the true artists, thought Brennan, the people to make sense of this mess? If a fifteen-year-old singer with a side sweep could shift records, it meant all now – but it meant nothing – where were the arbiters? Had they gone too? If they had gone – those point-men for the human race – then the rest of us weren't far behind. No one stood up any more to say we had all lost our way; we had supplanted our souls with rhinestone or dust or paste – anything vacuous and empty, anything worthless, meaningless.

Brennan felt like the only one who cared; he was old enough to remember a different way, a different world. Was he simply being nostalgic? he wondered. Had it really been that much better to hear a song he'd enjoyed on the radio had reached number one on *Top of the Pops*? Did it mean anything? It was just another fond memory from his youth that triggered deeper memories – reminded him that those times were now gone, passed, and would not be coming back. Was it further evidence of his growing discontent? Brennan knew that the world he had dwelt in as a younger man had vanished and the promise it offered had never materialised. He felt let down, duped; and every reminder of the fact dug at his battered heart.

The mobile phone on the passenger seat beside him started to ring; he picked it up. The caller ID said Joyce. He flicked on the blinkers, pulled into the side of the road.

Brennan took a deep breath before he answered, 'Hello, Joyce.'

She started on him immediately, 'That was some trick to pull.' Her voice was high, forceful. She had taken time to let her wrath simmer. 'I mean, to drag your daughter out of school is one thing, but to not even tell me, to leave me waiting at home . . . Wondering where in the name of Christ she was.'

'Shut up, Joyce.'

There was a single second of silence, then indignation bit once more, 'What did you say to me?'

Brennan answered calmly, he let the flat tone of his voice lead her opinion more than his words. 'I think you heard, I think you're being unfair, and I think you know it.'

Her teeth clacked on the other end of the line, 'I don't believe I'm hearing this.'

'Neither do I . . . did you just call to bawl me out?' Brennan could tell from the tone of his wife's voice that she had no intention of making a valid point about him collecting Sophie from school. She was not concerned about where she had been or whom she was with; Joyce had called to vent unspoken frustrations. She wanted to tell him that she was the one who had decamped to the moral high ground, she was the one who stayed home, looked after their daughter. He, by contrast, had to be reminded he was the adulterer, not fit to remain under their roof. That was her message, however she attempted to relay it.

233

'She went straight to her room and stayed there all night, never spoke a word. Do you realise the psychological damage you could have done to our daughter?'

Brennan tutted into the phone, it came out as a more guttural noise than he intended, but he wasn't entirely dissatisfied with the effect. 'Jesus Christ, woman . . . Will you listen to yourself? I took my daughter for coffee, one coffee and I delivered her to the door.' He paused, 'And, I have to say, she was in fine form when I left her . . .'

'And what's that supposed to mean?'

'It means what it means.'

Joyce's voice broke bluntly, 'I see . . .' she at once seemed to sense the futility of her situation. 'Well I called to tell you I will not tolerate anything like that in future . . . If you want access to my daughter you can apply through the courts.'

'Sophie is *our* daughter, Joyce.' A cat ran from a shaded wynd as Brennan waited for his wife's reply; none came. 'Joyce? . . .'

She had hung up.

The memory of the night he had met Joyce had grown opaque now. There had been a party, one of the weekly crop of them that had sprung up that long summer of his early twenties. At some point they had got chatting – he seemed to think it was in the kitchen, but that might have been maturity rearranging memory for convenience sake; hadn't all his party appearances convened in the kitchen? She wore her hair up and had a beautiful, slender neck that he had longed to kiss, that much was credible fact. He stored the image of her like a daguerreotype and brought it out when he had mourned its passing. Joyce was no longer the clubbable, girly party-goer, was no longer smooth

234

skinned or supple necked. He wasn't so superficial a man as to be swayed by her physical diminution – what plagued Brennan was the boy who had once been stripped of all reason, all sense, by the sight of a pretty girl. What he saw now was the vision of Joyce laid bare – the subcutaneous woman – and that was something he had failed to notice on their early encounters.

There was a harshness in Joyce, not a meanness of spirit exactly but a nagging, dispiriting malaise at the singular unfairness of life. He had wondered – had it always been there, his wife's bitterness? Or, had it been a late surfacing – perhaps even brought about by a sense of lack at their own station in life, or, indeed, her own reassessment of her poor early judgement. But he dismissed this. That was Brennan the detective doing his due diligence; Joyce's underlying angst, her enmity, had always been there. The markers were not hard to find. He could recall cutting, carping comments directed at their social circle that had irritated him at first. They sprouted in sparse patches like paving weeds – unsightly, certainly unwelcome, but always overlooked. As her opinions became entrenched, became a dogma she preached, the weeds proliferated. There was no point in him passing his own remarks – lobbing rejoinders – he had admitted early on he couldn't compete. His spleen wasn't strong enough for the counter-attack, and when attacked – when faced with her insensitivity – the issue itself became an irrelevance, bawled out by the censure of a caterwauling harpy. The weed-skirted edges of their exist-ence had soon been supplanted by rainforests of animosity – dark and impenetrable lands that swallowed up even the strongest of constitutions.

When he thought about it, about Joyce and the choice

he had made to marry her, Brennan was perplexed now. He had seen the signs – even as an inexperienced, naïve young man – and yet he'd avowed himself to her. He had willingly signed up for a life of misery and discontent, wilfully ignorant of the roaring sirens warning him to get out of the way. Should he regret it now? Should he regret any of his erroneous, hasty, foolhardy decisions taken in his youth? Yes, he thought – but also – no. He could mourn the lost lives he may have lived. The happy, fulfilled, sun-lit, soft-focused days that played on the screen of his mind like ruddy-cheeked children were phantoms. They no more existed in reality than wishes. He was where he was and nothing could change that. Not now. Decoupling from Joyce had been the rational thing to do but – he knew in retrospect – rational thought was not the proclivity of a young man.

Brennan looked out to the grey–purple wash of the sky, and sighed. He reached for the door handle, opened the car and stepped out; some fragments of red tail-light glass crushed under his shoes as he walked to the edge of the road and lit a cigarette. A loud motorbike roared past, dragging his attention back to the present.

He cursed out, 'Fucking hell.'

Brennan inhaled deep on the cigarette; at first his breathing felt constricted but then the anodyne rush of nicotine worked its way into his lungs. He exhaled slowly through his nostrils, looked towards the burning tip of the cigarette. He knew his mind was cartwheeling; was it the job? His life? He ran a hand through his hair and sighed as he stubbed out the remainder of the cigarette and returned to the car. Inside he sat with the door open for a bit, his head leaning back. He knew he needed to refocus, he needed to get his mind on the job, the case; he had let far too many infinitesimal distractions take him from his aim lately. He sat forward, rested his brow on the rim of the steering wheel for a moment; a damp patch stared back at him as he withdrew it. What was going on? What was happening to him? Brennan had never questioned his career choice before, he had never felt the weariness that now settled on him. He wondered where this uncertainty, this questioning of his lot had come from, and, where was it leading? The answer to the last part of the question scalded him; he knew there was no place on the force for someone who was conflicted like him, the job required more. But how could he give it his full attention when his life was imploding?

A chill wind blew down the wide sweep of the street. Brennan watched it carry an empty take-away carton with it and closed the car door. A sneer rose on his face as he reached for his mobile phone and brought up the contacts. He scanned the names, found what he was looking for and hoped might be a solution of sorts: Wullie Stuart – he pressed 'call'.

Ringing.

Brennan cleared his throat.

Wullie answered on the fourth ring, 'Hello.'

'Hello, auld fella,' said Rob; his voice sounded lyrical.

'Rob Brennan . . . Haven't heard from you for donkey's.'

His conscience pricked, 'Well, sorry about that . . . How are you keeping?'

Wullie's voice dropped. 'Aye not bad. And you? How's the job?'

Brennan steered the conversation back to where he wanted it to be, 'Well, there's time enough to get round to that, I was wondering if I could take you for a pint?'

'A pint . . . Christ Almighty, Rob . . . you must be in some bother if you're after a pint with me!'

Chapter 33

BRENNAN DREW UP OUTSIDE THE Sloans' house, stilled the car's engine. He sat for a brief moment, then yanked on the handbrake and reached for the door handle. His thoughts were whirring as he stepped onto the road. The long straight street was silent, save for occasional stirrings of dulcet birdsong in the chill air. He looked up to the whitewashed sky, caught no sight of the culprits and headed for the kerb. Brennan felt conscious of himself, his role, and what he was there to do as he paced forward, heavy-footing the soles of his shoes on the tarmac. He didn't want to bring any more grief to the household, he knew there was already plenty there. He remembered his last visit and the way Mrs Sloan had looked: she was wrecked with loss. How could she be anything else? She had mentioned Sophie when she came into the station and Brennan felt her deep hurt at the sounding of his daughter's name; she had lost her own daughter and the thought burned him. He didn't know how any mother or father moved on from the loss of a child. To see people destroyed by the actions of others was the hardest part of his job; he had seen too much of it and felt the past visions were accumulating inside him like a cancer. Where was the good in this world? he wondered. Where was the happiness? Where was *his* happiness? He knew it had been there once, when he was a boy – when he was growing up, with Andy – but it all seemed so long ago now, another world away. Did life have to be like this? he thought. Did moments of happiness have to be stored away, brought out and imbibed like a drug in times of grim despair? He didn't want to think his best days were already behind him, but the distance between him and his solid memories of happiness seemed to be growing every day and the job only added to the mileage.

The Sloans' gate was secured with an iron hasp; Brennan released it and moved onto the garden path. His steps felt heavy on the paving stones; made too much noise. The home looked well kept, tidy: the windows had been washed recently and the path swept. The grass could have taken another cut – blades overhung the lawn's edge – but the recent rain had kept the mower away. He looked up and down the height of the building, stalled for a second or two as he watched the curtains for movement, then he steadied himself before the door. As he reached forward, rung the doorbell, the sound of a dog barking began inside; it seemed to echo from the other end of the house, through the building, and then a small white blur scratched at the frosted glass of the door.

Brennan stood square-footed on the path, brushed down the shoulders of his overcoat as he watched a figure appear behind the glass. It swayed a little, seemed to steady itself, and then the DI heard the sound of someone reaching for the lock. The door's hinges squealed as Mr Sloan pressed his head through the narrow gap between door and jamb. His wiry grey hair sat low on his brow as he reached a thin hand towards the wall and leaned his bodyweight there, 'It's you . . . Hello.'

Brennan felt an uneasy doubt seep into his mind; he had started out on the road to Pilrig with a bolt of anger turning in his gut following the *News* article. He knew he couldn't blame the Sloans for that, they had no idea what they were doing, they were hurting and reaching out for something to relieve the pain. As Brennan looked at Mr Sloan – stooped and beaten before him – he felt his pulse still. He didn't feel welcome there, but how could he? He was the public face of a murder investigation – their daughter's murder. 'I'm sorry to bother you again, Mr Sloan . . .'

The man interrupted, widened the door and stepped back. He looked worn, seemed to have lost so much weight that his shoulders poked through his cardigan. 'No, it's quite all right . . .' Mr Sloan bowed, grabbed the little white dog's collar, 'Will you come in?'

As Brennan crossed the step, Mr Sloan released the dog; it ran into the living room in a mood of high excitement that seemed wholly out of place to Brennan. He halted in the hall and waited as Mr Sloan closed the door behind him. The dog returned with a fat tongue lolling from the side of its jaws.

Mr Sloan's voice came softly as he walked, 'Has there been any . . . developments?' He seemed to drag out the last word, as if it pained him to say it.

Brennan stifled an urge to walk back to the door he had just come through; there had indeed been developments, only not the type he had been hoping for. He wanted to be able to tell the Sloans he had found their daughter's murderer, that he had the killer in custody and ready to face the full force of the courts. He knew this wasn't the case, however. As he looked at Mr Sloan's dark-ringed eyes he understood he was holding out a forlorn hope. Brennan motioned a hand towards the open living-room door, 'Can we sit down, please?'

Mr Sloan stood silently in the hallway. His face lay still as he eyed the DI quizzically for a moment, then his whole body sprang to life. 'Of course, yes.' He pointed with his open palm, 'Make your way through.'

In the living room Mrs Sloan sat straight backed on the edge of the sofa, her knees were held tight together, her hands fidgeting in her lap. She nodded to Brennan, then tucked a handkerchief in the cuff of her cardigan. Her hair was mussed, she pressed the sides of it with her hand as she spoke, 'Would you like some tea . . . coffee maybe?'

Brennan stood before her, smiled and shook his head.

Mr Sloan walked into the room, paced the carpet towards the sofa and sat himself down beside his wife, 'Please take a seat, Inspector.'

Mrs Sloan watched as Brennan turned his head, she seemed to predict his next movement and rose quickly; she removed a copy of the *News* from the chair next to the window and placed it on a low-slung side table.

Brennan fanned the tails of his overcoat behind him as he lowered himself onto the chair, his hand brushed the newspaper as he and Mrs Sloan sat down. 'Actually, my visit's not unrelated to this.'

The couple looked blankly at him; Mr Sloan was first to speak, his voice rising with a note of optimism, 'Oh, really?' His tone suggested he was unaware that talking to the press would have any impact on the investigation other than a positive one.

Brennan crossed his legs, he felt his movements being scrutinised. His shoe, sitting stiff against his ankle, suddenly reminded him it should have been polished some days ago. He lowered his leg again, said, 'We had hoped to put the media to use on the case in due course . . .' his words sounded too formal to him, they verged on corporate-speak, but how did you find the right words to address the parents of a recently murdered young girl? There was nothing he could say that was going to make a difference now, there were no words that could mend what had happened to Lindsey Sloan and the aftermath her family was now dealing with. If there were words, any he could say, he would have uttered them. Brennan forced himself to continue, he knew he had to. He couldn't show the Sloans that he was anything less than a professional – they needed to know that someone was there for them, on their side; someone who would right the wrong. 'I thought I should warn you that there will likely be a substantial amount of interest in this case now.'

Mrs Sloan looked at her husband, all the light seemed to have faded from her eyes, her voice droned, 'What's he saying, Davie?'

Her husband shrugged, his face was immobile as he turned back to the DI, then he drew a solitary breath and his thin lips began to move, 'Has there been some development you're not telling us about?'

Brennan felt the rhythm of his heart change as he looked at the couple; he had started out with the idea of persuading the Sloans to appear in a televised appeal for witnesses but that plan seemed to have been waylaid the moment he stepped inside the door. He needed to give them something, they looked at him with pleading in their eyes; these people wanted someone to make sense of what had happened, to bring them back to a life with some humanity in it. Brennan edged forward on his chair, pressed his fingers together in a dome above his thighs. His breathing thinned as he prepared to speak, 'Look, I really don't want to alarm you . . .' he smoothed the corners of his mouth with his finger and thumb, 'But we believe Lindsey's murder may be related to another case which is very similar.'

Mr Sloan's dark eyes sunk in his head, he parted his thin lips again and stared at Brennan for a moment. His wife spoke his name but he didn't seem to register it, then he suddenly tilted his gaze towards her. Mr Sloan took his wife's hand, she settled her head on his shoulder, said, 'Not another lassie, Davie . . . Not another one.'

Brennan picked at the crease in his trousers; as he watched the couple absorb the information he felt an urge to give them space. They needed to take it in, to process what he had just told them. He rose, stepped towards the window and looked out to the street and the sky. His knees locked as he girded his pose; an old Nissan spewed smoke as it started in a neighbouring driveway. Brennan knew the information would release a press frenzy if they ever got hold of it. One brutal murder of a young girl was enough for them to go on for now; if they got hold of the fact that the force was pursuing links to Fiona Gow's murder as well then the headlines didn't bear thinking about. He knew the Chief Super would have him on a spit, but the Sloans deserved to know the facts. They deserved at least the facts.

When Brennan turned round, the couple were staring at him.

'Who . . . I mean, when?' said Mr Sloan.

'There was another murder, some years ago . . .' The DI's voice strained on the details, he caught the act before it became a habit and stilled his register. 'A local girl, called Gow.'

The Sloans looked blankly ahead, the name didn't mean anything to them. Brennan watched as moisture welled in Mrs Sloan's eyes. 'And you think . . .?'

'We're almost certain it's the same perpetrator.' Brennan crossed the carpet to the chair he had risen from, lowered himself back to the Sloans' eye level, said, 'We have some forensic evidence.'

'Evidence?' said Mr Sloan.

'It's indisputable . . . I'd sooner not go into too much detail but you need to understand that this is a very delicate time for the investigation. We need to tread very carefully with the press . . . If they get hold of this then they will blow the whole case up and we could lose our chance of catching our man.'

'Alert him, you mean?'

Brennan felt his face tighten, his brow held firm. 'We're dealing with an extremely resourceful individual.' He stopped himself, held his thoughts in check, made sure he wasn't about to say anything that would cause more damage to them. 'But we have the best possible people working on this case, I can assure you of that.'

Mr Sloan looked towards his wife, said, 'We understand, Inspector . . .' he paused, turned to face Brennan, his dark eyes burned, 'Just tell us you'll get this bastard.'

The DI nodded; some rain started to patter on the window outside. He looked out towards the sky, the room suddenly felt cramped. Brennan turned back to the couple, they sat very still before him like they had been carved into the wall by a sculptor. 'There is one more thing . . .'

'What's that?' said Mr Sloan; he barely moved as he spoke.

'I need to ask you both . . .' He stalled, made sure he connected with them on the right level, 'And I know it's hard for you . . .'

Mrs Sloan cut in, sounded impatient. 'What is it?'

Brennan raised his hands, pushing his elbows out at a jagged angle, 'I'd like you both to make a television appearance.' His voice felt stiff as he spoke. 'I know it won't be easy for either of you, but at this stage I think it could assist the investigation.'

Mrs Sloan released her husband's hand; she stood up and stared into Brennan's eyes. For an instant the DI thought she was about to rage at him, she loomed there, her face creased and her mouth twisted. When she spoke, her words came as a blast. 'And how in God's name will that help *us*?'

Mr Sloan reached out to his wife; his hand was quickly pushed away. 'We're already painted as martyrs in the paper . . . Nothing's going to bring our Lindsey back. Nothing!' She turned, paced towards the open door. Mr Sloan and Brennan watched in silence as she left the room. All the air seemed to have been sucked out in her wake, replaced by a tense electricity.

'She's taking it hard,' said Mr Sloan.

'I understand.'

'She wanted to draw a line under it all.' He nodded towards the newspaper where it sat next to Brennan on the side table. 'She wanted to talk about Lindsey but they twisted it round, made us sound, I don't know, needy . . .' He got to his feet, walked to the door and looked towards the staircase as if he expected to see his wife standing there. He turned back to the room, faced Brennan. 'It just wasn't supposed to be about us,' he said. 'It's about Lindsey. And

245

we can't get her back now, Inspector . . . She's gone for good . . . we know that.'

Mr Sloan followed his wife out the door, said, 'I have to go to her.'

'Of course.' Brennan stood alone.

Chapter 34

THE WHEATSHEAF STARTED FILLING UP, but hadn't quite reached the point where it could be described as busy. A disconsolate gathering of old men sat at the bar with half-pint tumblers in their hands, nodding towards the flickering portable television that showed a snooker match. The picture was grainy, almost a snowstorm; Henderson watched for a moment, saw a red ball sink in the middle pocket, then turned to the barman. 'Need to give the aerial a shoogle, I think.' The man looked at him with hooded eyes, rubbed at his ribcage and cleared all expression from his face; he seemed to be waiting for Henderson to speak again.

'Pint, mate,' he said, his voice sounded higher now, more lyrical.

The barman nodded, took up a glass from beneath the counter and started to look at the pumps. Henderson tilted his head towards the one marked McEwans, smiled. 'I'm, eh . . .' he leaned forward, rested his elbows on the scratched and scarred bar top, 'on the lookout for one of your regulars.'

The barman continued pouring until the pint glass was filled; he clipped the pump up, put it in line with the counter top and placed the full pint of McEwans on the bar in front of Henderson; some white froth escaped the brim and slid down the side of the glass, settled on the bar surface. The barman studied Henderson; each of his eyes contained a solitary pinpoint of light – he held his expression still for a moment and then briskly waved a dismissive hand, 'I pour pints, that's all.'

Henderson sniffed, cached away his emotions. His mouth opened and closed like he was exercising his jaw as he searched for words. 'You know who I'm after.' He placed a ten-pound note in the barman's open palm, 'Come on, mate . . . I can tell, y'know.'

The barman took the money, curled it in his fist and turned to the till. The cash drawer rattled noisily as it opened, then again when it was closed. He scratched the back of his shaven head, the glow of the bar lights reflected on his crown for a moment. Henderson watched, clamping his teeth as the barman stretched around and placed his change on the counter. He didn't make eye contact again, returned to the other end of the bar and picked up a copy of the *News*.

Henderson kept his gaze fixed on him; he could feel his stomach start to cramp as he tensed his muscles. He picked up his pint, quaffed the head and strolled around the bar and the old men seated beside him. His legs ached now, the muscles started to feel heavy. He'd exerted himself more than usual; even working the clutch on the car had set up a twinge in his calf. He knew he was in no shape for confrontation, but he wasn't there to be ignored. As he strolled to the end of the bar, the door opened and an office worker walked in shaking out the wet from her hair; her earrings swayed in time with the turning of her head. Henderson watched her pass him by, touched the package of money sitting in his pocket, and waited for a gap to appear at the counter. He felt his cheeks flush as he approached the sulky barman.

'Look, mate, do me a favour, eh . . . I have something here for,' he dropped his head, lowered his voice, 'Shaky.'

The barman eyed him over the newspaper for a few moments, lowered it, folded a crease down its middle. Henderson saw the cold pustules of sweat sitting out on his forehead as he rose, crossed the short distance to the bar and slapped down the *News*, said, 'Wait here.'

Henderson followed the back of the barman's shaven head as he walked away from him, turned at the end of the bar and raised the counter. In a few steps he was lost in the blur of bodies. The room had filled up. Henderson felt himself tune in to the birr of unknown voices and settled himself on a stool. He took up his pint again, gulped a mouthful and wiped his lips with the back of his hand. He felt uncomfortable now, his neck tensed and set up the same aches and pains as his stomach and legs. Shaky was unpredictable, he told himself, but he wasn't stupid. He had asked to be paid, sent one of his pugs round; he could hardly complain. Surely Shaky wanted to be paid. He felt himself struggle to find comfort on the bar stool, he settled his weight first on his right thigh, then his left. Nothing seemed to work. He rose, pushed in the stool and raked the room for a familiar face, but found none. He picked up the copy of the *News* that the barman had left behind, idly turned over the pages. He continued skimming until he alighted upon a story that

249

took his attention: the parents of the murdered girl found at Straiton had given an interview.

'Jesus Christ,' he said. They had given details how she had been tied up, choked on her own underwear and her genitals mutilated. Henderson felt a flash of heat in his gut, he wanted to return to Crawley; he had been too soft on him. He took the page from the newspaper, folded it in two, then folded it again and slipped it into the back pocket of his jeans. He was finishing off the dregs of his pint when the barman reappeared, his slack jowls slapping on his neck as he walked. At the end of the bar he raised the counter again, eased himself under it and paced the distance between himself and Henderson. He kept his eyes dipped towards the bare boards as he walked. 'Right, come here,' the barman flicked his head to the side as he spoke.

Henderson took a step closer, watched as the barman picked up the copy of the *News* then slapped it on the bar counter again.

'Are you Hendy?'

'Aye'

The man prodded the paper with his index finger. 'If you've got something for Boaby, put it in there.' He still hadn't made eye contact with Henderson; his teeth clicked as he clamped his jaw shut.

Henderson cleared his throat, he felt the tension sitting between them like an air of thick cigarette smoke. He removed the cash from his jacket pocket and placed it on top of the newspaper; he watched as the barman folded over the front page and picked up the bundle. He swiftly placed it under the counter, looked back towards Henderson and for the first time since he'd walked in, made eye contact. He said, 'Now fuck off.'

Henderson's eyes receded, he riled, 'What if I want another pint?'

The barman's voice rasped, took on a harder edge. 'No pints here for you.'

Henderson felt a needle jab his intestines, he had settled a large share of his debt to Shaky – he felt entitled to better treatment. The thought of his true worth stung him. He stood staring at the barman, turned his head to the door, then glanced back: the barman's firm gaze was still fixed in Henderson's direction. 'You not hear me? Fuck off . . . Now.' He took a step forward and Henderson backed away.

As he went, an old man at the bar raised a finger, pushed his way past him, and ordered a pint. The bare wood boards creaked as Henderson walked towards the line of white light that sat beneath the door. As he took the handle the flat wall dimly reflected the street lights outside the bar. The wind bit as he stepped onto the pavement; bitter rain lashed his face as he walked.

Crawley's car had been ticketed where he had parked; Henderson leaned over and grabbed the sticker from the windscreen, scrunched it up. The wind caught the piece of paper as it dropped towards the gutter; he watched it roll down the street, picking up pace. He opened the door, slumped inside the car and slotted the key in the ignition. As he released the handbrake, the wheels spun on the wet road and he accelerated towards the city centre through the falling rain.

By Crawley's house, Henderson had released and clamped his teeth so many times that his molars ached. He felt a still fury bubbling inside him as he slung the wheel towards the driveway and braked heavily. For a moment he sat staring out the window at the lashing rain then a set of twitching curtains in a neighbouring property grabbed his attention. The act seemed to jar him back to consciousness; he reached for the door handle and opened up. In the pathway towards Crawley's home, Henderson jogged, cupping his burning cigarette in his hand to shelter it from the wind and rain. He had always smoked like this – even before prison – but the movement reminded him of life on the inside once again, of smoking in the yard. What had he done? he thought. He'd taken a man prisoner. What was it Crawley had called it? Kidnapping. Mistaken identity.

'Bullshit,' said Henderson.

He knew Crawley was guilty, he didn't need a judge and jury to confirm it. The man was a nonce, a beast. He'd preyed on young girls; he'd terrified Angela. He tried to remind himself of this as he opened up the door to Crawley's home. Henderson still felt ice in his veins from the reception he'd received at the Wheatsheaf, but it mattered less to him now. He would take the rest of the cash from Crawley's accounts tomorrow and he'd settle some more of that score then. He'd be free of Boaby Stevens eventually and he'd be able to think about his next move.

Henderson called out as he closed the door, 'Here's Johnny!'

There was no reply; the place seemed too quiet.

Henderson lowered the keys onto the hallway table, rubbed the rain from his hair. He settled his breathing for a moment to listen for movement: he heard nothing. The place was silent. He leaned forward, rested the palm of his hand on the banister, looked up the stairs; the house had darkened now but there was no sign of lights burning. He scratched an itch on his brow, said, 'Get a grip, Hendy . . .'

Henderson knew he had the situation under control:

he'd tied Crawley up in the front room, he'd checked the knots, they were tight, secure. He smiled to himself, moved towards the living room door. As he grabbed for the handle he felt his breathing still, he double-blinked, halted his action and stopped still.

Something wasn't right, it was too quiet.

He felt his heart rate ramp as he turned the handle.

The living room was in darkness. The curtains were still open, the night outside showed a catenation of street lamps burning, bathing the pavement in a sickly orange glow. It took Henderson's eyes a moment to adjust to the darkness, then he settled on where he had left Crawley, tied and bound, before he left to pay his debt to Boaby Stevens. There was a pale patch of carpet and a long loop of unfurled nylon rope, but no Crawley.

Henderson stepped forward, turned towards the wall and groped in the darkness for the light switch.

When the room became illuminated he called out, 'Crawley, you fucking bastard!'

Chapter 35

ANGELA MICKLE PULLED HER KNEES up before her where she sat on the filthy mattress. She rocked on her bony rear and ran the palms of her hands down the fronts of her skinny legs. A car's horn sounded beyond the window, making her wince; at once she raised her hands to her ears and held them there, tried to block out the world beyond the mattress. Angela knew she should be out on the Links, scoring punters, scoring drugs. She knew that was why she felt the way she did – why her insides felt like they were being slow-cooked over an open flame – but there was a reason why she couldn't face the Links.

She didn't know how long Henderson had been away, she found it hard to record the passing of time – all time was withdrawal, minutes soon became hours, which became days. She knew, however, the longer he stayed away, the greater danger she may be in. Henderson didn't know Colin Crawley; not like she did.

'No. No. No.'

The memories returned when she thought about him.

254

Angela didn't want to remember what knowing Crawley had meant.

She turned, twisted herself on the mattress to face the wall. 'No.' It didn't matter how many times she said it though, the images, the pictures and the words, *his* words, were still there.

'Angela,' he was calling to her.

'Angela . . .' She could hear his voice, it hadn't changed. As a young girl she had been flattered by the voice to begin with. He was a grown-up, an adult. Mr Crawley was her teacher, her gymnastics coach. No one had shown any interest in her until he had. She felt special – he made her feel special.

'Angela . . .' The word set her muscles harder, her toes curled into the mattress. She closed her eyes and tried to think of something else but he was there, taunting her wherever she looked. Henderson thought he was just a square peg, a teacher, but he wasn't. She had tried to tell him that he was a danger, but it hadn't registered.

'He's a fucking beast, Ange,' he'd said. 'A beast! I've dealt with them before.'

She didn't want to know what he planned to do with Crawley, she didn't want to think about it, but the longer he was away from her the more scared she became. With Henderson around she felt safe, he looked after her on the Links and made sure no harm came to her from the punters or the girls. But Crawley was different, he was capable of much worse than Henderson imagined; she knew, she'd seen it. She remembered again his eyes bulging as he wrestled her to the ground and then she felt his hot breath on her neck as he pressed himself onto her in the field.

'Oh, God . . .' Ange's voice was low and strained,

strangled in her vocal cords. A dull gaze settled in her eyes as she looked towards the window and the street below. It was as good as dark. The street lamps were on. She began to feel the walls of the small flat enclosing her.

She rose, ran to the opposite end of the room and stood by the window. A packet of cigarettes sat on the ledge, a box of matches on top – she snatched them up. Her hands trembled as she clawed open the box and shook out a cigarette. She got the filter to her mouth and struck a match; the tobacco smoke tasted good but was a poor substitute for what she really wanted. As she smoked, Angela noticed the dark black crescents that sat under her nails – Henderson had always warned her about that, said it put off the punters; she somehow felt engulfed by a great sadness at the thought of Henderson now and wondered what had become of him.

'Neil, Neil . . . where are you?'

The cigarette burned quickly and when it was finished she stubbed the dowp on the windowsill and let the cold night breeze take the crushed filter tip away. She had seen worse nights; it was dry. A crowd of people had gathered on the other side of the road by the bus stop; it made her feel safe to see so many strangers, but at the same time the loneliness she felt in the empty flat started to prod her. Angela picked up the cigarettes and the matches and walked to the door; her shoes lay beside the skirting, she fitted her feet into them and reached for her coat. She stowed away the cigarettes and checked she had a store of condoms. Her heart was pounding as she opened the front door and walked towards the stairwell.

Angela gripped the banister tightly as she descended the staircase. Her high heels sounded noisily on the stone steps and she tried to raise herself up on her toes to compensate.

She felt self-conscious, but she longed to be around people now – the flat seemed suddenly unsafe. Her thoughts had left Henderson, she was preoccupied with herself and her survival through the night; she believed if she could score enough money for drugs then at least she wouldn't need to think about Crawley; that would be taken care of.

Outside a moonless sky sat low and dark like a backcloth to the tenements. The wind swept litter along the street and struck at Angela's bare legs. She dug her hands deeper in her pockets, balled fists as she scanned the faces in the crowd. Crawley was out there, she knew it, sensed it. She wished Henderson was here, he would talk sense to her; Angela knew she was always letting her thoughts run away with her, that's what Henderson had said: 'Leave the thinking to me, Ange, you're not fit for it.' She liked that, liked the feeling of putting all the responsibility in someone else's hands. But what if something had happened to him? What if Crawley had got the better of Henderson? She knew it could happen, she knew what he was capable of. She could never forget what Crawley was capable of.

Angela picked up her pace, her heels clacked on the hard paving flags; her heart rate started to ramp up. A tightening in her chest began to constrict her breathing and she slowed, balancing herself on the wall of the late-night grocer's store with an outstretched palm. She started to cough, spat up some gelatinous bile. People walking past stared at her, she caught one of them shaking her head in her direction.

'What's your fucking problem, eh?'

The woman looked away, grabbed at the scarf around her neck, tightened it as she strode off at an increased pace.

'Aye, nothing to fucking say, eh?' Angela roared at her; she found her breath again, felt emboldened as she started off for the Links with the sounds of the street and the traffic ululating in her ears.

Cars had started to patrol the edges of the Links already. Old Cavaliers with middle-aged men craning their necks over the dash to check out the flesh on offer. Angela spotted one of the girls getting into a Volvo; there was a 'Baby on Board' sticker visible through the back window – it made her smile to think of the punter going back to his family after spending hard-earned wages on a tumble with a whore. No one was innocent, she thought. Everyone was tainted in some way, there was none of us perfect. She knew why she was walking the Links, what had driven her to this low in her life. She could have been somebody else once, she knew that too. She could have been the stay-at-home wife with the babies and the big telly and the weekends away; but she could also have been married to the bastard driving the Volvo, they weren't better than her just because they lived a different way. People were trash, she'd met enough of them to form that judgement.

After an hour on the Links Angela had collected close to ninety pounds; it wasn't enough. She doubted whether Henderson would be back to take his share – she had come to that conclusion before she left the flat – but even so, ninety wasn't enough for her needs. She drew her jacket tight round her shoulders, looked towards the sky. The gloom of the night had settled above the rooftops where a blunt moon had appeared, partitioning the street and the Links with a waxy sheen. Angela withdrew a cigarette, asked one of the girls for a light.

'Quiet night, now,' said Kirsty.

'Might pick up.'

'Doubt it, think there must be a game on.'

Angela looked up the road; there was a man standing beyond the glare of the street lamp. 'Here's a punter now.'

'Lucky you . . .'

Angela smiled, 'I only need one and I'm off, Kirsty.'

'Think I'll be ahead of you.' The brass walked away, in the opposite direction, as Angela strode out towards the man on the other side of the street. He was hunched against the wall, his face hidden. He wore a long baggy coat and the breeze caught the folds, sending them flapping like sails.

Angela called out to him, 'You looking for business?'

There was no answer; the man barely moved, only seemed to shrink further into the shadow.

Angela took a last drag on her cigarette, flicked the butt into the street and hurried her steps. Punters were wary, some would bolt if they thought they might have been seen. She knew to play cautious; as the man turned and made for the lane, she followed. Angela was only two or three steps into the darkness when Crawley turned and clasped a hand on her mouth and dragged her kicking and trying to scream towards the depths of the narrow passage.

Angela's eyes flickered as she watched Crawley's features come into focus. She tried to yell out but there was no power left in her voice; she couldn't even breathe as Crawley held his hand over her mouth and nostrils. She thought she might pass out and for a second she hoped she would – that would be the end of it surely; if she passed out, she wouldn't come round. Something caused her to struggle with what strength she had; it was as if she was drowning, flailing her arms to keep her afloat. She felt herself lifted off the ground; one of her shoes came off and then the other made contact with the wall of the lane and she pushed herself away with all her remaining strength.

'Stop struggling, Angela,' said Crawley. His voice was calm, familiar. It flung her back in time. 'That's better. I always knew you were a smart girl.' Crawley released his grip on Angela's face and neck; he looked down at her.

'Wha . . .' Angela tried to speak but the words were trapped in her.

Crawley pushed into her, she backed away. She put her hands out to feel her way, there was a recess; she backed into it and Crawley followed.

'What d-do you want with me?'

Crawley continued to push towards her, she felt the back of the doorway. There was a handle, she turned to face it, grabbed it, but it didn't move. She rested her head on the door, sobbed. 'Please . . .'

'Angela, come on now . . . You know me better than that, surely?'

She cried harder now. 'Are you going to kill me?'

'Why would I want to do that . . . *here*?' Crawley raised his hands at his sides as if he was weighing the air.

Angela turned back to face him; her eyes widened as she took in the full glare of Crawley's face. 'I-I don't know.'

'And neither do I, Angela . . . You do know why I am here, though, don't you?'

She shook, tried to move to her side but Crawley copied her movements and blocked her way. 'What have you done with Neil?'

'Ah, your boyfriend . . . Now we're getting to the crux of the matter. So you knew he came to see me at school, did you? Of course, you must have, how else would he have found out if you hadn't told him?' There was a sound of movement at the entrance to the lane; Crawley turned away, a cat mewed and he seemed to settle. He put his

260

hand in his pocket, removed a bunch of plastic cable ties, started to loop them together.

'What are you doing?' she said.

'You made a mistake, Angela . . . You should never have told anyone about our little secret.'

'I didn't . . . I didn't tell . . .'

He reached forward, 'Give me your arms.'

'No.' She pinned herself against the doorway again, called out, 'Help! Help me . . .'

Crawley reached a hand to her throat, said, 'Now I'm warning you . . .'

Angela struggled harder, reached out with her nails. 'Help!'

'Stop fucking about!' Crawley grabbed one of her wrists, slipped her hand through the cable tie and tightened it. She pushed her way past him as he slipped the second loop over her other hand, then the sound of fast-moving footsteps from the lane seemed to still him.

'Ange! . . . Ange, you OK?' It was Kirsty.

Crawley loosened his grip on the ties and let Angela's hands fall to her side; as he bolted into the lane, she slumped against the door and sobbed.

Chapter 36

NEIL HENDERSON GIRDED HIMSELF AGAINST the cold wind as he walked, trying hard to still the rage he felt burning inside him. He cleared his throat as he approached the bus stop, spat fast onto the street. He raised his head to look over at the windows of the flat he shared with Angela; he didn't want to return there but knew he had no choice. Crawley had fled, but he couldn't have gone far; Henderson knew he wouldn't have gone far. There was no point: what would it take, a call? One call, that was all that was needed to put Crawley away. Henderson knew he had him; the beast would be back, had to be back, had to return to his home and face him. Henderson held all the cards, there was no question of that, the only thing he wondered about now was just what the hell Crawley thought he was playing at.

Henderson waited for a gap in the traffic, picked up his pace as he ran between a Lothian Bus and a blue Micra; the small car started to roll forward as he stepped in front of it and he stopped in his tracks.

'What the fuck you playing at?' he roared. He raised up his hands then slammed them down on the bonnet of the car; it was an old man behind the wheel, he looked at Henderson over the dash and shook his head. It came as incitement to the younger man. 'You fucking old prick!' He kicked at the bumper, sneered again and then walked off, saluting the V-sign as he went. By the other side of the street Henderson was still venting his anger, kicking out at the door to the stairwell and stomping in.

Inside the stair, Henderson slammed the door with the heel of his shoe and then leaned his back flat against it. He let out a long, slow exhalation of breath and then he groaned audibly as he banged the back of his head into the wood panel. He jerked his head forward, then back again. The sound came like a hard slap at first, but as he increased the intensity of the blows, dull thuds like heavy footfalls echoed up the stairwell. He clenched his teeth shut. A rigid sneer set on his face as he pushed himself off the door and took to the first step.

Outside the flat Henderson paused for a moment; his fingers tingled as he drew fists and released them quickly. His thoughts turned over; danced between Crawley and his disappearance and the humiliation he had felt trying to pay off Boaby Stevens in the Wheatsheaf. He felt trapped; nothing was going to plan. It was supposed to be easy: hit the beast for a few quid and move on. Get rid of the deadweight around his neck that Angela had become and make a fresh start. It didn't matter where, all that mattered was when. Henderson wanted to move on *now*. He grasped the door handle and walked in. 'Ange, where the fuck are you?'

There was a groan from the front room. Henderson felt his cheeks flush as he studied the hallway. The place was in darkness, save for the light from the street that fell through the uncovered window. As he trod the bare boards, a grey half moon appeared through the window pane and drew a sickly gleam over the contents of the room. His eyelids twitched as he let his vision adjust to the new setting; on the mattress, curled in a ball, was Angela.

'Jesus Christ . . . Look at the fucking state of you,' said Henderson.

She let out a dull, muddled trail of words. He knew at once she was wasted.

'Is this what you've been at tonight is it? . . . Fucking wasted again.' He grabbed her hair in his fist and turned her over; her cheekbones shone in the light of the half moon. 'You fucking piece of shit . . .'

'Hendy . . . I was . . .'

She didn't get the words out before she was thrown heavily towards the mattress. Henderson stood back, cleared all expression from his face as he watched her holding her stomach, writhing in drug-addled confusion. Something snapped in him; his blank features became animated as he pulled back his fist and brought it down on Angela's face.

She screamed out, at first it seemed in terror, and then, as the blows rained, her cries signalled a deeper agony. 'Stop. *Stop* . . .'

'I'll fucking stop all right . . . stop when you've had some fucking sense drummed into you!'

Henderson kept up his attack until he lost his strength; the blows became weaker, not worth his effort. As he raised himself, withdrew, Angela was a curled, sobbing, bleeding tangle of limbs on the floor. He watched her for a moment; she lay trembling and rocking, crying. He felt no sympathy for her, she was trash.

He moved to the side of the window and lit a cigarette. His cheeks creased at the corners of his mouth as he inhaled deeply. The nicotine stilled his surging pulse for a moment. He coughed, ran open fingers through his hair.

'Hendy . . .'

'Shut the fuck up!'

He turned towards the window, looked out at the throngs of people on the pavement, the lines of slow-moving traffic clogging the road. The wind soughed against the pane and shook the frame in a loose rattle above the sill. The chill air in the flat made his moist forehead tingle after his exertions. He took another draw on his cigarette, turned back to Angela. Her drowsy eyes flickered as she took him in.

'What's your fucking problem?' he said.

She scowled, pinching her bleeding nose and lips. 'I-I tried to tell you . . . I t-tried . . .'

'Tell me fucking what?' He pointed at her, shook his head and looked away. 'Ah, what the fuck do you know . . . fucking junkie.'

Angela pitched her voice higher, rose onto her knees. 'He came to the Links . . . I was out there, I saw him.'

Henderson spat, 'Crawley?'

Angela held out her hands, 'Yes, he grabbed m-me.'

His breathing had steadied now, but suddenly started to shorten again. 'Why . . . I mean, what did he want?'

Angela swayed; unsteady where she positioned herself beside the mattress, she reached out a hand to the edge of the door frame to hold herself up. 'He wanted to take me . . . He wanted to scare you.'

Henderson laughed, he scratched at the edge of his nose then quickly took another draw on the cigarette. 'He thinks . . .' he pointed to Angela with the tip of the cigarette, 'I give two fucks about you, he thought that?' He laughed, a spluttering guttural wheeze. The thought stuck in his chest like a winding. 'He's mistaken; fucking sorely so . . .'

Angela slumped to the side, reached out a hand to support herself as the delicate balance of her weight shifted. Her hair flopped in front of her eyes and she lowered her head towards the floor. Henderson watched her with a heavy thought settling on his mind; he stubbed his cigarette and headed towards the door. At the mattress he stood over Angela for a moment, contemplated levelling a boot at her head but the effort seemed unnecessary; she was already out of it. He reached under the mattress and removed the small mauve-coloured diary that she had shown him and tucked it in his jacket pocket. He bent over, grabbed her by the hair, raised her head off the floor a few inches, 'You better get that hole of yours out on those Links . . . There's no free fucking lunches in this world!' As he released his grip, Angela's head connected with the bare floorboards making a solid thud.

In Crawley's car, on the way back to the teacher's home, Henderson turned over his thoughts. His face sat tense as he held his jaw shut. There was a bitter taste in his mouth and his insides felt raw. What had Crawley been playing at? Showing up on the Links, trying to put a scare on Angela. Was he stupid? It was him Crawley needed to worry about, Henderson told himself. He gripped the wheel harder, felt his fingernails digging into the trim.

'Fucking daft prick,' he mouthed to himself.

The traffic had cleared, the roads starting to take on the deserted feel of this time of the night. Edinburgh gave over its centre to taxi cabs and stretch limos ferrying hen nights to and from the pubs and clubs after a certain hour. The

266

city wasn't a place for people who lived there at this time; it was for the out-of-towners, the party people.

Henderson passed girls, teetering on high heels in short, tight dresses, and rowdy groups of drunken revellers – boys, acting like men and their obverse: men who should know better than acting like boys. The place sickened Henderson at this time of night, it was all kebab shop fights and punters puking and pissing. He'd had enough of mixing it with their sort; where was his share of the good times? Where was his ease and comfort? He didn't want to hear another word out of Angela; he didn't want to be on the Links watching her back or watching to make sure she was on her back. He'd had enough. He wanted something else, something he felt he'd earned, felt he deserved.

As he pulled into Crawley's driveway, Henderson noticed the bulb burning in the front room: he was home. 'Cheeky prick,' he said. 'Fucking sitting there bold as brass . . .'

Henderson killed the engine, opened the door and stepped out. He stood on the driveway scree for a moment, turned towards the house and then slammed the car door as loud as possible. He waited to see if there would be any movement in the house: the sound of the back door opening or the light going out. Nothing. Crawley was either unfazed or fronting it out like he was. Henderson felt his throat stiffen and his nostrils widen as he gasped a deep breath.

The front door was unlocked. He moved in, closed it behind him. The lamp with the tassels in the hallway was burning. It looked all too cosy. Henderson set his gaze on the door to the living room and stretched out a pace towards where he knew Crawley would be waiting.

As he entered the room the television blared; *Coronation Street* was just going into a commercial break, the ginger

cat loping over the shed roof. Henderson watched the screen
for a second or two, then followed the light as it bounced
off the window pane. He moved towards the Venetian blinds,
closed them and then returned to the television and switched
it off. As he did so, Crawley appeared from the kitchen
holding a mug of tea. He stalled where he stood, splay-
footed, for a moment and then he proceeded into the living
room and resumed his place on the sofa.

'You must think I'm a fucking daftie, mate?' said
Henderson.

Crawley sipped his tea, rested the mug on the arm of the
sofa. 'I can't say I've given you much thought . . . Lately.'

Henderson walked in front of him, 'Just what the hell is
that supposed to mean? Have you fucking-well lost it?'

Crawley turned the handle of his mug to the other side,
raised the tea to his lips and started to blow on it. His lips
were pinched as Henderson slapped the mug from his hands
and gripped his throat. 'Don't get cocky with me, you little
cunt. I'm not a man who takes kindly to that.'

'I've cancelled my cards,' said Crawley.

'You what?'

'I think you heard. You'll get nothing more out of me.'

Henderson stepped back, his brows furrowed and lined.
His eyebrows sat low above his thinned eyes. 'I don't
believe what I'm hearing. Do you want me to pick up the
phone to the filth? Is that it, you got some hard-on for the
world to know you're a fucking beast all of a sudden?'

Crawley smiled, 'Ah, now that might have worked
earlier . . . But not now.'

'Oh, you think?'

'I know.'

Henderson stepped aside, raised a finger to wag in

Crawley's face. 'You think that because Ange is on the Links now that makes an ounce of difference . . . Fucking no chance. They'll toast your bollocks over a fire, beast.'

'I don't think so . . .'

Henderson smiled, 'I know you saw her, on the Links . . . You think putting a scare on her makes any difference? It's me you have to worry about.'

Crawley crossed his legs, started to drum a finger on his kneecap. '*You* threatened me . . . And *you* put a prostitute up to this. There's not a court in the land will take your claims seriously. But more than that, I'm sure Angela will be too delicate to go through with any plans you might have.'

Henderson edged forward, a truculent gleam lit in his eye. He dipped inside his jacket pocket and removed the diary, threw it into Crawley's lap. 'Read it and weep, beast.'

'What's this?' He raised the diary, turned over a few pages. 'Some kind of diary . . . A schoolgirl's diary.'

'It's Ange's diary . . . She kept it at school, and guess what, you feature quite prominently in there, beast.'

Crawley thumbed through the pages; his eyes scanned left to right. For a moment he stalled on one of the pages then turned it. He turned another page and seemed to tire of looking at the diary altogether. 'This is nothing . . . You can write anything on paper, it's hardly incriminating.'

Henderson snatched the diary back, tucked it in his pocket. He took his palm across Crawley's face; the smack lit a red streak from chin to brow. 'Don't fucking push it, beast . . . I could easy beat what I want out of you if you prefer.'

Crawley lifted his hands to his head; his crossed leg raised in time with the movement as his bravado left him. 'You've had all I have!'

'Bullshit.'

Crawley raised both feet from the floor and cowered on the sofa; he turned his head to look as Henderson raised his hand to level another blow. 'No. Stop . . .' Crawley reached into his trouser pocket and removed a bundle of notes, crumpled fives and tens. 'Here take it . . . take it!'

Henderson grabbed the cash. 'What the hell is this . . . Thirty-five fucking sheets!'

'It's all I have . . .'

'It's not enough!'

Crawley turned away, anticipating a blow, then sheltered his face beneath his elbow. 'I have twenty more . . . In my jacket, it's in the kitchen.'

Henderson's pallor darkened, 'You're taking the piss.' He slapped the top of Crawley's head with the flat of his hands, 'The piss, you're taking the fucking piss . . .' He brought another blow down, then gripped a fist. 'Do you know what we do inside with beasts who take the piss?' There was no answer. 'No. Well, you're going to fucking find out now, beast.'

Chapter 37

DI ROB BRENNAN PARKED ON the street outside
Robbie's Bar on Leith Walk. He had a strange tingling
sensation playing in the pit of his stomach that he knew
signalled apprehension. It had been some time since he had
met up with Wullie Stuart, a man he held the utmost respect
for since serving under him on the force. Wullie was old
school, what they used to call 'no nonsense' but would
probably be referred to these days as *unaware*, at best, as
difficult at worst. The last time Brennan encountered Wullie
he had been shocked, not by the physical deterioration of
the man – although that in itself was a sort of shock – but
by the way he had gone from a man of action to a man of
inaction in seemingly one fell swoop. It had worried
Brennan at the time – he felt for the old boy; but it had
also been a sobering glimpse of what the future might hold
in store for him when he gave up the DI's role; or indeed,
it gave up on him.

Robbie's was one of the more lauded of Edinburgh's
drinkers; a long, dark and little bedecked bar stretched from

the front door to the back where a mix of hardened blue-noses and tabard-clad office cleaners mingled with the shop and factory workers. It was not a place of shirts and ties, the sight of a mobile phone was greeted with disdain, down-turned mouths and headshakes. City people – Edinburgh's real warts-and-all occupants – held court in Robbie's. There was an unspoken chivalry that surrounded the interior like a poker-room pall; there were house rules here, but they weren't written up and framed on the wall. It was the kind of place where, one step inside, you knew it was different from all the corporate superpubs with their cocktail specials, their discount microwave meals and their shiny teenage servers spouting, 'Have a nice day, sir'.

Brennan walked through the door of the pub and took two paces towards the centre of the room. It was busy, Robbie's was always busy, but it was a kind of busy that Brennan liked. Not jammed; not jumping. Just filled with enough people to create a homely atmosphere that was far enough away from home to let you forget the cares of such a place. A couple at the bar eyed him cautiously; they had a way of appraising him that made him think they were criminals. Brennan was used to it; he knew police stuck out for them – there was a banner draped around his neck that read 'filth' for these people – but that was OK, the opposite was also true. The whole elaborate police–criminal *pas de deux* was as instinctual as the hair rising on a cat's back upon encountering a dog. It was as good a warning sign as any to remind them both to steer clear, or face the consequences, which were rarely pretty for either party. The key was toleration; social exclusivity was impossible and so they walked around each other, noting the other's presence but obviating its impact. Brennan turned a hand into his trouser pocket and drummed fingernails on the bar with his other as he raked the room with his gaze. For a moment he thought he had been the first to arrive but then he spotted Wullie sitting at the far end; the sight of him stung like a lash. His old mentor was slouched over a pint glass, his frame and face shrunken; it struck Brennan that after a certain age time became more precious, the path downhill steeper.

He nodded to the barman, 'Pint, mate . . .' and took a step towards the back of the room.

'I'll drop it over to you.'

'Cheers.'

Brennan tried to keep his mind in gear as he approached Wullie; he knew why he wanted to see him. The social stuff, the interaction that added up to friendship was never spoken of; it had to remain below the mask of manliness that their social mores had taught them to wear. Brennan might indeed have felt more for Wullie than his own father but the thought of ever expressing such inner workings was laughable to him. Years had passed in each other's company; secrets and hurts had been shared that would have felled many a man and yet they would both go to their graves knowing how much they had meant to each other but never having given voice to a single emotion. Did it matter? Did the words carry so much import that they needed to be said? Brennan knew the answer; some things could not be said with words, some things were only cheapened when brought into the open air.

'Hello, Wullie.' The older man shuffled his feet behind the table, placed his palms either side of his pint glass and went to push himself up. Brennan raised a hand, 'No, don't get up . . . I'm just going to sit down.'

Wullie nodded, 'Christ, you're looking well.'

A laugh. 'Well, I'm still here.'

'Always something.'

The barman appeared in front of them, put Brennan's pint on the table and retreated.

'Cheers, then.'

'Aye, I suppose so . . .' Wullie took a sip of his pint and placed it back on the beer mat. He fingered a stray drop that had landed on the tabletop. He seemed distracted, unsure of himself. 'Look, I really was sorry to hear about you and the wife.'

He obviously couldn't remember her name; maybe never knew it. That didn't matter thought Brennan; Wullie and himself had never been that type of friends. They had never entertained in each other's homes, they had never shared intimacies of their family lives. That kind of detail was sacred, another part of their existences that needed to be kept out of the light; if they were both family men, once, then those times had passed into ignominy like so much else.

'Don't be sorry.' Brennan's reply served as a stopper on the topic; it was stored away now, not to be returned to.

Wullie gulped another mouthful of his drink, 'So, you working a case?'

The old detective must know he was working a case; it was a conversational gambit. A verbal cue to commence with the real reason for Brennan's visit.

'Aye . . . bad one.'

'Children?' said Wullie.

Brennan shook his head, 'Well, as good as . . . teenagers.'

Wullie returned his pint to the table, rubbed at the spikes of white stubble on his chin. 'Christ, you've got the case they splashed all over the fucking papers . . .'

274

'You read it?'

'Of course I read it . . . Everyone in Edinburgh's read that. Jesus, painful for the families.'

Brennan eased himself back in his chair, the cushion sank to accommodate his frame. He reached out for his pint glass, raised it and gulped a long draught. The cold beer worked like a palliative; he wiped white foam from the tip of his lip and said, 'They're in bits. Can't blame them, anyone would be.'

Wullie was shaking his head, rubbing his fingers over his thighs. Brennan noticed the knees of his Farah trousers were shiny.

'Where are you at with it?' said Wullie.

Brennan exhaled a long breath, 'We have some forensic . . . It's a serial murder.'

'You got a profiler?'

'Joe Lorrimer.'

Wullie raised an eyebrow, 'Joe's good.'

Brennan reached into the blue folder he had in his document wallet, it was the profiler's report. He held it before Wullie. 'You want to see this?'

'Not got my glasses, want to give me the highlights?'

Brennan opened up the folder, 'OK, let me see . . .'

Wullie cut it, 'I warn you . . . first I hear of *constellated disadvantage* or the like, I'm off!'

The DI smiled, 'I'll edit as I go . . . Right, the psych fit is quite detailed: there's a strong methodical mind at work, systematic and a lover of routine. It's almost pathological so we're talking about an intense individual, someone likely to be able to keep that under wraps, though perhaps this could bubble to the surface now and again . . .'

'So he could hold down a good job.'

'Easy, no bother.' Brennan returned to the list, 'There's a superior streak which would make it hard to form intimate relationships . . . Perhaps as a result of a family trauma, likely a conflicted relationship with his mother.'

'A loner,' said Wullie.

Brennan nodded, returned to the file. 'The superiority complex manifests in a need to dominate.'

'A control freak.'

'. . . Any marital set-up would be unique, if not bizarre, because of the demands he'd place on obsequiousness. The home would be a microcosm of control, pseudo-moralising, elitism . . .'

Wullie held up a hand, 'OK, I think I get the picture before you delve any further into fucking psychobabble.'

Brennan closed the folder over, smiled. He raised his pint and watched Wullie do the same. 'So, what do you think?'

He sighed. 'Any trophies taken?'

'Eyes . . . And there was genital mutilation, but that was hidden on the corpses.'

'Jesus . . . a sick bastard.'

'True.'

Wullie scratched the edge of his mouth, 'This is a dangerous man you have on your hands; if the forensic matches the two killings then he could be lining up another kill.'

'Why would you say that?'

Wullie leaned back in his seat, crossed his legs. 'It's the control . . . That's what it's all about. You think he's the controller, but he's not, he's controlled . . . by impulses.'

'The impulse to kill?'

'He's ruled by impulses. The routines are impulse-driven, it's like an intense OCD, he regulates his life to ease the control impulses . . . That's what the killing is, he can't get away from that. He can store it up and up but then he's into a state of tension and fear and there's only one way to release that.'

Brennan leaned forward, 'Then why the gap, between the killings?'

'He feels remorse, not like you and I, but he feels differently to the victim afterwards. The tension's been released, he's been let off the hook . . . That might last some time, but the mindset isn't changed – can't change – the impulses come back eventually and they have to be dealt with.'

'So what triggers the impulse?'

'Fuck knows – brain chemistry, the mother was a control freak – does it matter? What matters is, Rob, this bastard is in your manor and he's going to strike again. He can't avoid it, and neither can you.'

Brennan drained the last of his pint, stood up. 'Another?'

'Why not.'

At the bar the DI mulled over what Wullie had told him; much of it was old news but what he had managed to glean was a decent second opinion. His own theories were well formed, Joe Lorrimer's were too, but what he needed was confirmation that neither of them were off course. If he had been missing something Wullie would have pointed it out, he always did, but the fact that he had merely confirmed Brennan's worst fears only added to the certainty that he would soon have another killing on his hands.

Brennan returned to the table with the drinks. Wullie stared vacantly into the middle distance.

'What is it?'

'Oh, Nothing . . . Just thinking about an old case.'

'Relevant?'

'Maybe.'

'Well, tell me more.'

Wullie uncrossed his legs, played with the perma-crease in his trousers. 'That profile, I'd say was missing one thing . . . These bastards usually have someone looking out for them, someone covering their tracks.'

'A wife you mean?'

'Maybe, aye . . . Or a parent. A sibling . . . It's a lot to organise, a lot to get right for one person. It's also a lot to go wrong, and with as much heat on the bastard as you're applying I'd say he could do with someone to help cover his tracks.'

Finding the killer was a big enough ask for Brennan; finding his helper could wait till after the event, he thought. But, it was something to think about, even though he had plenty to think about as it was. 'Look, there was something else I meant to ask you . . .'

Wullie's expression changed, he seemed to lighten around the shoulders, relax more. 'What was that?'

Brennan twisted round to face him, 'You got anything on Jim Gallagher?'

Wullie shrugged, 'Big Jim . . . Never liked the prick, is that enough?'

Brennan laughed, it was good to have another of his opinions endorsed. 'Join the club . . . No, it was just something Charlie said.'

The old man playfully landed a punch on the DI's arm, 'Och, he's meaning the raffle thing from years back. Fucker staged a raffle at the station, charity thing y'know, but he fiddled it so that himself and two vice ponces picked up the prizes . . . Was a big stooshie at the time, but Jim's a fly bastard and everybody knows it.'

Brennan bit, 'What do you mean, *fly*?'

'Just what I say, he's a bit wide. I wouldn't trust him as far as I could throw him, but he's not the only copper on the force like that . . . A lot of it will have to do with his upbringing, couldn't have been easy that. I always cut him some slack for the boys' home stuff.'

'Boys' home?'

Wullie creased his brows, 'He was brought up in a home, an orphanage, Dungarn it was, a right shit-hole . . . I think his parents died when he was about five or six, was a car crash in Fife, nasty business.'

Brennan picked up his pint, held it before his lips, said, 'Really, I didn't know that.'

Chapter 38

DI ROB BRENNAN WOKE TO the sound of the traffic's hum on Leith Walk. His neck ached and there was a solid, persistent pounding in his left temple. Was this the result of the few pints he'd had with Wullie the night before? He didn't think so. He could still handle a few pints, hadn't fallen that low, yet. He pushed his stocky frame off the sagging bed; the springs wheezed. As he looked down at the thin, flattened pillow he realised the culprit of his discomfort. He patted a hand on it, attempted to ruffle the contents, but it failed to make any difference to the deflated item. Brennan shook his head, felt another pang of pain in his neck, and rose. The springs sighed this time. He looked down at the bed and tried to remember the reason why he was living this way; how he had come to this sorry pass.

Brennan knew he was lonely, knew the symptoms. At times like this, disparate thoughts came to mind, floated, formed their own surreal mosaic. A laundry ticket, once lost, found tucked in a fold of his wallet. A girl he once knew called . . . now what was her name? She had played tennis and her parents were well off. His first watch – not a digital one – he'd wanted a digital one but his mother had said, 'No, Rob, they're just a fad!' Then there was the summer holiday, paddling on the shore. A wedding day – his wedding day – and the sense of dread wondering would she show? 'Why not, Rob?' his brother and his best man had said. 'She loves you, doesn't she?' Brennan stopped himself, flattened out the spiral of his thoughts. What was love anyway? He loved his wife once; he had a dog he loved once . . . and a brother.

The older Brennan got the more he found himself questioning. When he was younger he was filled with assumptions; random musings on everything and anything, arrived at from he knew not where. These opinions of his younger self became appropriated, became stamps of his own personality; he had had these thoughts – whether or not he had originated them didn't matter – they were opinions he wore like laurels. As he watched those laurels wither and die he discarded them, wondered why he had ever become so proud of them in the first place. And if he was being honest, felt an inward shame at the shallow vapidity of his sometime immaturity. He had moved on now, certainly; he was no longer that callow youth, or the preoccupied careerist determined to distinguish himself among other fools. But what was he now? He looked around the grimy bedsit that he couldn't bring himself to call home. Brennan felt like a failure, not because of the meagreness of his lodgings, nothing so superficial. He felt a failure because he had reached his forties and never felt less sure of himself, of who he was or where he was heading. At least in the past he felt like he was in the right – even when he was assuredly in the wrong – but now, he didn't know a thing; least of all himself. An old line from a play he had studied in secondary school came to him, 'This above all: to thine ownself be true.' Brennan smirked. He felt lost, if he was being truthful to himself.

On the road to Fettes Station, DI Rob Brennan attempted to distract himself from what lay ahead with the antics of a shock jock on the radio. He tried hard to tap into the show, to give himself over to the bear-pit atmosphere that had callers queuing up to rant at the host, but he couldn't do it. The subject of the show was the country's swing towards a nationalist government. The rights and wrongs of independence, of Scotland separating from its larger southern neighbour. It was a topical subject, a worthy subject, but the DJ treated it as mere entertainment to rattle the masses. That sort of thing was for other people, thought Brennan, not for him. It was not worthy of any space inside his mind, not alongside the brutal killing and mutilation of young girls that he would soon have to disburse to an expectant media. He was discomfited by the thought of what awaited him; knew that any contact with the press was likely to bring trouble in equal measure to reward. But this was the pass he had arrived at. There was a time when any action was better than inaction and that time had been reached; Wullie had said it himself the night before – this killer will strike again. Brennan didn't want to have another murder on his books, or his conscience. The memories he carried from the scene of Lindsey Sloan's murder were never far from the front of his mind; as was the pain of her grieving parents.

In the car park Brennan stilled the engine, turned off the radio and reached onto the passenger's seat to retrieve his document wallet. Some bubblegum wrappers caught his eye in the footwell – they had been left there by Sophie the last time she had been in the car – the sight of them dug at his heart. For a moment, Brennan had to ease himself back in his seat, draw a deep breath. It was at moments like this he realised how hard it was not to have his daughter in his life any more. He had grown accustomed to their regular daily sparring and its absence felt like a part of him had been excavated. He removed his mobile phone from his jacket, toyed with the idea of calling her but rejected it. She would be bemused by a call from her father at this hour, at any hour. As Joyce had said, he had brought this on himself. He returned the phone to his pocket and opened the car's door.

Inside the station Charlie looked up from the front desk and tapped a finger off his forehead, 'Morning, Rob.'

'Charlie.' The DI approached the desk and readied himself for the morning's first bulletin.

'The hack pack's in.'

Brennan nodded. 'Good numbers?'

'Telly crew and the usual suspects . . .' He leaned over the counter, folded his arms, 'Fucking Benny's in there already, giving the glad hand.'

'It's his job.'

Charlie turned down the corners of his mouth. 'I thought it was yours.'

Brennan knew Charlie well enough to pick up the subtext to his chatter. 'What's that supposed to mean?'

The desk sergeant looked down the hall, nodded. 'You better get moving, mate; way it's looking Jim Gallagher's going to be fronting things.'

Brennan felt a flash of heat in his chest, his shirt collar seemed to tighten suddenly. He knew Charlie was watching him for a reaction, and he knew to hide it. 'I see.' He let the words escape slowly and eased himself away to the corridor. 'Catch you later, Charlie.'

'Away to kick up are you?'

Brennan smiled, a subtle one. He walked off slowly.

If Benny had put Gallagher in the press conference then the task had just got a lot more difficult than it needed to be. Brennan knew the press were used to seeing only one representative of the force on the podium and if Gallagher was there too that could make for awkward questioning. He felt his grip on the document wallet tightening as he reached the door to the press conference. DS Stevie McGuire stood on the edge of a group near the Chief Superintendent; he caught sight of Brennan and eased himself away. As he crossed the floor he raised open palms. 'Good morning, boss.'

'Is it?' said Brennan. 'What the fuck is Gallagher doing in here?'

'Ah, I know . . . First I knew of it was when I got in ten minutes ago. Apparently you're sharing the stage.'

Brennan tipped back his head, 'Jesus Christ . . . That's all I need.'

McGuire put his hands in his pockets, stared down towards his shoes. 'Erm, does it seriously mess things up for you, or are you just pissed at Jim?'

Brennan shook his head, 'I don't want Gallagher front of house, full stop.' He edged around the DS, made a purposeful stride towards the Chief Super. As he reached the small gathering, Benny had already turned to face him. He placed a hand on Brennan's elbow and led him off to the side.

'I thought I'd put Jim in with you too . . .'

284

'I don't think that's a good idea . . .'

Benny stopped in his tracks, turned to face Brennan. 'You mistake me, I'm not consulting you on the matter. I'm telling you how it is.'

Brennan tried to speak, 'I really don't think . . .'

Benny cut in, 'Good. Don't think, leave that to me. Now get over there and say your piece.' The Chief Super moved away to the seating area and motioned the reporters and television crew to take their places.

Brennan heard his teeth click as he closed his mouth and walked towards the desk. There was a hum of movement, some chatter and the scraping of chairs on the hard flooring as the reporters moved into place. Two uniforms nodded towards the Chief Super as they were directed to leave the room, presumably, thought Brennan, to retrieve the Sloans. He didn't want to think about how they might react in front of the press pack, but then, he didn't want to think about how Gallagher would react either.

As he removed his overcoat, hung it on the back of the chair, Brennan checked the nameplates that had been put out – he was sitting next to Gallagher. He eased himself behind the long desk, and reached for the water carafe; he was half way to filling his glass as the Sloans appeared under the direction of the uniforms. Gallagher was behind them in a bright white shirt – obviously a new one – and a striped tie. He looked as if he was directing the uniforms, it set a cold needle of sweat running down Brennan's back. He was in charge, not Gallagher; who the bloody hell did he think he was? It was his investigation and he would be the one giving the directions, if there were any to be given.

Brennan watched as the Sloans shuffled behind the desk; he removed his chair and stood up, 'In here, Mrs Sloan.'

She was apprehensive, the colour of her skin a giveaway that she hadn't slept. 'Don't worry about a thing, this will be over in no time. They don't have that long a slot on the news for us . . .'

She returned a delicate smile, sat down. Mr Sloan pushed in the back of her chair, nodded towards Brennan, 'Good morning, Inspector.'

'Hello there . . . I was just saying, this won't take too long.'

Mr Sloan held up a piece of paper, 'I've got it all written down . . . What I need to say.'

'That's good. You better take a seat now.'

There was a moment of dead air, of silence and then the buzz of the overhead lights became apparent. Brennan felt the eyes of the room on him.

'Good morning, ladies and gentlemen, thank you for taking the time to come out here today. If I make some introductions,' he indicated the DI to his right, 'this is Detective Inspector Jim Gallagher, who is assisting in the investigation.' Brennan looked to his left, 'And as you are aware we are investigating the death of Lindsey Sloan and these are her parents who will be making a brief statement in a moment or two.'

A reporter in the front row raised a hand; Brennan flagged him down. 'I'd like you to keep all questions until after the brief statements if you don't mind.'

The reporter withdrew his arm, slunk back in his seat and opened a spiral-bound notebook.

Brennan was first to speak, 'Lothian and Borders Police Force is seeking the assistance of the public in the investigation of the death of Miss Lindsey Sloan.' He felt movement from the Sloans at his side; he continued,

'Lindsey was a local girl, raised in Edinburgh and schooled in Edinburgh. Her death has come as a shock to the community and all at Lothian and Borders Force. We would like to appeal to anyone who has any information, however slight, about her disappearance and subsequent death. I'd like to stress that no information can be considered insignificant in a murder investigation and I would like to assure everyone that all contact with the force will be treated in the strictest confidence.'

Brennan paused for a moment, then turned to Mr Sloan. 'I'd now like to hand you over to Lindsey's father who will make a brief statement on behalf of the family.'

Mr Sloan didn't seem to register Brennan's introduction, he sat holding the piece of paper before him and staring at the small printed words it contained. He looked cold, chilled to the bone. His hands trembled momentarily and the paper moved in time. Brennan wondered if he was going to bottle out but then a slow trail of words began to escape from his mouth.

'Lindsey, our daughter, was the centre of our world. We loved her and we cared for her and my wife and I have been lost without her. It's impossible to begin to describe how it feels to lose a daughter as young as Lindsey, and in the way we did, but we beg of you, please, don't let another family go through what we have been through . . .' He stalled; his wife gripped his hand and he raised his head once more, 'Please, if you have any information, no matter what it is, let the police know. I beg you as the grieving father of a much missed daughter.' On the last word Mr Sloan's frame seemed to deflate in the chair, he shrunk before the reporters and then the couple were led away by the uniforms.

'OK, any questions?' said Brennan.

The hack in the front row was first with his hand up, 'Do you have any suspects for the murder?'

Brennan provided a stock answer, 'We are pursuing definite lines of inquiry. Next question . . .'

The same hack raised his hand again; Brennan ignored him, pointed to a young woman in a red blouse. 'Yes, you have a question?'

'Will there be a reconstruction of Lindsey's final movements?'

Brennan rolled his eyes, 'I think that's a question for the television people.'

The pushy hack stood up, got his question out before being asked. 'Can you tell us why there are two Detective Inspectors on this investigation?'

Brennan shot him down, 'It's a very complicated investigation; I'm delighted to have someone of Jim Gallagher's experience on board.' He allowed himself a glance at the Chief Super as he concluded his answer.

The hack wasn't finished, 'And what is Inspector Gallagher's relevant experience?'

'Jim is a murder squad detective with many years' experience . . .' Brennan asserted himself, raised his tone. He sensed the Chief Super rising from his chair and making his way to the edge of the table. 'Look, I really don't see the relevance, can we keep the questions relevant please?'

The hack wasn't satisfied. 'I seem to recall Inspector Gallagher took part in another high-profile murder investigation some years ago . . .' He inserted a hand in the pocket of his jacket, removed a newspaper cutting and held it up. 'Fiona Gow was the girl's name.'

The room's attention became focused on Brennan's

reaction, he felt a flash of heat on the back of his neck. He saw the Chief Super walking towards the steps to the small stage the press conference desk was set upon.

The hack continued, 'Inspector Brennan, are you actively investigating links between the murder of Fiona Gow and Lindsey Sloan?'

The Chief Super increased his pace, crossed the final few yards to Brennan and clamped a hand on his shoulder and another on the table, 'That will be all ladies and gentlemen, thank you very much for your cooperation.'

A volley of voices erupted in the direction of the stage as Brennan and Gallagher were led from their chairs by the Chief Super.

Chapter 39

AS NEIL HENDERSON WALKED THROUGH the door of the flat he shared with Angela Mickle he gazed over the high bridge of his nose with vacant, shifting eyes. He seemed to have lost something, perhaps his sense of himself; or perhaps it was he who was lost. Angela rose from the mattress, stood before him, but he gazed through her as though she were glass. He stood splay-legged with his head tilted to the side. For a moment he was motionless, slightly groggy looking where he stood, and then a faint gleam entered his eyes. He registered her now, knew she was there. He jerked his head, his eyes front, and then he brought his feet together and shifted his weight to the right one. His demeanour altered too; it was as if Angela's presence stirred thoughts in him; he eyed her cautiously for a moment and then he took a step forward.

'Hello Ange,' he said.

'What is it, Hendy?' Her voice was shaky, seemed to carry a loose rattle that started somewhere in her chest and worked its way up her windpipe to her throat. 'W-what happened?'

He moved slowly, his broad shoulders easing forward and backward in harmony as each step sounded softly on the bare boards of the flat. His eyes narrowed now, took on a predatory glare as he started towards Angela. 'I saw your wee friend.'

'Crawley? You saw Crawley?' The timbre of her voice changed, grew higher.

'Aye, that's right.' Henderson watched Angela start to retreat from him; he smiled, a sly smile that slid up the side of his face and settled there like a scar.

'What did he say? W-will he come back?'

'Questions, questions . . .'

Angela put her hands out behind her as she backed up to the wall of the living room. Her thin frame looked insignificant against the broad expanse of plaster. She eased herself up to it and lifted her shoulder blades; the slow movement seemed to shrink her even more. 'What happened, Hendy? . . . I need to know.'

Henderson swayed in the doorway for a moment, he removed his hands from his trouser pockets and then entered the living room. He stared for a second at the dim bulb as it burned in the centre of the ceiling, then he reached for the switch to extinguish it. When his gaze returned to Angela her skin was the pale grey of prison walls. He sneered at her, registered her sour look and then he felt an unfathomable connection to her eyes. It was as if thoughts passed visibly between them, as if they were communicating without words, conveying more than language ever could.

'Hendy . . .'

The room felt cramped to him after the broad streets of Edinburgh with the wash of rain and the blow of wind. He felt closed in, not just within the confines of the room, but in his mind. He felt trapped there, with Angela. A succession of grim thoughts played inside his head. When he spoke, his voice was a coarse whispering rasp, 'He said you'd had words, Ange.'

Her mouth clamped shut, she turned her head to the side as if looking for an exit route. Her eyes closed tight and then reopened quickly as she flicked her head back to the front, towards Henderson.

'He said, he wasn't afraid of anything I had to say now.' His teeth gritted, 'Do you know why, Ange?'

She shook her head; her mouth remained tightly closed. Her fingertips worried at the seam of her dress as she looked at him with wide, staring eyes.

Henderson drank in Angela's fear, he bunched a fist, brought it before his face and bit into his knuckles. His eyes closed with the action, then reopened as he withdrew the knuckles from his mouth. 'You put him off, Ange.' His voice was louder now, firmer. 'He thinks he's safe because you fucked everything up.'

'No.'

'Yes . . . You ruined everything. All my hard work, wasted. What am I supposed to do now, Ange?' He leaned forward, placed his bunched fist under her chin, lifted her head back until it touched the hard wall. 'How am I supposed to get that beast bastard to pay up now, Ange? . . . You tell me that, eh . . .'

Angela tried to turn away from him, to push past his extended arm but he lowered his reach, splayed his fingers against the wall and blocked her path. She retreated, tried to manoeuvre herself in the other direction but Henderson stepped to the side and stood square-shouldered before her. 'Where do you think you're going, Ange?'

'Let me go . . .'

'Go . . . Go where? To Crawley? You going to go and see him and try and make it right?' Henderson drew in more of her fear. He wanted to see her scared, he knew she was the cause of his troubles and it lit a fuse inside him. He felt his stomach muscles tighten as he reached out and clutched her by the hair. Angela screamed out. He grabbed her throat and held her against the wall; he smothered her mouth with his free hand and watched as she struggled in his grip. She was nothing, trash. That's all she was. She had been useful to him once but she had outlived that usefulness a long time ago. 'You had to fuck it up, didn't you? . . . Just had to fucking ruin it. He was going to pay out, you knew that, and all you had to do was keep your trap shut, but you couldn't could you?'

She struggled harder, seemed to sense the anger that was burning inside of Henderson. He pressed his hand deeper into her face but her mouth seemed to widen to accommodate his palm and then she jerked forward and he felt the bite of her teeth on the fleshy underside of his hand.

'Ah, you fucking bitch!' He recoiled, turning his hand under his arm and folding himself over. The pain shot through him, he took his hand out, saw blood.

Angela ran from him towards the kitchen, her bare feet slapping on the boards as she went.

Henderson heard her opening the kitchen drawers, rattling cutlery. He straightened himself, looked down at the hand Angela had bitten. The palm throbbed, the thin flesh was torn and blood ran in a narrow trail towards his fingers. He could see her teeth marks, little puncture wounds that sat white above the skin. He shook out the sting of the wound, cursed, and ran after her. As he entered the kitchen Angela stood before him with her arms outstretched, her hands clutching at the haft of a large knife. She seemed unsteady on her feet but her jaw had set firm, signalling her resolve. She swiped the air before her with the knife.

'Are you off your fucking head?' said Henderson.

'You just leave me alone!' her voice screeched.

Henderson edged forward, smiling. He kicked out at the upturned drawer on the floor and closed in on her, 'I'm warning you, bitch, that knife comes anywhere near to connecting with me – even fucking close – and I'll use it to gut you.'

Angela screamed, 'Leave me!'

'Oh, I'll leave you . . . As I fucking found you.' He lunged forward to grab her arm, knock the knife away; Angela withdrew; lunging out with the blade in a sweeping arc she caught Henderson across the face and chest. He yelled as the knife fell to the floor.

Angela ran to the corner of the room and cowered there.

Henderson shouted out, 'Look what you've done!' He touched the blood spilling from his cheek and jaw, pressed the tear in his shirt fold. His chest tightened, the pain from the wound was intense but the rage beneath it felt as if someone had reached in and grabbed his heart, squeezed tight. 'You fucking bitch!'

He bent over and kicked the knife across the kitchen floor. As he did so, Angela stood against the wall with her eyes wide and her lips quivering. She pushed herself flat against the bare plaster and screamed out. 'Help!'

'You bitch!' said Henderson again. His brain itched; he felt queasy, the whole situation had the unreality of dreams. He took steps towards her but his legs didn't feel like his own, the sound of his footfalls was amplified, seemed to echo off the walls. 'You bitch! . . . You fucking bitch!' The words were a siren wailing in his head as his fingertips burned with a slow friction around her neck. He held her, pressed hard to the wall, for as long as it took the life to drain from her face. The eyes bulged out, then her mouth drooped open and her head lolled to the side, settled on her shoulder. He released his grip and watched Angela fall to the ground in a tangle of thin limbs. Her wide eyes protruded from within her grey–pink face as she lay on the floor.

'You stupid bitch!' he said. 'Couldn't leave well alone, could you?'

He stood over her, watching the motionless body she had once inhabited. He ran an open hand through his hair, gripped the crown and turned his face into the crook of his elbow. 'You had to fucking ruin it . . . Just had to.'

Henderson felt his heart pounding inside his chest; he removed his hand from his head and touched his bloodied shirt front. He walked towards the sink and started to run the tap. He removed his shirt, tearing the buttons off as he did so, and then dropped it on the floor beside Angela. The slash across his chest was a clean cut, deep enough to cause blood loss but he knew it wasn't so serious as to require hospital attention. He soaked a towel and dabbed with it; the raw tenderness of the cut caused him to wince but he continued to swab the wound and then held the towel in place with his hand for a moment to allow the blood to coagulate. As he looked down at Angela's twisted body he knew what he had to do next. He reached down to the floor and retrieved the kitchen knife she had attacked him with and held it in his hand.

'You asked for it, Ange . . . You know that.' Henderson

eyed the cold steel of the blade then pressed the knife's point in the counter to test its strength. As he did so, he caught Angela's wide-eyed stare and ran over to close her eyelids. 'You can fucking-well pack that in as well,' he said.

As he stepped back, looked at the woman he had killed lying on the floor, he started to laugh. 'Aye well, we might just get what we want out that beast bastard yet, Ange.' He removed the towel from his chest, blood was still weeping from the wound but only enough to line the skin's open fold. He reached down to grab Angela's wrist. As he dragged her from the kitchen he tucked the knife's blade into the back of his belt; he was surprised how heavy her lifeless body was.

Chapter 40

AS DI ROB BRENNAN WALKED into the Chief Super's office he eyed the back of Jim Gallagher's head with a burning contempt. Brennan had risen early, made a point of getting the first editions of the newspapers and listening to the radio news bulletin in the car on the way to the station. He had known what to expect from the evening news the night before but the sight of DI Gallagher in Benny's office threw up images of his worst nightmare coming true.

'Good morning, sir,' said Brennan.

'Let's dispense with the pleasantries, shall we?' said the Chief Super.

Brennan shrugged. 'If you like.'

'They do seem wholly inappropriate, wouldn't you agree?'

Brennan was tempted to add a smart-arse reply of his own, something like his mother saying manners cost nothing, but he let it slide. He was in enough trouble as it stood.

Gallagher shifted in his seat as Brennan drew level with him; there was no acknowledgement between the two men. The Chief Super shook his head and sighed, he raised both hands towards the ceiling in an exasperated salute and returned to his seat. 'Sit down, Rob,' he bellowed.

Brennan removed the chair in front of him, opened his coat and sat down. He watched as the Chief Super pressed his fingertips into his temples and massaged; he seemed stressed, even for a man whose natural state was to be stressed.

'Guess what's on my mind, Rob?' said the Chief Super.

'Sir?'

'No, go on, indulge me . . .'

Brennan crossed his legs. 'Well, if I was to hazard a guess it would be the Sloan case and . . .'

The Chief Super interrupted, 'And perhaps the way it's been portrayed in the press?'

Brennan paused, resumed his calm tone, 'Well, I was going to say, how it has been linked to the Fiona Gow cold case which,' he flagged a hand in Gallagher's direction, 'he gifted to the press yesterday.'

Gallagher leaned forward, turned to face Brennan. 'Now, come on.'

'Come on what, Jim? . . . Are you disputing that hack had your number from the moment you walked through the door? You should never have been within a mile of that press conference and you know it.'

The Chief Super raised his hands again, glanced upwards again. 'OK. Look, Rob, it was my idea to put Jim in the press call . . .'

Brennan tutted.

'Was that a tut, Inspector?' said the Chief Super.

'Sir, it was my press conference, and we wouldn't be in this bloody mess now if it had been left to me. Just like this is my case and it should be left to me.'

The Chief Super closed his mouth, leaned back in his chair. For a moment he paused before Brennan and Gallagher and then he opened a blue folder on his desk. 'When it's left to you, you go wild with overtime and hire profilers from Strathclyde!'

Brennan felt his throat freeze. 'I needed a profiler and he was the best man for the job.'

'That's not my point, Rob . . .'

'Well, then I'm missing the point, sir.'

The Chief Super leaned forward; he removed his glasses from his top pocket and put them on his nose. 'The point is you need to be closely supervised,' he ran his index finger down a column of figures, '. . . you appointed Lorrimer after I cautioned you about the overtime spending and I don't know what to expect from you next.'

Gallagher started to tap at the leg of his chair with his foot; Brennan turned away, held himself in check.

'No comment, Rob?' said the Chief Super.

Brennan flared, 'Look, Lorrimer is the best there is, what sort of a state do you think this investigation will be in without the best people on the job? You know we're in enough shit as it is with the press; if we don't get results soon we're going to be in even more . . . My job is catching criminals, not counting little rows of numbers in ledgers!'

'Wrong, Rob.' The Chief Super rose from his chair, pointed at Brennan. 'Your job is to do whatever I tell you to do. And not the bloody opposite!'

Brennan watched as the Chief Super kept his gaze fixed on him; he felt his mouth dry over and then a line of sweat formed on the back of his neck. He had seen Benny fire up before but never in front of anyone else; it should be a private affair – carpetings were something personal. This was new territory and it confused Brennan. If Benny had wanted to take the case from him, he would have done that by now; he sensed a shift. It could have been the fact that Brennan was now firmly fixed in the media's glare – he was leading the investigation – if he was suddenly stripped of command, that would make the force seem in turmoil. Moreover, Benny's favourite son – Gallagher – had been identified as the investigating officer from a similar unsolved case; Benny couldn't put Gallagher at the head of the team without attracting even more criticism. It was a stalemate. Brennan knew what that meant: the investigation might be his now but only in name; Benny would be calling the shots and that wouldn't ease up after the case was closed. Benny had been disgraced and he wanted Brennan to pay for that. The fact Gallagher had been shown up too was not to be ignored; circumstances had conspired to keep the investigating officer's role from him, but Gallagher would still need someone to blame, and Brennan knew who that would be.

The DI wiped the palms of his hands on his trouser legs as he prepared to reply to the Chief Super; there was a moment of dead calm in the room where even breathing seemed to have ceased and then, as he was about to speak, the phone on the Chief Super's desk started to ring.

'Yes, Hill . . .' his tone was firm, then suddenly changed, 'What? And the locus?'

Brennan caught Gallagher's eyes taking him in; they both looked away.

The Chief Super continued, 'And where are you now?

. . . Right, do not make a three-ring circus out of this, I do not want the press alerted!'

As the Chief Super returned the receiver to its cradle he seemed to have lost several shades of colour. He looked gloomily towards Brennan and spoke, 'We have another one.'

Brennan lunged forward in his seat, 'What did you say?'

'It's another murder . . . Same as the others.'

'Jesus Christ,' said Gallagher. 'Where about, same locale?'

The Chief Super nodded, 'Within a mile's radius . . . McGuire is on his way out there, and the SOCO squad.'

Brennan rose, 'Right. I better get on this.' He turned for the door.

'Rob, take Jim with you . . .'

Brennan halted mid-stride, 'Would you like me to carry him?'

'Very droll . . . This is not the time for jokes, Brennan.'

'I'm not joking, sir . . .' He turned to Gallagher, 'Shift your arse, Jim, I'm not waiting for you.'

As they left the Chief Super's office, Brennan noticed Benny had spun his seat to face the window. He sat staring out into the open sky like a man who had lost his way in the world.

On the stairs Brennan took out his mobile phone and dialled DS Stevie McGuire's number. The phone was answered on the third ring.

'Hello, sir . . .'

'Stevie, where are you now?'

'Erm, well, let me see . . .' there was a pause on the line, 'if you orientate yourself from the Straiton roundabout then we're about half a mile down the A720 . . . past the last crime scene.'

'Same side of the road?'

'Which road?'

'The bypass, Stevie.'

'Yes, same side . . . But the other side of the access road.'

'Right. I know where you are.'

Brennan let the front door of the station swing shut behind him; he watched Gallagher open it again himself and jog towards the VW Passat. When he was behind the wheel, he turned over the ignition and watched as Gallagher broke into a sprint. When the DI was in the passenger's seat, Brennan released the handbrake and pulled out.

They drove in complete quiet for the best part of the journey, until Gallagher broke the silence. 'Look, it wasn't my idea to put me in the press call. You can't blame me for that.'

Brennan bit. 'You've had your mind set on big-footing me from this investigation from the off, Jim; if it wasn't the press call it would have been something else.'

'That's some fucking ego you have . . . Why would I want your case?'

Brennan smirked at him, 'Because you're a glory hunter, always have been. You let your ambition get in the way of good sense. This time, it might have been Benny's idea for you to be on the panel but you could have said no . . . I mean, didn't you see that fucking hack there?'

'Jesus Christ, Rob, how many hacks are there? I can't be expected to remember every fucking one.'

Brennan took his eyes from the road, fleetingly put them on Gallagher, 'He remembered you well enough.'

The conversation ended as abruptly as it had begun. At the Straiton roundabout Brennan eased off the accelerator pedal and lowered the gears, took second. There were no officers viewable from the road. He scanned further down the exit and put his indicator on. At the point of the original crime scene Brennan started to look for the access road DS Stevie McGuire had mentioned; when he spotted it he started to slow again, dropped down through the gears once more.

'You know, Jim, there's something I don't quite understand.'

Gallagher sneered, 'Oh really, is that a doubt?'

Brennan turned the car into the access road, 'Oh I've got many a doubt about you, Jim . . . Maybe you can clear just one up for me.'

'Go on, then.'

'Right from the start, I've warned you off this case, *my* case, there's no way you could have been unaware that you weren't welcome. Yet, you persisted, and even after a spectacular downfall, you're still here. Why?'

Gallagher fell silent, for a moment he stared out into the fields and then he returned his gaze to Brennan. 'You don't get it do you?'

'Get what, Jim?'

'That you're not the only one who cares about the job.'

'Oh, I know I'm not. But I'll tell you what else I know: you're not one of the ones who gives two shits about this job, Jim. So don't be playing that old tune and expecting me to put coins in your cup.'

Gallagher smirked, exhaled a long breath and turned back to the fields.

Brennan glanced at him, stored away his expression. The doubts he harboured about Jim Gallagher's interest in the case remained intact as he pulled up to the crime scene fronted by two uniformed officers.

Brennan felt the wet beneath the wheels of the car as he

eased the vehicle into the verge. He motioned Gallagher to get out before he blocked his door with a dry-stone dyke. As he left the Passat, Brennan started to fasten his coat; he scanned the fields for members of the force, alighted on the sight of DS Stevie McGuire running towards him.

'All right, boss,' McGuire was breathless.

'Stevie . . . What's the SP?'

'Well, you're not going to like this.'

Brennan nodded, agreed with him inwardly. 'Try me anyway.'

McGuire brought himself up to the gate that separated the field he stood in from the road; he leaned his arms over the top rung and eyed the DI directly. 'It's a young girl, maybe early twenties . . .'

'We got a cause of death?'

'There's bruising to the neck and puncture wounds to the torso.'

Brennan eased himself over the gate, jumped down into the field and started to walk towards the small crowd of officers. 'Sounds familiar.'

McGuire raced after him, he was panting again as he spoke. 'Sir, that's not all that's familiar . . . There's the eye gouging and the genital mutilation as well. Boss, this is identical to the other cases; our man's struck again.'

Chapter 41

DI ROB BRENNAN TOOK THE blue coverings the SOCO handed out and slotted them over his shoes; he was already gloved as he turned the flap on the white tent and proceeded towards the murder scene. Jim Gallagher had reached the corpse before him, was hunched over staring at the victim, his hand pressed firm to his mouth. When he saw him, Brennan halted for a moment, placed an arm in front of DS McGuire and raised a finger to his mouth. As Brennan observed the older inspector at work he felt suddenly suffused with a new opinion of the man.

Brennan turned to McGuire, said, 'See that?'

'Oh, I saw it.'

'He's rattled, Stevie.'

'Certainly looks it.'

'Why though?'

McGuire turned to Brennan, spoke, 'Aren't you, boss?'

Brennan thinned his eyes, 'Not like that I'm not, no.' He lowered his arm, walked forward. As the detectives reached the corpse, Gallagher rose and placed his hands in his pockets. His complexion was pale, pasty. A patch of sweat formed on his brow as he looked at his colleagues.

'Everything OK, Jim?' said Brennan.

He paused, a thought seemed to spark in his mind; his countenance altered. 'I've got a bad feeling about this.'

Brennan rounded Gallagher, crouched low on his haunches and stared at the young girl lying on her back in the wet field. Her neck was heavily bruised, he identified the finger marks as being consistent with strangulation. Her dyed blonde hair had been soaked in the rain and her arms were splayed behind her, one beneath her torso, one to the side, as if she had been dumped. He ran his gaze head to toe; she was wearing only one shoe, a black high-heeled shoe, and there was more, but older, bruising on her knees. Above her thin white thighs was a covering of blood that matched the hacking scars on her pubis and extended over her stomach and the exposed parts of her thorax. Half of the girl's face was submerged in the soggy earth, the other half was bruised and blackened; some blood from a head wound ran from her hairline down her wide white cheekbone. As Brennan stared at her features he felt she looked young, and she looked scared.

'She's brass,' said Brennan.

Gallagher responded, 'That's what I thought. The knee bruising, and same with the wrists, it's old marks . . .'

'She's dressed like brass,' said McGuire.

Brennan rose, walked to the front of the tent and tilted his head as he looked down on the victim's features. He shook his head, 'This doesn't look right.'

McGuire and Gallagher followed Brennan's lead as he bent his knees and crouched down in front of the corpse. He leaned forward, removed a pencil from his inside pocket and stuck it in the girl's mouth.

'Sir, do you think you should?' said McGuire.

'Do you think I shouldn't, Stevie?'

'It's just, the doc hasn't been here yet and . . .'

'Fuck Pettigrew.'

Brennan prised open the girl's mouth; as he did so his face became contorted and creased. 'Jesus Christ . . .'

'Well?' said Gallagher.

'There's something in there . . . But not what I was expecting to see.' Brennan rose, fronted the two officers. 'She's been mutilated but it's inconsistent . . . The other two had their knickers in there as well.'

McGuire scratched his forehead, 'The eyes are gone though . . . That's consistent.'

Brennan removed his rubber gloves, they made a snapping noise as he turned from the others, said, 'Well that would be because the *News* printed that, Stevie . . . They never ran anything on the panties.' He lifted up the flap of the tent and walked out to the field. Two white-suited SOCOs stood outside the entrance; they were looking at a flip-chart but became distracted as Brennan approached.

'Sir . . .'

'Has she been printed?' said Brennan.

'Er, sorry, that would be John's line . . . We're casting the soil indents.'

Brennan widened his stance, slotted his hands in his pockets. 'I don't give a fuck whose job it is, I want it done. Now.'

'Yes, sir.'

'And move your arse; that girl's brass and I want her ID'd before I get back to the station . . . Do I make myself clear?'

'Sir.'

McGuire and Gallagher appeared behind Brennan and stood watching the SOCOs go to work. 'Where do you think you're going, Jim?' said Brennan.

A shrug.

'Get back in there and keep those fuckwits on their toes . . .'

'But . . .'

'No buts, Jim . . . Do it. And when Pettigrew decides to grace us with his presence tell him I want this girl on the slab and cut up today! Not tomorrow morning, tomorrow lunchtime or tomorrow fucking evening! Got that?'

Gallagher turned for the tent, said, 'Sir.' He took two steps then spun round, 'Oh, one thing, I take it we're on the same page with this.'

Brennan squared his shoulders, 'I doubt we're ever on the same page.' He nodded the DI towards the tent, 'Inconsistencies, Jim, that's what I want you looking for.'

As Brennan set out through the field towards his car, McGuire followed him. The inspector's steps were long and loping, the grass swished against his trouser legs and was flattened beneath his shoes as he went. McGuire broke into a trot to keep pace; his hair caught the breeze and was swept back from his high brow. The loud moan of traffic from the busy bypass skirted the field and pushed itself between the fast walking men. As Brennan scowled into the distance, a weakened sun sat low in the grey sky, sapping all the colour from the day.

At the fence, Brennan stalled, started to sway a little. His breathing had grown stertorous.

'Not a pretty sight is it, sir,' said McGuire.

Brennan's cheeks narrowed and reddened as he drew breath. 'That's what we're supposed to think.'

McGuire's eyes roved, 'What do you mean by that?'

'Isn't it obvious? . . . Our man never hacked that girl up.'

McGuire soaked up the information. 'You're saying it's a copy-cat killing?'

'Either that, or someone wants us to think it is.' He wiped at his brow with the sleeve of his jacket. 'Someone killed that brass and wants us to think it's one of our killer's . . .'

McGuire adopted the role of casuist. 'Why though? I mean, apart from the obvious that it would be hanging the blame on our serial killer.'

Brennan turned for the fence, placed his hands on the top rung, 'Maybe just that, Stevie . . . Or maybe something completely different. We'll be a damn sight closer to answering that question once we get that girl ID'd though.'

He climbed the fence, headed for the Passat; McGuire followed him, said, 'But it could turn out to be completely unrelated to the other cases . . . It could take us away from finding Fiona Gow and Lindsey Sloan's killer.'

Brennan fumbled for his keys, pointed at the car; the indicator lights flashed on then off as the central locking clicked. He rounded the bonnet and opened the driver's door. 'Yes, it could. Or it could be the break we're looking for. Keep your mind open . . . I'll see you back at the station.' Brennan was stepping inside the car when a thought struck, 'Oh, Stevie,' he stood up, leaned over the car's roof, 'how did you go with Mr Gow?'

The DS grimaced, lifted his hands from his sides and sighed. 'As well as could be expected, I suppose.'

'Meaning?'

'Meaning it's still all very raw for him . . . He is talking to the team today though.'

'Well, that's something. Make sure they know to cross-reference everything he tells us with the Sloan case. Remember Fiona Gow was Gallagher's case . . . Double check everything with Mr Gow . . . In fact, no, proceed as if he's never been interviewed. I don't trust Gallagher's investigation.'

McGuire pinched his brows, started to turn away from the car, 'Boss, are you serious?'

'Fucking deadly.'

McGuire removed his mobile phone, 'I'll let Lou know; he's in with Mr Gow now.'

Brennan got into the car, started the engine. His attempt at a three-point turn saw the wheels sliding about on the dirty road; he cursed as he rolled the gears between first and reverse and back again. The Passat was almost too long for the narrow access way but the DI managed to get the car turned around and facing the A720. A long line of traffic stretched from left to right; he anticipated a lengthy wait and then – from nowhere – a gap suddenly appeared and he floored the accelerator, slotted into the city-bound stream.

The traffic was slow moving, which suited Brennan; his mind was preoccupied with the latest turn of events. He knew the girl in the field was unlike the other victims, not just superficially. She was older, and she had all the classic markings of a prostitute; Brennan and the other investigators had seen enough dead prostitutes to make the leap, but his instincts also told him nothing was as it appeared. The case had shifted. All the old assumptions, the markers, the certainties, had been moved. Brennan knew he was in a different place entirely now, and the thought unsettled him. If the latest victim was linked to the others then he couldn't see the connection, and that worried him. However, if this victim was not linked to the others – as he surmised – then he was now looking for two killers.

At Liberton, Brennan stopped at the lights outside a newspaper shop. He looked over to the large window at the man on the till; he knew the hacks would have to be told about the latest killing, it couldn't be kept quiet for long. A day at most. There would have to be another press conference under the circumstances; the case demanded it. After that, the city would be thrown into blind panic. Three brutal murders, mutilation, young girls . . . Brennan knew he now had his own Ripper case to contend with. The thought brought a twisting pain to his stomach that seemed to strangle his intestines. He wondered what it was doing to the Chief Super's digestive tract. Benny – like all Chief Supers – didn't like media attention at the best of times, he was liable to be apoplectic after this recent turn of events. Brennan knew his job had never looked more difficult.

As he pulled into Fettes Station the DI stilled the Passat's engine and opened the driver's door. When he stepped out he realised he had driven all the way back from the A720 without his seatbelt on; as he went to lock the door he noticed a cigarette still burning in the ashtray. 'Fucking hell.' Brennan opened up the door, retrieved the cigarette and clamped it in his mouth. On the way to the station doors he inhaled deeply, drawing the tobacco into his lungs and sighing it back into the cold Edinburgh air.

The front desk was unattended, Brennan was glad not to have to exchange pleasantries with Charlie; he didn't feel very pleasant. On the stairs he sensed his pulse rate increase with the impending approach of the Chief Super's office but as he reached the top steps was relieved to see the door was closed. Benny would have to be faced, but that was a challenge for another time. Brennan headed for Incident Room One with an attenuated stride.

'How do, boss?' It was Collins, perched on the edge of a desk with a pencil behind his ear.

'Just dandy, why shouldn't I be?' said Brennan.

Collins seemed to have averred the tone of a serious man, rose smartly, removed the pencil from his ear. 'What's the word from the scene, sir?'

Brennan sighed, didn't bother to answer. He scanned the room. 'Where is everyone?'

'Erm, well lunch . . . And Lou and Brian are in with Mr Gow.'

Brennan withdrew his stare, took in Collins. 'And what the fuck's going on with the ID on our latest victim?'

'ID, sir?'

'Jesus Christ, do I have to do everything around here?' Brennan walked away from him, turned half way down the line of desks, 'We have a corpse in a field that I will bet a pound to a pail of shite is brass . . . If the SOCOs haven't got prints off her yet then I want you down there sticking that pencil up a few arseholes, get me?'

'Yes, sir.' Collins raked a telephone towards him, lifted the receiver and spoke, 'Scene of Crime . . .'

Brennan spun on his heels; something caught his attention on the desk to his left. It was the florid tie that he had previously seen around Gallagher's neck. The DI moved to the desk; he didn't know what he was looking for but something told him he should be looking. He opened the top drawer; a packet of McCoy's crisps and a Mars bar stared out at him. He opened the second drawer; on top of a loose pile of papers sat a blue folder marked 'Gymnastics'. Brennan retrieved the file, placed it on the desk and leafed through.

'Now, Jim, let's see what you've been up to . . .' The pages contained Gallagher's thin spidery scrawl in the margins, but there was nothing that stood out for Brennan. He knew what he was looking for – something to incriminate the DI, something to confirm his suspicions. As people began to trickle back from lunch, he turned more pages, then he was interrupted by Collins sprinting to his side.

'The ID's in . . . she's been in before and she's brass. Name's Angela Mickle . . .'

Brennan bit, 'Result.'

'That's not all, boss, we've got an address as well.'

Brennan closed the folder he was looking at, picked it up. 'Brilliant.'

'Want me to tell uniform to check it out?'

'Shit no, we'll do that.' Brennan called out to the room, 'Who's got a free minute?'

Elaine Docherty stood up, 'I can help out . . .' It was the first time Brennan had spoken to the WPC since the revelation that she was attached to McGuire; the awkward friction between them was palpable. 'I mean, if you need someone I can . . .'

'Great, Elaine.' Brennan choked back the tension. 'Can you take this file, make a photocopy and give it in to Lou and Brian . . .'

She looked disappointed, 'Oh, I thought . . .'

'What?'

'Aren't you going on a raid?' she said.

Collins laughed, 'Elaine's a bit of an adrenaline junkie, boss.'

'We are . . .' he handed over the file, 'but you're going to the interview rooms.'

'Yes, sir.'

Brennan nodded, 'And when you're finished . . . put it back in Jim's top drawer.' He tapped the side of his nose, grinned at her, 'Like it was never out of there, if you know what I mean.'

Elaine smiled back, 'Yes, sir.'

Brennan turned for the door, 'Right, Collins . . . You ready to rumble?'

Chapter 42

DI ROB BRENNAN PASSED THE car keys to Collins on the way down the stairs. There was too much going on inside his mind to concentrate on the task of driving. He had been right; he had followed his instinct and it had paid off. He knew that the latest victim in the field near Straiton was a prostitute, he had sensed it, and his suspicions had been confirmed by her fingerprints yielding a police record. He would go over the file, the whole team would, and search for something – anything – that could prove useful for the wider murder investigation, but at this precise moment, all Brennan wanted to do was catch the brass's killer.

He knew when people on the edge of society met their end in this way, their killers left a sticky trail behind them. There were no criminal masterminds working the Links. Life was brutal there, on the fringes. He had encountered so many slayings that were no more than arguments gone too far, an exchange of words that became an exchange of blows. Those deaths weren't planned; any planning came after the event, in a pathetic attempt at covering up.

In the car Brennan picked up the radio and made sure there was uniformed back-up on the way. The line crackled for a moment, then the radio room replied: 'Two cars are attending . . . Inspector.'

Brennan spoke into the hand-piece, 'Right, I don't want them going in guns blazing. They wait in the wings until I arrive and they wait quietly . . . Got it?'

The radio operator confirmed the request, 'The message has been relayed, the cars will wait for you, sir.'

Brennan put down the hand-piece but kept the volume high on the radio.

The address was for a flat in Leith; Brennan knew the location well. It was near the Links; there were good people living there, a community that objected to street walkers plying their trade in their midst, but Brennan knew there were good people everywhere. There were bad too; crime was never far, whoever you were.

The DI thought over the last few hours, and what they had unearthed. Another young woman had been killed, in horrific fashion. Angela Mickle might have been a prostitute, but Brennan wondered what chaos in her life had led her to be cut up and dumped in a field on the city's outskirts.

He spoke out, 'It doesn't make sense.'

Collins turned to face him, quickly drew his eyes back to the road. 'What's that, boss?'

'This brass . . . Why? I mean she's been killed and some bastard's hacked her up and dumped her in Straiton like the others.'

Collins dropped a gear, pressed the brake pedal, then accelerated again. 'You want my guess? . . . She's been offed by some nut-job – a punter, a boyfriend – and he's gone, "Shit what have I done, I'm in the frame for murder" . . .'

Brennan steadied his hand on the dash as the car leaned into a tight bend, 'And he's thought, I'll make it look like those murders out in Straiton . . . I don't buy that, Collins, he'd have to be fucking daft to think he'd get away with that . . .'

Collins spun the wheel, 'Aye, that's what I'm saying, a nut-job . . .'

'OK, well, let's follow your theory . . . Suppose your nut-job's successful in convincing us that he's killed this brass just like the others . . . Then that puts him in the frame for three murders, not one . . .'

'Well, if you put it like that, sir . . .'

'I do put it like that.'

They had reached the address; Collins slowed the car. Brennan and the DS stepped out of the vehicle and jogged towards the front door of the tenement building. Two officers from across the street started to move in their direction, another police car was parking up further down the road.

Brennan turned to Collins as they waited for the uniforms, 'No, if this nut-job of yours wanted to make this Mickle girl look like the others, he had to have another reason.'

'Like what, sir?'

Brennan shrugged, 'If I knew that, Collins . . . I'd have nothing to learn.'

The uniforms caught up with the officers, nodded towards the DI and stood patiently awaiting instructions. Brennan pressed the intercom buzzer, said, 'Police.'

The door sprang open.

On the stairs Brennan pointed one of the officers to the back door, said, 'Wait in the green . . . And keep an eye on the windows, eh.'

'Yes, sir.'

Brennan led the others up. He felt his thighs aching as he ascended the steep staircase at pace; he knew there was a time when he could run up and down Leith stairwells all day and never feel so much as a twitch, but he also knew those days had now gone. On the landing he rested a palm on the banister, looked towards Collins, 'Which one?'

The DS nodded down the hallway, 'Door on the end, there.'

Brennan waved the uniforms towards the door, told one to wait at the top of the stairs. 'Right, knock away,' he said.

Collins banged on the door with the heel of his hand, 'Open up, police!'

There was no reply.

He tried again, 'Open up, police!'

Silence.

'OK, knock it in,' said Brennan.

Collins and the DI stepped out of the way to let the uniforms kick into the door; it took only two swift pelts before the rotten wood behind the Yale lock gave way.

Brennan entered first, called out: 'Police!'

He checked the doors, left and right, a cupboard and a grimy bathroom. At the end of the narrow hallway was a dark room; he flicked the light switch and a bare bulb burned in the centre of the ceiling. He saw a filthy mattress in the middle of the floor, and a doorway leading to a small kitchen. He nodded Collins towards the kitchen, 'Check it out.'

Brennan looked over the mattress, it was stained and worn; empty condom packets and cigarette stubs lined its edges. He shook his head.

'All clear, sir . . . Stinks of disinfectant.'

318

'Oh, really . . .' The DI walked towards the kitchen; it looked scrubbed, quite a contrast to the rest of the flat. 'Get the SOCOs up here, Collins.'

'Yes, sir.' The DS removed his radio.

One of the uniforms had moved from the stairwell to the living room of the flat, he walked to the edge of the mattress and addressed Brennan. 'Sir, there's an old dear out here says the girl hasn't been in today.'

'That would be because she's up in Straiton, son.'

The uniform lowered his head, looked at his shoes.

'I'll have a word with her.'

Brennan followed the uniform back to the landing, the door to the flat next door stood open now. A woman in her bad sixties stood with a tabby cat in her arms, stroking its back. The cat purred like a Geiger counter.

'Hello, I'm Detective Inspector Brennan.'

The old woman's voice was reedy and high, 'Are you here about the noise? . . . Oh, the noise from that place was unbearable . . . I told them, you know.'

'Them?'

'The pair of them . . . Her and her fancy-man.'

Brennan put his hands in his pockets, tilted his head towards the open door he'd just walked through. 'There were two occupants of this flat?'

'Well, originally there was only the one, the girl.'

'That would be Angela Mickle?'

'I've no idea what her name was; she had a foul mouth, we never spoke.'

'And the other . . . The fancy-man?'

The woman removed her hand from the cat's back, raised a finger, 'Ah, now he was called Henderson. I know that because there was a tremendous scuffle on the landing outside the flat one day and he was bellowed at by another man . . . I think it was over money.'

'Henderson, that was the name he used? You're sure about that?'

The cat opened its eyes and stopped purring; it was a cue for the old woman to recommence the stroking of its back. 'Quite sure, Inspector.'

Brennan confirmed the uniform had taken a note of the name, returned his gaze to the woman, 'And when did this Henderson fellow move into the flat?'

'Oh, not long ago . . . Hardly any time at all. But my goodness, the rows, day and night.' She thinned her eyes, squinted beyond Brennan's shoulder, 'Has there been some sort of bother?'

The DI removed his hand from his pocket, touched the old woman's elbow, said, 'Thank you very much, love . . . That'll be all. If you could just give your details to the officer, I'd appreciate that a great deal.'

Brennan edged back towards the flat. Collins was putting away his radio as he entered the living room. 'Well?'

'Get back on that . . .' said the DI.

'What for?'

'Ask the station to check on any ex-cons called Henderson released in the last few weeks.'

Collins removed the radio again, held it before his mouth, but spoke to Brennan. 'Who's this, boss?'

'Likely our man . . . He was staying here,' Brennan waved a hand over the carnage of the room, 'I don't think you could call it living.'

Collins spoke into the radio, relayed Brennan's request and then held the hand-piece clear of his ear whilst he waited for a reply. 'So, he's a scrote?'

'By the sounds of it . . . A scrote that owes someone money too.'

'Money?'

Brennan looked around the room, picked at the peeling plaster on one of the walls. 'According to the neighbour there was a scuffle on the stairs . . . Sounds like Henderson was being noised-up for money.'

The radio crackled; Collins spoke into the hand-piece: 'Go ahead.'

The operator's voice came through a cloud of static: 'Only one . . . Neil Henderson released from Saughton; in for aggravated assault.'

Brennan nodded, 'That'll do us.'

'Thanks,' said Collins. 'Can you pull the files and drop them in Incident Room One?' He clicked off, turned to face Brennan. 'So what now, sir?'

'We punt Neil Henderson's face to the wooden tops . . .'

'And what about us, sir?'

Brennan started to fasten his coat, walk towards the open door. 'Well, you're coming with me. To check a few traps?'

Collins called out, 'Come again?'

'He's in hock . . .' said Brennan. 'And I don't think it's to the Royal Bank, do you?'

Collins smiled, 'I hear you.'

Brennan's quick footsteps made a steady repeating beat on the stone steps as the officers descended the stairs. A number of doors that were being held slightly ajar were closed tight as the officers came into view. Brennan smiled to himself and allowed a note of optimism to seep into his thoughts. He had a lead, a name. He'd been there before though, nothing could ever be taken for granted. But something told him that he now held information that was useful. The DI couldn't quite see where this Henderson character fitted into the overall scheme of things, but that was often the way an investigation went. What was opaque often became transparent only after a few shakes of the dice. He knew Henderson was no serial killer, that was for sure; the chaotic nature of his lifestyle didn't fit with Lorrimer's profile and, unless he was very much mistaken, he was dealing with a diminutive intelligence; how else could he account for the fact that he was confident he would have him in custody before the day was out.

On the street, some pigeons scratching for scraps on the paving flags scattered when Brennan and Collins appeared. As the pair headed for the Passat, the DI called out, 'Chuck me the keys over, eh.'

'You driving, boss?'

'Oh, I think so . . .'

Collins removed the keys from his trouser pocket, lobbed them towards the Inspector. 'So, where's first on our shady loanshark hit-list?'

Brennan pointed the keyring at the car; the blinkers flashed on then off, 'Well, I'm all for starting at the top . . . Where's Boaby Stevens hole up these days?'

Collins nodded, 'Shaky . . . Still the Wheatsheaf, isn't it?'

'Well, let's go and give him a wee rumble, eh.'

Chapter 43

AS DI ROB BRENNAN WALKED into the interview room, Neil Henderson turned his eyes towards the blank wall and sighed. DS Stevie McGuire entered after Brennan and slapped a blue folder down on the table: as he did so, a gust of dry air swept past Henderson catching his fringe. The sergeant removed a chair, dragged its legs across the floor as he kept a firm gaze on Henderson. When the chair was positioned adjacent to the interviewee, McGuire sat down and crossed his legs. He smiled at Henderson and then turned to Brennan and let out a wry laugh. The DI smiled back, walked to the other side of the desk and placed his hands at the edges of the folder; he tilted his head up to face Henderson and spoke, 'Well, well, Neil . . . Not had much luck have we?'

'Get fucked!' said Henderson.

Brennan turned over the folder and looked at the top page, scanned insouciantly. 'Quite a record you've got here.'

'I want a fag,' said Henderson.

'A fag . . . Tell me, Stevie, isn't that what they call arse-rape inside these days?'

McGuire sneered, 'I think so . . . That's where he's going anyway.'

'For sure and certain . . .'

Henderson leaned forward, extended his index finger and waved it at the officers, 'You pair can both fuck off . . .'

Brennan turned, moved his seat out, sat. He leaned forward on the desk, removed a packet of Embassy Regal and placed it before him. 'Now, now, Hendy, seems to me like you've not had much luck playing the hard man . . . I recommend you give it up.'

Henderson stared at the packet of cigarettes. 'What do you mean by that?'

'I mean, it took me under an hour to find you . . . You've no friends left in this town. If you ever had any.'

Henderson tapped his chest, 'I've got friends.'

'Oh aye,' said Brennan. 'And was Angela Mickle one of them?'

'Listen, you're not pinning that on me . . .'

Brennan knew he was engaged in a delicate balancing act. He was sure Henderson was responsible for Angela Mickle's death, but he didn't know how or why. The SOCOs' initial search of the flat had not turned up anything, but it was early enough for that to change. Still, without a definite link or a confession, the case against him was slight at the moment. Brennan knew he could pressure Henderson, make him sweat out a confession, but there was another matter to consider, two matters in fact: the deaths of Fiona Gow and Lindsey Sloan. The DI couldn't explain why Angela Mickle's death had been made to look like the others but he felt sure the postmortem would confirm his suspicions that he was dealing with a copy-cat killer. If Henderson was simply trying to cover

324

his murdering of Angela Mickle by making it look like the work of someone else, Brennan would gleefully drag that confession straight from his throat, but the thought, the possibility, that Henderson was in some way connected to the other girls' killer couldn't be ignored.

'Someone killed her, Hendy,' said Brennan.

'Look, I didn't do it!' He slapped his fist off the table, the papers in the blue folder shook. 'And you're not going to get me to say that I did.'

'Who would want to harm Angela, then?'

Henderson huffed. 'I'm saying nothing.'

Brennan turned to McGuire, then back to Henderson. 'Why not? You think someone's going to come to your rescue? No way, you're the only one we've got down for this, Hendy.'

'Then you're not doing your job right, are you?'

McGuire got out of his seat, walked around Henderson and picked up the packet of Embassy Regal. He lit a cigarette and blew the smoke towards Henderson as he spoke, 'Sounds to me like you know something that you're not letting on about, Hendy.'

He turned, put a stare on McGuire. He tapped his chest as he spoke, 'I know lots of things. Fucking loads.'

'Oh yeah,' said Brennan. 'Well, tell us something.'

Henderson turned away from McGuire; his eyes widened as he took in Brennan, then he dipped his gaze towards the cigarettes. 'Can I have one of them?'

'Go ahead . . .'

Henderson took the packet of Embassy Regal, withdrew a cigarette and tucked it in his mouth. McGuire brought the lighter's flame towards the cigarette and lit him up. 'Look, I'm not saying I know who did it or that, I'm not a fucking grass . . . But, what you were asking there, about who'd want to harm, Ange . . .' he paused.

'Go on,' said Brennan.

Henderson took a deep pull on the cigarette, took the smoke down into his lungs and held it there. As he spoke, the smoke escaped on his words, 'A little while back, right, I found something . . .'

'Found what?' said Brennan.

Henderson leaned forward, drew on the cigarette again, lowered his voice. 'It was . . . a diary.'

'Whose diary?'

'Well whose do you think? . . . Ange's.'

Brennan creased his brows, 'And why would I want to know about a brass's diary?'

Henderson shook his head, laughed. 'You fucking pigs, you just don't get it do you?'

'I don't think we do, Hendy,' said McGuire.

'No, maybe you should explain it to us,' said Brennan.

Henderson leaned back in the chair, he crossed his leg, raised his ankle and sat it on his knee. His white sports socks showed beneath his trouser leg. 'That diary, right, was all about a certain . . . individual.'

'And?'

'And . . . Well, that individual is the one that you should be asking the questions to.'

Brennan put his elbows on the desk, exhaled into his balled hands. 'Who are we talking about, Hendy?'

'I'm saying nothing more . . .' he flicked ash from his cigarette, 'nothing more, you'll have to read the diary. Surprised you haven't already, it's in the flat, under the bed isn't it.'

Brennan closed the folder in front of him and looked

towards McGuire; the DS stubbed his cigarette in the ashtray. As he rose, Brennan kept his tone low and serious, 'OK, Hendy, we'll check out this diary. But if this is stalling, you're not going to be doing yourself any favours.'

He shook his head, laughed. 'Fuck off the pair of you.'

Brennan and McGuire left the interview room. In the corridor, Brennan turned to the DS, said, 'What do you make of that?'

'He's very sure of himself.'

'Sure of himself . . . He's acting like he's fucking bullet proof.'

'Or nuts.'

Brennan scratched behind his ear, 'Well, he's that all right. Look, get the SOCOs to check for this diary; if they turn anything up, give it a look and get back to me . . . I've got some other stuff to check on.'

McGuire tapped his forehead, 'OK, boss.'

Brennan turned for the stairs; as he glanced out the window, a butyric sun melted on the rooftops. He took a moment to eye the scene, felt somehow calmed by the sight of a neon-red sky fading into the limitless distance. The world seemed to hold possibilities again; only a few short hours ago he had despaired, wondered if he would ever fit the puzzle together. He knew he was still some way from a resolution, but there was a peaceful, quiet feeling that came from having Neil Henderson in custody. Brennan couldn't explain it, it wasn't instinctual – optimistic, perhaps – but he felt a level of ease to have removed him from the streets. He knew he hadn't made the city a safer place – there would be a hundred others waiting to step into Henderson's place – but there was an assured feeling of release, relief.

Brennan ascended the remaining stairs and headed for

Incident Room One; as he opened the door he nodded to the first person he saw, WPC Elaine Docherty.

'Hello, sir.'

'Elaine . . . Any news on the postmortem?'

She touched the sleeve of her shirt, loaded the request in her mind, said, 'Erm, I haven't heard . . . Will I give the morgue a call?'

Brennan listened as the door's hinges sang out, turned to look behind him as Lou and Bri walked in. 'Yes, Elaine, call the morgue.' He turned to the others, 'Right . . . My office, now!'

Lou was removing his coat, 'Can I catch my breath first, sir?'

'No you fucking can't! . . . Office, now.' He pointed down to the other end of the room, stretched out his stride. As he walked, Brennan looked left to right, took in the level of activity, said, 'Right, come on you lot, we've got plenty to be getting on with now, I don't want to see anyone twiddling their fucking thumbs!' A blast of electricity ignited the room, seemed to jolt bodies into action. Brennan clapped his hands to gee-up the team.

In his small glassed-off office the DI suddenly felt cramped; he looked out to the reddening sky and the setting sun and felt the confinement more keenly. He turned away from the window, pulled out his chair and balanced his elbows on the desk. He was lacing his fingers into an arc as Lou and Bri appeared. 'Right, sit down,' he said. 'And tell me about Mr Gow's visit to the station.'

Bri was first to lower himself into the office chair, he thinned his eyes into tiny apertures as Lou sat, began to talk; he spoke in generalities, his speech as discursive and rambling as a child's.

Brennan raised a hand, 'Lou, for fuck's sake, I don't want to go all around the houses . . .'

Bri cut in, 'I think, what Lou's trying to say, boss, is that Mr Gow never really gave us very much.'

Brennan lowered his head, stared at the desk for a moment. He was still facing the laminated desktop as he spoke again, 'Look, didn't you get the folder I sent in?'

Lou lit up, 'Oh, aye . . . Well, we got that all right.'

'And?' said Brennan, raising his head.

'Fiona Gow did gymnastics, but we knew that, right?' Lou turned to Bri; the DS was turning over pages in a spiral-bound notebook.

'Erm, here we are,' said Bri, 'said she had champion potential . . . Well, her coach did, a Mr Crawley.'

Brennan felt his stomach tense, the muscles tightened like a cincture that sent a spasm all the way to his throat. 'What did you say?'

'What?' said Bri.

'The coach, Fiona Gow's gymnastics coach . . . What was his name?'

Bri returned to his notebook, inflated his chest and exhaled slowly. 'Let me see . . . Crawley.'

The DI absorbed the information like a blotter. He leaned back in his chair, raised his leg, resting his foot on an open drawer. 'Are you saying we are just getting this information now? . . . What I mean to say is, Jim Gallagher never flagged this earlier?'

Bri turned to Lou; the pair seemed to be confused by Brennan's reaction. Lou spoke, 'No, boss . . . at least, it wasn't in the file.'

Brennan rose, turned away from the others. He stood before the window and leaned over, placing his hands on the ledge. Clouds crossed the sky and the dying rays of the sun laced together in a liquid, bouncing light. The scene seemed to distract him, he couldn't focus. As he closed his eyes, tightened his facial muscles, he felt assailed by an army of possibilities – the chief being Gallagher must have known Crawley was now teaching at Edinburgh High, which was Lindsey Sloan's school. He thought back to their first encounter in the Sloans' home after Lindsey's death: Crawley had said she wasn't one of his pupils; but there was still the possibility of contact if he had been her gymnastics coach. The implications were obvious, but Gallagher's actions remained a mystery to him.

Brennan turned to face the others, 'Bring him in.'

Lou said, 'The teacher?'

'Nothing wrong with your hearing then.' As he spoke, the phone began to ring on his desk, he picked up. 'Brennan.'

It was Elaine Docherty. 'Sir, I have the morgue on the line, it's Dr Pettigrew.'

'Right, put him on.' Brennan turned back to the others as they left their seats, headed for the door. 'And whilst you're at it, get someone to do a full background check on Crawley . . . I want everything including his inside-leg measurement and fucking star sign.'

'Yes, sir,' the pair spoke together, left the office.

Brennan returned to the telephone, 'Hello . . .'

'Was this rush job really bloody necessary?' said Pettigrew.

Brennan smiled into the phone. 'Well, you tell me . . .'

Chapter 44

DI ROB BRENNAN HAD A set of specific questions about the death of Angela Mickle that he wanted answered by Dr Pettigrew's postmortem. Upon visiting the scene, just off the A720 where her battered corpse was uncovered, he had been immediately of the opinion that she was not a victim of the same killer as Fiona Gow and Lindsey Sloan. There were similarities – all three girls had been mutilated, their eyes had been removed and the location was within the same one-mile radius. But the level of unease he had felt at the latest crime scene was enough to make Brennan think something altogether different had occurred to Angela Mickle.

She was brass, a prostitute, that much was certain; and she was older, if only slightly, than the other girls. It was a fact that the investigation had been unable to establish any valid criteria that linked the girls – they could just as easily have been selected at random – but just because no similarities had been established didn't mean they were not there. He remembered a line from Wullie that had lodged in his mind: 'Facts don't cease to exist just because we don't know they exist, Rob.'

Brennan held the telephone receiver close to his ear as Dr Pettigrew spoke, listing off his initial actions of cutting the ribs and clavicles before removing the breastplate and taking samples of blood, bile and urine.

'I don't need the minute-by-minute version,' said Brennan.

Pettigrew bridled, 'Well, there is a point to my detailing the procedure.'

'And the point being?'

'I thought she was strangled and would have initiated the postmortem by cutting the scalp and removing brain tissue, but I thought you might want to have her drug usage confirmed if she was a prostitute.'

Brennan felt himself drawing breath slowly, he softened his tone, spoke into the phone. 'OK, doctor, and what did your analysis reveal?'

Pettigrew brightened, 'Well, I can confirm she was a very regular drug user, heroin . . . But that's not all I can confirm.' He paused. 'I said I thought she was strangled and that's borne out by the neck and head examination.'

Brennan's picture of Angela Mickle's final moments was coming together the more he spoke to the pathologist, but he still had questions he wanted answered. 'And what about the mutilation . . . How does that compare to the other victims?'

There was a gap on the line, 'Yes, I thought you'd ask that.'

'I am asking that,' said Brennan.

Pettigrew cleared his throat, spoke, 'The Gow and Sloan cases had striking similarities, the genital mutilation and the eyes, obviously, but there was also the fact that they had clearly been recently killed before any of the mutilation took place . . . Mickle, I'm not so sure. The strangulation was the cause of death but that could have happened some time before the desecration. And I have to say, the mutilation was frenzied and rough – not clean like the others – and you realise there were no undergarments found on this victim, whereas they'd been inserted into the mouth cavity with the genitalia . . .'

Brennan felt his shoulders tense as he listened to the doctor's assessment. He knew he'd been proven right. 'You're saying then, that it's your opinion we have two separate killers?'

'One for Gow and Sloan, and I would have to conclude another for Mickle.'

'So Mickle's a copy-cat case.'

'It would appear so, yes.'

Brennan massaged his jaw, bowed his head. As he raised his hand to his brow he felt a layer of moisture had settled there. He experienced no level of vindication to have been proven right by the pathologist's report; another young woman had died, it didn't matter to the DI that he believed he had her killer in custody already because there was nothing he could do about her death now. The law could take its course, justice could be served, but Angela Mickle would play no part in it; she would play no part in anything ever again.

Brennan spoke, 'Thank you, Doctor. I'll let you go.'

'My pleasure.'

He hung up.

Brennan eased himself back on the desk, the rim cut into his thighs as he leaned forward. He felt at once assailed by a mixture of hurt and anger. He saw the swaggering

Henderson in his mind's eye and the image cut into him like a saw blade. He had met his type before, boys from the schemes, wide as gates. They all felt the world owed them a living, felt justified in expressing their loathing for their bitter existences. Brennan didn't want to think too much about Henderson, or his type; when he did that he always found himself delving into other people's concerns. He didn't want to find excuses for why someone like Henderson would turn into a vicious killer. He didn't want to think about the social reasons, the economic exclusion, the deprivation, the way Edinburgh, or even Scotland, had developed. That was not his job, that was not for him to consider. He dealt in facts: provable, reasonable facts; the ifs and the buts were an intellectual exercise for middle managers and senior civil servants to debate between courses at New Town dinner parties. To Brennan it was black and white – he wanted the scum behind bars.

The DI raised himself from the desk, walked to the edge of the room and opened the venetian blinds. He faced the murder squad through the window as they went about their work in Incident Room One. He knew they had reached a fork in the road now; the case had split in two. He had three murders to think about and two killers to put away. He couldn't see any obvious link between the recent killing and the earlier two. He could guess at Henderson's reasons for copying the MO of the other killer but it was just that: guess work. He knew there was a wider set of possibilities at play; he only hoped they would come into focus soon. The media had been hovering since the disastrous press conference, they could only be kept at bay for so long, and there was the fact – as Wullie had pointed out – that there was a killer out there who was likely to strike again at any moment. Brennan felt the pressure of time gripping him as he turned the handle on his office door.

'Right, Collins, get over here,' he called out.

Collins made his way towards the DI, said, 'Yes, sir.'

'What did the SOCOs get out of Mickle's flat?'

The sergeant tucked a yellow pencil behind his ear, put his hands in his pockets, 'Nothing, so far as I know.'

Brennan bit, 'What do you mean nothing? They must have got fucking something!'

Collins removed his hands from his pockets, shrugged, 'Nothing in the way of evidence; there was blood in the kitchen but it wasn't the victim's.'

'Well whose was it?'

'His . . . Henderson's. Says he cut himself when he was drunk; there's a gash on his chest as well. Nasty. Had to get it looked at.'

Brennan shook his head, 'Cut himself when he was drunk, my arse.'

'Aye, more like cut himself trying to choke the life out of a brass with a knife in her mitt.'

Nods of approval. 'That's more like it.' Brennan raked the room with his gaze. 'Where's Gallagher?'

'Search me. Haven't seen him since this morning.'

Brennan thinned his eyes, looked further down the room as the door from the landing opened up. DS Stevie McGuire entered, started to remove his coat. He was hanging it on the stand as he spotted Brennan and Collins at the other end of the room watching him. McGuire nodded, reached into his coat pocket and removed a plastic bag with a small mauve-coloured object inside.

'Got the diary, boss.'

Brennan beckoned McGuire towards him, 'Right, bring it down here, we'll take a look at it in my office.'

'Diary?' said Collins.

'Angela Mickle's . . . according to Henderson.'

'And are you going to believe that scrote, sir?'

'Depends what's in it . . . Might suit us to believe him.'

Collins creased up his brows, edged to the side as McGuire swept past him and followed the DI into his office.

'Where was it?'

'Believe it or not,' said McGuire, 'exactly where he said it was.'

'And why's that surprising to you?'

'Well, it was the truth for a start . . . I'd say bugger all else we've had from him adds up.'

Brennan held out his hand, took the clear plastic bag from McGuire and opened the closed edge. He looked at the diary for a moment, glanced to the DS, then removed it and retreated to his seat. As he thumbed the first page over, he noticed the name was correct, written in a looping scroll that seemed to resemble his daughter's handwriting – little circles sat above the i's and the j's. As he took in the first few lines, he noticed it seemed to have been written by a much younger girl; he raised his head, addressed McGuire: 'Well, if he wrote this he's a good mimic, or knows something about channelling young lassies.'

McGuire looked confused, sat forward in his chair and stared at the page Brennan was reading, 'What do you mean, sir?'

'I mean, Stevie,' he looked up, 'this is genuine.'

'Then it might be of some use after all . . .'

'I don't know about that.'

McGuire rose, walked round to the same side of the

336

desk as the DI, said, 'Well, there's only one way we'll find out.'

Brennan huffed, lifted the diary and flicked through the pages, 'Suppose we'll have to read it all.'

'Maybe we could just skim.'

The DI frowned, turned back to the page. It felt somehow like an intrusion – Angela Mickle was dead – Brennan still remembered how her corpse looked in the field, exposed to the cold and rain of the Scottish morning. He wondered what it was about the artefacts of the dead that somehow made them feel sacred; was it a learned response? This was just a diary, words on a page, how could it be any more sanctified than any other piece of young girls' writing. But it was; he knew it. As Brennan read through the small pages he felt himself building an image of another side of Angela; she was no longer the murdered prostitute to him. Angela Mickle had some level of intelligence, that was evident, she had some integrity too and the words she put on the page revealed all of this and more.

'Look at this,' said Brennan.

McGuire read where the DI pointed, 'Gymnastics . . . another one.'

Brennan turned to face McGuire, 'I should be the one to tell you this, Stevie: I caught Jim Gallagher with his fingers in the cookie jar . . .'

'You what?'

Brennan sighed, marked his place in the diary and spoke, 'There was a teacher, a gymnastics coach called Crawley, linked to Gow and Sloan . . . and he buried the fact.'

'Are you sure?'

'As shooting. There's no way he couldn't have known.

I've sent Lou and Bri out to pick the teacher up; if he turns out to be our man . . .'

'Jesus, it doesn't bear thinking about. Have you told the Chief Super?'

Brennan turned back to the diary, 'No.'

McGuire touched the DI's elbow, 'Sir, you have to tell him . . . that sort of thing will be around the station like wildfire before you know it.'

'I know, Stevie.' Brennan thought about McGuire's remark for a moment; he did indeed have an obligation to inform the Chief Super, and he knew just how he would take it: badly. Benny had put his store of faith in Jim Gallagher and he'd wasted it all; it was going to look bad for the Chief Super, not as bad as it would for Gallagher, but bad enough. Brennan thought he would derive some form of satisfaction from being proven right about Gallagher but instead he felt only an emptiness inside. He didn't want to see a man's career ruined; he didn't want to see the man ruined, but he knew that was just what was going to happen. Suppressing evidence in a case of this magnitude was a serious matter, it went beyond any reprimand Benny could dole out. One question remained unanswered for Brennan, though: why? To risk his career, and more, had to come backed with heavyweight reasons. Detective Inspectors didn't take those kinds of risks unless they had no other choice and Brennan wanted to know what made Gallagher do it.

'Here, you take over, Stevie.' Brennan handed McGuire the diary, rose from his seat. He walked towards the window and looked out into Incident Room One. WPC Elaine Docherty was parading down between the desks with a clutch of papers in her hands. As she reached Brennan's office and prepared to knock on the door, he opened up.

'What have you got for me?'

'It's the backgrounder you asked for on that teacher . . .' Elaine handed over the bundle of papers.

'Does he have form?'

'Er, no, sir. This is all Education Department data . . .' she paused for a moment, 'I think you'll be interested in the stuff on page four.'

Brennan turned to the page she mentioned, it was a list of the places Crawley had taught; Elaine had highlighted Portobello Academy and Edinburgh High. In the margins beside the schools she had written in red ink the dates Fiona Gow, Lindsey Sloan and Angela Mickle had attended those schools – they all matched.

'Good work, Elaine,' said Brennan, he raised the sheets of paper in acknowledgement, turned back to his office; as he did so he was waylaid by DS McGuire brandishing the mauve-coloured diary.

'What was the name of that teacher?' said McGuire.

Brennan dipped his brows, turned towards the DS. 'Colin Crawley.'

McGuire dropped his arms, he seemed to be deflating, but in a second he raised the diary again, presented it to Brennan, 'I think we've found our man, sir.'

Chapter 45

DI ROB BRENNAN DID NOT feel good about what he was about to do. As he headed for the Chief Super's office he felt a slow trickle of sweat run the length of his spine. There was a dull ache in his chest, not a pain exactly, more like an emotion lodging itself there. He had felt the same ache when he had heard of his brother's death; he seemed to remember the ache started small, covered an area about the size of an egg, but then grew bigger until it had engulfed his entire chest, then later, his entire being. Brennan didn't anticipate the same reaction this time round, but he knew that the emotion he felt was for a passing: Jim Gallagher was finished.

Brennan realised he wasn't a brutal man, if anything, at times he felt too soft. He had spoken to Wullie about the way he felt some people operated and the old man had said they were just 'acting out their nature'. As a race we were a mix of personalities; where there were brutes and self-servers, there were also the opposites. Brennan knew he wasn't a polar opposite to the brutes – but there was enough humanity in him to know that a man was a man and he identified with Jim Gallagher's fall. He knew there were men on the force who, in his situation, would have been getting the rounds in – counting it as a result. But not Brennan. He felt saddened, if not sickened, and wanted more than anything to understand what had driven Gallagher to it. As he approached the Chief Super's office, reached out for the handle, and stepped in, he felt no level of satisfaction for the news he had to deliver.

Dee, the secretary, lit up as Brennan walked into the room. She gazed at him for a moment, seemed to take stock of his demeanour and suddenly changed her expression. 'Is there something wrong, Inspector?' she said.

'I need to see him,' Brennan raised a hand, 'no, don't get up, I'll announce myself.'

They both knew this was irregular, but somehow the news he carried with him automatically merited the change in procedure.

Dee nodded, 'Of course.'

As Brennan entered the long window-filled room, the Chief Super stayed bowed over a blue folder at his desk; it took some moments for him to register that Brennan was there. When he raised his head, the Chief Super looked first at Brennan and then at the door, as if checking it was properly closed. He motioned him to sit.

'You look like you've lost a pound and found a penny, Rob,' he said.

Brennan forced a smile onto his face, it sat there like an interloper for a second and then vanished. 'The murder investigation has taken a . . . turn, sir.'

Benny removed his glasses, 'For the better?'

'Well, the answer to that would be yes and no.'

The Chief Super closed the folder on his desk, laced his fingers. 'I think you better explain, Rob.'

Brennan leaned forward in his chair as he spoke, 'We have a prime suspect . . .'

'Excellent,' Benny opened his palms, clasped them together.

'Not quite, sir.'

'Well, are you bringing him in?'

'I have Lou and Bri on the way now . . .' Brennan scratched his forehead, 'there's complications, sir.'

'Go, on.'

'It's my belief that Detective Inspector Jim Gallagher identified this suspect some time ago, perhaps as far back as the Fiona Gow killing, and has suppressed it for reasons unknown.'

The Chief Super's eyes widened, a little gap appeared in his tight lips. For a moment he seemed frozen, closed off to the world and then he blinked rapidly and found words, 'That's quite an allegation, Inspector . . . You do realise that; I mean, you realise what you are saying?'

Brennan nodded slowly, 'Sir, there's a very definite paper trail; I wouldn't be stating this otherwise.'

The Chief Super rose from his desk, turned to face the window. He crossed his palms behind his back and looked out towards the sky and the line of the horizon. For a few seconds he was silent, and then, 'That'll be all, Rob.'

Brennan stared at the back of the Chief Super's head, 'I'll send in the paperwork.'

There was no reply.

As the DI raised himself from the chair, the dim scrape of the chair legs on the carpet tiles seemed to stir the atmosphere of the long office.

'Oh. One more thing, Rob,' the Chief Super turned, 'where is Inspector Gallagher?'

Brennan had reached the door, held the handle in his hand; he released it, turned to face Benny. 'Last I saw of him, he was at the scene in Straiton. He should be on his way in . . . I have instructed the team, those on the needs-to-know, to play dumb.'

'Thank you, Rob. Send him downstairs when he appears . . . And let me know, please.'

'Sir.'

Brennan reached for the handle, turned. As he walked out the door he spotted the Chief Super returning his gaze to the wide window.

The DI dipped his head towards Dee on the way out, 'Thanks,' he said.

In the hallway he took a deep breath, then removed his tie and opened the top button of his shirt. He felt somehow unclean to have talked to the Chief Super about Gallagher – like he was a schoolboy telling tales. He wondered if Wullie would have approved, he wondered if he approved of himself. Brennan tramped towards the coffee machine and rested a hand on the fascia; he ferreted for coins in his pockets and slotted the amount required for a black coffee. As the machine spat and gurgled, he waited, silently staring at the slow drain of black liquid into the plastic cup. When the machine quietened, he watched the last drops of coffee escape and then the bubbles resting on the surface, first in the centre, and then drifting to the sides. He reached down and removed the cup, walked away.

On the stairs, Brennan was met by DS Stevie McGuire, 'Ah, it's yourself . . . Ready for round two with Henderson?'

Brennan raised his coffee cup to his lips, blew. He looked

towards McGuire, turned and continued towards the interview rooms without uttering a word.

A few steps from the bottom of the staircase, McGuire
spoke again, 'Lou and Bri called in . . . Crawley's home's
deserted.'

'What do you mean, he's fled?'

'Well, it's empty. There was no sign of him, but . . . Jim
turned up.'

Brennan halted where he was. 'Jim lobbed up to Crawley's
house?'

McGuire nodded, 'Lou and Bri spotted him.'

Brennan scrunched a handful of hair from his fringe,
'Christ Almighty . . . That means he knows we're onto him.
Where is he now?'

'Lou and Bri are bringing him in.'

Brennan shook his head, 'Right, cells. But you tell me
when he's in – and before Benny knows . . .'

'Yes, sir.'

'Go on then, get onto the Brothers Grim, make sure they
fucking-well know the score as well.'

As McGuire removed his mobile phone, Brennan
proceeded down the corridor towards the interview rooms.
When he entered, Neil Henderson was sitting in the facing
seat, smiling to himself. Brennan placed his cup of coffee
on the table and started to remove his jacket. As he hung
it over the back of the chair, McGuire entered and nodded.

'All done?'

'Yes, sir.'

Henderson folded his arms, then just as quickly unfolded
them and showed his palms to the officers. 'Well, did you
get it . . . The diary?'

Brennan picked up his coffee and took a sip; he winced

344

a little, it was still too hot. He returned the cup to the table and removed a packet of Embassy Regal from his jacket. Henderson watched him as he moved, each turn followed by his twitching eyes.

'How did you come to know about the diary, Hendy?' said Brennan.

'She showed me it, didn't she.' He smirked as he finished his sentence.

'What just out of the blue . . . She tells you about Crawley.'

Henderson tapped on the table with a dirty fingernail. 'No, well, not really . . . It was after the thing on the news, about the murder and that.'

'Set her off did it?'

'Yeah, did a bit.'

McGuire crossed his legs, looked over Henderson. 'And so she turned to you as a sympathetic ear, is that right?'

'Yeah, I was all she had.'

Brennan leaned in, removed a cigarette from the packet and lit up. 'You were all she had . . . Bit sad that, isn't it? All she had was her pimp.'

Henderson brought his palm down on the table, 'Look, am I getting out of here or what? I gave you the fucking diary, you know who you should be looking for.'

Brennan and McGuire exchanged brief glances. The DI took a long draw on his cigarette, watched the slow trail of blue smoke making its way towards Henderson as he exhaled. 'I'm afraid it's not going to work like that, Hendy . . . You see, Crawley's done a runner, and I want to know who tipped him off. I think you might know Crawley a bit better than you're letting on.'

'Bullshit . . . He's a fucking beast.'

McGuire reached behind his seat, produced a blue folder

and placed it on the table. Brennan opened the folder, turned a few pages. 'You know what these are, Hendy?'

He shrugged, looked away.

'Well, let me explain . . . They're bank statements, Crawley's to be precise, and they tell an interesting story, say they were emptied up to the maximum amounts a wee while ago . . .'

Henderson remained impassive.

Brennan continued, 'Now when I spoke to a close friend of yours recently, Boaby Stevens that is, he told me you repaid a substantial part of your loan to him, and the amount matches the withdrawals from Crawley's bank accounts . . .'

Henderson sat back, stared at the wall. 'You can't prove anything.'

Brennan smiled, 'I don't fucking need to, Hendy, you're in enough shit as it is . . . Did I mention you're in the frame for Angela's death?'

'That was fucking Crawley!'

Brennan shook his head, stubbed his cigarette. 'The forensics team tell us a different story . . . Now, look, I'm going to be very generous to you, Hendy, so generous you'll be thanking your lucky stars you ever met me. I'm going to ask you, nicely, to tell me all about your involvement with Crawley, from your first meeting to your last. I want to know how much money you took from him, how much more you were planning to take, I want to know what you told him about Angela and her diary and I want to know, most importantly, where the hell he is now.'

Henderson stood up, knocking over his chair. 'Dream the fuck on!' Brennan watched him walk to the end of the interview room and kick out at the wall. He turned away from the officers and walked towards the other end of the room, launching at the opposite wall with a fist. He put his hands up to his head and stomped from left to right, then lashed out again. He continued in this pattern until he looked back to Brennan and pointed, 'Crawley's the fucking beast!'

Brennan reclined in his chair, put his hands in his pockets. He watched Henderson pace a little more and then kick over the chair. 'Pick it up, Hendy, sit yourself down and tell us what we want to know. You're going nowhere from here except a cell . . . How long you go there for depends on what you tell us, so grow some fucking sense.'

Henderson stood still for a moment; he watched Brennan through wide staring eyes and then he took a few steps towards the upturned chair and righted it. He sat down. 'Can I have a cigarette?'

Brennan nodded towards McGuire; the DS removed a cigarette from the pack and handed it to Henderson. As he placed the filter in his mouth, McGuire leaned over to light the tip.

Brennan spoke, 'Now, Hendy, in your own time . . . And don't leave anything out.'

Henderson's hand shook as he brought the cigarette towards his mouth, 'He knew what he'd done, knew I was onto him, and he was scared.'

'How do you know he was scared?' said Brennan.

Henderson lifted his head, 'Because he went to the Links, pulled up Ange . . . He was shitting himself.'

'But you told him he had nothing to fear, if he paid up, right?' said McGuire.

Henderson turned his gaze, his voice was a slow trail of words. 'Yeah . . . But he got all cocky, after he saw Ange.'

'What do you mean, cocky?'

'He'd put the shits up her, he thought she would be too frightened to tell anyone about him . . . That's when he said he wasn't going to pay up again, and I showed him the diary.'

Brennan removed his hands from his pockets, sat forward. 'And what did he make of that, seeing his name in there?'

'He was still acting cocky, trying to make out he didn't care . . . But I knew he would. I knew he was a fucking beast, he was trash . . .'

'But he had something you wanted didn't he, Hendy? Money. And when that wasn't getting coughed up easily that's when you thought you had to up the ante a bit wasn't it? . . . You killed Angela to scare him into giving you more money.'

Henderson had smoked the cigarette down to the filter tip. His fingers held the long trail of ash as he sat silently, unmoving. When the ash fell, landed on the floor, something sparked in him. Henderson's eyes widened as he turned to face the officers, 'It wasn't like that, she attacked me with a knife.'

'You struggled?' said McGuire, 'And then what?'

Henderson leaned forward, placed the empty filter tip on the table. 'She cut me, there was a lot of blood and . . . I just snapped. It wasn't until after that . . .'

Brennan pushed back the legs of his chair; the noise ricocheted off the walls of the interview room. He stood up and leaned on the edge of the table, 'Hendy, I want you to think very carefully about your next answer.' He reached out, placed a hand on his shoulder, 'Did you tell Crawley about Ange's death?'

Henderson looked towards Brennan's hand, turned his eyes towards his arm and followed all the way to his shoulder, and then his face. 'No. I-I was going to wait a bit . . .'

'What do you mean wait a bit, until the word got out?'

'I thought, y'know, after it was in the papers and that . . . He'd be easier to hit up.'

Brennan turned away from Henderson. He walked round behind the desk, sat down and closed the folder. He turned to McGuire, said, 'Charge this arsehole.'

Chapter 46

DI ROB BRENNAN STEPPED FROM the front door of the police station and removed a packet of cigarettes from his trouser pocket. There was only one cigarette left in the box of Embassy Regal; Brennan placed the filter tip in his mouth and scrunched the empty container. He lit the cigarette and stood staring into the distance as the tobacco filled his lungs. He could see the roofs of tenements catching the last rays of a tarrying sun. There had been a spill of rain earlier in the day, the pot-holed car park held dark pools of water that reflected the last of the day's light. It was cooling now, not just the temperature, but the sky's colour too, the cobalt expanses greying from the edges towards the centre. The scene set Brennan's pulse racing – time was ticking away. He knew what he needed to do before the sky turned from blue to black but he doubted whether he would be able to achieve it. There were too many uncertainties stacking up around him; too much he couldn't control.

As he drew the cigarette towards his mouth once more, the DI thought of Angela Mickle and the other girls. He had spent plenty of time going over the deaths of Fiona Gow and Lindsey Sloan but somehow he felt differently towards Angela. Her life had been ruined by what had happened in her past – Brennan recalled the entries she had made in her diary and wondered how the young girl who wrote them must have felt about the world and its new cruelties she was discovering. Brennan shook his head, took another drag on the cigarette and tried to regain his focus. He knew none of this was helping the investigation; was it helping him? He had always tried to compartmentalise his sympathies, store them away. It was a hindrance to have to feel like a normal human being at times like this; he wanted to be able to bring down the shutters, block out his emotions, but it was difficult when the victim was a young woman who had once been a young girl so much like his own daughter. How did these turns of fate transpire? he wondered. How did Angela Mickle go from one day being just another member of her school's gymnastics team to the object of a predatory paedophile's fantasy? Her fall from preyed-upon schoolgirl to preyed-upon prostitute looked like a long drop, but in reality – in her mind, he surmised – was probably no more than a matter of weeks. Angela Mickle had lost any grip she held on normality the day Crawley started to take an interest in her; when she met Neil Henderson, she lost everything else. He thought of the shabby flat the pair shared in Leith, the used condoms littering the floor, the dirty, stained mattress in the centre of the living room. They lived like animals, worse than animals. It struck Brennan that, perhaps, she was in a better place now – but he doubted it – it was a preprogrammed part of his brain lobbing out platitudes to make him feel better. One thing was for sure, wherever Angela Mickle was now, she was out of Crawley's clutches, and as far away from Neil Henderson's reach as could be.

Brennan scrunched his brows, flicked his cigarette into the car park. The amber tip fizzed as it came into contact with the wet tarmac. He watched the dim embers of the tobacco turn to grey as the white paper absorbed the moisture, and then a gust caught the cigarette butt and blew it out of sight. He felt the muscles stiffening in his shoulders as he braced against the sudden wind, his shirt sleeves billowing. He wanted to be away, somewhere else; he didn't want to think about the case and the deaths of three young women who he had only got to know once they had been killed. He thought it was too much for one man to have to deal with and then it struck him how strange it was for himself to have such a thought. He had dealt with many brutal murders before, so what was it about this case that sickened him so much? Was it his age, the age of his daughter, the end of his marriage? The fact that he had found one of his own officers covering up important evidence? He resigned himself to never know the answer, but the fact that he no longer had the stomach for the work was something he knew he would have to face.

The station doors swung open; DS Stevie McGuire stood in the jamb for a moment then paced into the cold. He was holding a blue folder. 'Thought I'd find you out here.'

Brennan nodded to the DS, 'And you did.'

'Henderson's charged . . .'

Brennan didn't answer.

McGuire continued, 'Bri was on the phone: they're on their way . . . Look, I was thinking you might want to cast an eye over this before they get here . . .'

Brennan took the folder from McGuire; it contained the

file – so far as it stood – on Crawley and the complete file on DI Jim Gallagher. 'Cheers, I'll have a deck at this before I see him.'

McGuire started to rub at his arms, 'Jesus, brass-monkeys out here isn't it?' He seemed to register Brennan's lack of interest in communicating. 'Right, I'll get away, boss . . .'

'OK.'

McGuire opened the station door, said, 'Look, do you want me to tell Benny that Gallagher's in . . . not right away, obviously, I mean when you've had a chat with him.'

Brennan kept his face front, 'No, Stevie, I need to see Benny about something else . . .'

'Oh, right . . . What's that?'

Brennan turned, a thin smile played on the side of his face, 'Just something.'

McGuire winked, made for the door, 'Say no more.'

Left on his own, Brennan turned to the folder he had been handed and started to go through it. He had seen much of the information on Crawley earlier, but as he turned the pages over he alighted on a piece of information that jabbed at him like a knife point.

'Jesus Christ!' said Brennan.

The DI shut Crawley's file and started to thumb through the early pages of DI Jim Gallagher's file; he was closing down on the information he sought when a navy-blue Mondeo drove into the car park and pulled up before the station's entrance.

Bri exited the passenger's door and nodded to Brennan, 'How goes it, boss?'

As Brennan replied, Lou left the driver's side and went to open the back door; DI Jim Gallagher was sitting in the back seat. 'Where do you want him, sir?'

Brennan snapped the blue folder shut, roared, 'Get him in the fucking door, now!' He turned for the entrance, jerked the handle and stomped into the station. As he stood waiting for the others he wondered if he would be able to face Gallagher and then the thought became a sounding board in him that he knew he would have to test. As Lou and Bri led in the DI, Brennan turned to face him squarely and said, 'What were you doing at Crawley's house, Jim?'

Gallagher's eyes were glassy under his moist brow, then he flashed a weak smile across his face, 'Rob, for crying out loud . . . I heard the call on the radio and went to check it out. Is that what all this is about?'

Brennan watched the others exchange glances, then he fixed his glare on Gallagher. 'No you never, Jim . . . Because we didn't put that on the radio.'

'But, I-I . . .'

'Take him down to the cells, lads.'

Gallagher bridled, seemed to dig in his heels where he stood. 'The cells? Is that really necessary, Rob, we can talk this through surely . . .'

Brennan nodded towards the steps, 'Not my orders, Jim . . . That comes straight from Benny.'

As Lou and Bri led Gallagher away, he turned, tried to catch Brennan's eye, but the DI dipped his head towards the folder in his hand. He let them get out of sight before he started to follow them. As he did so, he glanced towards the front desk; Charlie sat silently, his mouth clamped tight shut. Brennan acknowledged the desk sergeant and proceeded towards him.

'Give me that keyboard there,' he said.

Charlie handed over the grey office keyboard and turned

the monitor screen to face Brennan. 'Anything else I can do?' he said.

'No, this is fine . . . Just need to check something out on the database.'

Brennan reached over and picked up the mouse, placed it on the counter. He started to scroll through a few screens and then opened the blue folder to the page he was reading from earlier. He wanted to check the dates Jim Gallagher had attended Dungarn Boys Home, and cross-reference them with an idea that was germinating inside him. He located the dates, then closed down the screen and returned the keyboard to Charlie.

'All OK?' said Charlie.

Brennan nodded, lifted the phone and dialled Incident Room One. 'It's Rob, give me Stevie.'

'Yes, sir.'

The phone's receiver clunked on the hardwood desk and then was picked up a few moments later, 'McGuire.'

'Stevie, I want you to check something out for me . . . Now, you'll have to do this right away. Get into the files and search for Dungarn Boys Home . . .'

'Why on earth . . .'

'Don't ask, I need to know about the place, just get me the full SP . . . Can you do that?'

'Yes, sure . . . I just don't see the . . .'

Brennan cut in, 'You don't need to, Stevie . . . I'm going to see Gallagher, I'll be downstairs, so anything you turn up, bring it in right away. I don't have long with him before I'll have to hand him over to Benny.'

'OK, Boss. I'll get right on it.'

Brennan hung up the phone; he put a stare on Charlie as he turned from the desk and headed for the back steps towards the cells. He knew that the fount of all station gossip would have plenty to say on this matter one day, but he also knew he could rely on him to keep it to himself right now – some subjects, by their very nature, rendered themselves above gossip and Brennan knew that instinctively; even Charlie understood that.

As he descended the stairs towards the cells, Brennan played over in his mind the moments that had led up to this point. He had been suspicious of Jim Gallagher from the first but had no real evidence to back up his assumptions. He knew Gallagher was a glory hunter and he had witnessed his cozening of the Chief Super at first hand; however, what he had never considered was that Gallagher's involvement was criminal. He had covered up vital evidence in a triple murder case that had attracted widespread media attention; the force would not be kind to him, never mind the law. What really galled Brennan, however, was the fact that the murderer was still out there, and Gallagher knew it. Why would he sabotage the case like this? How many lives of innocent young girls did he want on his hands?

Brennan felt his stomach tighten, then turn sharply. He felt a sickening grip his heart and threaten to topple him. He steadied himself on the grey wall, reached out a hand and then placed the flat of his back on the cold plaster. For a moment everything spun; thoughts of the case laced with thoughts of Gallagher's actions. Nothing made sense any more; perhaps, above everything, that was what wounded Brennan. He felt like he had lost his edge, like the job was no longer within his ken.

He stood before the cell door where the word Gallagher had been chalked up, looked down the hallway and nodded towards the duty officer, 'Want to open up this one, Davie?'

The broad officer padded towards Brennan and removed a bunch of keys attached to a chain on his belt. He looked like he might speak, pass comment on the cell's occupant, but then he thinned his lips as if suddenly thinking better of it. Brennan spoke as he entered the cell, 'I'll give you a shout when I'm done.'

'OK, sir.'

In the cell, Gallagher sat on the edge of the narrow bed with his sleeves rolled up and his shirt open at the collar. His laces had been removed from his grey shoes and their tongues sat upwards like gravestones. He looked at Brennan when he walked in the room but then lowered his head as if resigned to his fate. He displayed a bald patch at the back of his head, stray hairs scraped over the pate showed like fence palings. For a moment Brennan stood before Gallagher, listened to the key turning in the door, and then he paced towards him.

'There's no way back, Jim,' said Brennan; he reached into his pocket for a cigarette and then recalled he had finished the pack. 'The Chief Super knows all about your antics . . .'

Gallagher huffed, 'Antics? . . . And what would they be, Rob?'

Brennan positioned himself on the adjacent wall, planted the sole of his shoe there to support him, 'Crawley . . . You cut him out the investigation. Why?'

Gallagher brought his hands up to the sides of his head; he splayed out his fingers and touched the temples. 'You don't know what you're talking about.'

'Why Jim? Why did you cover for him . . . If there is some kind of excuse, if he had something over you, I can live with that, but you have to tell me.'

357

Gallagher's fingers started to massage his head, first the sides, and then the crown, mussing what remained of his hair. 'You've no fucking clue, Rob.'

'Well, fill me in . . .'

Gallagher sat up straight; his eyes were rimmed in red. His face seemed to have lost several shades of colour as he spoke, 'Do you have a cigarette?'

Brennan tapped at his pockets, shook his head. 'Hold on, I'll get some.' He walked to the door and opened the Judas hole to attract the duty officer. When Davie appeared he motioned with two fingers towards his mouth to signify he wanted cigarettes. The officer opened up the door, held it ajar. 'Hold on, I've got a pack in the doocot,' he said.

As Brennan waited for Davie to return, the main door to the cells opened up and DS Stevie McGuire passed through; as he saw Brennan he increased his pace. 'All right, boss . . .'

'Stevie, what did you get for me?'

He held up a single sheet of paper, 'Not much to go on, but . . .'

Brennan raised his hand, read the copy of an original charge sheet that detailed the manslaughter of John Burnside by Colin McCabe, both residents of Dungarn Boys Home. He turned his gaze back towards Gallagher in the cell as he spoke again, 'Right, Stevie, go on . . .'

'I ran the name through . . . Colin McCabe . . . it's Crawley.'

Davie appeared with the cigarettes; Brennan took the packet of Silk Cut and a box of Swan Vestas matches and returned to the cell. As the door closed and the key turned once more, Brennan lit two cigarettes and handed one to Gallagher. The strong smell of tobacco lingered in the enclosed area as he walked back to his place at the wall and looked at the charge sheet. He kept the paper in his hand for a moment then leaned forward, placed it on the bed next to the prisoner.

Gallagher picked it up and read. His voice came weakly, 'That's good work, Rob . . . You were always a good copper.'

Brennan raised his cigarette, inhaled deep. 'Tell me what happened at Dungarn, Jim.'

He sneered, thin white lines appeared at the sides of his red eyes. 'It would be easier to tell you what didn't happen at that place.'

Brennan allowed Gallagher a moment, then pressed again. 'That boy, on the charge sheet . . .'

'Colin McCabe . . . It's Crawley, he changed his name years back, way before the Education Board started looking into that kind of thing.'

Brennan frowned, 'No, I didn't mean him . . . The victim, John Burnside, tell me about him.'

Gallagher raised the cigarette to his mouth and took a deep draw on it; his hand seemed to flutter before his face as he held the cigarette. He pinched his lips and blew out a thin trail of blue smoke as he spoke with a trembling voice, 'He was a cunt . . . What do you want me to say, Rob. He arse-fucked us all . . . He was a fucking animal. What we did, he had it coming.'

Brennan watched the ash fall from the tip of Gallagher's cigarette, stepped forward. 'What *we* did?'

Gallagher's head turned sharply; his eyes were wide as he took in the DI. 'You're the detective . . . Why the fuck do you think I'm here?'

Brennan stood before Gallagher, bent his knees to face him. He had taken in Gallagher's words, absorbed their implication, but their true meaning seemed to have escaped him. The logical answer had been given, but Brennan's mind seemed to be having difficulty keeping up. 'We, Jim?'

Gallagher lowered his head again, the cigarette in his fingers fell to the ground as he clutched at the back of his neck and sobbed. 'Colin and me, we killed him . . . Colin took the weight, they had it down as manslaughter but it should have been murder because we killed him, we both did.'

Brennan felt an urge to reach out to Gallagher, to place a hand on his shoulder and offer him some comfort; the man was hurting, but there was no sympathy on offer to him. Brennan rose, turned away towards the cell door. As he gathered his breath, his strength, he tried to process the information he had just received.

Gallagher called out to him, 'What'll they do to me, Rob?'

Brennan turned back, his heart was pounding beneath his shirt front. 'What'll they not do to you, Jim.'

Chapter 47

DI ROB BRENNAN MADE HIS way towards the main staircase at the front of the station. He paused before placing a foot on the first step and felt himself pulled towards the main desk; as he turned, Brennan locked eyes with Charlie for a moment. The desk sergeant had observed the earlier arrival of DI Jim Gallagher and had been silenced by the shock of his removal to the cells. The unusual display of taciturnity sent a jolt through Brennan: he knew Charlie was a barometer of the station's mood, and looking into his hollowed, lined face, the reading he took was for stormy weather to come.

It unnerved Brennan to think of the way he would be perceived in the station after Gallagher's betrayal, but he shoved it to a part of his mind where he seldom retreated to. What people thought of him was of little concern to Brennan at this stage of his life – he had never been one to cultivate colleagues for his own ends, or any other reason – nor was he concerned with winning any popularity contests. The force could think what it liked about him – he'd stared down opprobrium in the past but he knew now the rest of them would have to get used to being on the receiving end. This was what bothered Brennan more: the force was going to share the blame for Gallagher's wrongdoing; he had no doubts about that at all.

Brennan kept a fixed glare on Charlie for a moment and then the older man tipped back his head in acknowledgement; it was an unspoken concurrence – passed between them like radio waves, and would have been just as impossible to execute without the correct equipment. They had both been around long enough to know that the shame Gallagher had brought on himself, and all of them, was not a perennial experience; it was as if the sheer scale of what he had done was beyond words, beyond reason. Brennan returned Charlie's nod and took the first step towards the Chief Super's office.

The DI had vowed to inform Benny of Gallagher's return to the station right away – he hadn't done that, but disobeying direct instructions from the Chief Super seemed like a low-grade offence today. He knew his superior would have to reassess his priorities too: it was not the time to go after slightly wayward DIs when his own best boy had stepped beyond the limits of all known boundaries. Benny's priority would now be damage limitation – his own arse was on the line, thought Brennan, why would he care about settling old scores? The DI replayed recent decisions he'd been challenged on by Benny: there was the overtime ban; the appointment of a profiler from Strathclyde; and there was the press conference which had descended into complete and utter farce. Brennan felt himself gripping the banister tighter as he ascended the stairs; he knew that, even a few hours ago, he would not have been able to go to the Chief Super to seek support for his next move, but the axis of power had shifted now. The DI knew Benny was a greatly diminished force; he would have to put his faith in solving the case – that would be his redeemer – and there was only one man left capable of delivering that for him since Gallagher had dropped out of the picture.

Brennan grabbed the handle to the Chief Super's door; he felt ready to flay any opposition to his desired course of action, but he knew that the situation would require some degree of subtlety. It never helped to overplay your hand, he thought, and he knew that what he was about to propose was risky; getting Benny's support would be the easy part.

The boards beneath the carpet tiles creaked as Brennan entered the Chief Super's office. Benny stood staring out of the window, in much the same position he was when Brennan had last seen him, only now he seemed preoccupied with a ruckus of seagulls as they caterwauled over fresh deposits in the station's bins. The DI scratched at his cheekbone as he waited for the Chief Super to turn around; the sky had settled into a dark-purple wash.

'Ah, Rob, you're here,' said Benny.

Brennan lowered his hand, nodded, said, 'I thought you'd like to know that Detective Inspector Gallagher is . . .'

He cut in, 'Yes, I know . . . I still have some ears and eyes in this station, Rob.'

Brennan let the remark slide, but absorbed its implication. He watched the Chief Super take a seat, motion him towards the chair in front of the desk. As he sat down, the DI felt the atmosphere in the room tighten around him; 'I spoke to him,' he said.

Deep lines creased Benny's brow, two dark declivities sat beneath his eyes as he wet his grey lips, 'Was there any . . . justification?'

Brennan felt a corkscrew turn in his gut, he gripped the chair's arm with his closed hand as he spoke. 'Murder; you could call that justification . . . of sorts.'

The Chief Super cleared his throat, made a guttural noise as his facial muscles tightened into the shape of incredulity. '*What*?'

As Brennan outlined Gallagher's confession, and his claims of abuse, Benny groaned audibly; his eyes receded and his gaze looked distant, out of focus, as he slumped further into his chair. It started to darken in the room and the silence between the two men added to the unwholesome air. Brennan felt his earlier thoughts coalesce with an entirely new emotion: pity; he felt sorry for the Chief Super. As he watched him, almost writhing before him, Brennan knew the man felt unable to withstand the latest barrage to his authority. He wondered if Benny too entertained thoughts, doubts about whether he had chosen the right career path. The notion seemed fantastic, he was always so sure of himself, 'a puffed-up wee prick' Wullie had called him once; but now he appeared all too human and the thought gored Brennan. For a second or two he wondered how many times in the past he had made ill-founded decisions about people and then he checked himself, corrected his thinking. He was a DI, he reminded himself, and he had a triple murder case on his hands. The press were talking about an Edinburgh Ripper.

'Sir, I need to ask your approval for the next stage of the investigation,' said Brennan.

The words seemed to fall on Benny like blows, 'What? . . . I mean, what do you need, er, want to do?'

Brennan leaned forward in his chair, 'I believe our suspect may make a move to kill again, sir.'

Benny cut in, 'Yes, yes . . . Well, that doesn't change if Angela Mickle was killed by Henderson.'

Brennan watched the day closing through the window, said, 'Our suspect doesn't know about the Mickle killing, but the press pack will soon enough, if not already; we need a blanket ban on reporting on the case for the next twenty-four-hours.'

'Oh, Christ, Rob . . .' The Chief Super shook his head. 'Have you any idea of the complexity, the hoops I have to jump through to . . .'

Brennan raised a hand, 'Sir, in about an hour it's going to be pitch dark. I think that's going to be our last chance to catch this bastard . . . He doesn't know Mickle is dead, he thinks she's alive and he thinks she's holding incriminating evidence . . .'

'The diary?'

'Yes.' Brennan rose, tapped an index finger heavily on the desk in front of him, 'I think he'll try and reclaim it, and I think he'll try and silence Angela Mickle . . . if we can convince him she's alive.'

The Chief Super picked up a fountain pen from his desk, started to roll it between thumb and forefinger. His eyes darted, left to right. 'You're talking about a set-up . . . Something at Angela Mickle's flat?'

'I'm talking about that yes, but we'd need to bait the trap.'

'Oh, Jesus . . .' Benny's face fell like a stone.

'I think there's a WPC on the team who would fit the bill, and I'd supervise the operation personally.'

The Chief Super rose from his chair, faced Brennan across

the desk. As he spoke, he pointed at the DI with the tip of his fountain pen, 'You are asking me to sanction putting a member of my force into the clutches of the worst serial killer we've seen in a generation . . .'

Brennan shook his head. 'I think we can contain the risks, sir . . . And I don't think we have any other options. When the press reveal Mickle's death, and Gallagher's involvement, we're not going to see Crawley again . . . He's resourceful; if he goes to ground, we miss our chance.'

Benny gnawed on the edge of his lip, his eyes slanted towards the darkening window and then he lunged forward and flicked on the desk lamp. His face became illuminated in a bright white light that seemed too strong for him; he turned towards the window again and started to roll his fountain pen between his palms. His sloped shoulders deflated as he leaned towards the glass and spoke. 'OK, Rob, you make this work,' he turned around, his skin sat in grey-white folds beneath his eyes, 'because if you don't, it's not just your neck on the line.'

Brennan rose from his chair; as he put eyes on the Chief Super he noticed his lips seemed dry, chalky. There was a sensation of relief playing in his chest but he knew the hard work had not even begun. The DI turned for the door and listened as the boards creaked once again. He made a half smile as Dee greeted him; she was putting on her coat, heading for home. Brennan felt the extent of her world wouldn't fill the four walls around them. She would get in her car, collect some groceries and cook for an ungrateful brood before watching some brain-wash television and then go to bed. He didn't know whether to feel sympathy or envy for her.

As he entered Incident Room One, Brennan felt he had stepped into a spotlight; the squad stilled all activity and turned towards him. As he looked around the room he wondered what they all wanted as they stared at him, and then his thoughts aligned with theirs.

'If you're looking for the latest on Jim Gallagher, you'll have a long wait,' said Brennan. He walked towards the coat stand and fished in the pockets of his overcoat for cigarettes, but found none.

Collins walked towards Brennan with an outstretched hand; as the DI looked down he saw the packet of cigarettes and a plastic Bic lighter. 'Cheers,' he said.

'So, what now, boss?' said Collins.

Brennan removed a cigarette from the packet of B&H, looked at the clock on the wall. He knew what he wanted to be able to say, but it relied on one more person offering him the support he needed. 'Where's Elaine?' he said.

'Erm,' Collins seemed unsure of his response. 'Good question.'

As the room turned, started to hum with possibilities, the WPC and DS Stevie McGuire walked through the door; they were smiling together, but the smiles evaporated as they came into contact with the others' stares.

'What's going on?' said McGuire.

Brennan lit his cigarette, blew smoke into the room. He set his gaze on Elaine, 'I need a volunteer, I need a WPC to tease out our suspect.'

McGuire turned from Brennan and walked towards his desk; the DI tipped back his head as he awaited a response. 'Well, do you think you're up to it?'

Elaine nodded briskly, 'Yes, sure . . . What do I have to do?'

As she responded, Brennan felt his pulse settle, he brought the cigarette towards his mouth and inhaled deeply. 'That's great, Elaine. I'll fill you in on the logistics soon,' he flicked ash from his cigarette tip onto the carpet tiles, 'but you'll be impersonating our recent victim, playing possum at her flat.'

She smiled, 'Will I need my high heels, sir?'

'You just might.'

Brennan patted Elaine's shoulder, returned the cigarettes and lighter to Collins and walked towards McGuire's desk. The DS was poring over a folder, making annotations in the margin with a Biro.

'Stevie, got time for a word?' said Brennan.

The DS dropped the pen, slapped the folder closed, and stood up. He made no eye contact with Brennan as he quick-stepped towards his office at the end of Incident Room One. As Brennan watched McGuire, he felt as if he had made a miscalculation somewhere along the line, but he wasn't sure where. In his office, Brennan closed the door gently, then walked around to the other side of the desk and said, 'Take a seat, Stevie.'

'I'd sooner stand . . . sir.'

Brennan turned down the corners of his mouth, 'Suit yourself.' He watched as McGuire turned away from him, folded his arms. It seemed a petulant stance, like one a teenager would adopt. It was tempting to slap sense into the lad thought Brennan, and then he calmed his spirits. 'Is there something bothering you, Stevie?'

The DS sighed audibly, 'Oh, let me see . . . Now what could that be, sir?'

'She'll be perfectly safe, she'll be wired.'

McGuire leaned forward, 'Jesus Christ Almighty . . . Is that going to make an ounce of difference?' He turned his shoulder, raised an arm towards the incident room, 'Have you seen those pictures up there on the board? . . . What chance is she going to have against that bastard?'

Brennan placed his elbows on the desk, locked his fingers together. He allowed a few seconds of silence to settle in the room, gave McGuire a moment of reflection. 'I wouldn't put her in any danger; come on Stevie, I don't see Elaine complaining.'

McGuire reeled back, placed his hands on his hips, 'That's because she's too fucking ambitious for her own good . . . And you're just taking advantage of that!'

'No, I'm not. She's been working the clubs with Collins and she's proven herself . . . She's the best person for the job.'

McGuire stared at Brennan, lifted his hands from his hips and smacked them off his thighs, 'Fuck the job!'

Brennan rose from his chair; he could see eyes directed at him through the glass. 'Stevie, now calm down.'

'I'm serious; look at the state of this case: Gallagher's made cunts of us all and now all you're concerned about is getting him back, righting wrongs any old way . . .'

'Stevie, that's not true.'

'Bullshit! . . . I thought you would never put your team in danger, thought you looked out for people, but I was wrong.' He turned for the door, yanked the handle. As he exited, the door swung behind him then clattered into the frame.

Brennan pressed his fingernails into the edge of the desk, lowered himself into his chair. He watched McGuire stride through the office at pace, all heads turning towards him; as he left the main door of Incident Room One the DS had lost none of his fervour.

Chapter 48

DI ROB BRENNAN TRAVELLED IN the front of the van with Collins driving; there was a hint of rain in the air outside but the threat of more to come hadn't materialised by the time they reached the roundabout at the Playhouse Theatre. There was already a number of people queuing in the taxi rank – young girls in short skirts and young boys looking them over, digging elbows in each other's sides as they went. Brennan felt a shudder of despair as he looked out at the familiar landscape of the Edinburgh streets. He was tired of the city, nothing there offered him any surprises now. In another hour or so the shivering teenage girls would be holding their shoes in their hands, staggering and puking into the gutter. The boys would be throwing fists and holding burst noses or pissing against shop doorways. Edinburgh never changed; the city was like a production line throwing off skinny, spotty yobs who blocked the streets and cells and made the DI wonder when or if he would ever be free of it. He knew he was being hard on the place, but it was his job to know the real city behind the Georgian façade of the New Town and the whisky-soaked bonhomie of the Old Town. Brennan recalled the statistic that in London you were never more than six feet from a rat; in Edinburgh, he knew, the same distance could be applied to junkies, pimps and pushers with some degree of accuracy.

'The state of that,' said Collins, nodding towards a drunk negotiating a zigzagging path towards the traffic lights.

'He'll not last the night,' said Brennan.

'He'll be lucky to last to the end of the street before some wee ned has him pummelled . . .' Collins turned briefly to face the DI, 'rite of passage these days, isn't it.'

Brennan watched the drunk hanging on to the light at the pedestrian crossing, but didn't answer Collins. He started to roll down his window and took out a cigarette from a new packet of Embassy Regal. The cold wind from the street filled the cab and sent Collins reaching for the heater. Brennan took the hint and rolled the window up a little but left enough of a gap for him to knock the ash from the tip of his cigarette onto the road. As the van rolled onto Leith Walk, he thought about his temporary lodgings on nearby Montgomery Street and wondered what there was to keep him in the city now. He knew, of course, the answer was his daughter. Sophie was still here and she needed him, even if she didn't know it and would certainly never admit it. As he took stock of his life's worth, Brennan knew it was a thin tally to account for his time on the planet; he hoped for better for his daughter, didn't all fathers?

Brennan knew Angela Mickle had deserved better too, as had Fiona Gow and Lindsey Sloan. None of them deserved what their tragically short lives had amounted to. It hurt Brennan to think of the way they had suffered, how their families had suffered. None of it was remotely comprehensible to the DI, but then he knew that was the way it should be – it would take a sick mind to understand the likes of Crawley. The teacher had preyed on youngsters in his care and moulded them into objects of his sick fantasies. Brennan knew there would be lawyers and psychiatrists who would try to explain away Crawley's actions, but the thought of any kind of clemency for him made Brennan's guts tighten. He felt only revulsion for the man. There were two clear sides: the victims and the perpetrator, and Brennan knew which side of the chalk line he stood on. He felt his teeth locking tight as he thought of Crawley; there had never been a time when he had strayed completely from his duties as a police officer but Brennan knew he would reverse all of that to give Crawley a glimpse of the true terror he had brought to those young lives. The case had worked its way under Brennan's skin; had he grown too close to the investigation? he wondered. Yes, probably. But he was only human, he had seen the faces of those victims, heard the cries of grieving parents – how could it not affect him? As they turned off Leith Walk, the DI knew for certain that if he failed to catch Crawley the job was over for him; too much damage had been inflicted on him already, another blow would be his last.

Brennan threw his cigarette butt from the window, and pointed Collins towards a gap in the traffic. 'Pull in there.'

As Collins parked up, Brennan looked out towards the grey tenements sitting under the fast-darkening sky. He tapped a fingernail off the dashboard and turned round towards the back of the van, 'You guys set?'

The pair monitoring the wire nodded, raised thumbs. 'Sir.'

Brennan turned to Collins, 'Right, let's join them.'

As they moved towards the back of the van, they collected headsets – the DI spoke into his, 'Stevie, you in position?'

The line crackled, 'I'm on the back green.'

'What's the SP?' said Brennan.

'No movement, I have WPC Docherty in plain view . . .'

Brennan nudged himself up in the back of the van; it was cramped with four grown men in such a confined space but he hoped they wouldn't be there for too long. The DI had gambled on Crawley taking the risk of tackling Angela Mickle to remove the diary that Henderson had flaunted in front of him. It was, he knew, a long shot; but Crawley's profile indicated a strong risk-taking streak and he had already approached the victim with threats. Brennan knew there was also the fact that both Lorrimer and Wullie had confirmed his own fear that Crawley was destined to kill again – had an urge to – and he had a ready-made target in Angela Mickle, knew she could offer little resistance.

Brennan spoke into the microphone, 'Elaine, can you hear me all right?'

A whisper, 'Yes, sir.'

'Good. We'll keep contact to a minimum. If he shows, don't try to engage him physically . . . If he speaks, we'll be listening in, but the second he gets actually threatening you know what to do.'

The WPC's voice was soft, low. 'Yes, sir.'

'*Bluebell* . . . Just say the panic word and we're in there.'

Brennan looked out towards the tenement through the one-way glass on the side of the van; he could see the WPC standing in the window, staring down at the street. She was in the same style of black dress that he had seen Angela Mickle wearing on the day she was found in the field out at Straiton. Her hair had been styled in the same, unkempt fashion as the murder victim; as she brought a cigarette up to her mouth, Brennan felt the similarity between the two young women strike him; he suddenly felt the unease of another life on his conscience.

'OK, Elaine, move back from the window and put the light on,' said Brennan. 'After that, you can pass the window, but don't get up too close . . .'

There was no reply. The men in the van waited for the light to go on in the flat; as it illuminated the room, Collins spoke, 'Showtime.'

Brennan pushed the back of his head against the side of the van and sighed. 'Let's hope so.'

Collins covered his microphone as he engaged the DI, 'Do you think he'll appear?'

Brennan shrugged. 'There's a hope.'

'He's never been to the flat before, how will he find it?'

'He found her on the Links . . . And she was a brass turning tricks at home, how hard can it be?'

Collins removed his hand from the front of the mike, craned his neck towards the street. A man driving a blue Fiesta was pulling into a parking space on the other side of the road. 'What kind of car does Crawley have?'

'A silver Corolla,' said Brennan.

'Nah, that's a Fiesta.'

The DI looked at his watch; the iridescent flashes on the hands shone out. He knew it was still early, but already a void of tension had set up in his chest. Outside the van, the full gloom of the night sky settled over the street and the rooftops. The orange haze of street lamps burned against the black road and a thin moon reflected on the scene. Brennan listened to the hiss of static on the wire but heard

375

nothing; he felt an urge to prompt the team but stilled it as he became distracted by noise beyond the van. A woman's laughter came interspersed with loud clacking heels on paving flags but was quickly drowned out by a booming stereo from a passing car. The fast-moving vehicle shook the van where it sat in the street and prompted Collins to roll his eyes.

'Some wee boy racer.'

Brennan nodded. The laughing woman came into view, held up by a man in a business suit; his tie caught the wind and came to rest on his shoulder. The occupants of the van watched as the pair lolled down the street, stopping every few steps to grab handfuls of flesh and press their mouths together in violent gulping motions.

'Someone's on a promise,' said Brennan.

Collins broke into guffaws, 'Going to be a knee trembler tonight.'

The officers watched as the man positioned his hands on the woman's backside, allowed one to stray beneath the line of her skirt. 'Well, it's good to know romance isn't dead,' said Brennan.

'Jesus, get a room,' said Collins, '. . . A close at least.'

The man in the business suit let his second hand join the other one beneath the woman's skirt; as he did so, the woman started to raise her leg, hooked it round the back of the man's knee. For a moment the eagerness of the coupling intensified, both heads thrashed backwards and forwards like a drunken Punch and Judy show. The woman teetered on her one heel and dropped the leg she had raised; as she stepped back she ran hands down the man's shirt front, then started to unbuckle his belt.

'Fucking hell, she's only getting him out,' said Collins.

The wire operators leaned closer to the window, 'Should have cameras on this, it's urban porno!'

Brennan creased his brow as he felt the van start to dip to one side; he pressed his hand against the ceiling as he attempted to raise himself in readiness for an outburst, and then the wire lit with the sound of movement from the flat. WPC Elaine Docherty spoke, 'There's a knock at the door.'

Brennan clamped down the motion in the van, 'OK, Elaine, go to the door, answer it . . . but remember what we said.'

The occupants of the van fell into a tense silence as they monitored the wire; Brennan felt the skin tightening on his forehead as he brought a hand towards the earpiece and frowned. A green light flashed on the radio equipment in front of him and a jagged line was traced from one side of a small, flat screen to the next. The sound of the door's lock turning was the first thing the DI heard and then the hinge creaked, quietly at first, and then noisily. A thud like a board being kicked echoed down the line and then the hinges screamed once more and the door was slammed hard against the frame.

'Who the hell are you?' The voice was Crawley's.

The team waited for Elaine's reply; it came after a pause, her words quivering over the wire, 'Are you looking for business?'

'Where's Angela?'

There was a rustle of clothing, like an outdoor jacket, an anorak. Footsteps trailed along exposed boards.

'S-she's out.'

'Where is she?' Crawley's voice was high-pitched and sharp, he sounded agitated.

'Just . . . out.'

The sound of the anorak rustling came again, there was a muffled burst and some static on the line and then nothing.

'What's happened?' said Brennan.

One of the operators leaned forward, flicked a switch. The jagged line disappeared from the screen then he flicked the switch again and it reappeared as a single straight rule dissecting the screen. 'Don't know . . . Hang on.'

DS Stevie McGuire spoke, 'What the fuck's going on?'

'Hold tight, Stevie.'

McGuire's tone pitched up a notch, 'I'm going in. Fuck this!'

'Stevie, stay in the back . . . Do you hear me? Stay where you are.'

The operators worked over their equipment, pressed buttons, turned dials. Their arms jumped between the various controls, smacking into each other as they went. Neither seemed able to return the WPC's voice to the line.

Brennan removed his headset and said to Collins, 'We've fucking lost her . . . Come on.'

The van doors flew open as the officers ran into the darkened street. Collins shouted into his radio, 'We're going in. That's a go.'

Lou and Brian ran from further down the street as Brennan raced for the front door of the tenement. 'Stevie, where are you?'

There was no reply.

'Shit!' The DI entered the stairwell, reached out and grabbed the banister, took two steps at a time as he lunged upwards. His heart was pounding, a million thoughts rushed through his mind – predominant being where the hell was WPC Elaine Docherty?

At the first landing, Brennan leaned into the curve of the stairwell, looked upwards; he saw DS Stevie McGuire racing ahead of him. He knew this meant the back door was unguarded; he switched his point of view, turned eyes downwards but saw no more movement. As Collins caught up with him, Brennan straightened and threw himself back into the chase. He paced the hallway, then ran for the steps once more. He felt the sweat breaking on his chest and back. Collins was close behind him.

At the final landing, he saw the door to Angela Mickle's flat lying open. Brennan pushed himself, panting and out of breath, towards it. His lungs twinged, the air felt hot around his head as he entered the front room and took in the sight of DS Stevie McGuire knees bent, sitting on his haunches, holding his hair bunched in a fist.

'They're fucking gone!' he said.

Brennan wheezed forward, 'What?'

McGuire rose, fronted his superior. 'I said Elaine's gone . . . He's fucking taken her!' He pointed a finger, forced it into Brennan's chest, 'I told you, I fucking told you this would happen!'

The DI stepped back, raised a hand towards McGuire – the DS knocked it away, he inflated his chest as he stepped towards Brennan.

'Whoa, hang on, Stevie,' said Collins; he pushed himself between the officers, moved McGuire towards the window.

Brennan turned from them, made for the kitchen – he took two steps inside, looked the place up and down, and then ran through the living room and back to fling open the doors leading from the hallway. As he checked the empty rooms he felt his heart rate ramping even higher; a sickly feeling encircled his stomach as he became dimly

aware of the fact that he had lost his prime suspect and
WPC Elaine Docherty. His instinct was to keep looking but
he knew they were not there. He halted his pacing, he could
hear Lou and Bri entering the scene; their voices trailed
from incredulity to sparring with the bellicose McGuire.
Brennan touched his parched lips, pressed his hand tight to
his mouth. He wanted to hit out, to strike the wall or door
with fists but he knew that wasn't going to help – he needed
to think, to act.

Brennan called out to the others, 'Get to the back close!
Now . . . fucking move it!' He ran out of the front door.

The group converged in the narrow hallway, scrambled
to the stairwell. Coat tails flew out as the sound of leather-
soled shoes slapped the stone steps. Brennan felt the others'
panic as they descended behind him; he knew they were
all thinking ahead, wondering how to explain their roles in
the mess. He wanted them to concentrate on what was
happening right now, but he could sense the tension and
fear the team exuded like a poisonous gas.

The DI was first through the back door; the poorly-lit
yard felt spacious after the stairs but odd items littered the
path: a tin bath, a number of bicycles, a rusting lawnmower.
Brennan followed the flags to the back wall, placed his foot
on a pile of bricks and aimed his line of vision into the
next garden. He jumped back down, cursed, 'Shit . . .'

'Nothing?' said Collins.

'What do you think? . . . We've lost them. Get on that
radio – I want every uniform within a country mile in Leith
– now!'

'Yes, sir . . .'

As Collins removed his radio, Brennan jogged back
towards the others; a painful stitch had set up in his side,

his breathing felt strained, painful. When he reached the edge of the tin-roofed shed by the back doorway, Brennan bent himself over and gagged. His stomach contents whirred inside him for a moment and then presented themselves with a whoosh, splashing on the paving flags. His throat burned, and was immediately backed by a further burning, throbbing pain in the front of his forehead. The sight of the vomit, the smell and the dim-green wash of the lighting made Brennan's head spin. His eddying thoughts added to the distilled feeling of fear he now had for WPC Docherty; the fear seemed to be centred in his stomach but was spreading. As he straightened himself, Brennan had his knees loosen; he reached out a hand to steady himself on the shed, but was soon jerking it up into a guard.

'You fucking bastard!' spat McGuire.

The sergeant's fist connected cleanly with Brennan's jaw, dropping him to the ground in a moaning, writhing heap.

Chapter 49

AS DI ROB BRENNAN PUSHED his face from the dirt-strewn yard, a new feeling engulfed him: embarrassment. Lou and Bri had DS Stevie McGuire restrained; as he waved a hand in protest, Brennan got his feet under him, raised himself from the ground and started to brush the dirt and soil from his jacket and trousers.

'Let him go for Christ's sake,' he said.

'Are you sure, sir?' said Lou.

Brennan walked towards the three officers; his head hurt and his jaw ached. The shame he felt at being struck by McGuire had started to subside as he regained his sense of himself; he knew who was in the right and who was in the wrong. As the DI pointed inside the door, his words came like grunts, 'Get in there!'

'What for?' said McGuire.

'Go on, take a look.' Brennan staggered a few steps towards the DS. 'See what's behind the fucking door to the yard, Stevie.'

Lou and Bri let down their arms; the unrestrained McGuire

pushed himself away and shrugged past the DI on his way to the back door. As he went, sirens from police cars started to rake the cold air all around them. Collins came running from the bottom of the close, nodded to the others.

Brennan rubbed his jaw as he watched McGuire. 'Well, what do you see?'

McGuire looked like a petulant child as he peered behind the lee of the door. 'Another door . . . Under the stairs.'

Brennan shook his head, raised a finger and pointed it in McGuire's direction. His voice roared, 'A coal cellar! Test the door, I bet it's open!'

McGuire obliged him, the door opened in his hand. 'You're right.'

'I fucking know I am . . . Where did I tell you to stay put, Stevie? The back close, and if you had, the bastard wouldn't have been able to hide in the cupboard under the fucking stairs with Elaine whilst you ran up to the flat, would he?'

McGuire's stare seemed to lose all intensity, he wet his lips, ran the back of his hand over his mouth, then closed the door. 'You don't know that for sure.'

Lou and Bri huffed, shuffled past McGuire; the two officers' shoulders barged the DS as they made their way out, forcing him flat against the wall. He suddenly looked an isolated figure.

Brennan waited for Collins to join the others on their way to the front of the building; when he was sure they were out of earshot, he said, 'All you had to do was what you were told, Stevie.' He placed a hand on McGuire's arm, spun him round. 'Come on, we've got to get out there.'

'She's gone, sir . . .'

Brennan prodded McGuire in the back, 'Get moving, Stevie, I want you in that car and on the road in under a minute.'

'But what if we don't find her?'

'I don't do *what ifs*, laddie . . . Get your arse into gear!'

McGuire removed the car keys for the VW Passat from his trouser pocket, broke into a jog. Brennan followed at his back, rubbing at his jaw as they went. On the street, Lou and Bri were already in their car, revving the engine and pulling out in front of the DI and the DS. Lou rolled down the passenger's window. 'Where do you want us, sir?'

The DI halted in the street; he pitched his fingers under his belt and tucked in his shirt tails. 'Get out to Crawley's house . . . It's a long shot but you never know.'

'Right, sir.'

'And stay in contact; if the plan changes I'll want you both right away.'

Lou nodded towards Brennan; the wheels screamed on the car as he raced up the street. As Brennan turned, McGuire already had the Passat in gear and pulled up beside him. 'Where to?' he said.

Brennan opened the passenger door, stepped inside and buckled his seatbelt. 'Head out Liberton way . . .'

'Sir?' It was a question, McGuire obviously had doubts.

'Do it, Stevie . . . now!'

The car took off down the road, turned a hairpin into Duke Street. The burning stench of car tyres filled Brennan's nostrils, made him feel queasy again; he reached for the button to lower the window and stuck his face against the gushing air. The cold wind seemed to help, buffeted his hot brow and aching jaw. The DI raised his fingertips to where McGuire's fist had connected; he felt the swelling, knew there would be a bruise, but it was the damage to his self-esteem that mattered more. Brennan had taken a risk leaving WPC Docherty alone in Angela Mickle's flat. He had used her as bait. He now wondered how he could have been so reckless. He knew McGuire had every right to blame him for what had happened; in the final analysis it had been his decision to mount the operation and he would have to take responsibility for that.

Brennan raised a hand to the roof as McGuire spun the wheel through the roundabout at the top of the Walk. He punched an imaginary brake with his right foot as the Passat veered towards the back of a black cab, then the DS dropped a gear and overtook in the left-hand lane. The DI made a glance in McGuire's direction, caught sight of the locked gaze he presented to the windscreen. Brennan knew McGuire wasn't the only one who would hold him responsible for tonight's failures: there was the Chief Super to consider. He felt his fists tightening and his lower lip curling over his teeth as he thought about the prospect of explaining himself to Benny. He had nowhere left to go with his superior; he had exhausted all options on the case and the sting at Angela Mickle's flat was – he understood perfectly – his last opportunity to get it right. The Chief Super was already looking for a way out of the mess: there would be an inquiry into the Gallagher affair, certainly the Fiona Gow case would be re-examined and those of Lindsey Sloan and Angela Mickle too. Brennan knew he was in the clear – he had taken few liberties on the job – but he also knew how the force worked: scapegoats were sought and found. If it came down to it, Benny would fight to protect himself, and Chief Superintendents brought more weight to the ring than Detective Inspectors.

McGuire flashed his headlights at a Lothian bus driver, blasted the horn and stuck his head out the window. 'Move your arse!'

Brennan snapped out of his introspection as McGuire gestured angrily at the flashing blue light on the roof. 'All right, Stevie, take the middle lane and keep the head.'

McGuire dropped a gear, rolled the car towards the centre of the road. He was still cursing as he found an open stretch of Nicolson Street and pressed the accelerator down.

'This traffic is hellish . . . Are you sure about coming out this way, sir?'

Brennan gripped the seatbelt, 'Just keep going, head for the A720, and then lap the area . . .'

McGuire shot a glance in Brennan's direction; the DI and the DS seemed to share thoughts for a moment, but neither wanted to give voice to them.

Brennan's heart rate had reduced, his focus had returned, but his thoughts had taken him to a place he would sooner not be. WPC Docherty had been snatched by Crawley, that was the fact they were facing. He knew why it was his first instinct to head for the fields at Straiton: Crawley was a serial killer. He had killed two young women and was ready to kill a third – Angela Mickle – to silence her and his urges. Brennan knew Crawley could only suppress his urges to kill for so long before he needed to strike again – both Lorrimer and Wullie's experience had confirmed that – it was more than probable Crawley would act on his instinct to kill when confronted with Elaine Docherty. It was reckless, but if he thought she was a prostitute, he could afford to be reckless. He also had his protector, or so he believed.

The radio silence was broken by Lou's voice: 'Sir, we've reached the Crawley residence . . . All quiet.'

Brennan looked at McGuire who slapped an open palm off the wheel and grimaced. The DI picked up the handset, 'OK, Lou, what's occurring back in Leith?'

The line crackled, then, 'No reported sightings. Uniform's moving on foot round the Mickle flat and we've got the dogs out . . .'

Brennan touched his head with the edge of the handset. 'OK, Lou – join them.'

The car neared the roundabout at the bypass and Brennan craned his neck towards the dark fields. As McGuire flicked the headlights to full beam, Brennan felt his shoulders stiffen. The thudding of his heart increased again, the DI knew that his whole career was now on the line; it was as if all his work over the years had reached this point and yet he didn't seem to care whether he remained on the force or not. Brennan's mind was occupied with his previous visits to the grim stretch of farmland where he had seen the mutilated bodies of the two young women. The pictures that had been pinned on the board of Incident Room One came back to him, he heard the words from the pathologist's report again and he remembered the looks on the faces of the Sloans as he spoke to them about their daughter. Brennan knew he couldn't take the news of another death; he knew McGuire would be finished by the loss of Elaine too. The thoughts swirled in him, marched through his mind like an unholy pain brigade and made him shake his head in an effort to block them out.

'Fucking hell, slow it down, Stevie!' he yelled. 'How are we supposed to see anything if you're up to sixty!'

The DS depressed the brake, brought the speed of the car

down. Brennan reached for the buttons to lower the windows, a chill wind blew through the vehicle as they dropped. 'Can you hear anything?' he said.

McGuire shook his head, 'Nothing . . . No.'

'Right, get on the back road . . .'

Brennan watched McGuire turn on the blinkers, drop a gear and slot the car into the side road where they had driven towards the site of Angela Mickle's body. The DI blocked his emotions, gulped down all fears he held and became an automaton, searching the dark fields for a chink of light, listening for a shrill cry from WPC Elaine Docherty. He knew Crawley had a routine, he knew the serial killer had acted out the routine before and had never been caught, or even witnessed by anyone; but Brennan held out the hope that, until now, no one had been looking in the right place, or at the right time.

'Stop the car, Stevie . . .'

'What, here?'

Brennan smacked the dash with the flat of his hand, 'Yes, here . . .'

As the car slowed, the DI undid his seatbelt, started to open his door. His feet were dangling over the dirt road as the car came to a halt. He stepped out, turned towards the dry-stone dyke skirting the field. The ground was wet; long grass holding plenty of moisture brushed him as he positioned his feet on the stones of the wall and raised himself to a point where he could view the full mile radius of the murder scenes.

'See anything?' said McGuire.

Brennan flagged a hand and said, 'Shh-h, I'm trying to listen.'

The night was silent, black.

The DI felt the stone he stood on move beneath him, he

repositioned himself and felt McGuire's hand steady him. He could hear nothing, see nothing. As he stared out into complete and utter blackness, Brennan felt the immensity of the world conspiring against him. He felt like an insignificant speck as he raked his eyes over the miles of inky darkness. There was nothing there. It felt like the end of the world; it felt like the end of everything he had ever known, as if his whole life had been ineluctably aiming towards this point to prove just how futile all his struggles with existence were.

'What was that?' said McGuire.

'What was what?'

'A noise . . . a *click*.'

Brennan lowered his gaze, looked towards McGuire, 'Where?'

'Over there,' the DS pointed.

Brennan turned towards the direction McGuire indicated; as he roved the sublunary night he could only pick out the pinpricks of white stars burning above him, and then, a different colour of darkness appeared. A small shape at first, but it seemed to widen as Brennan's eyes adjusted.

'You see something?'

Brennan held his gaze firmly; now he saw a car's interior light burning, he saw movement, a figure, and then there was a sound like a door closing and the light disappeared from view.

'There's a car out there!' Brennan jumped down from the wall, ran for the Passat. The engine was still ticking over as he got behind the wheel and engaged the gears. McGuire dived into the passenger's side as Brennan spun the tyres on the dirt track. The car took off down the narrow side road and then suddenly stopped as Brennan applied the brakes.

'Hold on!'

He reversed the vehicle a few feet, turning the wheel to line the front of the car with a wooden gate that divided the dry-stone dyke.

'Jesus, you're going through it?' said McGuire.

'Fucking right!'

The car jolted forward in a lunging motion, wheels screeching beneath them; as the bumper connected, the sound of cracking wood erupted and then the gate was unmoored from its postings and struck the windscreen. The loud crack of glass caused the officers to raise hands to their faces and for a second the car veered to the right before McGuire swept clear the screen. Brennan gripped the wheel again and pressed forward into the black field. The pair rocked in their seats as the car progressed on the bumpy terrain. The lights flashed up and down, illuminating the immediate stretches of green grass before them and then darting to the further reaches of the field.

'There! There!' said McGuire.

'I see it . . .'

Brennan floored the pedal, the steering wheel spun in his hands and the tyres slid on the moist grass. They had their target in their sights now, the silver Corolla reflecting the lights of the police car like a beacon in the middle of the field. The DI tried to make out what was going on and how many people there were, but the ride was too bumpy, jolting his line of vision in and out of focus.

'Can you see anything, Stevie?'

'Just the car.'

They were getting nearer; Brennan started to apply the

brakes, dropped a gear. He wondered why he couldn't see anyone; surely they must be there, he thought, they must be in view by now. As he gripped the wheel he tried to scan further into the field, past the silver Corolla, but he still couldn't detect any movement. For a moment, his stomach started to cramp as he had the dreaded feeling that they had arrived too late.

'Where the fuck are they?' said McGuire.

'I don't know . . . Watch out.' Brennan felt the car slide to the side as he skidded to a halt. The officers pushed open the doors and ran to the other vehicle.

'Nothing . . .' said McGuire. 'Where the hell are they?'

Brennan opened the Corolla's door; the interior light came on and he spotted a length of nylon rope in the foot well. As he reached in, he felt a needle of pain slice into his back; he jolted himself from the car as a woman's scream raked the night air.

McGuire was already running towards the sound as Brennan turned; the DI took off after him. The pair went headlong into the darkness, Brennan following the thud of McGuire's footfalls and heavy breathing. The night air was cold and the men's warm breath was lit by the moonlight as they went. They had only travelled a few metres when they seemed to drop sharply into a ditch that halted them mid-stride. As Brennan fell downwards he extended his hands and felt his palms connecting soundly with solid earth. For a second he was jolted, as his shoulders absorbed the full shock of his body weight, and then his elbows bent and his chest smacked off the wet ground. He rolled to the side, tracing the ditch's declivity, and then came to a halt. As he righted himself, regained his senses, he saw the torchlight burning in Crawley's grip. WPC Elaine Docherty

391

was on the ground beneath him; her hands were tied behind her back but her legs kicked out as she thrashed and lunged at her attacker.

'Crawley, step away!' yelled Brennan as he tried to rise.

McGuire groaned at his side, turned over on his knees holding his elbow; Brennan saw the blood trailing over the sergeant's knuckles; the arm sat at an unnatural angle.

He got up, turned from McGuire and ran into the torch-light. Crawley stood frozen as Brennan crossed the few short yards between them and tackled him to the ground. The torch fell into the grass as Brennan landed heavily on Crawley, forcing him to cry out. The DI righted himself, rose up on his knees as he straddled the felled Crawley; for a moment Brennan was lost to himself, he put his hands on the killer's neck, tightened his grip and watched him writhe beneath him. He felt a powerful urge to watch Crawley's life drain away; his pulse was racing, his mind welling with animus as he pressed his hands deeper into Crawley's throat. He watched the killer's eyes widen, his lips splayed in a rictus and the dark tongue inside pressed into the air. Crawley started to gag, white froth gathering at the edges of his mouth. Brennan knew he was seconds from death, he felt the tension in his own aching jaw where he gripped his teeth tight and saw the real terror that was in Crawley's face. For a moment, Brennan understood nothing about himself and everything about the killer he gripped in his hands, and the thought stabbed at him; flashing into his mind with fresh perspicacity. It was as if an unseen hand was holding him back: some part of him didn't want to take revenge. Brennan knew the primal instinct to kill wasn't in him; he was a police officer, not a murderer. He gasped for breath and released his grip.

392

Brennan watched as Crawley raised hands to his throat; he coughed and spluttered as he gasped the night air greedily. His face was reddened, his eyes, still wide, showed the brightness of burst capillaries webbing their edges. He tried to turn over, to escape the hold Brennan had on him, but the DI grabbed his flailing arms and attached handcuffs to his wrists. As Crawley lay with his face in the dirt, spitting at the grass and muck, Brennan leaned forward, brought his mouth close to his ear and yelled in a ragged, emotional voice, 'Get used to fucking chains, beast!'

Brennan rose, gasped for breath himself as he turned to take in the sight of McGuire kneeling to comfort Elaine; he had his one good arm round her; she rocked in steady tears as they huddled together on the ground like lost children. The DI walked towards them, his steps heavy and uncertain, adrenaline receding, his mouth drooping as he took in air.

'It's over,' said McGuire to Elaine. 'All over.' As the DI appeared at his side, he looked up, said, 'It is, isn't it, sir?'

Brennan nodded; he placed a shaking hand on McGuire's shoulder. 'It's over, Stevie.' He turned away, looked to the dark night sky and caught the dim glow of the city of Edinburgh in the distance. 'It's well and truly over.'

ALSO BY TONY BLACK

Truth Lies Bleeding

Four teenagers find the mutilated body of a young girl crammed into a dumpster in an Edinburgh alleyway. Who is she? Where has she come from? Who has killed her – and why?

Inspector Rob Brennan, recently back from psychiatric leave, is still shocked by the senseless shooting of his only brother. The case of the dumpster girl looks perfect for getting him back on track. But Rob Brennan has enemies within the force, stacks of unfinished business, and a nose for trouble.

What he discovers about the murdered girl blows the case – and his life – wide open.

'Tony Black is one of those excellent perpetrators of Scottish noir ... a compelling and convincing portrait of raw emotions in a vicious milieu' *The Times*

'Fizzles with vicious verismilitude' *Guardian*

arrow books